THE
BEAUTIFUL
AND DAMNED

F. Scott Fitzgerald

COLLINS
CLASSICS

Harper Press
An imprint of HarperCollins*Publishers*
77–85 Fulham Palace Road
Hammersmith
London W6 8JB

This Harper Press paperback edition published 2013

F. Scott Fitzgerald asserts the moral right to be identified as the author of this work

A catalogue record for this book is available from the British Library

ISBN: 978-0-00-792535-3

Printed and bound in Great Britain by Clays Ltd, St Ives plc

MIX
Paper from
responsible sources
FSC
www.fsc.org   **FSC® C007454**

FSC™ is a non-profit international organisation established to promote the
responsible management of the world's forests. Products carrying the FSC label
are independently certified to assure consumers that they come
from forests that are managed to meet the social, economic and
ecological needs of present and future generations.

Find out more about HarperCollins and the environment at
www.harpercollins.co.uk/green

Life & Times section © HarperCollins*Publishers* Ltd
Gerard Cheshire asserts his moral rights as author of the Life & Times section
Classic Literature: Words and Phrases adapted from
Collins English Dictionary
Typesetting in Kalix by Palimpsest Book Production Limited,
Falkirk, Stirlingshire

All rights reserved. No part of this publication may be reproduced,
stored in a retrieval system, or transmitted, in any form or by any means,
electronic, mechanical, photocopying, recording or otherwise,
without the prior permission of the publishers.

This book is sold subject to the condition that it shall not, by way of trade
or otherwise, be lent, re-sold, hired out or otherwise circulated without the
publisher's prior consent in any form of binding or cover other than that
in which it is published and without a similar condition including
this condition being imposed on the subsequent purchaser.

10 9 8 7 6 5 4

History of Collins

In 1819, millworker William Collins from Glasgow,
Scotland, set up a company for printing and publishing
pamphlets, sermons, hymn books and prayer books. That
company was Collins and was to mark the birth of
HarperCollins Publishers as we know it today. The long
tradition of Collins dictionary publishing can be traced back
to the first dictionary William published in 1824, *Greek
and English Lexicon*. Indeed, from 1840 onwards, he began
to produce illustrated dictionaries and even obtained a
licence to print and publish the Bible.

Soon after, William published the first Collins novel,
Ready Reckoner, however it was the time of the Long
Depression, where harvests were poor, prices were high,
potato crops had failed and violence was erupting in
Europe. As a result, many factories across the country were
forced to close down and William chose to retire in 1846,
partly due to the hardships he was facing.

Aged 30, William's son, William II took over the
business. A keen humanitarian with a warm heart and a
generous spirit, William II was truly 'Victorian' in his
outlook. He introduced new, up-to-date steam presses and
published affordable editions of Shakespeare's works and
The Pilgrim's Progress, making them available to the
masses for the first time. A new demand for educational
books meant that success came with the publication of
travel books, scientific books, encyclopaedias and
dictionaries. This demand to be educated led to the later
publication of atlases and Collins also held the monopoly
on scripture writing at the time.

In the 1860s Collins began to expand and diversify

and the idea of 'books for the millions' was developed. Affordable editions of classical literature were published and in 1903 Collins introduced 10 titles in their Collins Handy Illustrated Pocket Novels. These proved so popular that a few years later this had increased to an output of 50 volumes, selling nearly half a million in their year of publication. In the same year, The Everyman's Library was also instituted, with the idea of publishing an affordable library of the most important classical works, biographies, religious and philosophical treatments, plays, poems, travel and adventure. This series eclipsed all competition at the time and the introduction of paperback books in the 1950s helped to open that market and marked a high point in the industry.

HarperCollins is and has always been a champion of the classics and the current Collins Classics series follows in this tradition – publishing classical literature that is affordable and available to all. Beautifully packaged, highly collectible and intended to be reread and enjoyed at every opportunity.

Life & Times

Fitzgerald's books provide a curious window into a world that has been and gone. A world where elements of US society had drowned themselves in a moral and ethical sump. His novels are a warning about what can happen when people become decadent and dishonourable, and appeal because the reader enjoys voyeuristically peering in to view the lives of those who are ridiculed as being exotic, foolish and beguiled, and is grateful not to be a part of it.

There is a moral judgement involved in the process of reading such stories and Fitzgerald's work can be compared to that of the British author Thomas Hardy, who takes the same view that people tend to get what they deserve in life and that the real victims are those who get caught up, either by accident or by attraction. There is a definite register of contempt penned by both of these authors, as if to suggest that they have chosen to point the spotlight at those for whom they have little time in real life.

As its title suggests, *The Beautiful and Damned* (1922) is about the superficiality of café society in New York during the Jazz Age. This was the period when jazz music became hugely popular, when the smart set enjoyed living to excess in the heady days before the Great Depression. Fitzgerald observed that these people were often attractive and glamorous in appearance, but flawed and shallow in personality. He isn't simply writing a condemnation of fey types, however, as the novel is essentially autobiographical, about himself and his wife Zelda.

In fact, Fitzgerald is clever enough to illustrate that this apparent superficiality is underscored by profound character complexity. The overt superficiality veils a covert diversity of hang-ups, anxieties, desires, needs, neuroses, passions, emotions, ambitions and failings. In short, the novel is a dissection of human nature, which is fundamentally the same in any social group, no matter what the outward impression.

Nevertheless, Fitzgerald's view is a rather unsympathetic one. He regards this social set as destined for personal disaster, because they are too subjectively obsessed to be objective about life. As a result, they lack the ability to save themselves from their indulgences, both internal and external. Ultimately Fitzgerald is saying that they lack the ingredients to keep themselves grounded, leaving their priorities in disarray. Their failure to reflect and maintain perspective on life means they inevitably lack the wisdom to make the right decisions and consequently they head for a fall.

It is this insight and analysis that makes Fitzgerald a great writer – he is just as interested in the human condition as he is in telling an entertaining story. *The Beautiful and Damned* is really a self-morality play, as the consequences it presents are self-impacting. The sub-society he describes is self-contained, like fermenting yeast in a demijohn, destined to destroy itself with the products of its own metabolism.

Later Works

There can be few novels as divisive as F. Scott Fitzgerald's *The Great Gatsby* in terms of people's opinion of its literary worth. It registered disappointing sales upon its publication in 1925 which led to Fitzgerald slipping into obscurity despite his having established a reasonable reputation with his earlier books. Following his death, in 1940, the book was included on a list of titles to be provided free to US service men and women fighting in World War Two. This meant that 150,000 copies began circulating through the armed forces until the book became familiar to overseas Americans. As a result it had inadvertently worked its way into the American psyche and won favour where otherwise it would have been forgotten.

The story itself is essentially about the moral decay that ensued in America during the 1920s. Although other countries had class divisions, the US had the equivalent of an upper class in the form of patricians or members of long-established wealthy families. These New World aristocrats lorded themselves above other people and spent much of their lives partying their way through the Jazz Age. In addition, 1920 had seen the prohibition of alcohol, with the result that organized criminals had seen a way to make good money by bootlegging, or illegally selling liquor. When both of these groups came together they formed a social order of dilettantism – people who assumed and cultivated pretensions of sophistication. The story of *The Great Gatsby* spirals into tragedy as the book progresses with a succession of events – manslaughter, murder and then suicide – tragedy that seems all the more horrific after the spirited and frothy excesses that have come before.

In stark contrast to *The Great Gatsby* came Fitzgerald's final novel *Tender is the Night* (1934), which is auto-biographical at its heart. At the time of writing the book Fitzgerald's wife was being treated for schizophrenia and the author holed-up in a house near the hospital in Baltimore, Maryland. There he wrestled with the book and indulged his alcoholism, from which he had suffered for most of his adult life. The story is about a couple who become involved because he is a psychoanalyst and she his patient. She is wealthy and fragile of mind, while he is poor and strong of mind. However, the tables are eventually turned as he becomes dependent on the demon drink and his behaviour sends him on a downward spiral, while she finds someone else and divorces him for a better life.

There are evidently themes in the book that run a close parallel with the real lives of the Fitzgeralds, so it seems that the author used the work as a way of unloading his darkest thoughts. It wasn't so much a catharsis as a confessional, for

Fitzgerald was laying his human flaws and desires bare for all to see, admitting that he had a drink problem and that his wife was his crutch. He was also known to have financial problems due to his frivolities and extravagancies and had turned to other women to satisfy his emotional and carnal desires. Much of his relationship with his wife had been spent as an amateur psychoanalyst, helping her to deal with her diminishing sanity.

Just six years after *Tender is the Night* was published, Fitzgerald was dead. His self-abuse had caught up with him at the age of only 44 years old, with a massive cardiac arrest. It seems that his last book was also a prophecy of his impending demise from alcohol. It was only a matter of time before his mortal being abandoned his immortal ambition. Fitzgerald the legendary writer has now outlived Fitzgerald the man several times over.

Fitzgerald and Hemingway

Fitzgerald was friends with arguably the greatest American writer, Ernest Hemingway. Hemingway encouraged Fitzgerald to pursue his prose with artistic integrity, but grew frustrated with Fitzgerald's tendency towards making his literature commercial. However, most of Fitzgerald's novels did not perform that well, so a large part of his income came from magazine work, writing short stories which, by their very nature, had to conform to editorial requirements. Nine years after *The Great Gatsby*, he had struggled to complete his final novel, *Tender is the Night*. Unfortunately for Fitzgerald the book was received with disappointment and the decline of his writing career continued unabated. In the latter half of the 1930s he found work developing movie scripts and carried out further commercial writing. By the time of his death his literary career had died, too.

In hindsight Fitzgerald's work is regarded variously, but *The Great Gatsby* has become the quintessential American classic. Some feel that Fitzgerald's talent would have been better focused on his novel writing, but fiscal matters always dictated that he continue with his commercial work. However, Hemingway may have been a heavyweight writer but he was certainly not a contented man. For him the praise he garnered for each new book was a fix. When he ran out of ideas he suffered severe depression and ultimately took his own life with a shotgun. Fitzgerald battled on in a workmanlike manner even when plaudits were a distant memory.

THE
BEAUTIFUL
AND DAMNED

The victor belongs to the spoils.

—ANTHONY PATCH

TO SHANE LESLIE, GEORGE JEAN NATHAN AND
MAXWELL PERKINS

IN APPRECIATION OF MUCH LITERARY HELP AND
ENCOURAGEMENT

CONTENTS

BOOK ONE

CHAPTER 1

ANTHONY PATCH

In 1913, when Anthony Patch was twenty-five, two years were already gone since irony, the Holy Ghost of this later day, had, theoretically at least, descended upon him. Irony was the final polish of the shoe, the ultimate dab of the clothes-brush, a sort of intellectual "There!"—yet at the brink of this story he has as yet gone no further than the conscious stage. As you first see him he wonders frequently whether he is not without honor and slightly mad, a shameful and obscene thinness glistening on the surface of the world like oil on a clean pond, these occasions being varied, of course, with those in which he thinks himself rather an exceptional young man, thoroughly sophisticated, well adjusted to his environment, and somewhat more significant than any one else he knows.

This was his healthy state and it made him cheerful, pleasant, and very attractive to intelligent men and to all women. In this state he considered that he would one day accomplish some quiet subtle thing that the elect would deem worthy and, passing on, would join the dimmer stars in a nebulous, indeterminate heaven half-way between death and immortality. Until the time came for this effort he would be

Anthony Patch—not a portrait of a man but a distinct and dynamic personality, opinionated, contemptuous, functioning from within outward—a man who was aware that there could be no honor and yet had honor, who knew the sophistry of courage and yet was brave.

A WORTHY MAN AND HIS GIFTED SON

Anthony drew as much consciousness of social security from being the grandson of Adam J. Patch as he would have had from tracing his line over the sea to the crusaders. This is inevitable; Virginians and Bostonians to the contrary notwithstanding, an aristocracy founded sheerly on money postulates wealth in the particular.

Now Adam J. Patch, more familiarly known as "Cross Patch," left his father's farm in Tarrytown early in sixty-one to join a New York cavalry regiment. He came home from the war a major, charged into Wall Street, and amid much fuss, fume, applause, and ill will he gathered to himself some seventy-five million dollars.

This occupied his energies until he was fifty-seven years old. It was then that he determined, after a severe attack of sclerosis, to consecrate the remainder of his life to the moral regeneration of the world. He became a reformer among reformers. Emulating the magnificent efforts of Anthony Comstock, after whom his grandson was named, he levelled a varied assortment of uppercuts and body-blows at liquor, literature, vice, art, patent medicines, and Sunday theatres. His mind, under the influence of that insidious mildew which eventually forms on all but the few, gave itself up furiously to every indignation of the age. From an armchair in the office of his Tarrytown estate he directed against the enormous hypothetical enemy, unrighteousness, a campaign which went on through fifteen years, during which he displayed himself a rabid monomaniac, an unqualified nuisance, and an intolerable bore. The year in which this story opens found him wearying; his campaign had grown desultory; 1861 was creeping up slowly on 1895; his thoughts ran a great deal on the Civil War, somewhat on his dead wife and son, almost infinitesimally on his grandson Anthony.

Early in his career Adam Patch had married an anemic lady of thirty, Alicia Withers, who brought him one hundred thousand dollars and an impeccable entrée into the banking circles of New York. Immediately and rather spunkily she had borne him a son and, as if completely devitalized by the magnificence of this performance, she had thenceforth effaced herself within the shadowy dimensions of the nursery. The boy, Adam Ulysses Patch, became an inveterate joiner of clubs, connoisseur of good form, and driver of tandems—at the astonishing age of twenty-six he began his memoirs under the title "New York Society as I Have Seen It." On the rumor of its conception this work was eagerly bid for among publishers, but as it proved after his death to be immoderately verbose and overpoweringly dull, it never obtained even a private printing.

This Fifth Avenue Chesterfield married at twenty-two. His wife was Henrietta Lebrune, the Boston "Society Contralto," and the single child of the union was, at the request of his grandfather, christened Anthony Comstock Patch. When he went to Harvard, the Comstock dropped out of his name to a nether hell of oblivion and was never heard of thereafter.

Young Anthony had one picture of his father and mother together—so often had it faced his eyes in childhood that it had acquired the impersonality of furniture, but every one who came into his bedroom regarded it with interest. It showed a dandy of the nineties, spare and handsome, standing beside a tall dark lady with a muff and the suggestion of a bustle. Between them was a little boy with long brown curls, dressed in a velvet Lord Fauntleroy suit. This was Anthony at five, the year of his mother's death.

His memories of the Boston Society Contralto were nebulous and musical. She was a lady who sang, sang, sang, in the music room of their house on Washington Square—sometimes with guests scattered all about her, the men with their arms folded, balanced breathlessly on the edges of sofas, the women with their hands in their laps, occasionally making little whispers to the men and always clapping very briskly and uttering cooing cries after each song—and often she sang to Anthony alone, in Italian or French or in a strange and terrible dialect which she imagined to be the speech of the Southern negro.

His recollections of the gallant Ulysses, the first man in America to roll the lapels of his coat, were much more vivid. After Henrietta Lebrune Patch had "joined another choir," as her widower huskily remarked from time to time, father and son lived up at grampa's in Tarrytown, and Ulysses came daily to Anthony's nursery and expelled pleasant, thick-smelling words for sometimes as much as an hour. He was continually promising Anthony hunting trips and fishing trips and excursions to Atlantic City, "oh, some time soon now"; but none of them ever materialized. One trip they did take; when Anthony was eleven they went abroad, to England and Switzerland, and there in the best hotel in Lucerne his father died with much sweating and grunting and crying aloud for air. In a panic of despair and terror Anthony was brought back to America, wedded to a vague melancholy that was to stay beside him through the rest of his life.

PAST AND PERSON OF THE HERO

At eleven he had a horror of death. Within six impressionable years his parents had died and his grandmother had faded off almost imperceptibly, until, for the first time since her marriage, her person held for one day an unquestioned supremacy over her own drawing room. So to Anthony life was a struggle against death, that waited at every corner. It was as a concession to his hypochondriacal imagination that he formed the habit of reading in bed—it soothed him. He read until he was tired and often fell asleep with the lights still on.

His favorite diversion until he was fourteen was his stamp collection; enormous, as nearly exhaustive as a boy's could be—his grandfather considered fatuously that it was teaching him geography. So Anthony kept up a correspondence with a half dozen "Stamp and Coin" companies and it was rare that the mail failed to bring him new stamp-books or packages of glittering approval sheets—there was a mysterious fascination in transferring his acquisitions interminably from one book to another. His stamps were his greatest happiness and he bestowed impatient frowns on any one who interrupted him at play with them; they devoured his allowance every month, and he lay awake at night musing untiringly on their variety and many-colored splendor.

At sixteen he had lived almost entirely within himself, an inarticulate boy, thoroughly un-American, and politely bewildered by his contemporaries. The two preceding years had been spent in Europe with a private tutor, who persuaded him that Harvard was the thing; it would "open doors," it would be a tremendous tonic, it would give him innumerable self-sacrificing and devoted friends. So he went to Harvard—there was no other logical thing to be done with him.

Oblivious to the social system, he lived for a while alone and unsought in a high room in Beck Hall—a slim dark boy of medium height with a shy sensitive mouth. His allowance was more than liberal. He laid the foundations for a library by purchasing from a wandering bibliophile first editions of Swinburne, Meredith, and Hardy, and a yellowed illegible autograph letter of Keats's, finding later that he had been amazingly overcharged. He became an exquisite dandy, amassed a rather pathetic collection of silk pajamas, brocaded dressing-gowns, and neckties too flamboyant to wear; in this secret finery he would parade before a mirror in his room or lie stretched in satin along his window-seat looking down on the yard and realizing dimly this clamor, breathless and immediate, in which it seemed he was never to have a part.

Curiously enough he found in senior year that he had acquired a position in his class. He learned that he was looked upon as a rather romantic figure, a scholar, a recluse, a tower of erudition. This amused him but secretly pleased him—he began going out, at first a little and then a great deal. He made the Pudding. He drank—quietly and in the proper tradition. It was said of him that had he not come to college so young he might have "done extremely well." In 1909, when he graduated, he was only twenty years old.

Then abroad again—to Rome this time, where he dallied with architecture and painting in turn, took up the violin, and wrote some ghastly Italian sonnets, supposedly the ruminations of a thirteenth-century monk on the joys of the contemplative life. It became established among his Harvard intimates that he was in Rome, and those of them who were abroad that year looked him up and discovered with him, on many moonlight excursions, much in the city that was older than the Renaissance or indeed than the republic. Maury Noble, from Philadelphia, for instance, remained two months, and together they realized the peculiar charm of Latin women and had a delightful sense of being very young and free in a civilization that was very old and free. Not a few acquaintances of his grandfather's called on him, and had he so desired he might have been *persona grata* with the diplomatic set—indeed, he found that his inclinations tended more and more toward conviviality, but that long adolescent aloofness and consequent shyness still dictated to his conduct.

He returned to America in 1912 because of one of his grandfather's sudden illnesses, and after an excessively tiresome talk with the perpetually convalescent old man he decided to put off until his grandfather's death the idea of living permanently abroad. After a prolonged search he took an apartment on Fifty-second Street and to all appearances settled down.

In 1913 Anthony Patch's adjustment of himself to the universe was in process of consummation. Physically, he had improved since his undergraduate days—he was still too thin but his shoulders had widened and his brunette face had lost the frightened look of his freshman year. He was secretly orderly and in person spick and span—his friends declared that they had never seen his hair rumpled. His nose was too sharp; his mouth was one of those unfortunate mirrors of mood inclined to droop perceptibly in moments of unhappiness, but his blue eyes were charming, whether alert with intelligence or half closed in an expression of melancholy humor.

One of those men devoid of the symmetry of feature essential to the Aryan ideal, he was yet, here and there, considered handsome—moreover, he was very clean, in appearance and in reality, with that especial cleanness borrowed from beauty.

THE REPROACHLESS APARTMENT

Fifth and Sixth Avenues, it seemed to Anthony, were the uprights of a gigantic ladder stretching from Washington Square to Central Park. Coming up-town on top of a bus toward Fifty-second Street invariably gave him the sensation of hoisting himself hand by hand on a series of treacherous rungs, and when the bus jolted to a stop at his own rung he found something akin to relief as he descended the reckless metal steps to the sidewalk.

After that, he had but to walk down Fifty-second Street half a block, pass a stodgy family of brownstone houses—and then in a jiffy he was under the high ceilings of his great front room. This was entirely satisfactory. Here, after all, life began. Here he slept, breakfasted, read, and entertained.

The house itself was of murky material, built in the late nineties; in response to the steadily growing need of small apartments each floor had been thoroughly remodelled and rented individually. Of the four apartments Anthony's, on the second floor, was the most desirable.

The front room had fine high ceilings and three large windows that loomed down pleasantly upon Fifty-second Street. In its appointments it escaped by a safe margin being of any particular period; it escaped stiffness, stuffiness, bareness, and decadence. It smelt neither of smoke nor of incense—it was tall and faintly blue. There was a deep lounge of the softest brown leather with somnolence drifting about it like a haze. There was a high screen of Chinese lacquer chiefly concerned with geometrical fishermen and huntsmen in black and gold; this made a corner alcove for a voluminous chair guarded by an orange-colored standing lamp. Deep in the fireplace a quartered shield was burned to a murky black.

Passing through the dining-room, which, as Anthony took only breakfast at home, was merely a magnificent potentiality, and down a comparatively long hall, one came to the heart and core of the apartment—Anthony's bedroom and bath.

Both of them were immense. Under the ceilings of the former even the great canopied bed seemed of only average size. On the floor an exotic rug of crimson velvet was soft as fleece on his bare feet. His bathroom, in contrast to the rather portentous character of his bedroom, was gay, bright, extremely habitable and even faintly facetious. Framed around the walls were photographs of four celebrated thespian beauties of the day: Julia Sanderson as "The Sunshine Girl," Ina Claire as "The Quaker Girl," Billie Burke as "The Mind-the-Paint Girl," and Hazel Dawn as "The Pink Lady." Between Billie Burke and Hazel Dawn hung a print representing a great stretch of snow presided over by a cold and formidable sun—this, claimed Anthony, symbolized the cold shower.

The bathtub, equipped with an ingenious bookholder,

was low and large. Beside it a wall wardrobe bulged with sufficient linen for three men and with a generation of neckties. There was no skimpy glorified towel of a carpet—instead, a rich rug, like the one in his bedroom a miracle of softness, that seemed almost to massage the wet foot emerging from the tub. . . .

All in all a room to conjure with—it was easy to see that Anthony dressed there, arranged his immaculate hair there, in fact did everything but sleep and eat there. It was his pride, this bathroom. He felt that if he had a love he would have hung her picture just facing the tub so that, lost in the soothing steamings of the hot water, he might lie and look up at her and muse warmly and sensuously on her beauty.

NOR DOES HE SPIN

The apartment was kept clean by an English servant with the singularly, almost theatrically, appropriate name of Bounds, whose technic was marred only by the fact that he wore a soft collar. Had he been entirely Anthony's Bounds this defect would have been summarily remedied, but he was also the Bounds of two other gentlemen in the neighborhood. From eight until eleven in the morning he was entirely Anthony's. He arrived with the mail and cooked breakfast. At nine-thirty he pulled the edge of Anthony's blanket and spoke a few terse words—Anthony never remembered clearly what they were and rather suspected they were deprecative; then he served breakfast on a card-table in the front room, made the bed and, after asking with some hostility if there was anything else, withdrew.

In the mornings, at least once a week, Anthony went to see his broker. His income was slightly under seven thousand a year, the interest on money inherited from his mother. His grandfather, who had never allowed his own son to graduate from a very liberal allowance, judged that this sum was sufficient for young Anthony's needs. Every Christmas he sent him a five-hundred-dollar bond, which Anthony usually sold, if possible, as he was always a little, not very, hard up.

The visits to his broker varied from semi-social chats to discussions of the safety of eight per cent investments, and Anthony always enjoyed them. The big trust company building seemed to link him definitely to the great fortunes whose solidarity he respected and to assure him that he was adequately chaperoned by the hierarchy of finance. From these hurried men he derived the same sense of safety that he had in contemplating his grandfather's money—even more, for the latter appeared, vaguely, a demand loan made by the world to Adam Patch's own moral righteousness, while this money down-town seemed rather to have been grasped and held by sheer indomitable strengths and tremendous feats of will; in addition, it seemed more definitely and explicitly—money.

Closely as Anthony trod on the heels of his income, he considered it to be enough. Some golden day, of course, he would have many millions; meanwhile he possessed a *raison d'etre* in the theoretical creation of essays on the popes of the Renaissance. This flashes back to the conversation with his grandfather immediately upon his return from Rome.

He had hoped to find his grandfather dead, but had learned by telephoning from the pier that Adam Patch was comparatively well again—the next day he had concealed his disappointment and gone out to Tarrytown. Five miles from the station his taxicab entered an elaborately groomed drive that threaded a veritable maze of walls and wire fences guarding the estate—this, said the public, was because it was definitely known that if the Socialists had their way, one of the first men they'd assassinate would be old Cross Patch.

Anthony was late and the venerable philanthropist was awaiting him in a glass-walled sun parlor, where he was glancing through the morning papers for the second time. His secretary, Edward Shuttleworth—who before his regeneration had been gambler, saloon-keeper, and general reprobate—ushered

Anthony into the room, exhibiting his redeemer and benefactor as though he were displaying a treasure of immense value.

They shook hands gravely. "I'm awfully glad to hear you're better," Anthony said.

The senior Patch, with an air of having seen his grandson only last week, pulled out his watch.

"Train late?" he asked mildly.

It had irritated him to wait for Anthony. He was under the delusion not only that in his youth he had handled his practical affairs with the utmost scrupulousness, even to keeping every engagement on the dot, but also that this was the direct and primary cause of his success.

"It's been late a good deal this month," he remarked with a shade of meek accusation in his voice—and then after a long sigh, "Sit down."

Anthony surveyed his grandfather with that tacit amazement which always attended the sight. That this feeble, unintelligent old man was possessed of such power that, yellow journals to the contrary, the men in the republic whose souls he could not have bought directly or indirectly would scarcely have populated White Plains, seemed as impossible to believe as that he had once been a pink-and-white baby.

The span of his seventy-five years had acted as a magic bellows—the first quarter-century had blown him full with life, and the last had sucked it all back. It had sucked in the cheeks and the chest and the girth of arm and leg. It had tyrannously demanded his teeth, one by one, suspended his small eyes in dark-bluish sacks, tweeked out his hairs, changed him from gray to white in some places, from pink to yellow in others—callously transposing his colors like a child trying over a paintbox. Then through his body and his soul it had attacked his brain. It had sent him night-sweats and tears and unfounded dreads. It had split his intense normality into credulity and suspicion. Out of the coarse material of his enthusiasm it had cut dozens of meek but petulant obsessions; his energy was shrunk to the bad temper of a spoiled child, and for his will to power was substituted a fatuous puerile desire for a land of harps and canticles on earth.

The amenities having been gingerly touched upon, Anthony felt that he was expected to outline his intentions—and simultaneously a glimmer in the old man's eye warned him against broaching, for the present, his desire to live abroad. He wished that Shuttleworth would have tact enough to leave the room—he detested Shuttleworth—but the secretary had settled blandly in a rocker and was dividing between the two Patches the glances of his faded eyes.

"Now that you're here you ought to *do* something," said his grandfather softly, "accomplish something."

Anthony waited for him to speak of "leaving something done when you pass on." Then he made a suggestion:

"I thought—it seemed to me that perhaps I'm best qualified to write—"

Adam Patch winced, visualizing a family poet with a long hair and three mistresses.

"—history," finished Anthony.

"History? History of what? The Civil War? The Revolution?"

"Why—no, sir. A history of the Middle Ages." Simultaneously an idea was born for a history of the Renaissance popes, written from some novel angle. Still, he was glad he had said "Middle Ages."

"Middle Ages? Why not your own country? Something you know about?"

"Well, you see I've lived so much abroad—"

"Why you should write about the Middle Ages, I don't know. Dark Ages, we used to call 'em. Nobody knows what happened, and nobody cares, except that they're over now." He continued for some minutes on the uselessness of such information, touching, naturally, on the Spanish Inquisition and the "corruption of the monasteries." Then:

"Do you think you'll be able to do any work in New York—or do you really intend to work at all?" This last with soft, almost imperceptible, cynicism.

"Why, yes, I do, sir."

"When'll you be done?"

"Well, there'll be an outline, you see—and a lot of preliminary reading."

"I should think you'd have done enough of that already."

The conversation worked itself jerkily toward a rather abrupt conclusion, when Anthony rose, looked at his watch, and remarked that he had an engagement with his broker that afternoon. He had intended to stay a few days with his grandfather, but he was tired and irritated from a rough crossing, and quite unwilling to stand a subtle and sanctimonious browbeating. He would come out again in a few days, he said.

Nevertheless, it was due to this encounter that work had come into his life as a permanent idea. During the year that had passed since then, he had made several lists of authorities, he had even experimented with chapter titles and the division of his work into periods, but not one line of actual writing existed at present, or seemed likely ever to exist. He did nothing—and contrary to the most accredited copy-book logic, he managed to divert himself with more than average content.

AFTERNOON

It was October in 1913, midway in a week of pleasant days, with the sunshine loitering in the cross-streets and the atmosphere so languid as to seem weighted with ghostly falling leaves. It was pleasant to sit lazily by the open window finishing a chapter of "Erewhon." It was pleasant to yawn about five, toss the book on a table, and saunter humming along the hall to his bath.

"To . . . you . . . beaut-if-ul lady," he was singing as he turned on the tap.

> "I raise . . . my . . . eyes;
> To . . . you . . . beaut-if-ul la-a-dy
> My . . . heart . . . cries—"

He raised his voice to compete with the flood of water pouring into the tub, and as he looked at the picture of Hazel Dawn upon the wall he put an imaginary violin to his shoulder and softly caressed it with a phantom bow. Through his closed lips he made a humming noise, which he vaguely imagined resembled the sound of a violin. After a moment his hands ceased their gyrations and wandered to his shirt, which he began to unfasten. Stripped, and adopting an athletic posture like the tiger-skin man in the advertisement, he regarded himself with some satisfaction in the mirror, breaking off to dabble a tentative foot in the tub. Readjusting a faucet and indulging in a few preliminary grunts, he slid in.

Once accustomed to the temperature of the water he relaxed into a state of drowsy content. When he finished his bath he would dress leisurely and walk down Fifth Avenue to the Ritz, where he had an appointment for dinner with his two most frequent companions, Dick Caramel and Maury Noble. Afterward he and Maury were going to the theatre— Caramel would probably trot home and work on his book, which ought to be finished pretty soon.

Anthony was glad *he* wasn't going to work on *his* book. The notion of sitting down and conjuring up, not only words in which to clothe thoughts but thoughts worthy of being clothed—the whole thing was absurdly beyond his desires.

Emerging from his bath he polished himself with the meticulous attention of a bootblack. Then he wandered into the bedroom, and whistling the while a weird, uncertain melody, strolled here and there buttoning, adjusting, and enjoying the warmth of the thick carpet on his feet.

He lit a cigarette, tossed the match out the open top of the window, then paused in his tracks with the cigarette two inches from his mouth—which fell faintly ajar. His eyes were focussed upon a spot of brilliant color on the roof of a house farther down the alley.

It was a girl in a red negligé, silk surely, drying her hair by the still hot sun of late afternoon. His whistle died upon the stiff air of the room; he walked cautiously another step nearer the window with a sudden impression that she was beautiful. Sitting on the stone parapet beside her was a cushion the same color as her garment and she was leaning both arms upon it as she looked down into the sunny areaway, where Anthony could hear children playing.

He watched her for several minutes. Something was stirred in him, something not accounted for by the warm smell of the afternoon or the triumphant vividness of red. He felt persistently that the girl was beautiful—then of a sudden he understood: it was her distance, not a rare and precious distance of soul but still distance, if only in terrestrial yards. The autumn air was between them, and the roofs and the blurred voices. Yet for a not altogether explained second, posing perversely in time, his emotion had been nearer to adoration than in the deepest kiss he had ever known.

He finished his dressing, found a black bow tie and adjusted it carefully by the three-sided mirror in the bathroom. Then yielding to an impulse he walked quickly into the bedroom and again looked out the window. The woman was standing up now; she had tossed her hair back and he had a full view of her. She was fat, full thirty-five, utterly undistinguished. Making a clicking noise with his mouth he returned to the bathroom and reparted his hair.

"To . . . you . . . beaut-if-ul lady,"

he sang lightly,

> "I raise . . . my . . . eyes—"

Then with a last soothing brush that left an iridescent surface of sheer gloss he left his bathroom and his apartment and walked down Fifth Avenue to the Ritz-Carlton.

THREE MEN

At seven Anthony and his friend Maury Noble are sitting at a corner table on the cool roof. Maury Noble is like nothing so much as a large slender and imposing cat. His eyes are narrow and full of incessant, protracted blinks. His hair is smooth and flat, as though it has been licked by a possible—and, if so, Herculean—mother-cat. During Anthony's time at Harvard he had been considered the most unique figure in his class, the most brilliant, the most original—smart, quiet and among the saved.

This is the man whom Anthony considers his best friend. This is the only man of all his acquaintance whom he admires and, to a bigger extent than he likes to admit to himself, envies.

They are glad to see each other now—their eyes are full of kindness as each feels the full effect of novelty after a short separation. They are drawing a relaxation from each other's presence, a new serenity; Maury Noble behind that fine and absurdly catlike face is all but purring. And Anthony, nervous as a will-o'-the-wisp, restless—he is at rest now.

They are engaged in one of those easy short-speech conversations that only men under thirty or men under great stress indulge in.

ANTHONY: Seven o'clock. Where's the Caramel? *(Impatiently.)* I wish he'd finish that interminable novel. I've spent more time hungry——

MAURY: He's got a new name for it. "The Demon Lover"
—not bad, eh?

ANTHONY: *(interested)* "The Demon Lover"? Oh "woman
wailing"—No—not a bit bad! Not bad at all—d'you
think?

MAURY: Rather good. What time did you say?

ANTHONY: Seven.

MAURY:*(His eyes narrowing—not unpleasantly, but to express
a faint disapproval)* Drove me crazy the other day.

ANTHONY: How?

MAURY: That habit of taking notes.

ANTHONY: Me, too. Seems I'd said something night
before that he considered material but he'd forgotten
it—so he had at me. He'd say "Can't you try to concentrate?" And I'd say "You bore me to tears. How do I
remember?"

*(MAURY laughs noiselessly, by a sort of bland and appreciative
widening of his features.)*

MAURY: Dick doesn't necessarily see more than any one else.
He merely can put down a larger proportion of what he
sees.

ANTHONY: That rather impressive talent——

MAURY: Oh, yes. Impressive!

ANTHONY: And energy—ambitious, well-directed energy.
He's so entertaining—he's so tremendously stimulating
and exciting. Often there's something breathless in being
with him.

MAURY: Oh, yes. *(Silence, and then:)*

ANTHONY: *(With his thin, somewhat uncertain face at its
most convinced)* But not indomitable energy. Some day,
bit by bit, it'll blow away, and his rather impressive talent
with it, and leave only a wisp of a man, fretful and
egotistic and garrulous.

MAURY: *(With laughter)* Here we sit vowing to each other
that little Dick sees less deeply into things than we do.

And I'll bet he feels a measure of superiority on his side—creative mind over merely critical mind and all that.

ANTHONY: Oh, yes. But he's wrong. He's inclined to fall for a million silly enthusiasms. If it wasn't that he's absorbed in realism and therefore has to adopt the garments of the cynic he'd be—he'd be credulous as a college religious leader. He's an idealist. Oh, yes. He thinks he's not, because he's rejected Christianity. Remember him in college? just swallow every writer whole, one after another, ideas, technic, and characters, Chesterton, Shaw, Wells, each one as easily as the last.

MAURY:*(Still considering his own last observation)* I remember.

ANTHONY: It's true. Natural born fetish-worshipper. Take art—

MAURY: Let's order. He'll be—

ANTHONY: Sure. Let's order. I told him—

MAURY: Here he comes. Look—he's going to bump that waiter. *(He lifts his finger as a signal—lifts it as though it were a soft and friendly claw.)* Here y'are, Caramel.

A NEW VOICE: *(Fiercely)* Hello, Maury. Hello, Anthony Comstock Patch. How is old Adam's grandson? Débutantes still after you, eh?

In person RICHARD CARAMEL *is short and fair—he is to be bald at thirty-five. He has yellowish eyes—one of them startlingly clear, the other opaque as a muddy pool—and a bulging brow like a funny-paper baby. He bulges in other places—his paunch bulges, prophetically, his words have an air of bulging from his mouth, even his dinner coat pockets bulge, as though from contamination, with a dog-eared collection of time-tables, programmes, and miscellaneous scraps—on these he takes his notes with great screwings up of his unmatched yellow eyes and motions of silence with his disengaged left hand.*

When he reaches the table he shakes hands with ANTHONY and

MAURY. *He is one of those men who invariably shake hands, even with people whom they have seen an hour before.*

ANTHONY: Hello, Caramel. Glad you're here. We needed a comic relief.

MAURY: You're late. Been racing the postman down the block? We've been clawing over your character.

DICK: (*Fixing* ANTHONY *eagerly with the bright eye*) What'd you say? Tell me and I'll write it down. Cut three thousand words out of Part One this afternoon.

MAURY: Noble aesthete. And I poured alcohol into my stomach.

DICK: I don't doubt it. I bet you two have been sitting here for an hour talking about liquor.

ANTHONY: We never pass out, my beardless boy.

MAURY: We never go home with ladies we meet when we're lit.

ANTHONY: All in our parties are characterized by a certain haughty distinction.

DICK: The particularly silly sort who boast about being "tanks"! Trouble is you're both in the eighteenth century. School of the Old English Squire. Drink quietly until you roll under the table. Never have a good time. Oh, no, that isn't done at all.

ANTHONY: This from Chapter Six, I'll bet.

DICK: Going to the theatre?

MAURY: Yes. We intend to spend the evening doing some deep thinking over of life's problems. The thing is tersely called "The Woman." I presume that she will "pay."

ANTHONY: My God! Is that what it is? Let's go to the Follies again.

MAURY: I'm tired of it. I've seen it three times. (*To DICK:*) The first time, we went out after Act One and found a most amazing bar. When we came back we entered the wrong theatre.

ANTHONY: Had a protracted dispute with a scared young couple we thought were in our seats.

DICK: (*As though talking to himself*) I think—that when I've done another novel and a play, and maybe a book of short stories, I'll do a musical comedy.

MAURY: I know—with intellectual lyrics that no one will listen to. And all the critics will groan and grunt about "Dear old Pinafore." And I shall go on shining as a brilliantly meaningless figure in a meaningless world.

DICK: (*Pompously*) Art isn't meaningless.

MAURY: It is in itself. It isn't in that it tries to make life less so.

ANTHONY: In other words, Dick, you're playing before a grandstand peopled with ghosts.

MAURY: Give a good show anyhow.

ANTHONY: (To MAURY) On the contrary, I'd feel that it being a meaningless world, why write? The very attempt to give it purpose is purposeless.

DICK: Well, even admitting all that, be a decent pragmatist and grant a poor man the instinct to live. Would you want every one to accept that sophistic rot?

ANTHONY: Yeah, I suppose so.

MAURY: No, sir! I believe that every one in America but a selected thousand should be compelled to accept a very rigid system of morals—Roman Catholicism, for instance. I don't complain of conventional morality. I complain rather of the mediocre heretics who seize upon the findings of sophistication and adopt the pose of a moral freedom to which they are by no means entitled by their intelligences.

(*Here the soup arrives and what MAURY might have gone on to say is lost for all time.*)

NIGHT

Afterward they visited a ticket speculator and, at a price, obtained seats for a new musical comedy called "High Jinks." In the foyer of the theatre they waited a few moments to see the first-night crowd come in. There were opera cloaks stitched of myriad, many-colored silks and furs; there were jewels dripping from arms and throats and ear-tips of white and rose; there were innumerable broad shimmers down the middles of innumerable silk hats; there were shoes of gold and bronze and red and shining black; there were the high-piled, tight-packed coiffures of many women and the slick, watered hair of well-kept men—most of all there was the ebbing, flowing, chattering, chuckling, foaming, slow-rolling wave effect of this cheerful sea of people as to-night it poured its glittering torrent into the artificial lake of laughter. . . .

After the play they parted—Maury was going to a dance at Sherry's, Anthony homeward and to bed.

He found his way slowly over the jostled evening mass of Times Square, which the chariot race and its thousand satellites made rarely beautiful and bright and intimate with carnival. Faces swirled about him, a kaleidoscope of girls, ugly, ugly as sin—too fat, too lean, yet floating upon this autumn air as upon their own warm and passionate breaths poured out into the night. Here, for all their vulgarity, he thought, they were faintly and subtly mysterious. He inhaled carefully, swallowing into his lungs perfume and the not unpleasant scent of many cigarettes. He caught the glance of a dark young beauty sitting alone in a closed taxicab. Her eyes in the half-light suggested night and violets, and for a moment he stirred again to that half-forgotten remoteness of the afternoon.

Two young Jewish men passed him, talking in loud voices and craning their necks here and there in fatuous supercilious glances. They were dressed in suits of the exaggerated tight-ness then semi-fashionable; their turned over collars were notched at the Adam's apple; they wore gray spats and carried gray gloves on their cane handles.

Passed a bewildered old lady borne along like a basket of eggs between two men who exclaimed to her of the wonders of Times Square—explained them so quickly that the old lady, trying to be impartially interested, waved her head here and there like a piece of wind-worried old orange-peel. Anthony heard a snatch of their conversation:

"There's the Astor, mama!"

"Look! See the chariot race sign——"

"There's where we were to-day. No, *there!*"

"Good gracious! . . ."

"You should worry and grow thin like a dime." He recognized the current witticism of the year as it issued stridently from one of the pairs at his elbow.

"And I says to him, I says——"

The soft rush of taxis by him, and laughter, laughter hoarse as a crow's, incessant and loud, with the rumble of the subways underneath—and over all, the revolutions of light, the growings and recedings of light—light dividing like pearls— forming and reforming in glittering bars and circles and monstrous grotesque figures cut amazingly on the sky.

He turned thankfully down the hush that blew like a dark wind out of a cross-street, passed a bakery-restaurant in whose windows a dozen roast chickens turned over and over on an automatic spit. From the door came a smell that was hot, doughy, and pink. A drug-store next, exhaling medicines, spilt soda water and a pleasant undertone from the cosmetic counter; then a Chinese laundry, still open, steamy and stifling, smelling folded and vaguely yellow. All these depressed him; reaching Sixth Avenue he stopped at a corner cigar store and emerged feeling better—the cigar store was cheerful, humanity in a navy blue mist, buying a luxury. . . .

Once in his apartment he smoked a last cigarette, sitting in the dark by his open front window. For the first time in over a year he found himself thoroughly enjoying New York. There was a rare pungency in it certainly, a quality almost Southern. A lonesome town, though. He who had grown up alone had lately learned to avoid solitude. During the past several months he had been careful, when he had no engagement for the evening, to hurry to one of his clubs and find some one. Oh, there was a loneliness here——

His cigarette, its smoke bordering the thin folds of curtain with rims of faint white spray, glowed on until the clock in St. Anne's down the street struck one with a querulous fashionable beauty. The elevated, half a quiet block away, sounded a rumble of drums—and should he lean from his window he would see the train, like an angry eagle, breasting the dark curve at the corner. He was reminded of a fantastic romance he had lately read in which cities had been bombed from aerial trains, and for a moment he fancied that Washington Square had declared war on Central Park and that this was a north-bound menace loaded with battle and sudden death. But as it passed the illusion faded; it diminished to the faintest of drums—then to a far-away droning eagle.

There were the bells and the continued low blur of auto horns from Fifth Avenue, but his own street was silent and he was safe in here from all the threat of life, for there was his door and the long hall and his guardian bedroom—safe, safe! The arc-light shining into his window seemed for this hour like the moon, only brighter and more beautiful than the moon.

A FLASH-BACK IN PARADISE

Beauty, who was born anew every hundred years, sat in a sort of outdoor waiting room through which blew gusts of white wind and occasionally a breathless hurried star. The stars winked at her intimately as they went by and the winds made a soft incessant flurry in her hair. She was incomprehensible, for, in her, soul and spirit were one—the beauty of her body was the essence of her soul. She was that unity sought for by philosophers through many centuries. In this outdoor waiting room of winds and stars she had been sitting for a hundred years, at peace in the contemplation of herself.

It became known to her, at length, that she was to be born again. Sighing, she began a long conversation with a voice that was in the white wind, a conversation that took many hours and of which I can give only a fragment here.

BEAUTY: (*Her lips scarcely stirring, her eyes turned, as always, inward upon herself*) Whither shall I journey now?

THE VOICE: To a new country—a land you have never seen before.

BEAUTY: (*Petulantly*) I loathe breaking into these new civilizations. How long a stay this time?

THE VOICE: Fifteen years.

BEAUTY: And what's the name of the place?

THE VOICE: It is the most opulent, most gorgeous land on earth—a land whose wisest are but little wiser than its dullest; a land where the rulers have minds like little children and the law-givers believe in Santa Claus; where ugly women control strong men——

BEAUTY: (*In astonishment*) What?

THE VOICE: (*Very much depressed*) Yes, it is truly a melancholy spectacle. Women with receding chins and shapeless noses go about in broad daylight saying "Do this!" and "Do that!" and all the men, even those of great wealth, obey implicitly their women to whom they refer sonorously either as "Mrs. So-and-so" or as "the wife."

BEAUTY: But this can't be true! I can understand, of course, their obedience to women of charm—but to fat women? to bony women? to women with scrawny cheeks?

THE VOICE: Even so.

BEAUTY: What of me? What chance shall I have?

THE VOICE: It will be "harder going," if I may borrow a phrase.

BEAUTY: (*After a dissatisfied pause*) Why not the old lands, the land of grapes and soft-tongued men or the land of ships and seas?

THE VOICE: It's expected that they'll be very busy shortly.

BEAUTY: Oh!

THE VOICE: Your life on earth will be, as always, the interval between two significant glances in a mundane mirror.

BEAUTY: What will I be? Tell me?

THE VOICE: At first it was thought that you would go this time as an actress in the motion pictures but, after all, it's not advisable. You will be disguised during your fifteen years as what is called a "susciety gurl."

BEAUTY: What's that?

(*There is a new sound in the wind which must for our purposes be interpreted as* THE VOICE *scratching its head.*)

THE VOICE: (*At length*) It's a sort of bogus aristocrat.

BEAUTY: Bogus? What is bogus?

THE VOICE: That, too, you will discover in this land. You will find much that is bogus. Also, you will do much that is bogus.

BEAUTY: (*Placidly*) It all sounds so vulgar.

THE VOICE: Not half as vulgar as it is. You will be known during your fifteen years as a ragtime kid, a flapper, a jazz-baby, and a baby vamp. You will dance new dances neither more nor less gracefully than you danced the old ones.

BEAUTY: (*In a whisper*) Will I be paid?

THE VOICE: Yes, as usual—in love.

BEAUTY: (*With a faint laugh which disturbs only momentarily the immobility of her lips*) And will I like being called a jazz-baby?

THE VOICE: (*Soberly*) You will love it. . . .

(*The dialogue ends here, with* BEAUTY *still sitting quietly, the stars pausing in an ecstasy of appreciation, the wind, white and gusty, blowing through her hair.*

All this took place seven years before ANTHONY *sat by the front windows of his apartment and listened to the chimes of St. Anne's.*)

CHAPTER 2

PORTRAIT OF A SIREN

Crispness folded down upon New York a month later, bringing November and the three big football games and a great fluttering of furs along Fifth Avenue. It brought, also, a sense of tension to the city, and suppressed excitement. Every morning now there were invitations in Anthony's mail. Three dozen virtuous females of the first layer were proclaiming their fitness, if not their specific willingness, to bear children unto three dozen millionaires. Five dozen virtuous females of the second layer were proclaiming not only this fitness, but in addition a tremendous undaunted ambition toward the first three dozen young men, who were of course invited to each of the ninety-six parties—as were the young lady's group of family friends, acquaintances, college boys, and eager young outsiders. To continue, there was a third layer from the skirts of the city, from Newark and the Jersey suburbs up to bitter Connecticut and the ineligible sections of Long Island—and doubtless contiguous layers down to the city's shoes: Jewesses were coming out into a society of Jewish men and women, from Riverside to the Bronx, and looking forward to a rising young broker or jeweller and a kosher wedding; Irish girls were casting their eyes, with license at last to do so, upon a society of young Tammany politicians, pious undertakers, and grown-up choirboys.

And, naturally, the city caught the contagious air of entrée—the working girls, poor ugly souls, wrapping soap in the factories and showing finery in the big stores, dreamed that perhaps in the spectacular excitement of this winter they might obtain for themselves the coveted male—as in a muddled carnival crowd an inefficient pickpocket may consider his chances increased. And the chimneys commenced to smoke and the subway's foulness was freshened. And the actresses came out in new plays and the publishers came out with new books and the Castles came out with new dances. And the railroads came out with new schedules containing new mistakes instead of the old ones that the commuters had grown used to. . . .

The City was coming out!

Anthony, walking along Forty-second Street one afternoon under a steel-gray sky, ran unexpectedly into Richard Caramel emerging from the Manhattan Hotel barber shop. It was a cold day, the first definitely cold day, and Caramel had on one of those knee-length, sheep-lined coats long worn by the working men of the Middle West, that were just coming into fashionable approval. His soft hat was of a discreet dark brown, and from under it his clear eye flamed like a topaz. He stopped Anthony enthusiastically, slapping him on the arms more from a desire to keep himself warm than from playfulness, and, after his inevitable hand shake, exploded into sound.

"Cold as the devil—Good Lord, I've been working like the deuce all day till my room got so cold I thought I'd get pneumonia. Darn landlady economizing on coal came up when I yelled over the stairs for her for half an hour. Began explaining why and all. God! First she drove me crazy, then I began to think she was sort of a character, and took notes while she talked—so she couldn't see me, you know, just as though I were writing casually—"

He had seized Anthony's arm and walking him briskly up Madison Avenue.

"Where to?"

"Nowhere in particular."

"Well, then what's the use?" demanded Anthony.

They stopped and stared at each other, and Anthony wondered if the cold made his own face as repellent as Dick Caramel's, whose nose was crimson, whose bulging brow was blue, whose yellow unmatched eyes were red and watery at the rims. After a moment they began walking again.

"Done some good work on my novel." Dick was looking and talking emphatically at the sidewalk. "But I have to get out once in a while." He glanced at Anthony apologetically, as though craving encouragement.

"I have to talk. I guess very few people ever really *think*, I mean sit down and ponder and have ideas in sequence. I do my thinking in writing or conversation. You've got to have a start, sort of—something to defend or contradict—don't you think?"

Anthony grunted and withdrew his arm gently.

"I don't mind carrying you, Dick, but with that coat—"

"I mean," continued Richard Caramel gravely, "that on paper your first paragraph contains the idea you're going to damn or enlarge on. In conversation you've got your vis-à-vis's last statement—but when you simply *ponder*, why, your ideas just succeed each other like magic-lantern pictures and each one forces out the last."

They passed Forty-fifth Street and slowed down slightly. Both of them lit cigarettes and blew tremendous clouds of smoke and frosted breath into the air.

"Let's walk up to the Plaza and have an egg-nog," suggested Anthony. "Do you good. Air'll get the rotten nicotine out of your lungs. Come on—I'll let you talk about your book all the way."

"I don't want to if it bores you. I mean you needn't do it as a favor." The words tumbled out in haste, and though he tried to keep his face casual it screwed up uncertainly. Anthony was compelled to protest: "Bore me? I should say not!"

"Got a cousin—" began Dick, but Anthony interrupted by stretching out his arms and breathing forth a low cry of exultation.

"Good weather!" he exclaimed, "isn't it? Makes me feel about ten. I mean it makes me feel as I should have felt when I was ten. Murderous! Oh, God! one minute it's my world, and the next I'm the world's fool. To-day it's my world and everything's easy, easy. Even Nothing is easy!"

"Got a cousin up at the Plaza. Famous girl. We can go up and meet her. She lives there in the winter—has lately anyway—with her mother and father."

"Didn't know you had cousins in New York."

"Her name's Gloria. She's from home—Kansas City. Her mother's a practising Bilphist, and her father's quite dull but a perfect gentleman."

"What are they? Literary material?"

"They try to be. All the old man does is tell me he just met the most wonderful character for a novel. Then he tells me about some idiotic friend of his and then he says: '*There's* a character for you! Why don't you write him up? Everybody'd be interested in *him*.' Or else he tells me about Japan or Paris, or some other very obvious place, and says: 'Why don't you write a story about that place? That'd be a wonderful setting for a story!'"

"How about the girl?" inquired Anthony casually, "Gloria—Gloria what?"

"Gilbert. Oh, you've heard of her—Gloria Gilbert. Goes to dances at colleges—all that sort of thing."

"I've heard her name."

"Good-looking—in fact damned attractive."

They reached Fiftieth Street and turned over toward the Avenue.

"I don't care for young girls as a rule," said Anthony, frowning.

This was not strictly true. While it seemed to him that the average debutante spent every hour of her day thinking and talking about what the great world had mapped out for her to do during the next hour, any girl who made a living directly on her prettiness interested him enormously.

"Gloria's darn nice—not a brain in her head."

Anthony laughed in a one-syllabled snort.

"By that you mean that she hasn't a line of literary patter."

"No, I don't."

"Dick, you know what passes as brains in a girl for you. Earnest young women who sit with you in a corner and talk earnestly about life. The kind who when they were sixteen argued with grave faces as to whether kissing was right or wrong—and whether it was immoral for freshmen to drink beer."

Richard Caramel was offended. His scowl crinkled like crushed paper.

"No—" he began, but Anthony interrupted ruthlessly.

"Oh, yes; kind who just at present sit in corners and confer on the latest Scandinavian Dante available in English translation."

Dick turned to him, a curious falling in his whole countenance. His question was almost an appeal.

"What's the matter with you and Maury? You talk sometimes as though I were a sort of inferior."

Anthony was confused, but he was also cold and a little uncomfortable, so he took refuge in attack.

"I don't think your brains matter, Dick."

"Of course they matter!" exclaimed Dick angrily. "What do you mean? Why don't they matter?"

"You might know too much for your pen."

"I couldn't possibly."

"I can imagine," insisted Anthony, "a man knowing too much for his talent to express. Like me. Suppose, for instance, I have more wisdom than you, and less talent. It would tend to make me inarticulate. You, on the contrary, have enough water to fill the pail and a big enough pail to hold the water."

"I don't follow you at all," complained Dick in a crest-fallen tone. Infinitely dismayed, he seemed to bulge in protest. He was staring intently at Anthony and caroming off a succession of passers-by, who reproached him with fierce, resentful glances.

"I simply mean that a talent like Wells's could carry the intelligence of a Spencer. But an inferior talent can only be graceful when it's carrying inferior ideas. And the more narrowly you can look at a thing the more entertaining you can be about it."

Dick considered, unable to decide the exact degree of criticism intended by Anthony's remarks. But Anthony, with that facility which seemed so frequently to flow from him, continued, his dark eyes gleaming in his thin face, his chin raised, his voice raised, his whole physical being raised:

"Say I am proud and sane and wise—an Athenian among Greeks. Well, I might fail where a lesser man would succeed. He could imitate, he could adorn, he could be enthusiastic, he could be hopefully constructive. But this hypothetical me would be too proud to imitate, too sane to be enthusiastic, too sophisticated to be Utopian, too Grecian to adorn."

"Then you don't think the artist works from his intelligence?"

"No. He goes on improving, if he can, what he imitates in the way of style, and choosing from his own interpretation of the things around him what constitutes material. But after all every writer writes because it's his mode of living. Don't tell me you like this 'Divine Function of the Artist' business?"

"I'm not accustomed even to refer to myself as an artist."

"Dick," said Anthony, changing his tone, "I want to beg your pardon."

"Why?"

"For that outburst. I'm honestly sorry. I was talking for effect."

Somewhat mollified, Dick rejoined:

"I've often said you were a Philistine at heart."

It was a crackling dusk when they turned in under the white façade of the Plaza and tasted slowly the foam and yellow thickness of an egg-nog. Anthony looked at his companion. Richard Caramel's nose and brow were slowly approaching a like pigmentation; the red was leaving the one, the blue deserting the other. Glancing in a mirror, Anthony was glad to find that his own skin had not discolored. On the contrary, a faint glow had kindled in his cheeks—he fancied that he had never looked so well.

"Enough for me," said Dick, his tone that of an athlete in training. "I want to go up and see the Gilberts. Won't you come?"

"Why—yes. If you don't dedicate me to the parents and dash off in the corner with Dora."

"Not Dora—Gloria."

A clerk announced them over the phone, and ascending to the tenth floor they followed a winding corridor and knocked at 1088. The door was answered by a middle-aged lady—Mrs. Gilbert herself.

"How do you do?" She spoke in the conventional American lady-lady language. "Well, I'm *aw*fully glad to see you—"

Hasty interjections by Dick, and then:

"Mr. Pats? Well, do come in, and leave your coat there." She pointed to a chair and changed her inflection to a deprecatory laugh full of minute gasps. "This is really lovely—lovely. Why, Richard, you haven't been here for *so* long—no!—no!" The latter monosyllables served half as responses, half as periods, to some vague starts from Dick. "Well, do sit down and tell me what you've been doing."

One crossed and recrossed; one stood and bowed ever so gently; one smiled again and again with helpless stupidity; one wondered if she would ever sit down at length one slid thankfully into a chair and settled for a pleasant call.

"I suppose it's because you've been busy—as much as anything else," smiled Mrs. Gilbert somewhat ambiguously. The "as much as anything else" she used to balance all her more rickety sentences. She had two other ones: "at least that's the way I look at it" and "pure and simple"—these three, alternated, gave each of her remarks an air of being a general reflection on life, as though she had calculated all causes and, at length, put her finger on the ultimate one.

Richard Caramel's face, Anthony saw, was now quite normal. The brow and cheeks were of a flesh color, the nose politely inconspicuous. He had fixed his aunt with the bright-yellow eye, giving her that acute and exaggerated attention that young males are accustomed to render to all females who are of no further value.

"Are you a writer too, Mr. Pats? . . . Well, perhaps we can all bask in Richard's fame."—Gentle laughter led by Mrs. Gilbert.

"Gloria's out," she said, with an air of laying down an axiom from which she would proceed to derive results. "She's dancing somewhere. Gloria goes, goes, goes. I tell her I don't see how she stands it. She dances all afternoon and all night, until I think she's going to wear herself to a shadow. Her father is very worried about her."

She smiled from one to the other. They both smiled.

She was composed, Anthony perceived, of a succession of semicircles and parabolas, like those figures that gifted folk

35

make on the typewriter: head, arms, bust, hips, thighs, and ankles were in a bewildering tier of roundnesses. Well ordered and clean she was, with hair of an artificially rich gray; her large face sheltered weather-beaten blue eyes and was adorned with just the faintest white mustache.

"I always say," she remarked to Anthony, "that Richard is an ancient soul."

In the tense pause that followed, Anthony considered a pun—something about Dick having been much walked upon.

"We all have souls of different ages," continued Mrs. Gilbert radiantly; "at least that's what I say."

"Perhaps so," agreed Anthony with an air of quickening to a hopeful idea. The voice bubbled on:

"Gloria has a very young soul—irresponsible, as much as anything else. She has no sense of responsibility."

"She's sparkling, Aunt Catherine," said Richard pleasantly. "A sense of responsibility would spoil her. She's too pretty."

"Well," confessed Mrs. Gilbert, "all I know is that she goes and goes and goes—"

The number of goings to Gloria's discredit was lost in the rattle of the door-knob as it turned to admit Mr. Gilbert.

He was a short man with a mustache resting like a small white cloud beneath his undistinguished nose. He had reached the stage where his value as a social creature was a black and imponderable negative. His ideas were the popular delusions of twenty years before; his mind steered a wabbly and anaemic course in the wake of the daily newspaper editorials. After graduating from a small but terrifying Western university, he had entered the celluloid business, and as this required only the minute measure of intelligence he brought to it, he did well for several years—in fact until about 1911, when he began exchanging contracts for vague agreements with the moving picture industry. The moving picture industry had decided about 1912 to gobble him up, and at this time he was, so to speak, delicately balanced on its tongue. Meanwhile he was supervising manager of the Associated Mid-western Film Materials Company, spending six months of each year in New York and the remainder in Kansas City and St. Louis. He felt credulously that there was a good thing coming to him—and his wife thought so, and his daughter thought so too.

He disapproved of Gloria: she stayed out late, she never ate her meals, she was always in a mix-up—he had irritated her once and she had used toward him words that he had not thought were part of her vocabulary. His wife was easier. After fifteen years of incessant guerilla warfare he had conquered her—it was a war of muddled optimism against organized dulness, and something in the number of "yes's" with which he could poison a conversation had won him the victory.

"Yes-yes-yes-yes," he would say, "yes-yes-yes-yes. Let me see. That was the summer of—let me see—ninety-one or ninety-two—Yes-yes-yes-yes——"

Fifteen years of yes's had beaten Mrs. Gilbert. Fifteen further years of that incessant unaffirmative affirmative, accompanied by the perpetual flicking of ash-mushrooms from thirty-two thousand cigars, had broken her. To this husband of hers she made the last concession of married life, which is more complete, more irrevocable, than the first—she listened to him. She told herself that the years had brought her tolerance—actually they had slain what measure she had ever possessed of moral courage.

She introduced him to Anthony.

"This is Mr. Pats," she said.

The young man and the old touched flesh; Mr. Gilbert's hand was soft, worn away to the pulpy semblance of a squeezed grapefruit. Then husband and wife exchanged greetings—he told her it had grown colder out; he said he had walked down to a news-stand on Forty-fourth Street for a Kansas City paper. He had intended to ride back in the bus but he had found it too cold, yes, yes, yes, yes, too cold.

Mrs. Gilbert added flavor to his adventure by being impressed with his courage in braving the harsh air.

"Well, you *are* spunky!" she exclaimed admiringly. "You *are* spunky. I wouldn't have gone out for anything."

Mr. Gilbert with true masculine impassivity disregarded the awe he had excited in his wife. He turned to the two young men and triumphantly routed them on the subject of the weather. Richard Caramel was called on to remember the month of November in Kansas. No sooner had the theme been pushed toward him, however, than it was violently fished back to be lingered over, pawed over, elongated, and generally devitalized by its sponsor.

The immemorial thesis that the days somewhere were warm but the nights very pleasant was successfully propounded and they decided the exact distance on an obscure railroad between two points that Dick had inadvertently mentioned. Anthony fixed Mr. Gilbert with a steady stare and went into a trance through which, after a moment, Mrs. Gilbert's smiling voice penetrated:

"It seems as though the cold were damper here—it seems to eat into my bones."

As this remark, adequately yessed, had been on the tip of Mr. Gilbert's tongue, he could not be blamed for rather abruptly changing the subject.

"Where's Gloria?"

"She ought to be here any minute."

"Have you met my daughter, Mr.——?"

"Haven't had the pleasure. I've heard Dick speak of her often."

"She and Richard are cousins."

"Yes?" Anthony smiled with some effort. He was not used to the society of his seniors, and his mouth was stiff from superfluous cheerfulness. It was such a pleasant thought about Gloria and Dick being cousins. He managed within the next minute to throw an agonized glance at his friend.

Richard Caramel was afraid they'd have to toddle off.

Mrs. Gilbert was tremendously sorry.

Mr. Gilbert thought it was too bad.

Mrs. Gilbert had a further idea—something about being glad they'd come, anyhow, even if they'd only seen an old lady way too old to flirt with them. Anthony and Dick evidently considered this a sly sally, for they laughed one bar in three-four time.

Would they come again soon?

"Oh, yes."

Gloria would be *aw*fully sorry!

"Good-by——"

"Good-by——"

Smiles!

Smiles!

Bang!

Two disconsolate young men walking down the tenth-floor corridor of the Plaza in the direction of the elevator.

A LADY'S LEGS

Behind Maury Noble's attractive indolence, his irrelevance and his easy mockery, lay a surprising and relentless maturity of purpose. His intention, as he stated it in college, had been to use three years in travel, three years in utter leisure—and then to become immensely rich as quickly as possible.

His three years of travel were over. He had accomplished the globe with an intensity and curiosity that in any one else would have seemed pedantic, without redeeming spontaneity, almost the self-editing of a human Baedeker; but, in this case, it assumed an air of mysterious purpose and significant design—as though Maury Noble were some predestined anti-Christ, urged by a preordination to go everywhere there was to go along the earth and to see all the billions of humans who bred and wept and slew each other here and there upon it.

Back in America, he was sallying into the search for amusement with the same consistent absorption. He who had never taken more than a few cocktails or a pint of wine at a sitting, taught himself to drink as he would have taught himself Greek—like Greek it would be the gateway to a wealth of new sensations, new psychic states, new reactions in joy or misery.

His habits were a matter for esoteric speculation. He had three rooms in a bachelor apartment on Forty-forth street, but he was seldom to be found there. The telephone girl had received the most positive instructions that no one should even have his ear without first giving a name to be passed upon. She had a list of half a dozen people to whom he was never at home, and of the same number to whom he was always at home. Foremost on the latter list were Anthony Patch and Richard Caramel.

Maury's mother lived with her married son in Philadelphia, and there Maury went usually for the week-ends, so one Saturday night when Anthony, prowling the chilly streets in a fit of utter boredom, dropped in at the Molton Arms he was overjoyed to find that Mr. Noble was at home.

His spirits soared faster than the flying elevator. This was so good, so extremely good, to be about to talk to Maury— who would be equally happy at seeing him. They would look at each other with a deep affection just behind their eyes which both would conceal beneath some attenuated raillery. Had it been summer they would have gone out together and indolently sipped two long Tom Collinses, as they wilted their collars and watched the faintly diverting round of some lazy August cabaret. But it was cold outside, with wind around the edges of the tall buildings and December just up the street, so better far an evening together under the soft lamplight and a drink or two of Bushmill's, or a thimbleful of Maury's Grand Marnier, with the books gleaming like ornaments against the walls, and Maury radiating a divine inertia as he rested, large and catlike, in his favorite chair.

There he was! The room closed about Anthony, warmed him. The glow of that strong persuasive mind, that temperament almost Oriental in its outward impassivity, warmed Anthony's restless soul and brought him a peace that could be likened only to the peace a stupid woman gives. One must understand all—else one must take all for granted. Maury filled the room, tigerlike, godlike. The winds outside were stilled; the brass candlesticks on the mantel glowed like tapers before an altar.

"What keeps you here to-day?" Anthony spread himself over a yielding sofa and made an elbow-rest among the pillows.

"Just been here an hour. Tea dance—and I stayed so late I missed my train to Philadelphia."

"Strange to stay so long," commented Anthony curiously.

"Rather. What'd you do?"

"Geraldine. Little usher at Keith's. I told you about her."

"Oh!"

"Paid me a call about three and stayed till five. Peculiar little soul—she gets me. She's so utterly stupid."

Maury was silent.

"Strange as it may seem," continued Anthony, "so far as I'm concerned, and even so far as I know, Geraldine is a paragon of virtue."

He had known her a month, a girl of nondescript and nomadic habits. Someone had casually passed her on to Anthony, who considered her amusing and rather liked the chaste and fairylike kisses she had given him on the third night of their acquaintance, when they had driven in a taxi through the Park. She had a vague family—a shadowy aunt and uncle who shared with her an apartment in the labyrinthine hundreds. She was company, familiar and faintly intimate and restful. Further than that he did not care to experiment—not from any moral compunction, but from a dread of allowing any entanglement to disturb what he felt was the growing serenity of his life.

"She has two stunts," he informed Maury; "one of them is to get her hair over her eyes some way and then blow it out, and the other is to say 'You cra-a-azy!' when some one makes a remark that's over her head. It fascinates me. I sit there hour after hour, completely intrigued by the maniacal symptoms she finds in my imagination."

Maury stirred in his chair and spoke.

"Remarkable that a person can comprehend so little and yet live in such a complex civilization. A woman like that actually takes the whole universe in the most matter-of-fact way. From the influence of Rousseau to the bearing of the tariff rates on her dinner, the whole phenomenon is utterly strange to her. She's just been carried along from an age of spearheads and plunked down here with the equipment of an archer for going into a pistol duel. You could sweep away the entire crust of history and she'd never know the difference."

"I wish our Richard would write about her."

"Anthony, surely you don't think she's worth writing about."

"As much as anybody," he answered, yawning. "You know I was thinking to-day that I have a great confidence in Dick. So long as he sticks to people and not to ideas, and as long as his inspirations come from life and not from art, and always granting a normal growth, I believe he'll be a big man."

"I should think the appearance of the black note-book would prove that he's going to life."

Anthony raised himself on his elbow and answered eagerly:

"He tries to go to life. So does every author except the very worst, but after all most of them live on predigested food. The incident or character may be from life, but the writer usually interprets it in terms of the last book he read. For instance, suppose he meets a sea captain and thinks he's an original character. The truth is that he sees the resemblance between the sea captain and the last sea captain Dana created, or who-ever creates sea captains, and therefore he knows how to set this sea captain on paper. Dick, of course, can set down any consciously picturesque, character-like character, but could he accurately transcribe his own sister?"

Then they were off for half an hour on literature.

"A classic," suggested Anthony, "is a successful book that has survived the reaction of the next period or generation. Then it's safe, like a style in architecture or furniture. It's acquired a picturesque dignity to take the place of its fashion. . . ."

After a time the subject temporarily lost its tang. The interest of the two young men was not particularly technical. They were in love with generalities. Anthony had recently discovered Samuel Butler and the brisk aphorisms in the note-book seemed to him the quintessence of criticism. Maury, his whole mind so thoroughly mellowed by the very hardness of his scheme of life, seemed inevitably the wiser of the two, yet in the actual stuff of their intelligences they were not, it seemed, fundamentally different.

They drifted from letters to the curiosities of each other's day.

"Whose tea was it?"

"People named Abercrombie."

"Why'd you stay late? Meet a luscious débutante?"

"Yes."

"Did you really?" Anthony's voice lifted in surprise.

"Not a débutante exactly. Said she came out two winters ago in Kansas City."

"Sort of left-over?"

"No," answered Maury with some amusement, "I think that's the last thing I'd say about her. She seemed—well, somehow the youngest person there."

"Not too young to make you miss a train."

"Young enough. Beautiful child."

Anthony chuckled in his one-syllable snort.

"Oh, Maury, you're in your second childhood. What do you mean by beautiful?"

Maury gazed helplessly into space.

"Well, I can't describe her exactly—except to say that she was beautiful. She was—tremendously alive. She was eating gum-drops."

"What!"

"It was a sort of attenuated vice. She's a nervous kind—said she always ate gum-drops at teas because she had to stand around so long in one place."

"What'd you talk about—Bergson? Bilphism? Whether the one-step is immoral?"

Maury was unruffled; his fur seemed to run all ways.

"As a matter of fact we did talk on Bilphism. Seems her mother's a Bilphist. Mostly, though, we talked about legs."

Anthony rocked in glee.

"My God! Whose legs?"

"Hers. She talked a lot about hers. As though they were a sort of choice bric-à-brac. She aroused a great desire to see them."

"What is she—a dancer?"

"No, I found she was a cousin of Dick's."

Anthony sat upright so suddenly that the pillow he released stood on end like a live thing and dove to the floor.

"Name's Gloria Gilbert?" he cried.

"Yes. Isn't she remarkable?"

"I'm sure I don't know—but for sheer dullness her father—"

"Well," interrupted Maury with implacable conviction, "her family may be as sad as professional mourners but I'm inclined to think that she's a quite authentic and original character. The outer signs of the cut-and-dried Yale prom girl and all that—but different, very emphatically different."

"Go on, go on!" urged Anthony. "Soon as Dick told me she didn't have a brain in her head I knew she must be pretty good."

"Did he say that?"

"Swore to it," said Anthony with another snorting laugh.

"Well, what he means by brains in a woman is—"

"I know," interrupted Anthony eagerly, "he means a smattering of literary misinformation."

"That's it. The kind who believes that the annual moral let-down of the country is a very good thing or the kind who believes it's a very ominous thing. Either pince-nez or postures. Well, this girl talked about legs. She talked about skin too—her own skin. Always her own. She told me the sort of tan she'd like to get in the summer and how closely she usually approximated it."

"You sat enraptured by her low alto?"

"By her low alto! No, by tan! I began thinking about tan. I began to think what color I turned when I made my last exposure about two years ago. I did use to get a pretty good tan. I used to get a sort of bronze, if I remember rightly."

Anthony retired into the cushions, shaken with laughter.

"She's got you going—oh, Maury! Maury the Connecticut life-saver. The human nutmeg. Extra! Heiress elopes with coast-guard because of his luscious pigmentation! Afterward found to be Tasmanian strain in his family!"

Maury sighed; rising he walked to the window and raised the shade.

"Snowing hard."

Anthony, still laughing quietly to himself, made no answer.

"Another winter." Maury's voice from the window was almost a whisper. "We're growing old, Anthony. I'm twenty-seven, by God! Three years to thirty, and then I'm what an undergraduate calls a middle-aged man."

Anthony was silent for a moment.

"You *are* old, Maury," he agreed at length. "The first signs of a very dissolute and wabbly senescence—you have spent the afternoon talking about tan and a lady's legs."

Maury pulled down the shade with a sudden harsh snap.

"Idiot!" he cried, "that from you! Here I sit, young Anthony, as I'll sit for a generation or more and watch such gay souls as you and Dick and Gloria Gilbert go past me, dancing and singing and loving and hating one another and being moved, being eternally moved. And I am moved only by my lack of emotion. I shall sit and the snow will come—oh, for a Caramel to take notes—and another winter and I shall be thirty and you and Dick and Gloria will go on being eternally moved and dancing by me and singing. But after you've all gone I'll be saying things for new Dicks to write down, and listening to the disillusions and cynicisms and emotions of new Anthonys—yes, and talking to new Glorias about the tans of summers yet to come."

The firelight flurried up on the hearth. Maury left the window, stirred the blaze with a poker, and dropped a log upon the andirons. Then he sat back in his chair and the remnants of his voice faded in the new fire that spit red and yellow along the bark.

"After all, Anthony, it's you who are very romantic and young. It's you who are infinitely more susceptible and afraid of your calm being broken. It's me who tries again and again to be moved—let myself go a thousand times and I'm always me. Nothing—quite—stirs me.

"Yet," he murmured after another long pause, "there was something about that little girl with her absurd tan that was eternally old—like me."

TURBULENCE

Anthony turned over sleepily in his bed, greeting a patch of cold sun on his counterpane, crisscrossed with the shadows of the leaded window. The room was full of morning. The carved chest in the corner, the ancient and inscrutable wardrobe, stood about the room like dark symbols of the obliviousness of matter; only the rug was beckoning and perishable to his perishable feet, and Bounds, horribly inappropriate in his soft collar, was of stuff as fading as the gauze of frozen breath he uttered. He was close to the bed, his hand still lowered where he had been jerking at the upper blanket, his dark-brown eyes fixed imperturbably upon his master.

"Bows!" muttered the drowsy god. "Thachew, Bows?"

"It's I, sir."

Anthony moved his head, forced his eyes wide, and blinked triumphantly.

"Bounds."

"Yes, sir?"

"Can you get off—yeow-ow-oh-oh-oh God!—" Anthony yawned insufferably and the contents of his brain seemed to fall together in a dense hash. He made a fresh start.

"Can you come around about four and serve some tea and sandwiches or something?"

"Yes, sir."

Anthony considered with chilling lack of inspiration. "Some sandwiches," he repeated helplessly, "oh, some cheese sandwiches and jelly ones and chicken and olive, I guess. Never mind breakfast."

The strain of invention was too much. He shut his eyes wearily, let his head roll to rest inertly, and quickly relaxed what he had regained of muscular control. Out of a crevice of his mind crept the vague but inevitable spectre of the night before—but it proved in this case to be nothing but a seemingly interminable conversation with Richard Caramel, who had called on him at midnight; they had drunk four bottles of beer and munched dry crusts of bread while Anthony listened to a reading of the first part of "The Demon Lover."

—Came a voice now after many hours. Anthony

disregarded it, as sleep closed over him, folded down upon him, crept up into the byways of his mind.

Suddenly he was awake, saying: "What?"

"For how many, sir?" It was still Bounds, standing patient and motionless at the foot of the bed—Bounds who divided his manner among three gentlemen.

"How many what?"

"I think, sir, I'd better know how many are coming. I'll have to plan for the sandwiches, sir."

"Two," muttered Anthony huskily; "lady and a gentleman."

Bounds said, "Thank you, sir," and moved away, bearing with him his humiliating reproachful soft collar, reproachful to each of the three gentlemen, who only demanded of him a third.

After a long time Anthony arose and drew an opalescent dressing grown of brown and blue over his slim pleasant figure. With a last yawn he went into the bathroom, and turning on the dresser light (the bathroom had no outside exposure) he contemplated himself in the mirror with some interest. A wretched apparition, he thought; he usually thought so in the morning—sleep made his face unnaturally pale. He lit a cigarette and glanced through several letters and the morning *Tribune*.

An hour later, shaven and dressed, he was sitting at his desk looking at a small piece of paper he had taken out of his wallet. It was scrawled with semi-legible memoranda: "See Mr. Howland at five. Get hair-cut. See about Rivers' bill. Go book-store."

—And under the last: "Cash in bank, $690 (crossed out), $612 (crossed out), $607."

Finally, down at the bottom and in a hurried scrawl: "Dick and Gloria Gilbert for tea."

This last item brought him obvious satisfaction. His day, usually a jelly-like creature, a shapeless, spineless thing, had attained Mesozoic structure. It was marching along surely, even jauntily, toward a climax, as a play should, as a day should. He dreaded the moment when the backbone of the day should be broken, when he should have met the girl at last, talked to her, and then bowed her laughter out the door, returning only to the melancholy dregs in the teacups and the gathering staleness of the uneaten sandwiches.

There was a growing lack of color in Anthony's days. He felt it constantly and sometimes traced it to a talk he had had with Maury Noble a month before. That anything so ingenuous, so priggish, as a sense of waste should oppress him was absurd, but there was no denying the fact that some unwelcome survival of a fetish had drawn him three weeks before down to the public library, where, by the token of Richard Caramel's card, he had drawn out half a dozen books on the Italian Renaissance. That these books were still piled on his desk in the original order of carriage, that they were daily increasing his liabilities by twelve cents, was no mitigation of their testimony. They were cloth and morocco witnesses to the fact of his defection. Anthony had had several hours of acute and startling panic.

In justification of his manner of living there was first, of course, The Meaninglessness of Life. As aides and ministers, pages and squires, butlers and lackeys to this great Khan there were a thousand books glowing on his shelves, there was his apartment and all the money that was to be his when the old man up the river should choke on his last morality. From a world fraught with the menace of débutantes and the stupidity of many Geraldines he was thankfully delivered—rather should he emulate the feline immobility of Maury and wear proudly the culminative wisdom of the numbered generations.

Over and against these things was something which his brain persistently analyzed and dealt with as a tiresome complex but which, though logically disposed of and bravely trampled under foot, had sent him out through the soft slush of late November to a library which had none of the books he most wanted. It is fair to analyze Anthony as far as he could analyze himself; further than that it is, of course, presumption. He found in himself a growing horror and loneliness. The idea of eating alone frightened him; in preference he dined often with men he detested. Travel, which had once charmed him, seemed at length, unendurable, a business of color without substance, a phantom chase after his own dream's shadow.

—If I am essentially weak, he thought, I need work to do, work to do. It worried him to think that he was, after all, a facile mediocrity, with neither the poise of Maury nor the enthusiasm of Dick. It seemed a tragedy to want nothing—and yet he wanted something, something. He knew in flashes what it was—some path of hope to lead him toward what he thought was an imminent and ominous old age.

After cocktails and luncheon at the University Club Anthony felt better. He had run into two men from his class at Harvard, and in contrast to the gray heaviness of their conversation his life assumed color. Both of them were married: one spent his coffee time in sketching an extra-nuptial adventure to the bland and appreciative smiles of the other. Both of them, he thought, were Mr. Gilberts in embryo; the number of their "yes's" would have to be quadrupled, their natures crabbed by twenty years—then they would be no more than obsolete and broken machines, pseudo-wise and valueless, nursed to an utter senility by the women they had broken.

Ah, he was more than that, as he paced the long carpet in the lounge after dinner, pausing at the window to look into the harried street. He was Anthony Patch, brilliant, magnetic, the heir of many years and many men. This was his world now—and that last strong irony he craved lay in the offing.

With a stray boyishness he saw himself a power upon the earth; with his grandfather's money he might build his own pedestal and be a Talleyrand, a Lord Verulam. The clarity of his mind, its sophistication, its versatile intelligence, all at their maturity and dominated by some purpose yet to be born would find him work to do. On this minor his dream faded—work to do: he tried to imagine himself in Congress rooting around in the litter of that incredible pigsty with the narrow and porcine brows he saw pictured sometimes in the rotogravure sections of the Sunday newspapers, those glorified proletarians babbling blandly to the nation the ideas of high school seniors! Little men with copy-book ambitions who by mediocrity had thought to emerge from mediocrity into the lustreless and unromantic heaven of a government by the people—and the best, the dozen shrewd men at the top, egotistic and cynical, were content to lead this choir of white ties and wire collar-buttons in a discordant and amazing hymn, compounded of a vague confusion between wealth as a reward of virtue and wealth as a proof of vice, and continued cheers for God, the Constitution, and the Rocky Mountains!

Lord Verulam! Talleyrand!

Back in his apartment the grayness returned. His cocktails had died, making him sleepy, somewhat befogged and inclined to be surly. Lord Verulam—he? The very thought was bitter. Anthony Patch with no record of achievement, without courage, without strength to be satisfied with truth when it was given him. Oh, he was a pretentious fool, making careers out of cocktails and meanwhile regretting, weakly and secretly, the collapse of an insufficient and wretched idealism. He had garnished his soul in the subtlest taste and now he longed for the old rubbish. He was empty, it seemed, empty as an old bottle—

The buzzer rang at the door. Anthony sprang up and lifted the tube to his ear. It was Richard Caramel's voice, stilted and facetious:

"Announcing Miss Gloria Gilbert."

"How do you do?" he said, smiling and holding the door ajar.

Dick bowed.

"Gloria, this is Anthony."

"Well!" she cried, holding out a little gloved hand. Under her fur coat her dress was Alice-blue, with white lace crinkled stiffly about her throat.

"Let me take your things."

Anthony stretched out his arms and the brown mass of fur tumbled into them.

"Thanks."

"What do you think of her, Anthony?" Richard Caramel demanded barbarously. "Isn't she beautiful?"

"Well!" cried the girl defiantly—withal unmoved.

She was dazzling—alight; it was agony to comprehend her beauty in a glance. Her hair, full of a heavenly glamour, was gay against the winter color of the room.

Anthony moved about, magician-like, turning the mushroom lamp into an orange glory. The stirred fire burnished the copper andirons on the hearth—

"I'm a solid block of ice," murmured Gloria casually, glancing around with eyes whose irises were of the most delicate and transparent bluish white. "What a slick fire! We found a place where you could stand on an iron-bar grating, sort of, and it blew warm air up at you—but Dick wouldn't wait there with me. I told him to go on alone and let me be happy."

Conventional enough this. She seemed talking for her own pleasure, without effort. Anthony, sitting at one end of the sofa, examined her profile against the foreground of the lamp: the exquisite regularity of nose and upper lip, the chin, faintly decided, balanced beautifully on a rather short neck. On a photograph she must have been completely classical, almost cold—but the glow of her hair and cheeks, at once flushed and fragile, made her the most living person he had ever seen.

". . . Think you've got the best name I've heard," she was saying, still apparently to herself; her glance rested on him a moment and then flitted past him—to the Italian bracket-lamps clinging like luminous yellow turtles at intervals along the walls, to the books row upon row, then to her cousin on the other side. "Anthony Patch. Only you ought to look sort of like a horse, with a long narrow face—and you ought to be in tatters."

"That's all the Patch part, though. How should Anthony look?"

"You look like Anthony," she assured him seriously—he thought she had scarcely seen him—"rather majestic," she continued, "and solemn."

Anthony indulged in a disconcerted smile.

"Only I like alliterative names," she went on, "all except mine. Mine's too flamboyant. I used to know two girls named Jinks, though, and just think if they'd been named anything except what they were named—Judy Jinks and Jerry Jinks. Cute, what? Don't you think?" Her childish mouth was parted, awaiting a rejoinder.

"Everybody in the next generation," suggested Dick, "will be named Peter or Barbara—because at present all the piquant literary characters are named Peter or Barbara."

Anthony continued the prophecy:

"Of course Gladys and Eleanor, having graced the last generation of heroines and being at present in their social prime, will be passed on to the next generation of shop-girls—"

"Displacing Ella and Stella," interrupted Dick.

"And Pearl and Jewel," Gloria added cordially, "and Earl and Elmer and Minnie."

"And then I'll come along," remarked Dick, "and picking up the obsolete name, Jewel, I'll attach it to some quaint and attractive character and it'll start its career all over again."

Her voice took up the thread of subject and wove along with faintly upturning, half-humorous intonations for sentence ends—as though defying interruption—and intervals of shadowy laughter. Dick had told her that Anthony's man was named Bounds—she thought that was wonderful! Dick had made some sad pun about Bounds doing patchwork, but if there was one thing worse than a pun, she said, it was a person who, as the inevitable come-back to a pun, gave the perpetrator a mock-reproachful look.

"Where are you from?" inquired Anthony. He knew, but beauty had rendered him thoughtless.

"Kansas City, Missouri."

"They put her out the same time they barred cigarettes."

"Did they bar cigarettes? I see the hand of my holy grandfather."

"He's a reformer or something, isn't he?"

"I blush for him."

"So do I," she confessed. "I detest reformers, especially the sort who try to reform me."

"Are there many of those?"

"Dozens. It's 'Oh, Gloria, if you smoke so many cigarettes you'll lose your pretty complexion!' and 'Oh, Gloria, why don't you marry and settle down?'"

Anthony agreed emphatically while he wondered who had had the temerity to speak thus to such a personage.

"And then," she continued, "there are all the subtle reformers who tell you the wild stories they've heard about you and how they've been sticking up for you."

He saw, at length, that her eyes were gray, very level and cool, and when they rested on him he understood what Maury had meant by saying she was very young and very old. She talked always about herself as a very charming child might talk, and her comments on her tastes and distastes were unaffected and spontaneous.

"I must confess," said Anthony gravely, "that even I've heard one thing about you."

54

Alert at once, she sat up straight. Those eyes, with the grayness and eternity of a cliff of soft granite, caught his.

"Tell me. I'll believe it. I always believe anything any one tells me about myself—don't you?"

"Invariably!" agreed the two men in unison.

"Well, tell me."

"I'm not sure that I ought to," teased Anthony, smiling unwillingly. She was so obviously interested, in a state of almost laughable self-absorption.

"He means your nickname," said her cousin.

"What name?" inquired Anthony, politely puzzled.

Instantly she was shy—then she laughed, rolled back against the cushions, and turned her eyes up as she spoke:

"Coast-to-Coast Gloria." Her voice was full of laughter, laughter undefined as the varying shadows playing between fire and lamp upon her hair. "O Lord!"

Still Anthony was puzzled.

"What do you mean?"

"*Me*, I mean. That's what some silly boys coined for *me*."

"Don't you see, Anthony," explained Dick, "traveller of a nation-wide notoriety and all that. Isn't that what you've heard? She's been called that for years—since she was seventeen."

Anthony's eyes became sad and humorous.

"Who's this female Methuselah you've brought in here, Caramel?"

She disregarded this, possibly rather resented it, for she switched back to the main topic.

"What *have* you heard of me?"

"Something about your physique."

"Oh," she said, coolly disappointed, "that all?"

"Your tan."

"My tan?" She was puzzled. Her hand rose to her throat, rested there an instant as though the fingers were feeling variants of color.

"Do you remember Maury Noble? Man you met about a month ago. You made a great impression."

She thought a moment.

"I remember—but he didn't call me up."

"He was afraid to, I don't doubt."

It was black dark without now and Anthony wondered that his apartment had ever seemed gray—so warm and friendly were the books and pictures on the walls and the good Bounds offering tea from a respectful shadow and the three nice people giving out waves of interest and laughter back and forth across the happy fire.

DISSATISFACTION

On Thursday afternoon Gloria and Anthony had tea together in the grill room at the Plaza. Her fur-trimmed suit was gray—"because with gray you *have* to wear a lot of paint," she explained—and a small toque sat rakishly on her head, allowing yellow ripples of hair to wave out in jaunty glory. In the higher light it seemed to Anthony that her personality was infinitely softer—she seemed so young, scarcely eighteen; her form under the tight sheath, known then as a hobble-skirt, was amazingly supple and slender, and her hands, neither "artistic" nor stubby, were small as a child's hands should be.

As they entered, the orchestra were sounding the preliminary whimpers to a maxixe, a tune full of castanets and facile faintly languorous violin harmonies, appropriate to the crowded winter grill teeming with an excited college crowd, high-spirited at the approach of the holidays. Carefully, Gloria considered several locations, and rather to Anthony's annoyance paraded him circuitously to a table for two at the far side of the room. Reaching it she again considered. Would she sit on the right or on the left? Her beautiful eyes and lips were very grave as she made her choice, and Anthony thought again how naïve was her every gesture; she took all the things of life for hers to choose from and apportion, as though she were continually picking out presents for herself from an inexhaustible counter.

Abstractedly she watched the dancers for a few moments, commenting murmurously as a couple eddied near.

"There's a pretty girl in blue"—and as Anthony looked obediently—"there! No. behind you—there!"

"Yes," he agreed helplessly.

"You didn't see her."

"I'd rather look at you."

"I know, but she was pretty. Except that she had big ankles."

"Was she?—I mean, did she?" he said indifferently.

A girl's salutation came from a couple dancing close to them.

"Hello, Gloria! O Gloria!"

"Hello there."

"Who's that?" he demanded.

"I don't know. Somebody." She caught sight of another face. "Hello, Muriel!" Then to Anthony: "There's Muriel Kane. Now I think she's attractive, 'cept not very."

Anthony chuckled appreciatively.

"Attractive, 'cept not very," he repeated.

She smiled—was interested immediately.

"Why is that funny?" Her tone was pathetically intent.

"It just was."

"Do you want to dance?"

"Do you?"

"Sort of. But let's sit," she decided.

"And talk about you? You love to talk about you, don't you?"

"Yes." Caught in a vanity, she laughed.

"I imagine your autobiography would be a classic."

"Dick says I haven't got one."

"Dick!" he exclaimed. "What does he know about you?"

"Nothing. But he says the biography of every woman begins with the first kiss that counts, and ends when her last child is laid in her arms."

"He's talking from his book."

"He says unloved women have no biographies—they have histories."

Anthony laughed again.

"Surely you don't claim to be unloved!"

"Well, I suppose not."

"Then why haven't you a biography? Haven't you ever had a kiss that counted?" As the words left his lips he drew in his breath sharply as though to suck them back. This *baby*!

"I don't know what you mean 'counts,'" she objected.

"I wish you'd tell me how old you are."

"Twenty-two," she said, meeting his eyes gravely. "How old did you think?"

"About eighteen."

"I'm going to start being that. I don't like being twenty-two. I hate it more than anything in the world."

"Being twenty-two?"

"No. Getting old and everything. Getting married."

"Don't you ever want to marry?"

"I don't want to have responsibility and a lot of children to take care of."

Evidently she did not doubt that on her lips all things were good. He waited rather breathlessly for her next remark, expecting it to follow up her last. She was smiling, without amusement but pleasantly, and after an interval half a dozen words fell into the space between them:

"I wish I had some gum-drops."

"You shall!" He beckoned to a waiter and sent him to the cigar counter.

"D'you mind? I love gum-drops. Everybody kids me about it because I'm always whacking away at one—whenever my daddy's not around."

"Not at all.—Who are all these children?" he asked suddenly. "Do you know them all?"

"Why—no, but they're from—oh, from everywhere, I suppose. Don't you ever come here?"

"Very seldom. I don't care particularly for 'nice girls.'"

Immediately he had her attention. She turned a definite shoulder to the dancers, relaxed in her chair, and demanded:

"What *do* you do with yourself?"

Thanks to a cocktail Anthony welcomed the question. In a mood to talk, he wanted, moreover, to impress this girl whose interest seemed so tantalizingly elusive—she stopped to browse in unexpected pastures, hurried quickly over the inobviously obvious. He wanted to pose. He wanted to appear suddenly to her in novel and heroic colors. He wanted to stir her from that casualness she showed toward everything except herself.

"I do nothing," he began, realizing simultaneously that his words were to lack the debonair grace he craved for them. "I do nothing, for there's nothing I can do that's worth doing."

"Well?" He had neither surprised her nor even held her, yet she had certainly understood him, if indeed he had said aught worth understanding.

"Don't you approve of lazy men?"

She nodded.

"I suppose so, if they're gracefully lazy. Is that possible for an American?"

"Why not?" he demanded, discomfited.

But her mind had left the subject and wandered up ten floors.

"My daddy's mad at me," she observed dispassionately.

"Why? But I want to know just why it's impossible for an American to be gracefully idle"—his words gathered conviction—"it astonishes me. It—it—I don't understand why people think that every young man ought to go down-town and work

59

ten hours a day for the best twenty years of his life at dull, unimaginative work, certainly not altruistic work."

He broke off. She watched him inscrutably. He waited for her to agree or disagree, but she did neither.

"Don't you ever form judgments on things?" he asked with some exasperation.

She shook her head and her eyes wandered back to the dancers as she answered:

"I don't know. I don't know anything about—what you should do, or what anybody should do."

She confused him and hindered the flow of his ideas. Self-expression had never seemed at once so desirable and so impossible.

"Well," he admitted apologetically, "neither do I, of course, but—"

"I just think of people," she continued, "whether they seem right where they are and fit into the picture. I don't mind if they don't do anything. I don't see why they should; in fact it always astonishes me when anybody does anything."

"You don't want to do anything?"

"I want to sleep."

For a second he was startled, almost as though she had meant this literally.

"Sleep?"

"Sort of. I want to just be lazy and I want some of the people around me to be doing things, because that makes me feel comfortable and safe—and I want some of them to be doing nothing at all, because they can be graceful and companionable for me. But I never want to change people or get excited over them."

"You're a quaint little determinist," laughed Anthony. "It's your world, isn't it?"

"Well—" she said with a quick upward glance, "isn't it? As long as I'm—young."

She had paused slightly before the last word and Anthony

suspected that she had started to say "beautiful." It was unde-
niably what she had intended.

Her eyes brightened and he waited for her to enlarge on
the theme. He had drawn her out, at any rate—he bent forward
slightly to catch the words.

But "Let's dance!" was all she said.

That winter afternoon at the Plaza was the first of a
succession of "dates" Anthony made with her in the blurred
and stimulating days before Christmas. Invariably she was
busy. What particular strata of the city's social life claimed
her he was a long time finding out. It seemed to matter very
little. She attended the semi-public charity dances at the big
hotels; he saw her several times at dinner parties in Sherry's,
and once as he waited for her to dress, Mrs. Gilbert, apropos
of her daughter's habit of "going," rattled off an amazing
holiday programme that included half a dozen dances to which
Anthony had received cards.

He made engagements with her several times for lunch
and tea—the former were hurried and, to him at least, rather
unsatisfactory occasions, for she was sleepy-eyed and casual,
incapable of concentrating upon anything or of giving consecutive attention to his remarks. When after two of these sallow
meals he accused her of tendering him the skin and bones of
the day she laughed and gave him a tea-time three days off.
This was infinitely more satisfactory.

One Sunday afternoon just before Christmas he called
up and found her in the lull directly after some important
but mysterious quarrel: she informed him in a tone of mingled
wrath and amusement that she had sent a man out of her
apartment—here Anthony speculated violently—and that the
man had been giving a little dinner for her that very night
and that of course she wasn't going. So Anthony took her to
supper.

"Let's go to something!" she proposed as they went down
in the elevator. "I want to see a show, don't you?"

Inquiry at the hotel ticket desk disclosed only two Sunday night "concerts."

"They're always the same," she complained unhappily, "same old Yiddish comedians. Oh, let's go somewhere!"

To conceal a guilty suspicion that he should have arranged a performance of some kind for her approval Anthony affected a knowing cheerfulness.

"We'll go to a good cabaret."

"I've seen every one in town."

"Well, we'll find a new one."

She was in wretched humor; that was evident. Her gray eyes were granite now indeed. When she wasn't speaking she stared straight in front of her as if at some distasteful abstraction in the lobby.

"Well, come on, then."

He followed her, a graceful girl even in her enveloping fur, out to a taxicab, and, with an air of having a definite place in mind, instructed the driver to go over to Broadway and then turn south. He made several casual attempts at conversation but as she adopted an impenetrable armor of silence and answered him in sentences as morose as the cold darkness of the taxicab he gave up, and assuming a like mood fell into a dim gloom.

A dozen blocks down Broadway Anthony's eyes were caught by a large and unfamiliar electric sign spelling "Marathon" in glorious yellow script, adorned with electrical leaves and flowers that alternately vanished and beamed upon the wet and glistening street. He leaned and rapped on the taxi-window and in a moment was receiving information from a colored doorman: Yes, this was a cabaret. Fine cabaret. Bes' showina city!

"Shall we try it?"

With a sigh Gloria tossed her cigarette out the open door and prepared to follow it; then they had passed under the screaming sign, under the wide portal, and up by a stuffy elevator into this unsung palace of pleasure.

The gay habitats of the very rich and the very poor, the very dashing and the very criminal, not to mention the lately exploited very Bohemian, are made known to the awed high school girls of Augusta, Georgia, and Redwing, Minnesota, not only through the bepictured and entrancing spreads of the Sunday theatrical supplements but through the shocked and alarmful eyes of Mr. Rupert Hughes and other chroniclers of the mad pace of America. But the excursions of Harlem onto Broadway, the deviltries of the dull and the revelries of the respectable are a matter of esoteric knowledge only to the participants themselves.

A tip circulates—and in the place knowingly mentioned, gather the lower moral-classes on Saturday and Sunday nights—the little troubled men who are pictured in the comics as "the Consumer" or "the Public." They have made sure that the place has three qualifications: it is cheap; it imitates with a sort of shoddy and mechanical wistfulness the glittering antics of the great cafes in the theatre district; and—this, above all, important—it is a place where they can "take a nice girl," which means, of course, that every one has become equally harmless, timid, and uninteresting through lack of money and imagination.

There on Sunday nights gather the credulous, sentimental, underpaid, overworked people with hyphenated occupations: book-keepers, ticket-sellers, office-managers, salesmen, and, most of all, clerks—clerks of the express, of the mail, of the grocery, of the brokerage, of the bank. With them are their giggling, over-gestured, pathetically pretentious women, who grow fat with them, bear them too many babies, and float helpless and uncontent in a colorless sea of drudgery and broken hopes.

They name these brummagem cabarets after Pullman cars. The "Marathon"! Not for them the salacious similes borrowed from the cafés of Paris! This is where their docile patrons bring their "nice women," whose starved fancies are

63

only too willing to believe that the scene is comparatively gay and joyous, and even faintly immoral. This is life! Who cares for the morrow?

Abandoned people!

Anthony and Gloria, seated, looked about them. At the next table a party of four were in process of being joined by a party of three, two men and a girl, who were evidently late—and the manner of the girl was a study in national sociology. She was meeting some new men—and she was pretending desperately. By gesture she was pretending and by words and by the scarcely perceptible motionings of her eyelids that she belonged to a class a little superior to the class with which she now had to do, that a while ago she had been, and presently would again be, in a higher, rarer air. She was almost painfully refined—she wore a last year's hat covered with violets no more yearningly pretentious and palpably artificial than herself.

Fascinated, Anthony and Gloria watched the girl sit down and radiate the impression that she was only condescendingly present. For *me*, her eyes said, this is practically a slumming expedition, to be cloaked with belittling laughter and semi-apologetics.

—And the other women passionately poured out the impression that though they were in the crowd they were not of it. This was not the sort of place to which they were accustomed; they had dropped in because it was near by and convenient—every party in the restaurant poured out that impression . . . who knew? They were forever changing class, all of them—the women often marrying above their opportunities, the men striking suddenly a magnificent opulence: a sufficiently preposterous advertising scheme, a celestialized ice cream cone. Meanwhile, they met here to eat, closing their eyes to the economy displayed in infrequent changings of table-cloths, in the casualness of the cabaret performers, most of all in the colloquial carelessness and familiarity of the waiters. One was sure that these waiters were not impressed by their patrons. One expected that presently they would sit at the tables . . .

"Do you object to this?" inquired Anthony.

Gloria's face warmed and for the first time that evening she smiled.

"I love it," she said frankly. It was impossible to doubt her. Her gray eyes roved here and there, drowsing, idle or alert, on each group, passing to the next with unconcealed enjoyment, and to Anthony were made plain the different values of her profile, the wonderfully alive expressions of her mouth, and the authentic distinction of face and form and manner that made her like a single flower amidst a collection of cheap bric-à-brac. At her happiness, a gorgeous sentiment welled into his eyes, choked him up, set his nerves a-tingle, and filled his throat with husky and vibrant emotion. There was a hush upon the room. The careless violins and saxophones, the shrill rasping complaint of a child near by, the voice of the violet-hatted girl at the next table, all moved slowly out, receded, and fell away like shadowy reflections on the shining floor—and they two, it seemed to him, were alone and infinitely remote, quiet. Surely the freshness of her cheeks was a gossamer projection from a land of delicate and undiscovered shades; her hand gleaming on the stained table-cloth was a shell from some far and wildly virginal sea. . . .

Then the illusion snapped like a nest of threads; the room grouped itself around him, voices, faces, movement; the garish shimmer of the lights overhead became real, became portentous; breath began, the slow respiration that she and he took in time with this docile hundred, the rise and fall of bosoms, the eternal meaningless play and interplay and tossing and reiterating of word and phrase—all these wrenched his senses open to the suffocating pressure of life—and then her voice came at him, cool as the suspended dream he had left behind.

"I belong here," she murmured, "I'm like these people."

For an instant this seemed a sardonic and unnecessary paradox hurled at him across the impassable distances she created about herself. Her entrancement had increased—her eyes rested upon a Semitic violinist who swayed his shoulders to the rhythm of the year's mellowest fox-trot:

> "Something—goes
> Ring-a-ting-a-ling-a-ling
> Right in-your ear—"

Again she spoke, from the centre of this pervasive illusion of her own. It amazed him. It was like blasphemy from the mouth of a child.

"I'm like they are—like Japanese lanterns and crape paper, and the music of that orchestra."

"You're a young idiot!" he insisted wildly. She shook her blonde head.

"No, I'm not. I *am* like them. . . . You ought to see. . . . You don't know me." She hesitated and her eyes came back to him, rested abruptly on his, as though surprised at the last to see him there. "I've got a streak of what you'd call cheapness. I don't know where I get it but it's—oh, things like this and bright colors and gaudy vulgarity. I seem to belong here. These people could appreciate me and take me for granted, and these men would fall in love with me and admire me, whereas the clever men I meet would just analyze me and tell me I'm this because of this or that because of that."

—Anthony for the moment wanted fiercely to paint her, to set her down *now*, as she was, as, as with each relentless second she could never be again.

"What were you thinking?" she asked.

"Just that I'm not a realist," he said, and then: "No, only the romanticist preserves the things worth preserving."

Out of the deep sophistication of Anthony an understanding formed, nothing atavistic or obscure, indeed scarcely physical at all, an understanding remembered from the romancings of many generations of minds that as she talked and caught his eyes and turned her lovely head, she moved him as he had never been moved before. The sheath that held her soul had assumed significance—that was all. She was a sun, radiant, growing, gathering light and storing it—then after an eternity pouring it forth in a glance, the fragment of a sentence, to that part of him that cherished all beauty and all illusion.

CHAPTER 3

THE CONNOISSEUR OF KISSES

From his undergraduate days as editor of The Harvard Crimson Richard Caramel had desired to write. But as a senior he had picked up the glorified illusion that certain men were set aside for "service" and, going into the world, were to accomplish a vague yearnful something which would react either in eternal reward or, at the least, in the personal satisfaction of having striven for the greatest good of the greatest number.

This spirit has long rocked the colleges in America. It begins, as a rule, during the immaturities and facile impressions of freshman year—sometimes back in preparatory school. Prosperous apostles known for their emotional acting go the rounds of the universities and, by frightening the amiable sheep and dulling the quickening of interest and intellectual curiosity which is the purpose of all education, distil a mysterious conviction of sin, harking back to childhood crimes and to the ever-present menace of "women." To these lectures go the wicked youths to cheer and joke and the timid to swallow the tasty pills, which would be harmless if administered to farmers' wives and pious drug-clerks but are rather dangerous medicine for these "future leaders of men."

This octopus was strong enough to wind a sinuous tentacle about Richard Caramel. The year after his graduation it called him into the slums of New York to muck about with bewildered Italians as secretary to an "Alien Young Men's Rescue Association." He labored at it over a year before the monotony began to weary him. The aliens kept coming inexhaustibly—Italians, Poles, Scandinavians, Czechs, Armenians—with the same wrongs, the same exceptionally ugly faces and very much the same smells, though he fancied that these grew more profuse and diverse as the months passed. His eventual conclusions about the expediency of service were vague, but concerning his own relation to it they were abrupt and decisive. Any amiable young man, his head ringing with the latest crusade, could accomplish as much as he could with the débris of Europe—and it was time for him to write.

He had been living in a down-town Y.M.C.A., but when he quit the task of making sow-ear purses out of sows' ears, he moved up-town and went to work immediately as a reporter for *The Sun*. He kept at this for a year, doing desultory writing on the side, with little success, and then one day an infelicitous incident peremptorily closed his newspaper career. On a February afternoon he was assigned to report a parade of Squadron A. Snow threatening, he went to sleep instead before a hot fire, and when he woke up did a smooth column about the muffled beats of the horses' hooves in the snow . . . This he handed in. Next morning a marked copy of the paper was sent down to the City Editor with a scrawled note: "Fire the man who wrote this." It seemed that Squadron A had also seen the snow threatening—had postponed the parade until another day.

A week later he had begun "The Demon Lover.". . .

In January, the Monday of the months, Richard Caramel's nose was blue constantly, a sardonic blue, vaguely suggestive of the flames licking around a sinner. His book was nearly ready, and as it grew in completeness it seemed to grow also in its demands, sapping him, overpowering him, until he walked haggard and conquered in its shadow. Not only to Anthony and Maury did he pour out his hopes and boasts and indecisions, but to anyone who could be prevailed upon to listen. He called on polite but bewildered publishers, he discussed it with his casual vis-à-vis at the Harvard Club; it was even claimed by Anthony that he had been discovered, one Sunday night, debating the transposition of Chapter Two with a literary ticket-collector in the chill and dismal recesses of a Harlem subway station. And latest among his confidantes was Mrs. Gilbert, who sat with him by the hour and alternated between Bilphism and literature in an intense cross-fire.

"Shakespeare was a Bilphist," she assured him through a fixed smile. "Oh, yes! He was a Bilphist. It's been proved."

At this Dick would look a bit blank.

"If you've read 'Hamlet' you can't help but see."

"Well, he—he lived in a more credulous age—a more religious age."

But she demanded the whole loaf:

"Oh, yes, but you see Bilphism isn't a religion. It's the science of all religions." She smiled defiantly at him. This was the *bon mot* of her belief. There was something in the arrangement of words which grasped her mind so definitely that the statement became superior to any obligation to define itself. It is not unlikely that she would have accepted any idea encased in this radiant formula—which was perhaps not a formula; it was the *reductio ad absurdum* of all formulas.

Then eventually, but gorgeously, would come Dick's turn.

"You've heard of the new poetry movement. You haven't? Well, it's a lot of young poets that are breaking away from the old forms and doing a lot of good. Well, what I was going to say was that my book is going to start a new prose movement, a sort of renaissance."

"I'm sure it will," beamed Mrs. Gilbert. "I'm *sure* it will. I went to Jenny Martin last Tuesday, the palmist, you know, that everyone's *mad* about. I told her my nephew was engaged upon a work and she said she knew I'd be glad to hear that his success would be *extraordinary*. But she'd never seen you or known anything about you—not even your *name*."

Having made the proper noises to express his amazement at this astounding phenomenon, Dick waved her theme by him as though he were an arbitrary traffic policeman, and, so to speak, beckoned forward his own traffic.

"I'm absorbed, Aunt Catherine," he assured her, "I really am. All my friends are joshing me—oh, I see the humor in it and I don't care. I think a person ought to be able to take joshing. But I've got a sort of conviction," he concluded gloomily.

"You're an ancient soul, I always say."

"Maybe I am." Dick had reached the stage where he no longer fought, but submitted. He *must* be an ancient soul, he fancied grotesquely; so old as to be absolutely rotten. However, the reiteration of the phrase still somewhat embarrassed him and sent uncomfortable shivers up his back. He changed the subject.

"Where is my distinguished cousin Gloria?"

"She's on the go somewhere, with someone."

Dick paused, considered, and then, screwing up his face into what was evidently begun as a smile but ended as a terrifying frown, delivered a comment.

"I think my friend Anthony Patch is in love with her."

Mrs. Gilbert started, beamed half a second too late, and breathed her "Really?" in the tone of a detective play-whisper.

"I *think* so," corrected Dick gravely. "She's the first girl I've ever seen him with, so much."

"Well, of course," said Mrs. Gilbert with meticulous

carelessness, "Gloria never makes me her confidante. She's very secretive. Between you and me"—she bent forward cautiously, obviously determined that only Heaven and her nephew should share her confession—"between you and me, I'd like to see her settle down."

Dick arose and paced the floor earnestly, a small, active, already rotund young man, his hands thrust unnaturally into his bulging pockets.

"I'm not claiming I'm right, mind you," he assured the infinitely-of-the-hotel steel-engraving which smirked respectably back at him. "I'm saying nothing that I'd want Gloria to know. But I think Mad Anthony is interested—tremendously so. He talks about her constantly. In anyone else that'd be a bad sign."

"Gloria is a very young soul—" began Mrs. Gilbert eagerly, but her nephew interrupted with a hurried sentence:

"Gloria'd be a very young nut not to marry him." He stopped and faced her, his expression a battle map of lines and dimples, squeezed and strained to its ultimate show of intensity—this as if to make up by his sincerity for any indiscretion in his words. "Gloria's a wild one, Aunt Catherine. She's uncontrollable. How she's done it I don't know, but lately she's picked up a lot of the funniest friends. She doesn't seem to care. And the men she used to go with around New York were—" He paused for breath.

"Yes-yes-yes," interjected Mrs. Gilbert, with an anaemic attempt to hide the immense interest with which she listened.

"Well," continued Richard Caramel gravely, "there it is. I mean that the men she went with and the people she went with used to be first rate. Now they aren't."

Mrs. Gilbert blinked very fast—her bosom trembled, inflated, remained so for an instant, and with the exhalation her words flowed out in a torrent.

She knew, she cried in a whisper; oh, yes, mothers see these things. But what could she do? He knew Gloria. He'd seen enough of Gloria to know how hopeless it was to try to deal with her. Gloria had been so spoiled—in a rather complete and unusual way. She had been suckled until she was three, for instance, when she could probably have chewed sticks. Perhaps—one never knew—it was this that had given that health and *hardiness* to her whole personality. And then ever since she was twelve years old she'd had boys about her so thick—oh, so thick one couldn't *move*. At sixteen she began going to dances at preparatory schools, and then came the colleges; and everywhere she went, boys, boys, boys. At first, oh, until she was eighteen there had been so many that it never seemed one any more than the others, but then she began to single them out.

She knew there had been a string of affairs spread over about three years, perhaps a dozen of them altogether. Sometimes the men were undergraduates, sometimes just out of college—they lasted on an average of several months each, with short attractions in between. Once or twice they had endured longer and her mother had hoped she would be engaged, but always a new one came—a new one—

The men? Oh, she made them miserable, literally! There was only one who had kept any sort of dignity, and he had been a mere child, young Carter Kirby, of Kansas City, who was so conceited anyway that he just sailed out on his vanity one afternoon and left for Europe next day with his father. The others had been—wretched. They never seemed to know when she was tired of them, and Gloria had seldom been deliberately unkind. They would keep phoning, writing letters to her, trying to see her, making long trips after her around the country. Some of them had confided in Mrs. Gilbert, told her with tears in their eyes that they would never get over Gloria . . . at least two of them had since married, though. . . . But Gloria, it seemed, struck to kill—to this day Mr. Carstairs called up once a week, and sent her flowers which she no longer bothered to refuse.

Several times, twice, at least, Mrs. Gilbert knew it had gone as far as a private engagement—with Tudor Baird and that Holcome boy at Pasadena. She was sure it had, because—this must go no further—she had come in unexpectedly and found Gloria acting, well, very much engaged indeed. She had not spoken to her daughter, of course. She had had a certain sense of delicacy and, besides, each time she had expected an announcement in a few weeks. But the announcement never came; instead, a new man came.

Scenes! Young men walking up and down the library like caged tigers! Young men glaring at each other in the hall as one came and the other left! Young men calling up on the telephone and being hung up upon in desperation! Young men threatening South America! . . . Young men writing the most pathetic letters! (She said nothing to this effect, but Dick fancied that Mrs. Gilbert's eyes had seen some of these letters.)

. . . And Gloria, between tears and laughter, sorry, glad, out of love and in love, miserable, nervous, cool, amidst a great returning of presents, substitution of pictures in immemorial frames, and taking of hot baths and beginning again—with the next.

That state of things continued, assumed an air of permanency. Nothing harmed Gloria or changed her or moved her. And then out of a clear sky one day she informed her mother that undergraduates wearied her. She was absolutely going to no more college dances.

This had begun the change—not so much in her actual habits, for she danced, and had as many "dates" as ever—but they were dates in a different spirit. Previously it had been a sort of pride, a matter of her own vainglory. She had been, probably, the most celebrated and sought-after young beauty in the country. Gloria Gilbert of Kansas City! She had fed on it ruthlessly—enjoying the crowds around her, the manner in which the most desirable men singled her out; enjoying the fierce jealousy of other girls; enjoying the fabulous, not to say scandalous, and, her mother was glad to say, entirely unfounded rumors about her—for instance, that she had gone in the Yale swimming-pool one night in a chiffon evening dress.

And from loving it with a vanity that was almost masculine—it had been in the nature of a triumphant and dazzling career—she became suddenly anaesthetic to it. She retired. She who had dominated countless parties, who had blown fragrantly through many ballrooms to the tender tribute of many eyes, seemed to care no longer. He who fell in love with her now was dismissed utterly, almost angrily. She went listlessly with the most indifferent men. She continually broke engagements, not as in the past from a cool assurance that she was irreproachable, that the man she insulted would return like a domestic animal—but indifferently, without contempt or pride. She rarely stormed at men any more—she yawned at them. She seemed—and it was so strange—she seemed to her mother to be growing cold.

Richard Caramel listened. At first he had remained standing, but as his aunt's discourse waxed in content—it stands here pruned by half, of all side references to the youth of Gloria's soul and to Mrs. Gilbert's own mental distresses—he drew a chair up and attended rigorously as she floated, between tears and plaintive helplessness, down the long story of Gloria's life. When she came to the tale of this last year, a tale of the ends of cigarettes left all over New York in little trays marked "Midnight Frolic" and "Justine Johnson's Little Club," he began nodding his head slowly, then faster and faster, until, as she finished on a staccato note, it was bobbing briskly up and down, absurdly like a doll's wired head, expressing—almost anything.

In a sense Gloria's past was an old story to him. He had followed it with the eyes of a journalist, for he was going to write a book about her some day. But his interests, just at present, were family interests. He wanted to know, in particular, who was this Joseph Bloeckman that he had seen her with several times; and those two girls she was with constantly, "this" Rachael Jerryl and "this" Miss Kane—surely Miss Kane wasn't exactly the sort one would associate with Gloria!

But the moment had passed. Mrs. Gilbert having climbed the hill of exposition was about to glide swiftly down the ski-jump of collapse. Her eyes were like a blue sky seen through two round, red window-casements. The flesh about her mouth was trembling.

And at the moment the door opened, admitting into the room Gloria and the two young ladies lately mentioned.

TWO YOUNG WOMEN

"Well!"

"How do you do, Mrs. Gilbert!"

Miss Kane and Miss Jerryl are presented to Mr. Richard Caramel. "This is Dick" (laughter).

"I've heard so much about you," says Miss Kane between a giggle and a shout.

"How do you do," says Miss Jerryl shyly.

Richard Caramel tries to move about as if his figure were better. He is torn between his innate cordiality and the fact that he considers these girls rather common—not at all the Farmover type.

Gloria has disappeared into the bedroom.

"Do sit down," beams Mrs. Gilbert, who is by now quite herself. "Take off your things." Dick is afraid she will make some remark about the age of his soul, but he forgets his qualms in completing a conscientious, novelist's examination of the two young women.

Muriel Kane had originated in a rising family of East Orange. She was short rather than small, and hovered audaciously between plumpness and width. Her hair was black

and elaborately arranged. This, in conjunction with her handsome, rather bovine eyes, and her over-red lips, combined to
make her resemble Theda Bara, the prominent motion picture
actress. People told her constantly that she was a "vampire,"
and she believed them. She suspected hopefully that they
were afraid of her, and she did her utmost under all circumstances to give the impression of danger. An imaginative man
could see the red flag that she constantly carried, waving it
wildly, beseechingly—and, alas, to little spectacular avail. She
was also tremendously timely: she knew the latest songs, all
the latest songs—when one of them was played on the phonograph she would rise to her feet and rock her shoulders back
and forth and snap her fingers, and if there was no music
she would accompany herself by humming.

Her conversation was also timely: "I don't care," she
would say, "I should worry and lose my figure"—and again:
"I can't make my feet behave when I hear that tune. Oh,
baby!"

Her finger-nails were too long and ornate, polished to a
pink and unnatural fever. Her clothes were too tight, too
stylish, too vivid, her eyes too roguish, her smile too coy. She
was almost pitifully over-emphasized from head to foot.

The other girl was obviously a more subtle personality.
She was an exquisitely dressed Jewess with dark hair and a
lovely milky pallor. She seemed shy and vague, and these two
qualities accentuated a rather delicate charm that floated
about her. Her family were "Episcopalians," owned three
smart women's shops along Fifth Avenue, and lived in a
magnificent apartment on Riverside Drive. It seemed to Dick,
after a few moments, that she was attempting to imitate
Gloria—he wondered that people invariably chose inimitable
people to imitate.

"We had the most *hectic* time!" Muriel was exclaiming
enthusiastically. "There was a crazy woman behind us on the
bus. She was absitively, posolutely *nutty*! She kept talking to

herself about something she'd like to do to somebody or some-thing. I was *pet*rified, but Gloria simply *wouldn't* get off."

Mrs. Gilbert opened her mouth, properly awed.

"Really?"

"Oh, she was crazy. But we should worry, she didn't hurt us. Ugly! Gracious! The man across from us said her face ought to be on a night-nurse in a home for the blind, and we all *howled*, naturally, so the man tried to pick us up."

Presently Gloria emerged from her bedroom and in unison every eye turned on her. The two girls receded into a shadowy background, unperceived, unmissed.

"We've been talking about you," said Dick quickly, "— your mother and I."

"Well," said Gloria.

A pause—Muriel turned to Dick.

"You're a great writer, aren't you?"

"I'm a writer," he confessed sheepishly.

"I always say," said Muriel earnestly, "that if I ever had time to write down all my experiences it'd make a wonderful book."

Rachael giggled sympathetically; Richard Caramel's bow was almost stately. Muriel continued:

"But I don't see how you can sit down and do it. And poetry! Lordy, I can't make two lines rhyme. Well, I should worry!"

Richard Caramel with difficulty restrained a shout of laughter. Gloria was chewing an amazing gum-drop and staring moodily out the window. Mrs. Gilbert cleared her throat and beamed.

"But you see," she said in a sort of universal exposition, "you're not an ancient soul—like Richard."

The Ancient Soul breathed a gasp of relief—it was out at last.

Then as if she had been considering it for five minutes, Gloria made a sudden announcement:

THE BEAUTIFUL AND DAMNED

"I'm going to give a party."

"Oh, can I come?" cried Muriel with facetious daring.

"A dinner. Seven people: Muriel and Rachael and I, and you, Dick, and Anthony, and that man named Noble—I liked him—and Bloeckman."

Muriel and Rachael went into soft and purring ecstasies of enthusiasm. Mrs. Gilbert blinked and beamed. With an air of casualness Dick broke in with a question:

"Who is this fellow Bloeckman, Gloria?"

Scenting a faint hostility, Gloria turned to him.

"Joseph Bloeckman? He's the moving picture man. Vice-president of 'Films Par Excellence.' He and father do a lot of business."

"Oh!"

"Well, will you all come?"

They would all come. A date was arranged within the week. Dick rose, adjusted hat, coat, and muffler, and gave out a general smile.

"By-by," said Muriel, waving her hand gaily, "call me up some time."

Richard Caramel blushed for her.

DEPLORABLE END OF THE CHEVALIER O'KEEFE

It was Monday and Anthony took Geraldine Burke to luncheon at the Beaux Arts—afterward they went up to his apartment and he wheeled out the little rolling-table that held his supply of liquor, selecting vermouth, gin, and absinthe for a proper stimulant.

Geraldine Burke, usher at Keith's, had been an amusement of several months. She demanded so little that he liked her, for since a lamentable affair with a débutante the preceding summer, when he had discovered that after half a dozen kisses a proposal was expected, he had been wary of girls of his own class. It was only too easy to turn a critical eye on their imperfections: some physical harshness or a general lack of personal delicacy—but a girl who was usher at Keith's was approached with a different attitude. One could tolerate qualities in an intimate valet that would be unforgivable in a mere acquaintance on one's social level.

Geraldine, curled up at the foot of the lounge, considered him with narrow slanting eyes.

"You drink all the time, don't you?" she said suddenly.

"Why, I suppose so," replied Anthony in some surprise. "Don't you?"

"Nope. I go on parties sometimes—you know, about once a week, but I only take two or three drinks. You and your friends keep on drinking all the time. I should think you'd ruin your health."

Anthony was somewhat touched.

"Why, aren't you sweet to worry about me!"

"Well, I do."

"I don't drink so very much," he declared. "Last month I didn't touch a drop for three weeks. And I only get really tight about once a week."

"But you have something to drink every day and you're only twenty-five. Haven't you any ambition? Think what you'll be at forty?"

"I sincerely trust that I won't live that long."

She clicked her tongue with her teeth.

"You cra-azy!" she said as he mixed another cocktail—and then: "Are you any relation to Adam Patch?"

"Yes, he's my grandfather."

"Really?" She was obviously thrilled.

"Absolutely."

"That's funny. My daddy used to work for him."

"He's a queer old man."

"Is he nice?" she demanded.

"Well, in private life he's seldom unnecessarily disagreeable."

"Tell us about him."

"Why," Anthony considered "—he's all shrunken up and he's got the remains of some gray hair that always looks as though the wind were in it. He's very moral."

"He's done a lot of good," said Geraldine with intense gravity.

"Rot!" scoffed Anthony. "He's a pious ass—a chicken-brain."

Her mind left the subject and flitted on.

"Why don't you live with him?"

"Why don't I board in a Methodist parsonage?"

"You cra-azy!"

Again she made a little clicking sound to express disapproval. Anthony thought how moral was this little waif at heart—how completely moral she would still be after the inevitable wave came that would wash her off the sands of respectability.

"Do you hate him?"

"I wonder. I never liked him. You never like people who do things for you."

"Does he hate you?"

"My dear Geraldine," protested Anthony, frowning humorously, "do have another cocktail. I annoy him. If I smoke a cigarette he comes into the room sniffing. He's a prig, a bore, and something of a hypocrite. I probably wouldn't be telling you this if I hadn't had a few drinks, but I don't suppose it matters."

Geraldine was persistently interested. She held her glass, untasted, between finger and thumb and regarded him with eyes in which there was a touch of awe.

"How do you mean a hypocrite?"

"Well," said Anthony impatiently, "maybe he's not. But he doesn't like the things that I like, and so, as far as I'm concerned, he's uninteresting."

"Hm." Her curiosity seemed, at length, satisfied. She sank back into the sofa and sipped her cocktail.

"You're a funny one," she commented thoughtfully. "Does everybody want to marry you because your grandfather is rich?"

"They don't—but I shouldn't blame them if they did. Still, you see, I never intend to marry."

She scorned this.

"You'll fall in love someday. Oh, you will—I know." She nodded wisely.

"It'd be idiotic to be overconfident. That's what ruined the Chevalier O'Keefe."

"Who was he?"

"A creature of my splendid mind. He's my one creation, the Chevalier."

"Cra-a-azy!" she murmured pleasantly, using the clumsy rope ladder with which she bridged all gaps and climbed after her mental superiors. Subconsciously she felt that it eliminated distances and brought the person whose imagination had eluded her back within range.

"Oh, no!" objected Anthony, "oh, no, Geraldine. You mustn't play the alienist upon the Chevalier. If you feel yourself unable to understand him I won't bring him in. Besides, I should feel a certain uneasiness because of his regrettable reputation."

"I guess I can understand anything that's got any sense to it," answered Geraldine a bit testily.

"In that case there are various episodes in the life of the Chevalier which might prove diverting."

"Well?"

"It was his untimely end that caused me to think of him and made him apropos in the conversation. I hate to introduce him end foremost, but it seems inevitable that the Chevalier must back into your life."

"Well, what about him? Did he die?"

"He did! In this manner. He was an Irishman, Geraldine, a semi-fictional Irishman—the wild sort with a genteel brogue and 'reddish hair.' He was exiled from Erin in the late days of chivalry and, of course, crossed over to France. Now the Chevalier O'Keefe, Geraldine, had, like me, one weakness. He was enormously susceptible to all sorts and conditions of women. Besides being a sentimentalist he was a romantic, a vain fellow, a man of wild passions, a little blind in one eye and almost stone-blind in the other. Now a male roaming the world in this condition is as helpless as a lion without teeth, and in consequence the Chevalier was made utterly miserable for twenty years by a series of women who hated him, used him, bored him, aggravated him, sickened him, spent his money, made a fool of him—in brief, as the world has it, loved him.

"This was bad, Geraldine, and as the Chevalier, save for this one weakness, this exceeding susceptibility, was a man of penetration, he decided that he would rescue himself once and for all from these drains upon him. With this purpose he went to a very famous monastery in Champagne called—well, anachronistically known as St. Voltaire's. It was the rule at St. Voltaire's that no monk could descend to the ground story of the monastery so long as he lived, but should exist engaged in prayer and contemplation in one of the four towers, which were called after the four commandments of the monastery rule: Poverty, Chastity, Obedience, and Silence.

"When the day came that was to witness the Chevalier's farewell to the world he was utterly happy. He gave all his Greek books to his landlady, and his sword he sent in a golden sheath to the King of France, and all his mementos of Ireland he gave to the young Huguenot who sold fish in the street where he lived.

"Then he rode out to St. Voltaire's, slew his horse at the door, and presented the carcass to the monastery cook.

"At five o'clock that night he felt, for the first time,

free—forever free from sex. No woman could enter the monastery; no monk could descend below the second story. So as he climbed the winding stair that led to his cell at the very top of the Tower of Chastity he paused for a moment by an open window which looked down fifty feet on to a road below. It was all so beautiful, he thought, this world that he was leaving, the golden shower of sun beating down upon the long fields, the spray of trees in the distance, the vineyards, quiet and green, freshening wide miles before him. He leaned his elbows on the window casement and gazed at the winding road.

"Now, as it happened, Thérèse, a peasant girl of sixteen from a neighboring village, was at that moment passing along this same road that ran in front of the monastery. Five minutes before, the little piece of ribbon which held up the stocking on her pretty left leg had worn through and broken. Being a girl of rare modesty she had thought to wait until she arrived home before repairing it, but it had bothered her to such an extent that she felt she could endure it no longer. So, as she passed the Tower of Chastity, she stopped and with a pretty gesture lifted her skirt—as little as possible, be it said to her credit—to adjust her garter.

"Up in the tower the newest arrival in the ancient monastery of St. Voltaire, as though pulled forward by a gigantic and irresistible hand, leaned from the window. Further he leaned and further until suddenly one of the stones loosened under his weight, broke from its cement with a soft powdery sound—and, first headlong, then head over heels, finally in a vast and impressive revolution tumbled the Chevalier O'Keefe, bound for the hard earth and eternal damnation.

"Thérèse was so much upset by the occurrence that she ran all the way home and for ten years spent an hour a day in secret prayer for the soul of the monk whose neck and vows were simultaneously broken on that unfortunate Sunday afternoon.

"And the Chevalier O'Keefe, being suspected of suicide, was not buried in consecrated ground, but tumbled into a field near by, where he doubtless improved the quality of the soil for many years afterward. Such was the untimely end of a very brave and gallant gentleman. What do you think, Geraldine?"

But Geraldine, lost long before, could only smile roguishly, wave her first finger at him, and repeat her bridge-all, her explain-all:

"Crazy!" she said, "you cra-a-azy!"

His thin face was kindly, she thought, and his eyes quite gentle. She liked him because he was arrogant without being conceited, and because, unlike the men she met about the theatre, he had a horror of being conspicuous. What an odd, pointless story! But she had enjoyed the part about the stocking!

After the fifth cocktail he kissed her, and between laughter and bantering caresses and a half-stifled flare of passion they passed an hour. At four-thirty she claimed an engagement, and going into the bathroom she rearranged her hair. Refusing to let him order her a taxi she stood for a moment in the doorway.

"You *will* get married," she was insisting, "you wait and see."

Anthony was playing with an ancient tennis ball, and he bounced it carefully on the floor several times before he answered with a soupçon of acidity:

"You're a little idiot, Geraldine."

She smiled provokingly.

"Oh, I am, am I? Want to bet?"

"That'd be silly too."

"Oh, it would, would it? Well, I'll just bet you'll marry somebody inside of a year."

Anthony bounced the tennis ball very hard. This was one of his handsome days, she thought; a sort of intensity had displaced the melancholy in his dark eyes.

"Geraldine," he said, at length, "in the first place I have no one I want to marry; in the second place I haven't enough money to support two people; in the third place I am entirely opposed to marriage for people of my type; in the fourth place I have a strong distaste for even the abstract consideration of it."

But Geraldine only narrowed her eyes knowingly, made her clicking sound, and said she must be going. It was late.

"Call me up soon," she reminded him as he kissed her goodbye, "you haven't for three weeks, you know."

"I will," he promised fervently.

He shut the door and coming back into the room stood for a moment lost in thought with the tennis ball still clasped in his hand. There was one of his lonelinesses coming, one of those times when he walked the streets or sat, aimless and depressed, biting a pencil at his desk. It was a self-absorption with no comfort, a demand for expression with no outlet, a sense of time rushing by, ceaselessly and wastefully—assuaged only by that conviction that there was nothing to waste, because all efforts and attainments were equally valueless.

He thought with emotion—aloud, ejaculative, for he was hurt and confused.

"No *idea* of getting married, by *God*!"

Of a sudden he hurled the tennis ball violently across the room, where it barely missed the lamp, and, rebounding here and there for a moment, lay still upon the floor.

SIGNLIGHT AND MOONLIGHT

For her dinner Gloria had taken a table in the Cascades at the Biltmore, and when the men met in the hall outside a little after eight, "that person Bloeckman" was the target of six masculine eyes. He was a stoutening, ruddy Jew of about thirty-five, with an expressive face under smooth sandy hair—and, no doubt, in most business gatherings his personality would have been considered ingratiating. He sauntered up to the three younger men, who stood in a group smoking as they waited for their hostess, and introduced himself with a little too evident assurance—nevertheless it is to be doubted whether he received the intended impression of faint and ironic chill: there was no hint of understanding in his manner.

"You related to Adam J. Patch?" he inquired of Anthony, emitting two slender strings of smoke from nostrils overwide.

Anthony admitted it with the ghost of a smile.

"He's a fine man," pronounced Bloeckman profoundly. "He's a fine example of an American."

"Yes," agreed Anthony, "he certainly is."

—I detest these underdone men, he thought coldly. Boiled looking! Ought to be shoved back in the oven; just one more minute would do it.

Bloeckman squinted at his watch.

"Time these girls were showing up . . ."

—Anthony waited breathlessly; it came—

". . . but then," with a widening smile, "you know how women are."

The three young men nodded; Bloeckman looked casually about him, his eyes resting critically on the ceiling and then passing lower. His expression combined that of a Middle Western farmer appraising his wheat crop and that of an actor wondering whether he is observed—the public manner of all good Americans. As he finished his survey he turned back quickly to the reticent trio, determined to strike to their very heart and core.

"You college men? . . . Harvard, eh. I see the Princeton boys beat you fellows in hockey."

Unfortunate man. He had drawn another blank. They had been three years out and heeded only the big football games. Whether, after the failure of this sally, Mr. Bloeckman would have perceived himself to be in a cynical atmosphere is problematical, for—

Gloria arrived. Muriel arrived. Rachael arrived. After a hurried "Hello, people!" uttered by Gloria and echoed by the other two, the three swept by into the dressing room.

A moment later Muriel appeared in a state of elaborate undress and *crept* toward them. She was in her element: her ebony hair was slicked straight back on her head; her eyes were artificially darkened; she reeked of insistent perfume. She was got up to the best of her ability as a siren, more popularly a "vamp"—a picker up and thrower away of men, an unscrupulous and fundamentally unmoved toyer with affections. Something in the exhaustiveness of her attempt fascinated Maury at first sight—a woman with wide hips affecting a panther-like litheness! As they waited the extra three minutes for Gloria, and, by polite assumption, for Rachael, he was unable to take his eyes from her. She would turn her head away, lowering her eyelashes and biting her nether lip in an amazing exhibition of coyness. She would rest her hands on her hips and sway from side to side in tune to the music, saying:

"Did you ever hear such perfect ragtime? I just can't make my shoulders behave when I hear that."

Mr. Bloeckman clapped his hands gallantly.

"You ought to be on the stage."

"I'd like to be!" cried Muriel; "will you back me?"

"I sure will."

With becoming modesty Muriel ceased her motions and turned to Maury, asking what he had "seen" this year. He interpreted this as referring to the dramatic world, and they had a gay and exhilarating exchange of titles, after this manner:

MURIEL: Have you seen "Peg o' My Heart"?
MAURY: No, I haven't.
MURIEL: (*Eagerly*) It's wonderful! You want to see it.
MAURY: Have you seen "Omar, the Tentmaker"?

MURIEL: No, but I hear it's wonderful. I'm very anxious to
see it. Have you seen "Fair and Warmer"?

MAURY: (*Hopefully*) Yes.

MURIEL: I don't think it's very good. It's trashy.

MAURY: (*Faintly*) Yes, that's true.

MURIEL: But I went to "Within the Law" last night and I
thought it was fine. Have you seen "The Little Cafe"?. . .

This continued until they ran out of plays. Dick, meanwhile,
turned to Mr. Bloeckman, determined to extract what gold
he could from this unpromising load.

"I hear all the new novels are sold to the moving pictures
as soon as they come out."

"That's true. Of course the main thing in a moving
picture is a strong story."

"Yes, I suppose so."

"So many novels are all full of talk and psychology. Of
course those aren't as valuable to us. It's impossible to make
much of that interesting on the screen."

"You want plots first," said Richard brilliantly.

"Of course. Plots first—" He paused, shifted his gaze.
His pause spread, included the others with all the authority
of a warning finger. Gloria followed by Rachael was coming
out of the dressing room.

Among other things it developed during dinner that
Joseph Bloeckman never danced, but spent the music time
watching the others with the bored tolerance of an elder
among children. He was a dignified man and a proud one.
Born in Munich he had begun his American career as a peanut
vender with a travelling circus. At eighteen he was a side
show ballyhoo; later, the manager of the side show, and, soon
after, the proprietor of a second-class vaudeville house. Just
when the moving picture had passed out of the stage of a
curiosity and become a promising industry he was an ambitious young man of twenty-six with some money to invest,

nagging financial ambitions and a good working knowledge of the popular show business. That had been nine years before. The moving picture industry had borne him up with it where it threw off dozens of men with more financial ability, more imagination, and more practical ideas . . . and now he sat here and contemplated the immortal Gloria for whom young Stuart Holcome had gone from New York to Pasadena—watched her, and knew that presently she would cease dancing and come back to sit on his left hand.

He hoped she would hurry. The oysters had been standing some minutes.

Meanwhile Anthony, who had been placed on Gloria's left hand, was dancing with her, always in a certain fourth of the floor. This, had there been stags, would have been a delicate tribute to the girl, meaning "Damn you, don't cut in!" It was very consciously intimate.

"Well," he began, looking down at her, "you look mighty sweet to-night."

She met his eyes over the horizontal half foot that separated them.

"Thank you—Anthony."

"In fact you're uncomfortably beautiful," he added. There was no smile this time.

"And you're very charming."

"Isn't this nice?" he laughed. "We actually approve of each other."

"Don't you, usually?" She had caught quickly at his remark, as she always did at any unexplained allusion to herself, however faint.

He lowered his voice, and when he spoke there was in it no more than a wisp of badinage.

"Does a priest approve the Pope?"

"I don't know—but that's probably the vaguest compliment I ever received."

"Perhaps I can muster a few bromides."

"Well, I wouldn't have you strain yourself. Look at Muriel! Right here next to us."

He glanced over his shoulder. Muriel was resting her brilliant cheek against the lapel of Maury Noble's dinner coat and her powdered left arm was apparently twisted around his head. One was impelled to wonder why she failed to seize the nape of his neck with her hand. Her eyes, turned ceiling-ward, rolled largely back and forth; her hips swayed, and as she danced she kept up a constant low singing. This at first seemed to be a translation of the song into some foreign tongue but became eventually apparent as an attempt to fill out the metre of the song with the only words she knew—the words of the title—

> "He's a rag-picker,
> A rag-picker;
> A rag-time picking man,
> Rag-picking, picking, pick, pick,
> Rag-pick, pick, pick."

—and so on, into phrases still more strange and barbaric. When she caught the amused glances of Anthony and Gloria she acknowledged them only with a faint smile and a half-closing of her eyes, to indicate that the music entering into her soul had put her into an ecstatic and exceedingly seductive trance.

The music ended and they returned to their table, whose solitary but dignified occupant arose and tendered each of them a smile so ingratiating that it was as if he were shaking their hands and congratulating them on a brilliant performance.

"Blockhead never will dance! I think he has a wooden leg," remarked Gloria to the table at large. The three young men started and the gentleman referred to winced perceptibly.

This was the one rough spot in the course of Bloeckman's acquaintance with Gloria. She relentlessly punned on his name. First it had been "Block-house." lately, the more invidious "Blockhead." He had requested with a strong undertone of irony that she use his first name, and this she had done obediently several times—then slipping, helpless, repentant but dissolved in laughter, back into "Blockhead."

It was a very sad and thoughtless thing.

"I'm afraid Mr. Bloeckman thinks we're a frivolous crowd," sighed Muriel, waving a balanced oyster in his direction.

"He has that air," murmured Rachael. Anthony tried to remember whether she had said anything before. He thought not. It was her initial remark.

Mr. Bloeckman suddenly cleared his throat and said in a loud, distinct voice:

"On the contrary. When a man speaks he's merely tradition. He has at best a few thousand years back of him. But woman, why, she is the miraculous mouthpiece of posterity."

In the stunned pause that followed this astounding remark, Anthony choked suddenly on an oyster and hurried his napkin to his face. Rachael and Muriel raised a mild if somewhat surprised laugh, in which Dick and Maury joined, both of them red in the face and restraining uproariousness with the most apparent difficulty.

"—My God!" thought Anthony. "It's a subtitle from one of his movies. The man's memorized it!"

Gloria alone made no sound. She fixed Mr. Bloeckman with a glance of silent reproach.

"Well, for the love of Heaven! Where on earth did you dig that up?"

Bloeckman looked at her uncertainly, not sure of her intention. But in a moment he recovered his poise and assumed the bland and consciously tolerant smile of an intellectual among spoiled and callow youth.

The soup came up from the kitchen—but simultaneously the orchestra leader came up from the bar, where he had absorbed the tone color inherent in a seidel of beer. So the soup was left to cool during the delivery of a ballad entitled "Everything's at Home Except Your Wife."

Then the champagne—and the party assumed more amusing proportions. The men, except Richard Caramel, drank freely; Gloria and Muriel sipped a glass apiece; Rachael Jerryl took none. They sat out the waltzes but danced to everything else—all except Gloria, who seemed to tire after a while and preferred to sit smoking at the table, her eyes now lazy, now eager, according to whether she listened to Bloeckman or watched a pretty woman among the dancers. Several times Anthony wondered what Bloeckman was telling her. He was chewing a cigar back and forth in his mouth, and had expanded after dinner to the extent of violent gestures.

Ten o'clock found Gloria and Anthony beginning a dance. Just as they were out of ear-shot of the table she said in a low voice:

"Dance over by the door. I want to go down to the drug-store."

Obediently Anthony guided her through the crowd in the designated direction; in the hall she left him for a moment, to reappear with a cloak over her arm.

"I want some gum-drops," she said, humorously apologetic; "you can't guess what for this time. It's just that I want to bite my finger-nails, and I will if I don't get some gum-drops." She sighed, and resumed as they stepped into the empty elevator: "I've been biting 'em all day. A bit nervous, you see. Excuse the pun. It was unintentional—the words just arranged themselves. Gloria Gilbert, the female wag."

Reaching the ground floor they naïvely avoided the hotel candy counter, descended the wide front staircase, and walking through several corridors found a drug-store in the Grand Central Station. After an intense examination of the perfume counter she made her purchase. Then on some mutual unmentioned impulse they strolled, arm in arm, not in the direction from which they had come, but out into Forty-third Street.

The night was alive with thaw; it was so nearly warm that a breeze drifting low along the sidewalk brought to Anthony a vision of an unhoped-for hyacinthine spring. Above in the blue oblong of sky, around them in the caress of the drifting air, the illusion of a new season carried relief from the stiff and breathed-over atmosphere they had left, and for a hushed moment the traffic sounds and the murmur of water flowing in the gutters seemed an illusive and rarefied prolongation of that music to which they had lately danced. When Anthony spoke it was with surety that his words came from something breathless and desirous that the night had conceived in their two hearts.

"Let's take a taxi and ride around a bit!" he suggested, without looking at her.

Oh, Gloria, Gloria!

A cab yawned at the curb. As it moved off like a boat on a labyrinthine ocean and lost itself among the inchoate night masses of the great buildings, among the now stilled, now strident, cries and clangings, Anthony put his arm around the girl, drew her over to him and kissed her damp, childish mouth.

She was silent. She turned her face up to him, pale under the wisps and patches of light that trailed in like moonshine through a foliage. Her eyes were gleaming ripples in the white lake of her face; the shadows of her hair bordered the brow with a persuasive unintimate dusk. No love was there, surely; nor the imprint of any love. Her beauty was cool as this damp breeze, as the moist softness of her own lips.

"You're such a swan in this light," he whispered after a moment. There were silences as murmurous as sound. There were pauses that seemed about to shatter and were only to be snatched back to oblivion by the tightening of his arms about her and the sense that she was resting there as a caught, gossamer feather, drifted in out of the dark. Anthony laughed, noiselessly and exultantly, turning his face up and away from her, half in an overpowering rush of triumph, half lest her sight of him should spoil the splendid immobility of her expression. Such a kiss—it was a flower held against the face, never to be described, scarcely to be remembered; as though her beauty were giving off emanations of itself which settled transiently and already dissolving upon his heart.

. . . The buildings fell away in melted shadows; this was the Park now, and after a long while the great white ghost of the Metropolitan Museum moved majestically past, echoing sonorously to the rush of the cab.

"Why, Gloria! Why, Gloria!"

Her eyes appeared to regard him out of many thousand years: all emotion she might have felt, all words she might have uttered, would have seemed inadequate beside the adequacy of her silence, ineloquent against the eloquence of her beauty—and of her body, close to him, slender and cool.

"Tell him to turn around," she murmured, "and drive pretty fast going back. . . ."

Up in the supper room the air was hot. The table, littered with napkins and ash-trays, was old and stale. It was between dances as they entered, and Muriel Kane looked up with roguishness extraordinary.

"Well, where have *you* been?"

"To call up mother," answered Gloria coolly. "I promised her I would. Did we miss a dance?"

Then followed an incident that though slight in itself Anthony had cause to reflect on many years afterward. Joseph Bloeckman, leaning well back in his chair, fixed him with a peculiar glance, in which several emotions were curiously and inextricably mingled. He did not greet Gloria except by rising, and he immediately resumed a conversation with Richard Caramel about the influence of literature on the moving pictures.

MAGIC

The stark and unexpected miracle of a night fades out with the lingering death of the last stars and the premature birth of the first newsboys. The flame retreats to some remote and platonic fire; the white heat has gone from the iron and the glow from the coal.

Along the shelves of Anthony's library, filling a wall amply, crept a chill and insolent pencil of sunlight touching with frigid disapproval Thérèse of France and Ann the Superwoman, Jenny of the Orient Ballet and Zuleika the Conjurer—and Hoosier Cora—then down a shelf and into the years, resting pityingly on the over-invoked shades of Helen, Thaïs, Salome, and Cleopatra.

Anthony, shaved and bathed, sat in his most deeply cushioned chair and watched it until at the steady rising of the sun it lay glinting for a moment on the silk ends of the rug—and went out.

It was ten o'clock. *The Sunday Times,* scattered about his feet, proclaimed by rotogravure and editorial, by social revelation and sporting sheet, that the world had been tremendously engrossed during the past week in the business of moving toward some splendid if somewhat indeterminate goal. For his part Anthony had been once to his grandfather's, twice to his broker's, and three times to his tailor's—and in the last hour of the week's last day he had kissed a very beautiful and charming girl.

When he reached home his imagination had been teeming with high pitched, unfamiliar dreams. There was suddenly no question on his mind, no eternal problem for a solution and resolution. He had experienced an emotion that was neither mental nor physical, nor merely a mixture of the two, and the love of life absorbed him for the present to the exclusion of all else. He was content to let the experiment remain isolated and unique. Almost impersonally he was convinced that no woman he had ever met compared in any way with Gloria. She was deeply herself; she was immeasurably sincere—of these things he was certain. Beside her the two dozen schoolgirls and debutantes, young married women and waifs and strays whom he had known were so many females, in the word's most contemptuous sense, breeders and bearers, exuding still that faintly odorous atmosphere of the cave and the nursery.

So far as he could see, she had neither submitted to any will of his nor caressed his vanity—except as her pleasure in his company was a caress. Indeed he had no reason for thinking she had given him aught that she did not give to others. This was as it should be. The idea of an entanglement growing out of the evening was as remote as it would have been repugnant. And she had disclaimed and buried the incident with a decisive untruth. Here were two young people with fancy enough to distinguish a game from its reality—who by the very casualness with which they met and passed on would proclaim themselves unharmed.

Having decided this he went to the phone and called up the Plaza Hotel.

Gloria was out. Her mother knew neither where she had gone nor when she would return.

It was somehow at this point that the first wrongness in the case asserted itself. There was an element of callousness, almost of indecency, in Gloria's absence from home. He suspected that by going out she had intrigued him into a disadvantage. Returning she would find his name, and smile. Most discreetly! He should have waited a few hours in order to drive home the utter inconsequence with which he regarded the incident. What an asinine blunder! She would think he considered himself particularly favored. She would think he was reacting with the most inept intimacy to a quite trivial episode.

He remembered that during the previous month

his janitor, to whom he had delivered a rather muddled lecture on the "brother-hoove man," had come up next day and, on the basis of what had happened the night before, seated himself in the window seat for a cordial and chatty half-hour. Anthony wondered in horror if Gloria would regard him as he had regarded that man. Him—Anthony Patch! Horror!

It never occurred to him that he was a passive thing, acted upon by an influence above and beyond Gloria, that he was merely the sensitive plate on which the photograph was made. Some gargantuan photographer had focussed the camera on Gloria and *snap*!—the poor plate could but develop, confined like all things to its nature.

But Anthony, lying upon his couch and staring at the orange lamp, passed his thin fingers incessantly through his dark hair and made new symbols for the hours. She was in a shop now, it seemed, moving lithely among the velvets and the furs, her own dress making, as she walked, a debonair rustle in that world of silken rustles and cool soprano laughter and scents of many slain but living flowers. The Minnies and Pearls and jewels and jennies would gather round her like courtiers, bearing wispy frailties of Georgette crepe, delicate chiffon to echo her cheeks in faint pastel, milky lace to rest in pale disarray against her neck—damask was used but to cover priests and divans in these days, and cloth of Samarand was remembered only by the romantic poets.

She would go elsewhere after a while, tilting her head a hundred ways under a hundred bonnets, seeking in vain for mock cherries to match her lips or plumes that were graceful as her own supple body.

Noon would come—she would hurry along Fifth Avenue, a Nordic Ganymede, her fur coat swinging fashionably with her steps, her cheeks redder by a stroke of the wind's brush, her breath a delightful mist upon the bracing air—and the doors of the Ritz would revolve, the crowd would divide, fifty masculine eyes would start, stare, as she gave back forgotten dreams to the husbands of many obese and comic women.

One o'clock. With her fork she would tantalize the heart of an adoring artichoke, while her escort served himself up in the thick, dripping sentences of an enraptured man.

Four o'clock: her little feet moving to melody, her face distinct in the crowd, her partner happy as a petted puppy and mad as the immemorial hatter. . . . Then—then night would come drifting down and perhaps another damp. The signs would spill their light into the street. Who knew? No wiser than he, they haply sought to recapture that picture done in cream and shadow they had seen on the hushed Avenue the night before. And they might, ah, they might! A thousand taxis would yawn at a thousand corners, and only to him was that kiss forever lost and done. In a thousand guises Thaïs would hail a cab and turn up her face for loving. And her pallor would be virginal and lovely, and her kiss chaste as the moon. . . .

He sprang excitedly to his feet. How inappropriate that she should be out! He had realized at last what he wanted— to kiss her again, to find rest in her great immobility. She was the end of all restlessness, all malcontent.

Anthony dressed and went out, as he should have done long before, and down to Richard Caramel's room to hear the last revision of the last chapter of "The Demon Lover." He did not call Gloria again until six. He did not find her in until eight and—oh, climax of anticlimaxes!—she could give him no engagement until Tuesday afternoon. A broken piece of gutta-percha clattered to the floor as he banged up the phone.

BLACK MAGIC

Tuesday was freezing cold. He called at a bleak two o'clock and as they shook hands he wondered confusedly whether he had ever kissed her; it was almost unbelievable—he seriously doubted if she remembered it.

"I called you four times on Sunday," he told her.

"Did you?"

There was surprise in her voice and interest in her expression. Silently he cursed himself for having told her. He might have known her pride did not deal in such petty triumphs. Even then he had not guessed at the truth—that never having had to worry about men she had seldom used the wary subterfuges, the playings out and haulings in, that were the stock in trade of her sisterhood. When she liked a man, that was trick enough. Did she think she loved him—there was an ultimate and fatal thrust. Her charm endlessly preserved itself.

"I was anxious to see you," he said simply. "I want to talk to you—I mean really talk, somewhere where we can be alone. May I?"

"What do you mean?"

He swallowed a sudden lump of panic. He felt that she knew what he wanted.

"I mean, not at a tea table," he said.

"Well, all right, but not to-day. I want to get some exercise. Let's walk!"

It was bitter and raw. All the evil hate in the mad heart of February was wrought into the forlorn and icy wind that cut its way cruelly across Central Park and down along Fifth Avenue. It was almost impossible to talk, and discomfort made him distracted, so much so that he turned at Sixty-first Street to find that she was no longer beside him. He looked around. She was forty feet in the rear standing motionless, her face half hidden in her fur coat collar, moved either by anger or laughter—he could not determine which. He started back.

"Don't let me interrupt your walk!" she called.

"I'm mighty sorry," he answered in confusion. "Did I go too fast?"

"I'm cold," she announced. "I want to go home. And you walk too fast."

"I'm very sorry."

Side by side they started for the Plaza. He wished he could see her face.

"Men don't usually get so absorbed in themselves when they're with me."

"I'm sorry."

"That's very interesting."

"It *is* rather too cold to walk," he said, briskly, to hide his annoyance.

She made no answer and he wondered if she would dismiss him at the hotel entrance. She walked in without speaking, however, and to the elevator, throwing him a single remark as she entered it:

"You'd better come up."

He hesitated for the fraction of a moment.

"Perhaps I'd better call some other time."

"Just as you say." Her words were murmured as an aside. The main concern of life was the adjusting of some stray wisps of hair in the elevator mirror. Her cheeks were brilliant, her eyes sparkled—she had never seemed so lovely, so exquisitely to be desired.

Despising himself, he found that he was walking down the tenth-floor corridor a subservient foot behind her; was in the sitting room while she disappeared to shed her furs. Something had gone wrong—in his own eyes he had lost a shred of dignity; in an unpremeditated yet significant encounter he had been completely defeated.

However, by the time she reappeared in the sitting-room he had explained himself to himself with sophistic satisfaction. After all he had done the strongest thing, he thought. He had wanted to come up, he had come. Yet what happened later on that afternoon must be traced to the indignity he had experienced in the elevator; the girl was worrying him intolerably, so much so that when she came out he involuntarily drifted into criticism.

"Who's this Bloeckman, Gloria?"

"A business friend of father's."

"Odd sort of fellow!"

"He doesn't like you either," she said with a sudden smile.

Anthony laughed.

"I'm flattered at his notice. He evidently considers me a—" He broke off with "Is he in love with you?"

"I don't know."

"The deuce you don't," he insisted. "Of course he is. I remember the look he gave me when we got back to the table. He'd probably have had me quietly assaulted by a delegation of movie supes if you hadn't invented that phone call."

"He didn't mind. I told him afterward what really happened."

"You told him!"

"He asked me."

"I don't like that very well," he remonstrated.

She laughed again.

"Oh, you don't?"

"What business is it of his?"

"None. That's why I told him."

Anthony in a turmoil bit savagely at his mouth.

"Why should I lie?" she demanded directly. "I'm not ashamed of anything I do. It happened to interest him to know that I kissed you, and I happened to be in a good humor, so I satisfied his curiosity by a simple and precise 'yes.' Being rather a sensible man, after his fashion, he dropped the subject."

"Except to say that he hated me."

"Oh, it worries you? Well, if you must probe this stupendous matter to its depths he didn't say he hated you. I simply know he does."

"It doesn't wor——"

"Oh, let's drop it!" she cried spiritedly. "It's a most uninteresting matter to me."

With a tremendous effort Anthony made his acquiescence a twist of subject, and they drifted into an ancient question-and-answer game concerned with each other's pasts, gradually warming as they discovered the age-old, immemorial resemblances in tastes and ideas. They said things that were more revealing than they intended—but each pretended to accept the other at face, or rather word, value.

The growth of intimacy is like that. First one gives off his best picture, the bright and finished product mended with bluff and falsehood and humor. Then more details are required and one paints a second portrait, and a third—before long the best lines cancel out—and the secret is exposed at last; the planes of the pictures have intermingled and given us away, and though we paint and paint we can no longer sell a picture. We must be satisfied with hoping that such fatuous accounts of ourselves as we make to our wives and children and business associates are accepted as true.

"It seems to me," Anthony was saying earnestly, "that the position of a man with neither necessity nor ambition is unfortunate. Heaven knows it'd be pathetic of me to be sorry for myself—yet, sometimes I envy Dick."

Her silence was encouragement. It was as near as she ever came to an intentional lure.

"—And there used to be dignified occupations for a gentleman who had leisure, things a little more constructive than filling up the landscape with smoke or juggling some one else's money. There's science, of course: sometimes I wish I'd taken a good foundation, say at Boston Tech. But now, by golly, I'd have to sit down for two years and struggle through the fundamentals of physics and chemistry."

She yawned.

"I've told you I don't know what anybody ought to do,"

she said ungraciously, and at her indifference his rancor was
born again.

"Aren't you interested in anything except yourself?"

"Not much."

He glared; his growing enjoyment in the conversation
was ripped to shreds. She had been irritable and vindictive
all day, and it seemed to him that for this moment he hated
her hard selfishness. He stared morosely at the fire.

Then a strange thing happened. She turned to him and
smiled, and as he saw her smile every rag of anger and hurt
vanity dropped from him—as though his very moods were but
the outer ripples of her own, as though emotion rose no longer
in his breast unless she saw fit to pull an omnipotent control-
ling thread.

He moved closer and taking her hand pulled her ever so
gently toward him until she half lay against his shoulder. She
smiled up at him as he kissed her.

"Gloria," he whispered very softly. Again she had made
a magic, subtle and pervading as a spilt perfume, irresistible
and sweet.

Afterward, neither the next day nor after many years,
could he remember the important things of that afternoon.
Had she been moved? In his arms had she spoken a little—or
at all? What measure of enjoyment had she taken in his kisses?
And had she at any time lost herself ever so little?

Oh, for him there was no doubt. He had risen and
paced the floor in sheer ecstasy. That such a girl should be;
should poise curled in a corner of the couch like a swallow
newly landed from a clean swift flight, watching him with
inscrutable eyes. He would stop his pacing and, half shy
each time at first, drop his arm around her and find her
kiss.

She was fascinating, he told her. He had never met any
one like her before. He besought her jauntily but earnestly
to send him away; he didn't want to fall in love. He wasn't

coming to see her any more—already she had haunted too many of his ways.

What delicious romance! His true reaction was neither fear nor sorrow—only this deep delight in being with her that colored the banality of his words and made the mawkish seem sad and the posturing seem wise. He *would* come back— eternally. He should have known!

"This is all. It's been very rare to have known you, very strange and wonderful. But this wouldn't do—and wouldn't last." As he spoke there was in his heart that tremulousness that we take for sincerity in ourselves.

Afterward he remembered one reply of hers to something he had asked her. He remembered it in this form—perhaps he had unconsciously arranged and polished it:

"A woman should be able to kiss a man beautifully and romantically without any desire to be either his wife or his mistress."

As always when he was with her she seemed to grow gradually older until at the end ruminations too deep for words would be wintering in her eyes.

An hour passed, and the fire leaped up in little ecstasies as though its fading life was sweet. It was five now, and the clock over the mantel became articulate in sound. Then as if a brutish sensibility in him was reminded by those thin, tinny beats that the petals were falling from the flowered afternoon, Anthony pulled her quickly to her feet and held her helpless, without breath, in a kiss that was neither a game nor a tribute.

Her arms fell to her side. In an instant she was free.

"Don't!" she said quietly. "I don't want that."

She sat down on the far side of the lounge and gazed straight before her. A frown had gathered between her eyes. Anthony sank down beside her and closed his hand over hers. It was lifeless and unresponsive.

"Why, Gloria!" He made a motion as if to put his arm about her but she drew away.

"I don't want that," she repeated.

"I'm very sorry," he said, a little impatiently. "I—I didn't know you made such fine distinctions."

She did not answer.

"Won't you kiss me, Gloria?"

"I don't want to." It seemed to him she had not moved for hours.

"A sudden change, isn't it?" Annoyance was growing in his voice.

"Is it?" She appeared uninterested. It was almost as though she were looking at someone else.

"Perhaps I'd better go."

No reply. He rose and regarded her angrily, uncertainly. Again he sat down.

"Gloria, Gloria, won't you kiss me?"

"No." Her lips, parting for the word, had just faintly stirred.

Again he got to his feet, this time with less decision, less confidence.

"Then I'll go."

Silence.

"All right—I'll go."

He was aware of a certain irremediable lack of originality in his remarks. Indeed he felt that the whole atmosphere had grown oppressive. He wished she would speak, rail at him, cry out upon him, anything but this pervasive and chilling silence. He cursed himself for a weak fool; his clearest desire was to move her, to hurt her, to see her wince. Helplessly, involuntarily, he erred again.

"If you're tired of kissing me I'd better go."

He saw her lips curl slightly and his last dignity left him. She spoke, at length:

"I believe you've made that remark several times before."

He looked about him immediately, saw his hat and coat on a chair—blundered into them, during an intolerable moment. Looking again at the couch he perceived that she had not turned, not even moved. With a shaken, immediately regretted "good-by" he went quickly but without dignity from the room.

For over a moment Gloria made no sound. Her lips were still curled; her glance was straight, proud, remote. Then her eyes blurred a little, and she murmured three words half aloud to the death-bound fire:

"Good-by, you ass!" she said.

PANIC

The man had had the hardest blow of his life. He knew at last what he wanted, but in finding it out it seemed that he had put it forever beyond his grasp. He reached home in misery, dropped into an armchair without even removing his overcoat, and sat there for over an hour, his mind racing the paths of fruitless and wretched self-absorption. She had sent him away! That was the reiterated burden of his despair. Instead of seizing the girl and holding her by sheer strength until she became passive to his desire, instead of beating down her will by the force of his own, he had walked, defeated and powerless, from her door, with the corners of his mouth drooping and what force there might have been in his grief and rage hidden behind the manner of a whipped schoolboy. At one minute she had liked him tremendously—ah, she had nearly loved him. In the next he had become a thing of indifference to her, an insolent and efficiently humiliated man.

He had no great self-reproach—some, of course, but there were other things dominant in him now, far more urgent. He was not so much in love with Gloria as mad for her. Unless he could have her near him again, kiss her, hold her close and acquiescent, he wanted nothing more from life. By her three minutes of utter unwavering indifference the girl had lifted herself from a high but somehow casual position in his mind, to be instead his complete preoccupation. However much his wild thoughts varied between a passionate desire for her kisses and an equally passionate craving to hurt and mar her, the residue of his mind craved in finer fashion to possess the triumphant soul that had shone through those three minutes. She was beautiful—but especially she was without mercy. He must own that strength that could send him away.

At present no such analysis was possible to Anthony. His clarity of mind, all those endless resources which he thought his irony had brought him were swept aside. Not only for that night but for the days and weeks that followed his books were to be but furniture and his friends only people who lived and walked in a nebulous outer world from which he was trying to escape—that world was cold and full of bleak wind, and for a little while he had seen into a warm house where fires shone.

About midnight he began to realize that he was hungry. He went down into Fifty-second Street, where it was so cold that he could scarcely see; the moisture froze on his lashes and in the corners of his lips. Everywhere dreariness had come down from the north, settling upon the thin and cheerless street, where black bundled figures blacker still against the night, moved stumbling along the sidewalk through the shrieking wind, sliding their feet cautiously ahead as though they were on skis. Anthony turned over toward Sixth Avenue, so absorbed in his thoughts as not to notice that several passers-by had stared at him. His overcoat was wide open, and the wind was biting in, hard and full of merciless death.

. . . After a while a waitress spoke to him, a fat waitress with black-rimmed eye-glasses from which dangled a long black cord.

"Order, please!"

Her voice, he considered, was unnecessarily loud. He looked up resentfully.

"You wanna order or doncha?"

"Of course," he protested.

"Well, I ast you three times. This ain't no rest-room."

He glanced at the big clock and discovered with a start that it was after two. He was down around Thirtieth Street somewhere, and after a moment he found and translated the

CHILD'S

in a white semicircle of letters upon the glass front. The place was inhabited sparsely by three or four bleak and half-frozen night-hawks.

"Give me some bacon and eggs and coffee, please."

The waitress bent upon him a last disgusted glance and, looking ludicrously intellectual in her corded glasses, hurried away.

God! Gloria's kisses had been such flowers. He remembered as though it had been years ago the low freshness of her voice, the beautiful lines of her body shining through her clothes, her face lily-colored under the lamps of the street—under the lamps.

Misery struck at him again, piling a sort of terror upon the ache and yearning. He had lost her. It was true—no denying it, no softening it. But a new idea had seared his sky—what of Bloeckman! What would happen now? There was a wealthy man, middle-aged enough to be tolerant with a beautiful wife, to baby her whims and indulge her unreason, to wear her as she perhaps wished to be worn—a bright flower in his button-hole, safe and secure from the things she feared. He felt that she had been playing with the idea of marrying Bloeckman, and it was well possible that this disappointment in Anthony might throw her on sudden impulse into Bloeckman's arms.

The idea drove him childishly frantic. He wanted to kill Bloeckman and make him suffer for his hideous presumption. He was saying this over and over to himself with his teeth tight shut, and a perfect orgy of hate and fright in his eyes.

But, behind this obscene jealousy, Anthony was in love

at last, profoundly and truly in love, as the word goes between man and woman.

His coffee appeared at his elbow and gave off for a certain time a gradually diminishing wisp of steam. The night manager, seated at his desk, glanced at the motionless figure alone at the last table, and then with a sigh moved down upon him just as the hour hand crossed the figure three on the big clock.

WISDOM

After another day the turmoil subsided and Anthony began to exercise a measure of reason. He was in love—he cried it passionately to himself. The things that a week before would have seemed insuperable obstacles, his limited income, his desire to be irresponsible and independent, had in this forty hours become the merest chaff before the wind of his infatuation. If he did not marry her his life would be a feeble parody on his own adolescence. To be able to face people and to endure the constant reminder of Gloria that all existence had become, it was necessary for him to have hope. So he built hope desperately and tenaciously out of the stuff of his dream, a hope flimsy enough, to be sure, a hope that was cracked and dissipated a dozen times a day, a hope mothered by mockery, but, nevertheless, a hope that would be brawn and sinew to his self-respect.

Out of this developed a spark of wisdom, a true perception of his own from out the effortless past.

"Memory is short," he thought.

So very short. At the crucial point the Trust President is on the stand, a potential criminal needing but one push to be a jailbird, scorned by the upright for leagues around. Let him be acquitted—and in a year all is forgotten. "Yes, he did have some trouble once, just a technicality, I believe." Oh, memory is very short!

Anthony had seen Gloria altogether about a dozen times, say two dozen hours. Supposing he left her alone for a month, made no attempt to see her or speak to her, and avoided every place where she might possibly be. Wasn't it possible, the more possible because she had never loved him, that at the end of that time the rush of events would efface his personality from her conscious mind, and with his personality his offense and humiliation? She would forget, for there would be other men. He winced. The implication struck out at him—other men. Two months—God! Better three weeks, two weeks——

He thought this the second evening after the catastrophe when he was undressing, and at this point he threw himself down on the bed and lay there, trembling very slightly and looking at the top of the canopy.

Two weeks—that was worse than no time at all. In two weeks he would approach her much as he would have to now, without personality or confidence—remaining still the man who had gone too far and then for a period that in time was but a moment but in fact an eternity, whined. No, two weeks was too short a time. Whatever poignancy there had been for her in that afternoon must have time to dull. He must give her a period when the incident should fade, and then a new period when she should gradually begin to think of him, no matter how dimly, with a true perspective that would remember his pleasantness as well as his humiliation.

He fixed, finally, on six weeks as approximately the interval best suited to his purpose, and on a desk calendar he marked the days off, finding that it would fall on the ninth of April. Very well, on that day he would phone and ask her if he might call. Until then—silence.

After his decision a gradual improvement was manifest. He had taken at least a step in the direction to which hope pointed, and he realized that the less he brooded upon her the better he would be able to give the desired impression when they met.

In another hour he fell into a deep sleep.

THE INTERVAL

Nevertheless, though, as the days passed, the glory of her hair dimmed perceptibly for him and in a year of separation might have departed completely, the six weeks held many abominable days. He dreaded the sight of Dick and Maury, imagining wildly that they knew all—but when the three met it was Richard Caramel and not Anthony who was the centre of attention; "The Demon Lover" had been accepted for immediate publication. Anthony felt that from now on he moved apart. He no longer craved the warmth and security of Maury's society which had cheered him no further back than November. Only Gloria could give that now and no one else ever again. So Dick's success rejoiced him only casually and worried him not a little. It meant that the world was going ahead—writing and reading and publishing—and living. And he wanted the world to wait motionless and breathless for six weeks—while Gloria forgot.

TWO ENCOUNTERS

His greatest satisfaction was in Geraldine's company. He took her once to dinner and the theatre and entertained her several times in his apartment. When he was with her she absorbed him, not as Gloria had, but quieting those erotic sensibilities in him that worried over Gloria. It didn't matter how he kissed Geraldine. A kiss was a kiss—to be enjoyed to the utmost for its short moment. To Geraldine things belonged in definite pigeonholes: a kiss was one thing, anything further was quite another; a kiss was all right; the other things were "bad."

When half the interval was up two incidents occurred

on successive days that upset his increasing calm and caused a temporary relapse.

The first was—he saw Gloria. It was a short meeting. Both bowed. Both spoke, yet neither heard the other. But when it was over Anthony read down a column of *The Sun* three times in succession without understanding a single sentence.

One would have thought Sixth Avenue a safe street! Having forsworn his barber at the Plaza he went around the corner one morning to be shaved, and while waiting his turn he took off coat and vest, and with his soft collar open at the neck stood near the front of the shop. The day was an oasis in the cold desert of March and the sidewalk was cheerful with a population of strolling sun-worshippers. A stout woman upholstered in velvet, her flabby cheeks too much massaged, swirled by with her poodle straining at its leash—the effect being given of a tug bringing in an ocean liner. Just behind them a man in a striped blue suit, walking slue-footed in white-spatted feet, grinned at the sight and catching Anthony's eye, winked through the glass. Anthony laughed, thrown immediately into that humor in which men and women were graceless and absurd phantasms, grotesquely curved and rounded in a rectangular world of their own building. They inspired the same sensations in him as did those strange and monstrous fish who inhabit the esoteric world of green in the aquarium.

Two more strollers caught his eye casually, a man and a girl—then in a horrified instant the girl resolved herself into Gloria. He stood here powerless; they came nearer and Gloria, glancing in, saw him. Her eyes widened and she smiled politely. Her lips moved. She was less than five feet away.

"How do you do?" he muttered inanely.

Gloria, happy, beautiful, and young—with a man he had never seen before!

It was then that the barber's chair was vacated and he read down the newspaper column three times in succession.

The second incident took place the next day. Going into the Manhattan bar about seven he was confronted with Bloeckman. As it happened, the room was nearly deserted, and before the mutual recognition he had stationed himself within a foot of the older man and ordered his drink, so it was inevitable that they should converse.

"Hello, Mr. Patch," said Bloeckman amiably enough.

Anthony took the proffered hand and exchanged a few aphorisms on the fluctuations of the mercury.

"Do you come in here much?" inquired Bloeckman.

"No, very seldom." He omitted to add that the Plaza bar had, until lately, been his favorite.

"Nice bar. One of the best bars in town."

Anthony nodded. Bloeckman emptied his glass and picked up his cane. He was in evening dress.

"Well, I'll be hurrying on. I'm going to dinner with Miss Gilbert."

Death looked suddenly out at him from two blue eyes. Had he announced himself as his vis-à-vis's prospective murderer he could not have struck a more vital blow at Anthony. The younger man must have reddened visibly, for his every nerve was in instant clamor. With tremendous effort he mustered a rigid—oh, so rigid—smile, and said a conventional good-by. But that night he lay awake until after four, half wild with grief and fear and abominable imaginings.

WEAKNESS

And one day in the fifth week he called her up. He had been sitting in his apartment trying to read "L'Education Sentimental," and something in the book had sent his thoughts racing in the direction that, set free, they always took, like horses racing for a home stable. With suddenly quickened breath he walked to the telephone. When he gave the number it seemed to him that his voice faltered and broke like a schoolboy's. The Central must have heard the pounding of his heart. The sound of the receiver being taken up at the other end was a crack of doom, and Mrs. Gilbert's voice, soft as maple syrup running into a glass container, had for him a quality of horror in its single "Hello-o-ah?"

"Miss Gloria's not feeling well. She's lying down, asleep. Who shall I say called?"

"Nobody!" he shouted.

In a wild panic he slammed down the receiver; collapsed into his armchair in the cold sweat of breathless relief.

SERENADE

The first thing he said to her was: "Why, you've bobbed your hair!" and she answered: "Yes, isn't it gorgeous?"

It was not fashionable then. It was to be fashionable in five or six years. At that time it was considered extremely daring.

"It's all sunshine outdoors," he said gravely. "Don't you want to take a walk?"

She put on a light coat and a quaintly piquant Napoleon hat of Alice Blue, and they walked along the Avenue and into the Zoo, where they properly admired the grandeur of the elephant and the collar-height of the giraffe, but did not visit the monkey house because Gloria said that monkeys smelt so bad.

Then they returned toward the Plaza, talking about nothing, but glad for the spring singing in the air and for the warm balm that lay upon the suddenly golden city. To their right was the Park, while at the left a great bulk of granite and marble muttered dully a millionaire's chaotic message to whosoever would listen: something about "I worked and I saved and I was sharper than all Adam and here I sit, by golly, by golly!"

All the newest and most beautiful designs in

automobiles were out on Fifth Avenue, and ahead of them the Plaza loomed up rather unusually white and attractive. The supple, indolent Gloria walked a short shadow's length ahead of him, pouring out lazy casual comments that floated a moment on the dazzling air before they reached his ear.

"Oh!" she cried, "I want to go south to Hot Springs! I want to get out in the air and just roll around on the new grass and forget there's ever been any winter."

"Don't you, though!"

"I want to hear a million robins making a frightful racket. I sort of like birds."

"All women *are* birds," he ventured.

"What kind am I?"—quick and eager.

"A swallow, I think, and sometimes a bird of paradise. Most girls are sparrows, of course—see that row of nurse-maids over there? They're sparrows—or are they magpies? And of course you've met canary girls—and robin girls."

"And swan girls and parrot girls. All grown women are hawks, I think, or owls."

"What am I—a buzzard?"

She laughed and shook her head.

"Oh, no, you're not a bird at all, do you think? You're a Russian wolfhound."

Anthony remembered that they were white and always looked unnaturally hungry. But then they were usually photographed with dukes and princesses, so he was properly flattered.

"Dick's a fox terrier, a trick fox terrier," she continued.

"And Maury's a cat." Simultaneously it occurred to him how like Bloeckman was to a robust and offensive hog. But he preserved a discreet silence.

Later, as they parted, Anthony asked when he might see her again.

"Don't you ever make long engagements?" he pleaded,

"even if it's a week ahead, I think it'd be fun to spend a whole day together, morning and afternoon both."

"It would be, wouldn't it?" She thought for a moment. "Let's do it next Sunday."

"All right. I'll map out a programme that'll take up every minute."

He did. He even figured to a nicety what would happen in the two hours when she would come to his apartment for tea: how the good Bounds would have the windows wide to let in the fresh breeze—but a fire going also lest there be chill in the air—and how there would be clusters of flowers about in big cool bowls that he would buy for the occasion. They would sit on the lounge.

And when the day came they did sit upon the lounge. After a while Anthony kissed her because it came about quite naturally; he found sweetness sleeping still upon her lips, and felt that he had never been away. The fire was bright and the breeze sighing in through the curtains brought a mellow damp, promising May and world of summer. His soul thrilled to remote harmonies; he heard the strum of far guitars and waters lapping on a warm Mediterranean shore—for he was young now as he would never be again, and more triumphant than death.

Six o'clock stole down too soon and rang the querulous melody of St. Anne's chimes on the corner. Through the gathering dusk they strolled to the Avenue, where the crowds, like prisoners released, were walking with elastic step at last after the long winter, and the tops of the busses were thronged with congenial kings and the shops full of fine soft things for the summer, the rare summer, the gay promising summer that seemed for love what the winter was for money. Life was singing for his supper on the corner! Life was handing round cocktails in the street! Old women there were in that crowd who felt that they could have run and won a hundred-yard dash!

In bed that night with the lights out and the cool room swimming with moonlight, Anthony lay awake and played with every minute of the day like a child playing in turn with each one of a pile of long-wanted Christmas toys. He had told her gently, almost in the middle of a kiss, that he loved her, and she had smiled and held him closer and murmured, "I'm glad," looking into his eyes. There had been a new quality in her attitude, a new growth of sheer physical attraction toward him and a strange emotional tenseness, that was enough to make him clinch his hands and draw in his breath at the recollection. He had felt nearer to her than ever before. In a rare delight he cried aloud to the room that he loved her.

He phoned next morning—no hesitation now, no uncertainty—instead a delirious excitement that doubled and trebled when he heard her voice:

"Good morning—Gloria."

"Good morning."

"That's all I called you up to say-dear."

"I'm glad you did."

"I wish I could see you."

"You will, to-morrow night."

"That's a long time, isn't it?"

"Yes—" Her voice was reluctant. His hand tightened on the receiver.

"Couldn't I come to-night?" He dared anything in the glory and revelation of that almost whispered "yes."

"I have a date."

"Oh—"

"But I might—I might be able to break it."

"Oh!"—a sheer cry, a rhapsody. "Gloria?"

"What?"

"I love you."

Another pause and then:

"I—I'm glad."

Happiness, remarked Maury Noble one day, is only the

first hour after the alleviation of some especially intense misery. But oh, Anthony's face as he walked down the tenth-floor corridor of the Plaza that night! His dark eyes were gleaming—around his mouth were lines it was a kindness to see. He was handsome then if never before, bound for one of those immortal moments which come so radiantly that their remembered light is enough to see by for years.

He knocked and, at a word, entered. Gloria, dressed in simple pink, starched and fresh as a flower, was across the room, standing very still, and looking at him wide-eyed.

As he closed the door behind him she gave a little cry and moved swiftly over the intervening space, her arms rising in a premature caress as she came near. Together they crushed out the stiff folds of her dress in one triumphant and enduring embrace.

BOOK TWO

CHAPTER 1

THE RADIANT HOUR

After a fortnight Anthony and Gloria began to indulge in "practical discussions," as they called those sessions when under the guise of severe realism they walked in an eternal moonlight.

"Not as much as I do you," the critic of belles-lettres would insist. "If you really loved me you'd want everyone to know it."

"I do," she protested; "I want to stand on the street corner like a sandwich man, informing all the passers-by."

"Then tell me all the reasons why you're going to marry me in June."

"Well, because you're so clean. You're sort of blowy clean, like I am. There's two sorts, you know. One's like Dick: he's clean like polished pans. You and I are clean like streams and winds. I can tell whenever I see a person whether he is clean, and if so, which kind of clean he is."

"We're twins."

Ecstatic thought!

"Mother says"—she hesitated uncertainly—"mother says

that two souls are sometimes created together and—and in love before they're born."

Bilphism gained its easiest convert. . . . After a while he lifted up his head and laughed soundlessly toward the ceiling. When his eyes came back to her he saw that she was angry.

"Why did you laugh?" she cried, "you've done that twice before. There's nothing funny about our relation to each other. I don't mind playing the fool, and I don't mind having you do it, but I can't stand it when we're together."

"I'm sorry."

"Oh, don't say you're sorry! If you can't think of anything better than that, just keep quiet!"

"I love you."

"I don't care."

There was a pause. Anthony was depressed. . . . At length Gloria murmured:

"I'm sorry I was mean."

"You weren't. I was the one."

Peace was restored—the ensuing moments were so much more sweet and sharp and poignant. They were stars on this stage, each playing to an audience of two: the passion of their pretense created the actuality. Here, finally, was the quintessence of self-expression—yet it was probable that for the most part their love expressed Gloria rather than Anthony. He felt often like a scarcely tolerated guest at a party she was giving.

Telling Mrs. Gilbert had been an embarrassed matter. She sat stuffed into a small chair and listened with an intense and very blinky sort of concentration. She must have known it—for three weeks Gloria had seen no one else—and she must have noticed that this time there was an authentic difference in her daughter's attitude. She had been given special deliveries to post; she had heeded, as all mothers seem to heed, the hither end of telephone conversations, disguised but still rather warm—

—Yet she had delicately professed surprise and declared

herself immensely pleased; she doubtless was; so were the geranium plants blossoming in the window-boxes, and so were the cabbies when the lovers sought the romantic privacy of hansom cabs—quaint device—and the staid bill of fares on which they scribbled "you know I do," pushing it over for the other to see.

But between kisses Anthony and this golden girl quarrelled incessantly.

"Now, Gloria," he would cry, "please let me explain!"

"Don't explain. Kiss me."

"I don't think that's right. If I hurt your feelings we ought to discuss it. I don't like this kiss-and-forget."

"But I don't want to argue. I think it's wonderful that we *can* kiss and forget, and when we can't it'll be time to argue."

At one time some gossamer difference attained such bulk that Anthony arose and punched himself into his overcoat—for a moment it appeared that the scene of the preceding February was to be repeated, but knowing how deeply she was moved he retained his dignity with his pride, and in a moment Gloria was sobbing in his arms, her lovely face miserable as a frightened little girl's.

Meanwhile they kept unfolding to each other, unwillingly, by curious reactions and evasions, by distastes and prejudices and unintended hints of the past. The girl was proudly incapable of jealousy and, because he was extremely jealous, this virtue piqued him. He told her recondite incidents of his own life on purpose to arouse some spark of it, but to no avail. She possessed him now—nor did she desire the dead years.

"Oh, Anthony," she would say, "always when I'm mean to you I'm sorry afterward. I'd give my right hand to save you one little moment's pain."

And in that instant her eyes were brimming and she was not aware that she was voicing an illusion. Yet Anthony knew that there were days when they hurt each other purposely—taking almost a delight in the thrust. Incessantly she puzzled him: one hour so intimate and charming, striving desperately toward an unguessed, transcendent union; the next, silent and cold, apparently unmoved by any consideration of their love or anything he could say. Often he would eventually trace these portentous reticences to some physical discomfort—of these she never complained until they were over—or to some carelessness or presumption in him, or to an unsatisfactory dish at dinner, but even then the means by which she created the infinite distances she spread about herself were a mystery, buried somewhere back in those twenty-two years of unwavering pride.

"Why do you like Muriel?" he demanded one day.

"I don't very much."

"Then why do you go with her?"

"Just for some one to go with. They're no exertion, those girls. They sort of believe everything I tell them—but I rather like Rachael. I think she's cute—and so clean and slick, don't you? I used to have other friends—in Kansas City and at school—casual, all of them, girls who just flitted into my range and out of it for no more reason than that boys took us places together. They didn't interest me after environment stopped throwing us together. Now they're mostly married. What does it matter—they were all just people."

"You like men better, don't you?"

"Oh, much better. I've got a man's mind."

"You've got a mind like mine. Not strongly gendered either way."

Later she told him about the beginnings of her friendship with Bloeckman. One day in Delmonico's, Gloria and Rachael had come upon Bloeckman and Mr. Gilbert having luncheon and curiosity had impelled her to make it a party of four. She had liked him—rather. He was a relief from younger men, satisfied as he was with so little. He humored her and he laughed, whether he understood her or not. She met him several times, despite the open disapproval of her parents, and within a month he had asked her to marry him, tendering her everything from a villa in Italy to a brilliant career on the screen. She had laughed in his face—and he had laughed too.

But he had not given up. To the time of Anthony's arrival in the arena he had been making steady progress. She treated him rather well—except that she had called him always by an invidious nickname—perceiving, meanwhile, that he was figuratively following along beside her as she walked the fence, ready to catch her if she should fall.

The night before the engagement was announced she told Bloeckman. It was a heavy blow. She did not enlighten Anthony as to the details, but she implied that he had not hesitated to argue with her. Anthony gathered that the interview had terminated on a stormy note, with Gloria very cool and unmoved lying in her corner of the sofa and Joseph Bloeckman of "Films Par Excellence" pacing the carpet with eyes narrowed and head bowed. Gloria had been sorry for him but she had judged it best not to show it. In a final burst of kindness she had tried to make him hate her, there at the last. But Anthony, understanding that Gloria's indifference was her strongest appeal, judged how futile this must have been. He wondered, often but quite casually, about Bloeckman—finally he forgot him entirely.

HEYDAY

One afternoon they found front seats on the sunny roof of a bus and rode for hours from the fading Square up along the sullied river, and then, as the stray beams fled the westward streets, sailed down the turgid Avenue, darkening with ominous bees from the department stores. The traffic was clotted and gripped in a patternless jam; the busses were packed four deep like platforms above the crowd as they waited for the moan of the traffic whistle.

"Isn't it good!" cried Gloria. "Look!"

A miller's wagon, stark white with flour, driven by a

powdery clown, passed in front of them behind a white horse and his black team-mate.

"What a pity!" she complained; "they'd look so beautiful in the dusk, if only both horses were white. I'm mighty happy just this minute, in this city."

Anthony shook his head in disagreement.

"I think the city's a mountebank. Always struggling to approach the tremendous and impressive urbanity ascribed to it. Trying to be romantically metropolitan."

"I don't. I think it is impressive."

"Momentarily. But it's really a transparent, artificial sort of spectacle. It's got its press-agented stars and its flimsy, unenduring stage settings and, I'll admit, the greatest army of supers ever assembled—" He paused, laughed shortly, and added: "Technically excellent, perhaps, but not convincing."

"I'll bet policemen think people are fools," said Gloria thoughtfully, as she watched a large but cowardly lady being helped across the street. "He always sees them frightened and inefficient and old—they are," she added. And then: "We'd better get off. I told mother I'd have an early supper and go to bed. She says I look tired, damn it."

"I wish we were married," he muttered soberly; "there'll be no good night then and we can do just as we want."

"Won't it be good! I think we ought to travel a lot. I want to go to the Mediterranean and Italy. And I'd like to go on the stage some time—say for about a year."

"You bet. I'll write a play for you."

"Won't that be good! And I'll act in it. And then some time when we have more money"—old Adam's death was always thus tactfully alluded to—"we'll build a magnificent estate, won't we?"

"Oh, yes, with private swimming pools."

"Dozens of them. And private rivers. Oh, I wish it were now."

Odd coincidence—he had just been wishing that very

thing. They plunged like divers into the dark eddying crowd and emerging in the cool fifties sauntered indolently homeward, infinitely romantic to each other . . . both were walking alone in a dispassionate garden with a ghost found in a dream.

Halcyon days like boats drifting along slow-moving rivers; spring evenings full of a plaintive melancholy that made the past beautiful and bitter, bidding them look back and see that the loves of other summers long gone were dead with the forgotten waltzes of their years. Always the most poignant moments were when some artificial barrier kept them apart: in the theatre their hands would steal together, join, give and return gentle pressures through the long dark; in crowded rooms they would form words with their lips for each other's eyes—not knowing that they were but following in the footsteps of dusty generations but comprehending dimly that if truth is the end of life happiness is a mode of it, to be cherished in its brief and tremulous moment. And then, one fairy night, May became June. Sixteen days now—fifteen—fourteen——

THREE DIGRESSIONS

Just before the engagement was announced Anthony had gone up to Tarrytown to see his grandfather, who, a little more wizened and grizzly as time played its ultimate chuckling tricks, greeted the news with profound cynicism.

"Oh, you're going to get married, are you?" He said this with such a dubious mildness and shook his head up and down so many times that Anthony was not a little depressed. While he was unaware of his grandfather's intentions he presumed that a large part of the money would come to him. A good deal would go in charities, of course; a good deal to carry on the business of reform.

"Are you going to work?"

"Why—" temporized Anthony, somewhat disconcerted. "I *am* working. You know—"

"Ah, I mean work," said Adam Patch dispassionately.

"I'm not quite sure yet what I'll do. I'm not exactly a beggar, grampa," he asserted with some spirit.

The old man considered this with eyes half closed. Then almost apologetically he asked:

"How much do you save a year?"

"Nothing so far—"

"And so after just managing to get along on your money you've decided that by some miracle two of you can get along on it."

"Gloria has some money of her own. Enough to buy clothes."

"How much?"

Without considering this question impertinent, Anthony answered it.

"About a hundred a month."

"That's altogether about seventy-five hundred a year." Then he added softly: "It ought to be plenty. If you have any sense it ought to be plenty. But the question is whether you have any or not."

"I suppose it is." It was shameful to be compelled to endure this pious browbeating from the old man, and his next words were stiffened with vanity. "I can manage very well. You seem convinced that I'm utterly worthless. At any rate I came up here simply to tell you that I'm getting married in June. Good-by, sir." With this he turned away and headed for the door, unaware that in that instant his grandfather, for the first time, rather liked him.

"Wait!" called Adam Patch, "I want to talk to you."

Anthony faced about.

"Well, sir?"

"Sit down. Stay all night."

Somewhat mollified, Anthony resumed his seat.

"I'm sorry, sir, but I'm going to see Gloria to-night."

"What's her name?"

"Gloria Gilbert."

"New York girl? Someone you know?"

"She's from the Middle West."

"What business her father in?"

"In a celluloid corporation or trust or something. They're from Kansas City."

"You going to be married out there?"

"Why, no, sir. We thought we'd be married in New York—rather quietly."

"Like to have the wedding out here?"

Anthony hesitated. The suggestion made no appeal to him, but it was certainly the part of wisdom to give the old man, if possible, a proprietary interest in his married life. In addition Anthony was a little touched.

"That's very kind of you, grampa, but wouldn't it be a lot of trouble?"

"Everything's a lot of trouble. Your father was married here—but in the old house."

"Why—I thought he was married in Boston."

Adam Patch considered.

"That's true. He *was* married in Boston."

Anthony felt a moment's embarrassment at having made the correction, and he covered it up with words.

"Well, I'll speak to Gloria about it. Personally I'd like to, but of course it's up to the Gilberts, you see."

His grandfather drew a long sigh, half closed his eyes, and sank back in his chair.

"In a hurry?" he asked in a different tone.

"Not especially."

"I wonder," began Adam Patch, looking out with a mild, kindly glance at the lilac bushes that rustled against the windows, "I wonder if you ever think about the after-life."

"Why—sometimes."

"I think a great deal about the after-life." His eyes were dim but his voice was confident and clear. "I was sitting here to-day thinking about what's lying in wait for us, and somehow I began to remember an afternoon nearly sixty-five years ago, when I was playing with my little sister Annie, down where that summer-house is now." He pointed out into the long flower-garden, his eyes trembling of tears, his voice shaking.

"I began thinking—and it seemed to me that *you* ought to think a little more about the after-life. You ought to be—steadier"—he paused and seemed to grope about for the right word—"more industrious—why—"

Then his expression altered, his entire personality seemed to snap together like a trap, and when he continued the softness had gone from his voice.

"—Why, when I was just two years older than you," he rasped with a cunning chuckle, "I sent three members of the firm of Wrenn and Hunt to the poorhouse."

Anthony started with embarrassment.

"Well, good-by," added his grandfather suddenly, "you'll miss your train."

Anthony left the house unusually elated, and strangely sorry for the old man; not because his wealth could buy him "neither youth nor digestion" but because he had asked Anthony to be married there, and because he had forgotten something about his son's wedding that he should have remembered.

Richard Caramel, who was one of the ushers, caused Anthony and Gloria much distress in the last few weeks by continually stealing the rays of their spot-light. "The Demon Lover" had been published in April, and it interrupted the love affair as it may be said to have interrupted everything its author came in contact with. It was a highly original, rather overwritten piece of sustained description concerned with a Don Juan of the New York slums. As Maury and Anthony had said before, as the more hospitable critics were saying then, there was no writer in America with such power to describe the atavistic and unsubtle reactions of that section of society.

The book hesitated and then suddenly "went." Editions, small at first, then larger, crowded each other week by week. A spokesman of the Salvation Army denounced it as a cynical misrepresentation of all the uplift taking place in the under-world. Clever press-agenting spread the unfounded rumor that "Gypsy" Smith was beginning a libel suit because one of the principal characters was a burlesque of himself. It was barred from the public library of Burlington, Iowa, and a Mid-Western columnist announced by innuendo that Richard Caramel was in a sanitarium with delirium tremens.

The author, indeed, spent his days in a state of pleasant madness. The book was in his conversation three-fourths of the time—he wanted to know if one had heard "the latest"; he would go into a store and in a loud voice order books to be charged to him, in order to catch a chance morsel of recog-nition from clerk or customer. He knew to a town in what sections of the country it was selling best; he knew exactly what he cleared on each edition, and when he met anyone who had not read it, or, as it happened only too often, had not heard of it, he succumbed to moody depression.

So it was natural for Anthony and Gloria to decide, in their jealousy, that he was so swollen with conceit as to be a bore. To Dick's great annoyance Gloria publicly boasted that she had never read "The Demon Lover," and didn't intend to until everyone stopped talking about it. As a matter of fact, she had no time to read now, for the presents were pouring in—first a scattering, then an avalanche, varying from the bric-à-brac of forgotten family friends to the photographs of forgotten poor relations.

Maury gave them an elaborate "drinking set," which included silver goblets, cocktail shaker, and bottle-openers. The extortion from Dick was more conventional—a tea set from Tiffany's. From Joseph Bloeckman came a simple and exquisite travelling clock, with his card. There was even a cigarette-holder from Bounds; this touched Anthony and made him want to weep—indeed, any emotion short of hysteria seemed natural in the half-dozen people who were swept up by this tremendous sacrifice to convention. The room set aside in the Plaza bulged with offerings sent by Harvard friends and by associates of his grandfather, with remembrances of Gloria's Farmover days, and with rather pathetic trophies from her former beaux, which last arrived with esoteric, melancholy messages, written on cards tucked carefully inside, beginning "I little thought when—" or "I'm sure I wish you all the happiness—" or even "When you get this I shall be on my way to—"

The most munificent gift was simultaneously the most disappointing. It was a concession of Adam Patch's—a check for five thousand dollars.

To most of the presents Anthony was cold. It seemed to him that they would necessitate keeping a chart of the marital status of all their acquaintances during the next half-century. But Gloria exulted in each one, tearing at the tissue-paper and excelsior with the rapaciousness of a dog digging for a bone, breathlessly seizing a ribbon or an edge of metal and finally bringing to light the whole article and holding it up critically, no emotion except rapt interest in her unsmiling face.

"Look, Anthony!"

"Darn nice, isn't it!"

No answer until an hour later when she would give him a careful account of her precise reaction to the gift, whether it would have been improved by being smaller or larger, whether she was surprised at getting it, and, if so, just how much surprised.

Mrs. Gilbert arranged and rearranged a hypothetical house, distributing the gifts among the different rooms, tabulating articles as "second-best clock" or "silver to use *every* day," and embarrassing Anthony and Gloria by semi-facetious references to a room she called the nursery. She was pleased by old Adam's gift and thereafter had it that he was a very ancient soul, "as much as anything else." As Adam Patch never quite decided whether she referred to the advancing senility of his mind or to some private and psychic schema of her own, it cannot be said to have pleased him. Indeed he always spoke of her to Anthony as "that old woman, the mother," as though she were a character in a comedy he had seen staged many times before. Concerning Gloria he was unable to make up his mind. She attracted him but, as she herself told Anthony, he had decided that she was frivolous and was afraid to approve of her.

Five days!—A dancing platform was being erected on the lawn at Tarrytown. Four days!—A special train was chartered to convey the guests to and from New York. Three days!—

THE DIARY

She was dressed in blue silk pajamas and standing by her bed with her hand on the light to put the room in darkness, when she changed her mind and opening a table drawer brought out a little black book—a "Line-a-day" diary. This she had kept for seven years. Many of the pencil entries were almost illegible and there were notes and references to nights and afternoons long since forgotten, for it was not an intimate diary, even though it began with the immemorial "I am going to keep a diary for my children." Yet as she thumbed over the pages the eyes of many men seemed to look out at her from their half-obliterated names. With one she had gone to New Haven for the first time—in 1908, when she was sixteen and padded shoulders were fashionable at Yale—she had been flattered because "Touch down" Michaud had "rushed" her all evening. She sighed, remembering the grown-up satin dress she had been so proud of and the orchestra playing "Yama-yama, My Yama Man" and "Jungle-Town." So long ago!—the names: Eltynge Reardon, Jim Parsons, "Curly" McGregor, Kenneth Cowan, "Fish-eye" Fry (whom she had liked for being so ugly), Carter Kirby—he had sent her a present; so had Tudor Baird;—Marty Reffer, the first man she had been in love with for more than a day, and Stuart Holcome, who had run away with her in his automobile and tried to make her marry him by force. And Larry Fenwick, whom she had always admired because he had told her one night that if she wouldn't kiss him she could get out of his car and walk home. What a list!

. . . And, after all, an obsolete list. She was in love now, set for the eternal romance that was to be the synthesis of all romance, yet sad for these men and these moonlights and for the "thrills" she had had—and the kisses. The past—her past, oh, what a joy! She had been exuberantly happy.

Turning over the pages her eyes rested idly on the scattered entries of the past four months. She read the last few carefully.

"*April 1st.*—I know Bill Carstairs hates me because I was so disagreeable, but I hate to be sentimentalized over sometimes. We drove out to the Rockyear Country Club and the most wonderful moon kept shining through the trees. My silver dress is getting tarnished. Funny how one forgets the other nights at Rockyear—with Kenneth Cowan when I loved him so!

"*April 3rd.*—After two hours of Schroeder who, they inform me, has millions, I've decided that this matter of sticking to things wears one out, particularly when the things concerned are men. There's nothing so often overdone and from to-day I swear to be amused. We talked about 'love'—how banal! With how many men have I talked about love?

"*April 11th.*—Patch actually called up to-day! and when he forswore me about a month ago he fairly raged out the door. I'm gradually losing faith in any man being susceptible to fatal injuries.

"*April 20th.*—Spent the day with Anthony. Maybe I'll marry him some time. I kind of like his ideas—he stimulates all the originality in me. Blockhead came around about ten in his new car and took me out Riverside Drive. I liked him to-night: he's so considerate. He knew I didn't want to talk so he was quiet all during the ride.

"*April 21st.*—Woke up thinking of Anthony and sure enough he called and sounded sweet on the phone—so I broke a date for him. To-day I feel I'd break anything for him, including the ten commandments and my neck. He's coming at eight and I shall wear pink and look very fresh and starched——"

She paused here, remembering that after he had gone that night she had undressed with the shivering April air streaming in the windows. Yet it seemed she had not felt the cold, warmed by the profound banalities burning in her heart.

The next entry occurred a few days later:

"*April 24th.*—I want to marry Anthony, because husbands are so often 'husbands' and I must marry a lover.

"There are four general types of husbands.

"(1) The husband who always wants to stay in in the evening, has no vices and works for a salary. Totally undesirable!

"(2) The atavistic master whose mistress one is, to wait on his pleasure. This sort always considers every pretty woman 'shallow,' a sort of peacock with arrested development.

"(3) Next comes the worshipper, the idolater of his wife and all that is his, to the utter oblivion of everything else. This sort demands an emotional actress for a wife. God! it must be an exertion to be thought righteous.

"(4) And Anthony—a temporarily passionate lover with wisdom enough to realize when it has flown and that it must fly. And I want to get married to Anthony.

"What grubworms women are to crawl on their bellies through colorless marriages! Marriage was created not to be a background but to need one. Mine is going to be outstanding. It can't, shan't be the setting—it's going to be the performance, the live, lovely, glamorous performance, and the world shall be the scenery. I refuse to dedicate my life to posterity. Surely one owes as much to the current generation as to one's unwanted children. What a fate—to grow rotund and unseemly, to lose my self-love, to think in terms of milk, oatmeal, nurse, diapers. . . . Dear dream children, how much more beautiful you are, dazzling little creatures who flutter (all dream children must flutter) on golden, golden wings——

"Such children, however, poor dear babies, have little in common with the wedded state.

"*June 7th.*—Moral question: Was it wrong to make Bloeckman love me? Because I did really make him. He was almost sweetly sad to-night. How opportune it was that my throat is swollen plunk together and tears were easy to muster. But he's just the past—buried already in my plentiful lavender.

"*June 8th.*—And to-day I've promised not to chew my mouth. Well, I won't, I suppose—but if he'd only asked me not to eat!

"Blowing bubbles—that's what we're doing, Anthony and me. And we blew such beautiful ones to-day, and they'll explode and then we'll blow more and more, I guess—bubbles just as big and just as beautiful, until all the soap and water is used up."

On this note the diary ended. Her eyes wandered up the page, over the June 8th's of 1912, 1910, 1907. The earliest entry was scrawled in the plump, bulbous hand of a sixteen-year-old girl—it was the name, Bob Lamar, and a word she could not decipher. Then she knew what it was—and, knowing, she found her eyes misty with tears. There in a graying blur was the record of her first kiss, faded as its intimate afternoon, on a rainy veranda seven years before. She seemed to remember something one of them had said that day and yet she could not remember. Her tears came faster, until she could scarcely see the page. She was crying, she told herself, because she could remember only the rain and the wet flowers in the yard and the smell of the damp grass.

. . . After a moment she found a pencil and holding it unsteadily drew three parallel lines beneath the last entry. Then she printed FINIS in large capitals, put the book back in the drawer, and crept into bed.

BREATH OF THE CAVE

Back in his apartment after the bridal dinner, Anthony snapped out his lights and, feeling impersonal and fragile as a piece of china waiting on a serving table, got into bed. It was a warm night—a sheet was enough for comfort—and through his wide-open windows came sound, evanescent and summery, alive with remote anticipation. He was thinking that the young years behind him, hollow and colorful, had been lived in facile and vacillating cynicism upon the recorded emotions of men long dust. And there was something beyond that; he knew now. There was the union of his soul with Gloria's, whose radiant fire and freshness was the living material of which the dead beauty of books was made.

From the night into his high-walled room there came, persistently, that evanescent and dissolving sound—something the city was tossing up and calling back again, like a child playing with a ball. In Harlem, the Bronx, Gramercy Park, and along the water-fronts, in little parlors or on pebble-strewn, moon-flooded roofs, a thousand lovers were making this sound, crying little fragments of it into the air. All the city was playing with this sound out there in the blue summer dark, throwing it up and calling it back, promising that, in a little while, life would be beautiful as a story, promising happiness—and by that promise giving it. It gave love hope in its own survival. It could do no more.

It was then that a new note separated itself jarringly from the soft crying of the night. It was a noise from an areaway within a hundred feet from his rear window, the noise of a woman's laughter. It began low, incessant and whining—some servant-maid with her fellow, he thought—and then it grew in volume and became hysterical, until it reminded him of a girl he had seen overcome with nervous laughter at a vaudeville performance. Then it sank, receded, only to rise again and include words—a coarse joke, some bit of obscure horseplay he could not distinguish. It would break off for a moment and he would just catch the low rumble of a man's voice, then begin again—interminably; at first annoying, then strangely terrible. He shivered, and getting up out of bed went to the window. It had reached a high point, tensed and stifled, almost the quality of a scream—then it ceased and left behind it a silence empty and menacing as the greater silence overhead. Anthony stood by the window a moment longer before he returned to his bed. He found himself upset and shaken. Try as he might to strangle his reaction, some animal quality in that unrestrained laughter had grasped at his imagination, and for the first time in four months aroused his old aversion and horror toward all the business of life. The room had grown smothery. He wanted to be out in some cool and bitter breeze, miles above the cities, and to live serene and detached back in the corners of his mind. Life was that sound out there, that ghastly reiterated female sound.

"Oh, my *God*!" he cried, drawing in his breath sharply.

Burying his face in the pillows he tried in vain to concentrate upon the details of the next day.

MORNING

In the gray light he found that it was only five o'clock. He regretted nervously that he had awakened so early—he would appear fagged at the wedding. He envied Gloria who could hide her fatigue with careful pigmentation.

In his bathroom he contemplated himself in the mirror and saw that he was unusually white—half a dozen small imperfections stood out against the morning pallor of his complexion, and overnight he had grown the faint stubble of a beard—the general effect, he fancied, was unprepossessing, haggard, half unwell.

On his dressing table were spread a number of articles which he told over carefully with suddenly fumbling fingers—their tickets to California, the book of traveller's checks, his watch, set to the half minute, the key to his apartment, which he must not forget to give to Maury, and, most important of all, the ring. It was of platinum set around with small emeralds; Gloria had insisted on this; she had always wanted an emerald wedding ring, she said.

It was the third present he had given her; first had come the engagement ring, and then a little gold cigarette-case. He would be giving her many things now—clothes and jewels and friends and excitement. It seemed absurd that from now on he would pay for all her meals. It was going to cost: he wondered if he had not underestimated for this trip, and if he had not better cash a larger check. The question worried him.

Then the breathless impendency of the event swept his mind clear of details. This was the day—unsought, unsuspected six months before, but now breaking in yellow light through his east window, dancing along the carpet as though the sun were smiling at some ancient and reiterated gag of his own.

Anthony laughed in a nervous one-syllable snort.

"By God!" he muttered to himself, "I'm as good as married!"

THE USHERS

Six young men in CROSS PATCH'S *library growing more and more cheery under the influence of Mumm's Extra Dry, set surreptitiously in cold pails by the bookcases.*

THE FIRST YOUNG MAN: By golly! Believe me, in my next book I'm going to do a wedding scene that'll knock 'em cold!

THE SECOND YOUNG MAN: Met a débutante th'other day said she thought your book was powerful. As a rule young girls cry for this primitive business.

THE THIRD YOUNG MAN: Where's Anthony?

THE FOURTH YOUNG MAN: Walking up and down outside talking to himself.

SECOND YOUNG MAN: Lord! Did you see the minister? Most peculiar looking teeth.

FIFTH YOUNG MAN: Think they're natural. Funny thing people having gold teeth.

SIXTH YOUNG MAN: They say they love 'em. My dentist told me once a woman came to him and insisted on having two of her teeth covered with gold. No reason at all. All right the way they were.

FOURTH YOUNG MAN: Hear you got out a book, Dicky. 'Gratulations!

DICK: (*Stiffly*) Thanks.

FOURTH YOUNG MAN: (*Innocently*) What is it? College stories?

DICK: (*More stiffly*) No. Not college stories.

FOURTH YOUNG MAN: Pity! Hasn't been a good book about Harvard for years.

DICK: (*Touchily*) Why don't you supply the lack?

THIRD YOUNG MAN: I think I saw a squad of guests turn the drive in a Packard just now.

SIXTH YOUNG MAN: Might open a couple more bottles on the strength of that.

THIRD YOUNG MAN: It was the shock of my life when I heard the old man was going to have a wet wedding. Rabid prohibitionist, you know.

FOURTH YOUNG MAN: (*Snapping his fingers excitedly*) By gad! I knew I'd forgotten something. Kept thinking it was my vest.

DICK: What was it?

FOURTH YOUNG MAN: By gad! By gad!

SIXTH YOUNG MAN: Here! Here! Why the tragedy?

SECOND YOUNG MAN: What'd you forget? The way home?

DICK: (*Maliciously*) He forgot the plot for his book of Harvard stories.

FOURTH YOUNG MAN: No, sir, I forgot the present, by George! I forgot to buy old Anthony a present. I kept putting it off and putting it off, and by gad I've forgotten it! What'll they think?

SIXTH YOUNG MAN: (*Facetiously*) That's probably what's been holding up the wedding.

(THE FOURTH YOUNG MAN *looks nervously at his watch. Laughter.*)

FOURTH YOUNG MAN: By gad! What an ass I am!

SECOND YOUNG MAN: What d'you make of the bridesmaid who thinks she's Nora Bayes? Kept telling me she wished this was a ragtime wedding. Name's Haines or Hampton.

DICK: (*Hurriedly spurring his imagination*) Kane, you mean, Muriel Kane. She's a sort of debt of honor, I believe. Once saved Gloria from drowning, or something of the sort.

SECOND YOUNG MAN: I didn't think she could stop that perpetual swaying long enough to swim. Fill up my glass, will you? Old man and I had a long talk about the weather just now.

MAURY: Who? Old Adam?

SECOND YOUNG MAN: No, the bride's father. He must be with a weather bureau.

DICK: He's my uncle, Otis.

OTIS: Well, it's an honorable profession. (*Laughter.*)

SIXTH YOUNG MAN: Bride your cousin, isn't she?

DICK: Yes, Cable, she is.

CABLE: She certainly is a beauty. Not like you, Dicky. Bet she brings old Anthony to terms.

MAURY: Why are all grooms given the title of "old"? I think marriage is an error of youth.

DICK: Maury, the professional cynic.

MAURY: Why, you intellectual faker!

FIFTH YOUNG MAN: Battle of the highbrows here, Otis. Pick up what crumbs you can.

DICK: Faker yourself! What do *you* know?

MAURY: What do *you* know?

LICK: Ask me anything. Any branch of knowledge.

MAURY: All right. What's the fundamental principle of biology?

DICK: You don't know yourself.

MAURY: Don't hedge!

DICK: Well, natural selection?

MAURY: Wrong.

DICK: I give it up.

MAURY: Ontogony recapitulates phyllogony.

FIFTH YOUNG MAN: Take your base!

MAURY: Ask you another. What's the influence of mice on the clover crop? (*Laughter.*)

FOURTH YOUNG MAN: What's the influence of rats on the Decalogue?

MAURY: Shut up, you saphead. There *is* a connection.

DICK: What is it then?

MAURY: (*Pausing a moment in growing disconcertion*) Why, let's see. I seem to have forgotten exactly. Something about the bees eating the clover.

FOURTH YOUNG MAN: And the clover eating the mice! Haw! Haw!

MAURY: (*Frowning*) Let me just think a minute.

DICK: (*Sitting up suddenly*) Listen!

(*A volley of chatter explodes in the adjoining room. The six young men arise, feeling at their neckties.*)

DICK: (*Weightily*) We'd better join the firing squad. They're going to take the picture, I guess. No, that's afterward.

OTIS: Cable, you take the ragtime bridesmaid.

FOURTH YOUNG MAN: I wish to God I'd sent that present.

MAURY: If you'll give me another minute I'll think of that about the mice.

OTIS: I was usher last month for old Charlie McIntyre and——

(*They move slowly toward the door as the chatter becomes a babel and the practising preliminary to the overture issues in long pious groans from ADAM PATCH'S organ.*)

ANTHONY

There were five hundred eyes boring through the back of his cutaway and the sun glinting on the clergyman's inappropriately bourgeois teeth. With difficulty he restrained a laugh. Gloria was saying something in a clear proud voice and he tried to think that the affair was irrevocable, that every second was significant, that his life was being slashed into two periods and that the face of the world was changing before him. He tried to recapture that ecstatic sensation of ten weeks before. All these emotions eluded him, he did not even feel the physical nervousness of that very morning—it was all one gigantic aftermath. And those gold teeth! He wondered if the clergyman were married; he wondered perversely if a clergyman could perform his own marriage service. . . .

But as he took Gloria into his arms he was conscious of a strong reaction. The blood was moving in his veins now. A languorous and pleasant content settled like a weight upon him, bringing responsibility and possession. He was married.

GLORIA

So many, such mingled emotions, that no one of them was separable from the others! She could have wept for her mother, who was crying quietly back there ten feet and for the loveliness of the June sunlight flooding in at the windows. She was beyond all conscious perceptions. Only a sense, colored with delirious wild excitement, that the ultimately important was happening—and a trust, fierce and passionate, burning in her like a prayer, that in a moment she would be forever and securely safe.

Late one night they arrived in Santa Barbara, where the night clerk at the Hotel Lafcadio refused to admit them, on the grounds that they were not married.

The clerk thought that Gloria was beautiful. He did not think that anything so beautiful as Gloria could be moral.

"CON AMORE"

That first half-year—the trip West, the long months' loiter along the California coast, and the gray house near Greenwich where they lived until late autumn made the country dreary—those days, those places, saw the enraptured hours. The breathless idyll of their engagement gave way, first, to the intense romance of the more passionate relationship. The breathless idyll left them, fled on to other lovers; they looked around one day and it was gone, how they scarcely knew. Had either of them lost the other in the days of the idyll, the love lost would have been ever to the loser that dim desire without fulfilment which stands back of all life. But magic must hurry on, and the lovers remain. . . .

The idyll passed, bearing with it its extortion of youth. Came a day when Gloria found that other men no longer bored her; came a day when Anthony discovered that he could sit again late into the evening, talking with Dick of those tremendous abstractions that had once occupied his world. But, knowing they had had the best of love, they clung to what remained. Love lingered—by way of long conversations at night into those stark hours when the mind thins and sharpens and the borrowings from dreams become the stuff of all life, by way of deep and intimate kindnesses they developed toward each other, by way of their laughing at the same absurdities and thinking the same things noble and the same things sad.

It was, first of all, a time of discovery. The things they found in each other were so diverse, so intermixed and, moreover, so sugared with love as to seem at the time not so much discoveries as isolated phenomena—to be allowed for, and to be forgotten. Anthony found that he was living with a girl of tremendous nervous tension and of the most high-handed selfishness. Gloria knew within a month that her husband was an utter coward toward any one of a million phantasms created by his imagination. Her perception was intermittent, for this cowardice sprang out, became almost obscenely evident, then faded and vanished as though it had been only a creation of her own mind. Her reactions to it were not those attributed to her sex—it roused her neither to disgust nor to a premature feeling of motherhood. Herself almost completely without physical fear, she was unable to understand, and so she made the most of what she felt to be his fear's redeeming feature, which was that though he was a coward under a shock and a coward under a strain—when his imagination was given play—he had yet a sort of dashing recklessness that moved her on its brief occasions almost to admiration, and a pride that usually steadied him when he thought he was observed.

The trait first showed itself in a dozen incidents of little more than nervousness—his warning to a taxi-driver against fast driving, in Chicago; his refusal to take her to a certain tough café she had always wished to visit; these of course admitted the conventional interpretation—that it was of her he had been thinking; nevertheless, their culminative weight disturbed her. But something that occurred in a San Francisco hotel, when they had been married a week, gave the matter certainty.

It was after midnight and pitch dark in their room. Gloria was dozing off and Anthony's even breathing beside her made her suppose that he was asleep, when suddenly she saw him raise himself on his elbow and stare at the window.

"What is it, dearest?" she murmured.

147

F. SCOTT FITZGERALD

"Nothing"—he had relaxed to his pillow and turned toward her—"nothing, my darling wife."

"Don't say 'wife.' I'm your mistress. Wife's such an ugly word. Your 'permanent mistress' is so much more tangible and desirable. . . . Come into my arms," she added in a rush of tenderness; "I can sleep so well, so well with you in my arms."

Coming into Gloria's arms had a quite definite meaning. It required that he should slide one arm under her shoulder, lock both arms about her, and arrange himself as nearly as possible as a sort of three-sided crib for her luxurious ease. Anthony, who tossed, whose arms went tinglingly to sleep after half an hour of that position, would wait until she was asleep and roll her gently over to her side of the bed—then, left to his own devices, he would curl himself into his usual knots.

Gloria, having attained sentimental comfort, retired into her doze. Five minutes ticked away on Bloeckman's travelling clock; silence lay all about the room, over the unfamiliar, impersonal furniture and the half-oppressive ceiling that melted imperceptibly into invisible walls on both sides. Then there was suddenly a rattling flutter at the window, staccato and loud upon the hushed, pent air.

With a leap Anthony was out of the bed and standing tense beside it.

"Who's there?" he cried in an awful voice.

Gloria lay very still, wide awake now and engrossed not so much in the rattling as in the rigid breathless figure whose voice had reached from the bedside into that ominous dark.

The sound stopped; the room was quiet as before—then Anthony pouring words in at the telephone.

"Some one just tried to get into the room! . . .

"There's some one at the window!" His voice was emphatic now, faintly terrified.

"All right! Hurry!" He hung up the receiver; stood motionless.

. . . There was a rush and commotion at the door, a knocking—Anthony went to open it upon an excited night clerk with three bell-boys grouped staring behind him. Between thumb and finger the night clerk held a wet pen with the threat of a weapon; one of the bell-boys had seized a telephone directory and was looking at it sheepishly. Simultaneously the group was joined by the hastily summoned house-detective, and as one man they surged into the room.

Lights sprang on with a click. Gathering a piece of sheet about her Gloria dove away from sight, shutting her eyes to keep out the horror of this unpremeditated visitation. There was no vestige of an idea in her stricken sensibilities save that her Anthony was at grievous fault.

. . . The night clerk was speaking from the window, his tone half of the servant, half of the teacher reproving a schoolboy.

"Nobody out there," he declared conclusively; "my golly, nobody *could* be out there. This here's a sheer fall to the street of fifty feet. It was the wind you heard, tugging at the blind."

"Oh."

Then she was sorry for him. She wanted only to comfort him and draw him back tenderly into her arms, to tell them to go away because the thing their presence connotated was odious. Yet she could not raise her head for shame. She heard a broken sentence, apologies, conventions of the employee and one unrestrained snicker from a bell-boy.

"I've been nervous as the devil all evening," Anthony was saying; "somehow that noise just shook me—I was only about half awake."

"Sure, I understand," said the night clerk with comfortable tact; "been that way myself."

The door closed; the lights snapped out; Anthony crossed the floor quietly and crept into bed. Gloria, feigning to be heavy with sleep, gave a quiet little sigh and slipped into his arms.

"What was it, dear?"

"Nothing," he answered, his voice still shaken; "I thought there was somebody at the window, so I looked out, but I couldn't see anyone and the noise kept up, so I phoned downstairs. Sorry if I disturbed you, but I'm awfully darn nervous to-night."

Catching the lie, she gave an interior start—he had not gone to the window, nor near the window. He had stood by the bed and then sent in his call of fear.

"Oh," she said—and then: "I'm so sleepy."

For an hour they lay awake side by side, Gloria with her eyes shut so tight that blue moons formed and revolved against backgrounds of deepest mauve, Anthony staring blindly into the darkness overhead.

After many weeks it came gradually out into the light, to be laughed and joked at. They made a tradition to fit over it—whenever that overpowering terror of the night attacked Anthony, she would put her arms about him and croon, soft as a song:

"I'll protect my Anthony. Oh, nobody's ever going to harm my Anthony!"

He would laugh as though it were a jest they played for their mutual amusement, but to Gloria it was never quite a jest. It was, at first, a keen disappointment; later, it was one of the times when she controlled her temper.

The management of Gloria's temper, whether it was aroused by a lack of hot water for her bath or by a skirmish with her husband, became almost the primary duty of Anthony's day. It must be done just so—by this much silence, by that much pressure, by this much yielding, by that much force. It was in her angers with their attendant cruelties that her inordinate egotism chiefly displayed itself. Because she was brave, because she was "spoiled," because of her outrageous and commendable independence of judgment, and finally because of her arrogant consciousness that she had never seen a girl as beautiful as herself, Gloria had developed into a consistent, practising Nietzschean. This, of course, with overtones of profound sentiment.

There was, for example, her stomach. She was used to certain dishes, and she had a strong conviction that she could not possibly eat anything else. There must be a lemonade and a tomato sandwich late in the morning, then a light lunch with a stuffed tomato. Not only did she require food from a selection of a dozen dishes, but in addition this food must be prepared in just a certain way. One of the most annoying half hours of the first fortnight occurred in Los Angeles, when an unhappy waiter brought her a tomato stuffed with chicken salad instead of celery.

"We always serve it that way, madame," he quavered to the gray eyes that regarded him wrathfully.

Gloria made no answer, but when the waiter had turned discreetly away she banged both fists upon the table until the china and silver rattled.

"Poor Gloria!" laughed Anthony unwittingly, "you can't get what you want ever, can you?"

"I can't eat *stuff*!" she flared up.

"I'll call back the waiter."

"I don't want you to! He doesn't know anything, the darn *fool*!"

"Well, it isn't the hotel's fault. Either send it back, forget it, or be a sport and eat it."

"Shut up!" she said succinctly.

"Why take it out on me?"

"Oh, I'm *not*," she wailed, "but I simply *can't* eat it."

Anthony subsided helplessly.

"We'll go somewhere else," he suggested.

"I don't *want* to go anywhere else. I'm tired of being trotted around to a dozen cafés and not getting *one thing* fit to eat."

"When did we go around to a dozen cafés?"

"You'd *have* to in *this* town," insisted Gloria with ready sophistry.

Anthony, bewildered, tried another tack.

"Why don't you try to eat it? It can't be as bad as you think."

"Just—because—I—don't—like—chicken!"

She picked up her fork and began poking contemptuously at the tomato, and Anthony expected her to begin flinging the stuffings in all directions. He was sure that she was approximately as angry as she had ever been—for an instant he had detected a spark of hate directed as much toward him as toward any one else—and Gloria angry was, for the present, unapproachable.

Then, surprisingly, he saw that she had tentatively raised the fork to her lips and tasted the chicken salad. Her frown had not abated and he stared at her anxiously, making no comment and daring scarcely to breathe. She tasted another forkful—in another moment she was eating. With difficulty Anthony restrained a chuckle; when at length he spoke his words had no possible connection with chicken salad.

This incident, with variations, ran like a lugubrious fugue through the first year of marriage; always it left Anthony baffled, irritated, and depressed. But another rough brushing of temperaments, a question of laundry-bags, he found even more annoying as it ended inevitably in a decisive defeat for him.

One afternoon in Coronado, where they made the longest stay of their trip, more than three weeks, Gloria was arraying herself brilliantly for tea. Anthony, who had been down-stairs listening to the latest rumor bulletins of war in Europe, entered the room, kissed the back of her powdered neck, and went to his dresser. After a great pulling out and pushing in of drawers, evidently unsatisfactory, he turned around to the Unfinished Masterpiece.

"Got any handkerchiefs, Gloria?" he asked. Gloria shook her golden head.

"Not a one. I'm using one of yours."

"The last one, I deduce." He laughed dryly.

"Is it?" She applied an emphatic though very delicate contour to her lips.

"Isn't the laundry back?"

"I don't know."

Anthony hesitated—then, with sudden discernment, opened the closet door. His suspicions were verified. On the hook provided hung the blue bag furnished by the hotel. This was full of his clothes—he had put them there himself. The floor beneath it was littered with an astonishing mass of finery—lingerie, stockings, dresses, nightgowns, and pajamas—most of it scarcely worn but all of it coming indubitably under the general heading of Gloria's laundry.

He stood holding the closet door open.

"Why, Gloria!"

"What?"

The lip line was being erased and corrected according to some mysterious perspective; not a finger trembled as she manipulated the lip-stick, not a glance wavered in his direction. It was a triumph of concentration.

"Haven't you ever sent out the laundry?"

"Is it there?"

"It most certainly is."

"Well, I guess I haven't, then."

"Gloria," began Anthony, sitting down on the bed and trying to catch her mirrored eyes, "you're a nice fellow, you are! I've sent it out every time it's been sent since we left New York, and over a week ago you promised you'd do it for a change. All you'd have to do would be to cram your own junk into that bag and ring for the chambermaid."

"Oh, why fuss about the laundry?" exclaimed Gloria petulantly, "I'll take care of it."

"I haven't fussed about it. I'd just as soon divide the bother with you, but when we run out of handkerchiefs it's darn near time something's done."

Anthony considered that he was being extraordinarily logical. But Gloria, unimpressed, put away her cosmetics and casually offered him her back.

"Hook me up," she suggested; "Anthony, dearest, I forgot all about it. I meant to, honestly, and I will to-day. Don't be cross with your sweetheart."

What could Anthony do then but draw her down upon his knee and kiss a shade of color from her lips.

"But I don't mind," she murmured with a smile, radiant and magnanimous. "You can kiss all the paint off my lips any time you want."

They went down to tea. They bought some handkerchiefs in a notion store near by. All was forgotten.

But two days later Anthony looked in the closet and saw the bag still hung limp upon its hook and that the gay and vivid pile on the floor had increased surprisingly in height.

"Gloria!" he cried.

"Oh—" Her voice was full of real distress. Despairingly Anthony went to the phone and called the chambermaid.

"It seems to me," he said impatiently, "that you expect me to be some sort of French valet to you."

Gloria laughed, so infectiously that Anthony was unwise enough to smile. Unfortunate man! In some intangible manner his smile made her mistress of the situation—with an air of injured righteousness she went emphatically to the closet and began pushing her laundry violently into the bag. Anthony watched her—ashamed of himself.

"There!" she said, implying that her fingers had been worked to the bone by a brutal taskmaster.

He considered, nevertheless, that he had given her an object-lesson and that the matter was closed, but on the contrary it was merely beginning. Laundry pile followed laundry pile—at long intervals; dearth of handkerchief followed dearth of handkerchief—at short ones; not to mention dearth of sock, of shirt, of everything. And Anthony found at length that either he must send it out himself or go through the increasingly unpleasant ordeal of a verbal battle with Gloria.

GLORIA AND GENERAL LEE

On their way East they stopped two days in Washington, strolling about with some hostility in its atmosphere of harsh repellent light, of distance without freedom, of pomp without splendor—it seemed a pasty-pale and self-conscious city. The second day they made an ill-advised trip to General Lee's old home at Arlington.

The bus which bore them was crowded with hot, unprosperous people, and Anthony, intimate to Gloria, felt a storm brewing. It broke at the Zoo, where the party stopped for ten minutes. The Zoo, it seemed, smelt of monkeys. Anthony laughed; Gloria called down the curse of Heaven upon monkeys, including in her malevolence all the passengers of the bus and their perspiring offspring who had hied themselves monkey-ward.

Eventually the bus moved on to Arlington. There it met other busses and immediately a swarm of women and children were leaving a trail of peanut-shells through the halls of General Lee and crowding at length into the room where he was married. On the wall of this room a pleasing sign announced in large red letters "Ladies' Toilet." At this final blow Gloria broke down.

"I think it's perfectly terrible!" she said furiously, "the idea of letting these people come here! And of encouraging them by making these houses show-places."

"Well," objected Anthony, "if they weren't kept up they'd go to pieces."

"What if they did!" she exclaimed as they sought the

wide pillared porch. "Do you think they've left a breath of 1860 here? This has become a thing of 1914."

"Don't you want to preserve old things?"

"But you *can't*, Anthony. Beautiful things grow to a certain height and then they fail and fade off, breathing out memories as they decay. And just as any period decays in our minds, the things of that period should decay too, and in that way they're preserved for a while in the few hearts like mine that react to them. That graveyard at Tarrytown, for instance. The asses who give money to preserve things have spoiled that too. Sleepy Hollow's gone; Washington Irving's dead and his books are rotting in our estimation year by year—then let the graveyard rot too, as it should, as all things should. Trying to preserve a century by keeping its relics up to date is like keeping a dying man alive by stimulants."

"So you think that just as a time goes to pieces its houses ought to go too?"

"Of course! Would you value your Keats letter if the signature was traced over to make it last longer? It's just because I love the past that I want this house to look back on its glamourous moment of youth and beauty, and I want its stairs to creak as if to the footsteps of women with hoop skirts and men in boots and spurs. But they've made it into a blond-ined, rouged-up old woman of sixty. It hasn't any right to look so prosperous. It might care enough for Lee to drop a brick now and then. How many of these—these *animals*"—she waved her hand around—"get anything from this, for all the histories and guide-books and restorations in existence? How many of them who think that, at best, appreciation is talking in under-tones and walking on tiptoes would even come here if it was any trouble? I want it to smell of magnolias instead of peanuts and I want my shoes to crunch on the same gravel that Lee's boots crunched on. There's no beauty without poignancy and there's no poignancy without the feeling that it's going, men, names, books, houses—bound for dust—mortal—"

A small boy appeared beside them and, swinging a handful of banana-peels, flung them valiantly in the direction of the Potomac.

SENTIMENT

Simultaneously with the fall of Liège, Anthony and Gloria arrived in New York. In retrospect the six weeks seemed miraculously happy. They had found to a great extent, as most young couples find in some measure, that they possessed in common many fixed ideas and curiosities and odd quirks of mind; they were essentially companionable.

But it had been a struggle to keep many of their conversations on the level of discussions. Arguments were fatal to Gloria's disposition. She had all her life been associated either with her mental inferiors or with men who, under the almost hostile intimidation of her beauty, had not dared to contradict her; naturally, then, it irritated her when Anthony emerged from the state in which her pronouncements were an infallible and ultimate decision.

He failed to realize, at first, that this was the result partly of her "female" education and partly of her beauty, and he was inclined to include her with her entire sex as curiously and definitely limited. It maddened him to find she had no sense of justice. But he discovered that, when a subject did interest her, her brain tired less quickly than his. What he chiefly missed in her mind was the pedantic teleology—the sense of order and accuracy, the sense of life as a mysteriously correlated piece of patchwork, but he understood after a while that such a quality in her would have been incongruous.

Of the things they possessed in common, greatest of all was their almost uncanny pull at each other's hearts. The day they left the hotel in Coronado she sat down on one of the beds while they were packing, and began to weep bitterly.

"Dearest—" His arms were around her; he pulled her head down upon his shoulder. "What is it, my own Gloria? Tell me."

"We're going away," she sobbed. "Oh, Anthony, it's sort of the first place we've lived together. Our two little beds here—side by side—they'll be always waiting for us, and we're never coming back to 'em any more."

She was tearing at his heart as she always could. Sentiment came over him, rushed into his eyes.

"Gloria, why, we're going on to another room. And two other little beds. We're going to be together all our lives."

Words flooded from her in a low husky voice.

"But it won't be—like our two beds—ever again. Everywhere we go and move on and change, something's lost—something's left behind. You can't ever quite repeat anything, and I've been so yours, here—"

He held her passionately near, discerning far beyond any criticism of her sentiment, a wise grasping of the minute, if only an indulgence of her desire to cry—Gloria the idler, caresser of her own dreams, extracting poignancy from the memorable things of life and youth.

Later in the afternoon when he returned from the station with the tickets he found her asleep on one of the beds, her arm curled about a black object which he could not at first identify. Coming closer he found it was one of his shoes, not a particularly new one, nor clean one, but her face, tear-stained, was pressed against it, and he understood her ancient and most honorable message. There was almost ecstasy in waking her and seeing her smile at him, shy but well aware of her own nicety of imagination.

With no appraisal of the worth or dross of these two things, it seemed to Anthony that they lay somewhere near the heart of love.

THE GRAY HOUSE

It is in the twenties that the actual momentum of life begins to slacken, and it is a simple soul indeed to whom as many things are significant and meaningful at thirty as at ten years before. At thirty an organ-grinder is a more or less moth-eaten man who grinds an organ—and once he was an organ-grinder! The unmistakable stigma of humanity touches all those imper-sonal and beautiful things that only youth ever grasps in their impersonal glory. A brilliant ball, gay with light romantic laughter, wears through its own silks and satins to show the bare framework of a man-made thing—oh, that eternal hand!—a play, most tragic and most divine, becomes merely a succession of speeches, sweated over by the eternal plagia-rist in the clammy hours and acted by men subject to cramps, cowardice, and manly sentiment.

And this time with Gloria and Anthony, this first year of marriage, and the gray house caught them in that stage when the organ-grinder was slowly undergoing his inevitable metamorphosis. She was twenty-three; he was twenty-six.

The gray house was, at first, of sheerly pastoral intent. They lived impatiently in Anthony's apartment for the first fortnight after the return from California, in a stifled atmos-phere of open trunks, too many callers, and the eternal laundry-bags. They discussed with their friends the stupen-dous problem of their future. Dick and Maury would sit with them agreeing solemnly, almost thoughtfully, as Anthony ran through his list of what they "ought" to do, and where they "ought" to live.

"I'd like to take Gloria abroad," he complained, "except for this damn war—and next to that I'd sort of like to have a place in the country, somewhere near New York, of course, where I could write—or whatever I decide to do."

Gloria laughed.

"Isn't he cute?" she required of Maury. "'Whatever he

decides to do!' But what am *I* going to do if he works? Maury, will you take me around if Anthony works?"

"Anyway, I'm not going to work yet," said Anthony quickly.

It was vaguely understood between them that on some misty day he would enter a sort of glorified diplomatic service and be envied by princes and prime ministers for his beautiful wife.

"Well," said Gloria helplessly, "I'm sure I don't know. We talk and talk and never get anywhere, and we ask all our friends and they just answer the way we want 'em to. I wish somebody'd take care of us."

"Why don't you go out to—out to Greenwich or something?" suggested Richard Caramel.

"I'd like that," said Gloria, brightening. "Do you think we could get a house there?"

Dick shrugged his shoulders and Maury laughed.

"You two amuse me," he said. "Of all the unpractical people! As soon as a place is mentioned you expect us to pull great piles of photographs out of our pockets showing the different styles of architecture available in bungalows."

"That's just what I don't want," wailed Gloria, "a hot stuffy bungalow, with a lot of babies next door and their father cutting the grass in his shirt sleeves—"

"For Heaven's sake, Gloria," interrupted Maury, "nobody wants to lock you up in a bungalow. Who in God's name brought bungalows into the conversation? But you'll never get a place anywhere unless you go out and hunt for it."

"Go where? You say 'go out and hunt for it,' but where?"

With dignity Maury waved his hand paw-like about the room.

"Out anywhere. Out in the country. There're lots of places."

"Thanks."

"Look here!" Richard Caramel brought his yellow eye

rakishly into play. "The trouble with you two is that you're all disorganized. Do you know anything about New York State? Shut up, Anthony, I'm talking to Gloria."

"Well," she admitted finally, "I've been to two or three house parties in Portchester and around in Connecticut—but, of course, that isn't in New York State, is it? And neither is Morristown," she finished with drowsy irrelevance.

There was a shout of laughter.

"Oh, Lord!" cried Dick, "'neither is Morristown!' No, and neither is Santa Barbara, Gloria. Now listen. To begin with, unless you have a fortune there's no use considering any place like Newport or Southhampton or Tuxedo. They're out of the question."

They all agreed to this solemnly.

"And personally I hate New Jersey. Then, of course, there's upper New York, above Tuxedo."

"Too cold," said Gloria briefly. "I was there once in an automobile."

"Well, it seems to me there're a lot of towns like Rye between New York and Greenwich where you could buy a little gray house of some—"

Gloria leaped at the phrase triumphantly. For the first time since their return East she knew what she wanted.

"Oh, yes!" she cried. "Oh, yes! that's it: a little gray house with sort of white around and a whole lot of swamp maples just as brown and gold as an October picture in a gallery. Where can we find one?"

"Unfortunately, I've mislaid my list of little gray houses with swamp maples around them—but I'll try to find it. Meanwhile you take a piece of paper and write down the names of seven possible towns. And every day this week you take a trip to one of those towns."

"Oh, gosh!" protested Gloria, collapsing mentally, "why won't you do it for us? I hate trains."

"Well, hire a car, and—"

Gloria yawned.

"I'm tired of discussing it. Seems to me all we do is talk about where to live."

"My exquisite wife wearies of thought," remarked Anthony ironically. "She must have a tomato sandwich to stimulate her jaded nerves. Let's go out to tea."

As the unfortunate upshot of this conversation, they took Dick's advice literally, and two days later went out to Rye, where they wandered around with an irritated real estate agent, like bewildered babes in the wood. They were shown houses at a hundred a month which closely adjoined other houses at a hundred a month; they were shown isolated houses to which they invariably took violent dislikes, though they submitted weakly to the agent's desire that they "look at that stove—some stove!" and to a great shaking of doorposts and tapping of walls, intended evidently to show that the house would not immediately collapse, no matter how convincingly it gave that impression. They gazed through windows into interiors furnished either "commercially" with slab-like chairs and unyielding settees, or "home-like" with the melancholy bric-à-brac of other summers—crossed tennis rackets, fit-form couches, and depressing Gibson girls. With a feeling of guilt they looked at a few really nice houses, aloof, dignified, and cool—at three hundred a month. They went away from Rye thanking the real estate agent very much indeed.

On the crowded train back to New York the seat behind was occupied by a super-respiring Latin whose last few meals had obviously been composed entirely of garlic. They reached the apartment gratefully, almost hysterically, and Gloria rushed for a hot bath in the reproachless bathroom. So far as the question of a future abode was concerned both of them were incapacitated for a week.

The matter eventually worked itself out with unhoped-for romance. Anthony ran into the living room one afternoon fairly radiating "the idea."

"I've got it," he was exclaiming as though he had just caught a mouse. "We'll get a car."

"Gee whiz! Haven't we got troubles enough taking care of ourselves?"

"Give me a second to explain, can't you? just let's leave our stuff with Dick and just pile a couple of suitcases in our car, the one we're going to buy—we'll have to have one in the country anyway—and just start out in the direction of New Haven. You see, as we get out of commuting distance from New York, the rents'll get cheaper, and as soon as we find a house we want we'll just settle down."

By his frequent and soothing interpolation of the word "just" he aroused her lethargic enthusiasm. Strutting violently about the room, he simulated a dynamic and irresistible efficiency. "We'll buy a car to-morrow."

Life, limping after imagination's ten-league boots, saw them out of town a week later in a cheap but sparkling new roadster, saw them through the chaotic unintelligible Bronx, then over a wide murky district which alternated cheerless blue-green wastes with suburbs of tremendous and sordid activity. They left New York at eleven and it was well past a hot and beatific noon when they moved rakishly through Pelham.

"These aren't towns," said Gloria scornfully, "these are just city blocks plumped down coldly into waste acres. I imagine all the men here have their mustaches stained from drinking their coffee too quickly in the morning."

"And play pinochle on the commuting trains."

"What's pinochle?"

"Don't be so literal. How should I know? But it sounds as though they ought to play it."

"I like it. It sounds as if it were something where you sort of cracked your knuckles or something. . . . Let me drive."

Anthony looked at her suspiciously.

"You swear you're a good driver?"

"Since I was fourteen."

He stopped the car cautiously at the side of the road and they changed seats. Then with a horrible grinding noise the car was put in gear, Gloria adding an accompaniment of laughter which seemed to Anthony disquieting and in the worst possible taste.

"Here we go!" she yelled. "Whoo-oop!"

Their heads snapped back like marionettes on a single wire as the car leaped ahead and curved retchingly about a standing milk-wagon, whose driver stood up on his seat and bellowed after them. In the immemorial tradition of the road Anthony retorted with a few brief epigrams as to the grossness of the milk-delivering profession. He cut his remarks short, however, and turned to Gloria with the growing conviction that he had made a grave mistake in relinquishing control and that Gloria was a driver of many eccentricities and of infinite carelessness.

"Remember now!" he warned her nervously, "the man said we oughtn't to go over twenty miles an hour for the first five thousand miles."

She nodded briefly, but evidently intending to accomplish the prohibitive distance as quickly as possible, slightly increased her speed. A moment later he made another attempt.

"See that sign? Do you want to get us pinched?"

"Oh, for Heaven's sake," cried Gloria in exasperation, "you *always* exaggerate things so!"

"Well, I don't want to get arrested."

"Who's arresting you? You're so persistent—just like you were about my cough medicine last night."

"It was for your own good."

"Ha! I might as well be living with mama."

"What a thing to say to me!"

A standing policeman swerved into view, was hastily passed.

"See him?" demanded Anthony.

"Oh, you drive me crazy! He didn't arrest us, did he?"

"When he does it'll be too late," countered Anthony brilliantly.

Her reply was scornful, almost injured.

"Why, this old thing won't *go* over thirty-five."

"It isn't old."

"It is in spirit."

That afternoon the car joined the laundry-bags and Gloria's appetite as one of the trinity of contention. He warned her of railroad tracks; he pointed out approaching automobiles; finally he insisted on taking the wheel and a furious, insulted Gloria sat silently beside him between the towns of Larchmont and Rye.

But it was due to this furious silence of hers that the gray house materialized from its abstraction, for just beyond Rye he surrendered gloomily to it and re-relinquished the wheel. Mutely he beseeched her and Gloria, instantly cheered, vowed to be more careful. But because a discourteous street-car persisted callously in remaining upon its track Gloria ducked down a side-street—and thereafter that afternoon was never able to find her way back to the Post Road. The street they finally mistook for it lost its Post-Road aspect when it had gone five miles from Cos Cob. Its macadam became gravel, then dirt—moreover, it narrowed and developed a border of maple trees, through which filtered the weltering sun, making its endless experiments with shadow designs upon the long grass.

"We're lost now," complained Anthony.

"Read that sign!"

"Marietta—Five Miles. What's Marietta?"

"Never heard of it, but let's go on. We can't turn here and there's probably a detour back to the Post Road."

The way became scarred with deepening ruts and insidious shoulders of stone. Three farmhouses faced them momentarily, slid by. A town sprang up in a cluster of dull roofs around a white tall steeple.

Then Gloria, hesitating between two approaches, and making her choice too late, drove over a fire-hydrant and ripped the transmission violently from the car.

It was dark when the real-estate agent of Marietta showed them the gray house. They came upon it just west of the village, where it rested against a sky that was a warm blue cloak buttoned with tiny stars. The gray house had been there when women who kept cats were probably witches, when Paul Revere made false teeth in Boston preparatory to arousing the great commercial people, when our ancestors were gloriously deserting Washington in droves. Since those days the house had been bolstered up in a feeble corner, considerably repartitioned and newly plastered inside, amplified by a kitchen and added to by a side-porch—but, save for where some jovial oaf had roofed the new kitchen with red tin, Colonial it defiantly remained.

"How did you happen to come to Marietta?" demanded the real-estate agent in a tone that was first cousin to suspicion. He was showing them through four spacious and airy bedrooms.

"We broke down," explained Gloria. "I drove over a fire-hydrant and we had ourselves towed to the garage and then we saw your sign."

The man nodded, unable to follow such a sally of spontaneity. There was something subtly immoral in doing anything without several months' consideration.

They signed a lease that night and, in the agent's car, returned jubilantly to the somnolent and dilapidated Marietta Inn, which was too broken for even the chance immoralities and consequent gaieties of a country road-house. Half the night they lay awake planning the things they were to do there. Anthony was going to work at an astounding pace on his history and thus ingratiate himself with his cynical grandfather. . . . When the car was repaired they would explore the country and join the nearest "really nice" club, where

Gloria would play golf "or something" while Anthony wrote. This, of course, was Anthony's idea—Gloria was sure she wanted but to read and dream and be fed tomato sandwiches and lemonades by some angelic servant still in a shadowy hinterland. Between paragraphs Anthony would come and kiss her as she lay indolently in the hammock. . . . The hammock! a host of new dreams in tune to its imagined rhythm, while the wind stirred it and waves of sun undulated over the shadows of blown wheat, or the dusty road freckled and darkened with quiet summer rain. . . .

And guests—here they had a long argument, both of them trying to be extraordinarily mature and far-sighted. Anthony claimed that they would need people at least every other week-end "as a sort of change." This provoked an involved and extremely sentimental conversation as to whether Anthony did not consider Gloria change enough. Though he assured her that he did, she insisted upon doubting him. . . . Eventually the conversation assumed its eternal monotone: "What then? Oh, what'll we do then?"

"Well, we'll have a dog," suggested Anthony.

"I don't want one. I want a kitty." She went thoroughly and with great enthusiasm into the history, habits, and tastes of a cat she had once possessed. Anthony considered that it must have been a horrible character with neither personal magnetism nor a loyal heart.

Later they slept, to wake an hour before dawn with the gray house dancing in phantom glory before their dazzled eyes.

THE SOUL OF GLORIA

For that autumn the gray house welcomed them with a rush of sentiment that falsified its cynical old age. True, there were the laundry-bags, there was Gloria's appetite, there was Anthony's tendency to brood and his imaginative "nervousness," but there were intervals also of an unhoped-for serenity. Close together on the porch they would wait for the moon to stream across the silver acres of farmland, jump a thick wood and tumble waves of radiance at their feet. In such a moonlight Gloria's face was of a pervading, reminiscent white, and with a modicum of effort they would slip off the blinders of custom and each would find in the other almost the quintessential romance of the vanished June.

One night while her head lay upon his heart and their cigarettes glowed in swerving buttons of light through the dome of darkness over the bed, she spoke for the first time and fragmentarily of the men who had hung for brief moments on her beauty.

"Do you ever think of them?" he asked her.

"Only occasionally—when something happens that recalls a particular man."

"What do you remember—their kisses?"

"All sorts of things. . . . Men are different with women."

"Different in what way?"

"Oh, entirely—and quite inexpressibly. Men who had the most firmly rooted reputation for being this way or that would sometimes be surprisingly inconsistent with me. Brutal men were tender, negligible men were astonishingly loyal and lovable, and, often, honorable men took attitudes that were anything but honorable."

"For instance?"

"Well, there was a boy named Percy Wolcott from Cornell who was quite a hero in college, a great athlete, and saved a lot of people from a fire or something like that. But I soon found he was stupid in a rather dangerous way."

"What way?"

"It seems he had some naïve conception of a woman 'fit to be his wife,' a particular conception that I used to run into a lot and that always drove me wild. He demanded a girl who'd never been kissed and who liked to sew and sit home and pay tribute to his self-esteem. And I'll bet a hat if he's gotten an idiot to sit and be stupid with him he's tearing out on the side with some much speedier lady."

"I'd be sorry for his wife."

"I wouldn't. Think what an ass she'd be not to realize it before she married him. He's the sort whose idea of honoring and respecting a woman would be never to give her any excitement. With the best intentions, he was deep in the dark ages."

"What was his attitude toward you?"

"I'm coming to that. As I told you—or did I tell you?—he was mighty good-looking: big brown honest eyes and one of those smiles that guarantee the heart behind it is twenty-karat gold. Being young and credulous, I thought he had some discretion, so I kissed him fervently one night when we were riding around after a dance at the Homestead at Hot Springs. It had been a wonderful week, I remember—with the most luscious trees spread like green lather, sort of, all over the valley and a mist rising out of them on October mornings like bonfires lit to turn them brown—"

"How about your friend with the ideals?" interrupted Anthony.

"It seems that when he kissed me he began to think that perhaps he could get away with a little more, that I needn't be 'respected' like this Beatrice Fairfax glad-girl of his imagination."

"What'd he do?"

"Not much. I pushed him off a sixteen-foot embankment before he was well started."

"Hurt him?" inquired Anthony with a laugh.

"Broke his arm and sprained his ankle. He told the story all over Hot Springs, and when his arm healed a man named Barley who liked me fought him and broke it over again. Oh, it was all an awful mess. He threatened to sue Barley, and Barley—he was from Georgia—was seen buying a gun in town.

But before that mama had dragged me North again, much against my will, so I never did find out all that happened— though I saw Barley once in the Vanderbilt lobby."

Anthony laughed long and loud.

"What a career! I suppose I ought to be furious because you've kissed so many men. I'm not, though."

At this she sat up in bed.

"It's funny, but I'm so sure that those kisses left no mark on me—no taint of promiscuity, I mean—even though a man once told me in all seriousness that he hated to think I'd been a public drinking glass."

"He had his nerve."

"I just laughed and told him to think of me rather as a loving-cup that goes from hand to hand but should be valued none the less."

"Somehow it doesn't bother me—on the other hand it would, of course, if you'd done any more than kiss them. But I believe *you're* absolutely incapable of jealousy except as hurt vanity. Why don't you care what I've done? Wouldn't you prefer it if I'd been absolutely innocent?"

"It's all in the impression it might have made on you. *My* kisses were because the man was good-looking, or because there was a slick moon, or even because I've felt vaguely sentimental and a little stirred. But that's all—it's had utterly no effect on me. But you'd remember and let memories haunt you and worry you."

"Haven't you ever kissed anyone like you've kissed me?"

"No," she answered simply. "As I've told you, men have tried—oh, lots of things. Any pretty girl has that experience. . . . You see," she resumed, "it doesn't matter to me how many women you've stayed with in the past, so long as it was merely a physical satisfaction, but I don't believe I could endure the idea of your ever having lived with another woman for a protracted period or even having wanted to marry some possible girl. It's different somehow. There'd be all the

little intimacies remembered—and they'd dull that freshness
that after all is the most precious part of love."

Rapturously he pulled her down beside him on the
pillow.

"Oh, my darling," he whispered, "as if I remembered
anything but your dear kisses."

Then Gloria, in a very mild voice:

"Anthony, did I hear anybody say they were thirsty?"

Anthony laughed abruptly and with a sheepish and
amused grin got out of bed.

"With just a *little* piece of ice in the water," she added.
"Do you suppose I could have that?"

Gloria used the adjective "little" whenever she asked a
favor—it made the favor sound less arduous. But Anthony
laughed again—whether she wanted a cake of ice or a marble
of it, he must go down-stairs to the kitchen. . . . Her voice
followed him through the hall: "And just a *little* cracker with
just a *little* marmalade on it. . . ."

"Oh, gosh!" sighed Anthony in rapturous slang, "she's
wonderful, that girl! She *has* it!"

"When we have a baby," she began one day—this, it had
already been decided, was to be after three years—"I want it
to look like you."

"Except its legs," he insinuated slyly.

"Oh, yes, except his legs. He's got to have my legs. But
the rest of him can be you."

"My nose?"

Gloria hesitated.

"Well, perhaps my nose. But certainly your eyes—and
my mouth, and I guess my shape of the face. I wonder; I
think he'd be sort of cute if he had my hair."

"My dear Gloria, you've appropriated the whole baby."

"Well, I didn't mean to," she apologized cheerfully.

"Let him have my neck at least," he urged, regarding
himself gravely in the glass. "You've often said you liked my

neck because the Adam's apple doesn't show, and, besides, your neck's too short."

"Why, it is *not*!" she cried indignantly, turning to the mirror, "it's just right. I don't believe I've ever seen a better neck."

"It's too short," he repeated teasingly.

"Short?" Her tone expressed exasperated wonder.

"Short? You're crazy!" She elongated and contracted it to convince herself of its reptilian sinuousness. "Do you call *that* a short neck?"

"One of the shortest I've ever seen."

For the first time in weeks tears started from Gloria's eyes and the look she gave him had a quality of real pain.

"Oh, Anthony—"

"My Lord, Gloria!" He approached her in bewilderment and took her elbows in his hands. "Don't cry, *please*! Didn't you know I was only kidding? Gloria, look at me! Why, dearest, you've got the longest neck I've ever seen. Honestly."

Her tears dissolved in a twisted smile.

"Well—you shouldn't have said that, then. Let's talk about the b-baby."

Anthony paced the floor and spoke as though rehearsing for a debate.

"To put it briefly, there are two babies we could have, two distinct and logical babies, utterly differentiated. There's the baby that's the combination of the best of both of us. Your body, my eyes, my mind, your intelligence—and then there is the baby which is our worst—my body, your disposition, and my irresolution."

"I like that second baby," she said.

"What I'd really like," continued Anthony, "would be to have two sets of triplets one year apart and then experiment with the six boys—"

"Poor me," she interjected.

"—I'd educate them each in a different country and by

a different system and when they were twenty-three I'd call them together and see what they were like."

"Let's have 'em all with my neck," suggested Gloria.

THE END OF A CHAPTER

The car was at length repaired and with a deliberate vengeance took up where it left off the business of causing infinite dissension. Who should drive? How fast should Gloria go? These two questions and the eternal recriminations involved ran through the days. They motored to the Post-Road towns, Rye, Portchester, and Greenwich, and called on a dozen friends, mostly Gloria's, who all seemed to be in different stages of having babies and in this respect as well as in others bored her to a point of nervous distraction. For an hour after each visit she would bite her fingers furiously and be inclined to take out her rancor on Anthony.

"I loathe women," she cried in a mild temper. "What on earth can you say to them—except talk 'lady-lady'? I've enthused over a dozen babies that I've wanted only to choke. And every one of those girls is either incipiently jealous and suspicious of her husband if he's charming or beginning to be bored with him if he isn't."

"Don't you ever intend to see any women?"

"I don't know. They never seem clean to me—never—never. Except just a few. Constance Shaw—you know, the Mrs. Merriam who came over to see us last Tuesday—is almost the only one. She's so tall and fresh-looking and stately."

"I don't like them so tall."

Though they went to several dinner dances at various country clubs, they decided that the autumn was too nearly over for them to "go out" on any scale, even had they been so inclined. He hated golf; Gloria liked it only mildly, and though she enjoyed a violent rush that some undergraduates gave her one night and was glad that Anthony should be proud of her beauty, she also perceived that their hostess for the evening, a Mrs. Granby, was somewhat disquieted by the fact that Anthony's classmate, Alec Granby, joined with enthusiasm in the rush. The Granbys never phoned again, and though Gloria laughed, it piqued her not a little.

"You see," she explained to Anthony, "if I wasn't married it wouldn't worry her—but she's been to the movies in her day and she thinks I may be a vampire. But the point is that placating such people requires an effort that I'm simply unwilling to make. . . . And those cute little freshmen making eyes at me and paying me idiotic compliments! I've grown up, Anthony."

Marietta itself offered little social life. Half a dozen farm-estates formed a hectagon around it, but these belonged to ancient men who displayed themselves only as inert, gray-thatched lumps in the back of limousines on their way to the station, whither they were sometimes accompanied by equally ancient and doubly massive wives. The townspeople were a particularly uninteresting type—unmarried females were predominant for the most part—with school-festival horizons and souls bleak as the forbidding white architecture of the three churches. The only native with whom they came into close contact was the broad-hipped, broad-shouldered Swedish girl who came every day to do their work. She was silent and efficient, and Gloria, after finding her weeping violently into her bowed arms upon the kitchen table, developed an uncanny fear of her and stopped complaining about the food. Because of her untold and esoteric grief the girl stayed on.

Gloria's penchant for premonitions and her bursts of vague supernaturalism were a surprise to Anthony. Either some complex, properly and scientifically inhibited in the early years with her Bilphistic mother, or some inherited hypersensitiveness, made her susceptible to any suggestion of the psychic, and, far from gullible about the motives of people, she was inclined to credit any extraordinary happening attributed to the whimsical perambulations of the buried. The desperate squeakings about the old house on windy nights that to Anthony were burglars with revolvers ready in hand represented to Gloria the auras, evil and restive, of dead generations, expiating the inexpiable upon the ancient and romantic hearth. One night, because of two swift bangs down-stairs, which Anthony fearfully but unavailingly investigated, they lay awake nearly until dawn asking each other examination-paper questions about the history of the world.

In October Muriel came out for a two weeks' visit. Gloria had called her on long-distance, and Miss Kane ended the conversation characteristically by saying "All-ll-ll righty. I'll be there with bells!" She arrived with a dozen popular songs under her arm.

"You ought to have a phonograph out here in the country," she said, "just a little Vic—they don't cost much. Then whenever you're lonesome you can have Caruso or Al Jolson right at your door."

She worried Anthony to distraction by telling him that "he was the first clever man she had ever known and she got so tired of shallow people." He wondered that people fell in love with such women. Yet he supposed that under a certain impassioned glance even she might take on a softness and promise.

But Gloria, violently showing off her love for Anthony, was diverted into a state of purring content.

Finally Richard Caramel arrived for a garrulous and to Gloria painfully literary week-end, during which he discussed himself with Anthony long after she lay in childlike sleep up-stairs.

"It's been mighty funny, this success and all," said Dick. "Just before the novel appeared I'd been trying, without success, to sell some short stories. Then, after my book came out, I polished up three and had them accepted by one of the magazines that had rejected them before. I've done a lot of them since; publishers don't pay me for my book till this winter."

"Don't let the victor belong to the spoils."

"You mean write trash?" He considered. "If you mean deliberately injecting a slushy fade-out into each one, I'm not. But I don't suppose I'm being so careful. I'm certainly writing faster and I don't seem to be thinking as much as I used to. Perhaps it's because I don't get any conversation, now that you're married and Maury's gone to Philadelphia. Haven't the old urge and ambition. Early success and all that."

"Doesn't it worry you?"

"Frantically. I get a thing I call sentence-fever that must be like buck-fever—it's a sort of intense literary self-consciousness that comes when I try to force myself. But the really awful days aren't when I think I can't write. They're when I wonder whether any writing is worth while at all—I mean whether I'm not a sort of glorified buffoon."

"I like to hear you talk that way," said Anthony with a touch of his old patronizing insolence. "I was afraid you'd gotten a bit idiotic over your work. Read the damnedest interview you gave out——"

Dick interrupted with an agonized expression.

"Good Lord! Don't mention it. Young lady wrote it—most admiring young lady. Kept telling me my work was 'strong,' and I sort of lost my head and made a lot of strange pronouncements. Some of it was good, though, don't you think?"

"Oh, yes; that part about the wise writer writing for the youth of his generation, the critic of the next, and the schoolmaster of ever afterward."

"Oh, I believe a lot of it," admitted Richard Caramel with a faint beam. "It simply was a mistake to give it out."

In November they moved into Anthony's apartment, from which they sallied triumphantly to the Yale-Harvard and Harvard-Princeton football games, to the St. Nicholas ice-skating rink, to a thorough round of the theatres and to a miscellany of entertainments—from small, staid dances to the great affairs that Gloria loved, held in those few houses where lackeys with powdered wigs scurried around in magnificent Anglomania under the direction of gigantic majordomos. Their intention was to go abroad the first of the year or, at any rate, when the war was over. Anthony had actually completed a Chestertonian essay on the twelfth century by way of introduction to his proposed book and Gloria had done some extensive research work on the question of Russian sable coats—in fact the winter was approaching quite comfortably, when the Bilphistic demiurge decided suddenly in mid-December that Mrs. Gilbert's soul had aged sufficiently in its present incarnation. In consequence Anthony took a miserable and hysterical Gloria out to Kansas City, where, in the fashion of mankind, they paid the terrible and mind-shaking deference to the dead.

Mr. Gilbert became, for the first and last time in his life, a truly pathetic figure. That woman he had broken to wait upon his body and play congregation to his mind had ironically deserted him—just when he could not much longer have supported her. Never again would he be able so satisfactorily to bore and bully a human soul.

CHAPTER 2

SYMPOSIUM

Gloria had lulled Anthony's mind to sleep. She, who seemed of all women the wisest and the finest, hung like a brilliant curtain across his doorways, shutting out the light of the sun. In those first years what he believed bore invariably the stamp of Gloria; he saw the sun always through the pattern of the curtain.

It was a sort of lassitude that brought them back to Marietta for another summer. Through a golden enervating spring they had loitered, restive and lazily extravagant, along the California coast, joining other parties intermittently and drifting from Pasadena to Coronado, from Coronado to Santa Barbara, with no purpose more apparent than Gloria's desire to dance by different music or catch some infinitesimal variant among the changing colors of the sea. Out of the Pacific there rose to greet them savage rocklands and equally barbaric hostelries built that at tea-time one might drowse into a languid wicker bazaar glorified by the polo costumes of Southhampton and Lake Forest and Newport and Palm Beach. And, as the waves met and splashed and glittered in the most placid of the bays, so they joined this group and that, and with them shifted stations, murmuring ever of those strange unsubstantial gaieties in wait just over the next green and fruitful valley.

A simple healthy leisure class it was—the best of the men not unpleasantly undergraduate—they seemed to be on a perpetual candidates list for some etherealized "Porcellian" or "Skull and Bones" extended out indefinitely into the world; the women, of more than average beauty, fragilely athletic, somewhat idiotic as hostesses but charming and infinitely decorative as guests. Sedately and gracefully they danced the steps of their selection in the balmy tea hours, accomplishing with a certain dignity the movements so horribly burlesqued by clerk and chorus girl the country over. It seemed ironic that in this lone and discredited offspring of the arts Americans should excel, unquestionably.

Having danced and splashed through a lavish spring, Anthony and Gloria found that they had spent too much money and for this must go into retirement for a certain period. There was Anthony's "work," they said. Almost before they knew it they were back in the gray house, more aware now that other lovers had slept there, other names had been called over the banisters, other couples had sat upon the porch steps watching the gray-green fields and the black bulk of woods beyond.

It was the same Anthony, more restless, inclined to quicken only under the stimulus of several high-balls, faintly, almost imperceptibly, apathetic toward Gloria. But Gloria—she would be twenty-four in August and was in an attractive but sincere panic about it. Six years to thirty! Had she been less in love with Anthony her sense of the flight of time would have expressed itself in a reawakened interest in other men, in a deliberate intention of extracting a transient gleam of romance from every potential lover who glanced at her with lowered brows over a shining dinner table. She said to Anthony one day:

"How I feel is that if I wanted anything I'd take it. That's what I've always thought all my life. But it happens that I want you, and so I just haven't room for any other desires."

They were bound eastward through a parched and lifeless Indiana, and she had looked up from one of her beloved moving picture magazines to find a casual conversation suddenly turned grave.

Anthony frowned out the car window. As the track crossed a country road a farmer appeared momentarily in his wagon; he was chewing on a straw and was apparently the same farmer they had passed a dozen times before, sitting in silent and malignant symbolism. As Anthony turned to Gloria his frown intensified.

"You worry me," he objected; "I can imagine *wanting* another woman under certain transitory circumstances, but I can't imagine taking her."

"But I don't feel that way, Anthony. I can't be bothered resisting things I want. My way is not to want them—to want nobody but you."

"Yet when I think that if you just happened to take a fancy to some one—"

"Oh, don't be an idiot!" she exclaimed. "There'd be nothing casual about it. And I can't even imagine the possibility."

This emphatically closed the conversation. Anthony's unfailing appreciation made her happier in his company than in anyone's else. She definitely enjoyed him—she loved him. So the summer began very much as had the one before.

There was, however, one radical change in ménage. The icy-hearted Scandinavian, whose austere cooking and sardonic manner of waiting on table had so depressed Gloria, gave way to an exceedingly efficient Japanese whose name was Tanalahaka, but who confessed that he heeded any summons which included the dissyllable "Tana."

Tana was unusually small even for a Japanese, and

displayed a somewhat naïve conception of himself as a man of the world. On the day of his arrival from "R. Gugimoniki, Japanese Reliable Employment Agency," he called Anthony into his room to see the treasures of his trunk. These included a large collection of Japanese postcards, which he was all for explaining to his employer at once, individually and at great length. Among them were half a dozen of pornographic intent and plainly of American origin, though the makers had modestly omitted both their names and the form for mailing. He next brought out some of his own handiwork—a pair of American pants, which he had made himself, and two suits of solid silk underwear. He informed Anthony confidentially as to the purpose for which these latter were reserved. The next exhibit was a rather good copy of an etching of Abraham Lincoln, to whose face he had given an unmistakable Japanese cast. Last came a flute; he had made it himself but it was broken: he was going to fix it soon.

After these polite formalities, which Anthony conjectured must be native to Japan, Tana delivered a long harangue in splintered English on the relation of master and servant from which Anthony gathered that he had worked on large estates but had always quarrelled with the other servants because they were not honest. They had a great time over the word "honest," and in fact became rather irritated with each other, because Anthony persisted stubbornly that Tana was trying to say "hornets," and even went to the extent of buzzing in the manner of a bee and flapping his arms to imitate wings.

After three-quarters of an hour Anthony was released with the warm assurance that they would have other nice chats in which Tana would tell "how we do in my countree."

Such was Tana's garrulous première in the gray house— and he fulfilled its promise. Though he was conscientious and honorable, he was unquestionably a terrific bore. He seemed unable to control his tongue, sometimes continuing from paragraph to paragraph with a look akin to pain in his small brown eyes.

Sunday and Monday afternoons he read the comic sections of the newspapers. One cartoon which contained a facetious Japanese butler diverted him enormously, though he claimed that the protagonist, who to Anthony appeared clearly Oriental, had really an American face. The difficulty with the funny paper was that when, aided by Anthony, he had spelled out the last three pictures and assimilated their context with a concentration surely adequate for Kant's "Critique," he had entirely forgotten what the first pictures were about.

In the middle of June Anthony and Gloria celebrated their first anniversary by having a "date." Anthony knocked at the door and she ran to let him in. Then they sat together on the couch calling over those names they had made for each other, new combinations of endearments ages old. Yet to this "date" was appended no attenuated good-night with its ecstasy of regret.

Later in June horror leered out at Gloria, struck at her and frightened her bright soul back half a generation. Then slowly it faded out, faded back into that impenetrable darkness whence it had come—taking relentlessly its modicum of youth.

With an infallible sense of the dramatic it chose a little railroad station in a wretched village near Portchester. The station platform lay all day bare as a prairie, exposed to the dusty yellow sun and to the glance of that most obnoxious type of countryman who lives near a metropolis and has attained its cheap smartness without its urbanity. A dozen of these yokels, red-eyed, cheerless as scarecrows, saw the incident. Dimly it passed across their confused and uncomprehending minds, taken at its broadest for a coarse joke, at its subtlest for a "shame." Meanwhile there upon the platform a measure of brightness faded from the world.

With Eric Merriam, Anthony had been sitting over a decanter of Scotch all the hot summer afternoon, while Gloria and Constance Merriam swam and sunned themselves at the Beach Club, the latter under a striped parasol-awning, Gloria stretched sensuously upon the soft hot sand, tanning her inevitable legs. Later they had all four played with inconsequential sandwiches; then Gloria had risen, tapping Anthony's knee with her parasol to get his attention.

"We've got to go, dear."

"Now?" He looked at her unwillingly. At that moment nothing seemed of more importance than to idle on that shady porch drinking mellowed Scotch, while his host reminisced interminably on the byplay of some forgotten political campaign.

"We've really got to go," repeated Gloria. "We can get a taxi to the station. . . . Come on, Anthony!" she commanded a bit more imperiously.

"Now see here—" Merriam, his yarn cut off, made conventional objections, meanwhile provocatively filling his guest's glass with a high-ball that should have been sipped through ten minutes. But at Gloria's annoyed "We really *must!*" Anthony drank it off, got to his feet and made an elaborate bow to his hostess.

"It seems we 'must,'" he said, with little grace.

In a minute he was following Gloria down a garden-walk between tall rose-bushes, her parasol brushing gently the June-blooming leaves. Most inconsiderate, he thought, as they reached the road. He felt with injured naïvete that Gloria should not have interrupted such innocent and harmless enjoyment. The whiskey had both soothed and clarified the restless things in his mind. It occurred to him that she had taken this same attitude several times before. Was he always to retreat from pleasant episodes at a touch of her parasol or a flicker of her eye? His unwillingness blurred to ill will, which rose within him like a resistless bubble. He kept silent, perversely inhibiting a desire to reproach her. They found a taxi in front of the Inn; rode silently to the little station. . . .

Then Anthony knew what he wanted—to assert his will against this cool and impervious girl, to obtain with one magnificent effort a mastery that seemed infinitely desirable.

"Let's go over to see the Barneses," he said without looking at her. "I don't feel like going home."

—Mrs. Barnes, née Rachael Jerryl, had a summer place several miles from Redgate.

"We went there day before yesterday," she answered shortly.

"I'm sure they'd be glad to see us." He felt that that was not a strong enough note, braced himself stubbornly, and added: "I want to see the Barneses. I haven't any desire to go home."

"Well, I haven't any desire to go to the Barneses."

Suddenly they stared at each other.

"Why, Anthony," she said with annoyance, "this is Sunday night and they probably have guests for supper. Why we should go in at this hour—"

"Then why couldn't we have stayed at the Merriams'?" he burst out. "Why go home when we were having a perfectly decent time? They asked us to supper."

"They had to. Give me the money and I'll get the railroad tickets."

"I certainly will not! I'm in no humor for a ride in that damn hot train."

Gloria stamped her foot on the platform.

"Anthony, you act as if you're tight!"

"On the contrary, I'm perfectly sober."

But his voice had slipped into a husky key and she knew with certainty that this was untrue.

"If you're sober you'll give me the money for the tickets."

But it was too late to talk to him that way. In his mind was but one idea—that Gloria was being selfish, that she was always being selfish and would continue to be unless here and now he asserted himself as her master. This was the occasion of all occasions, since for a whim she had deprived him of a pleasure. His determination solidified, approached momentarily a dull and sullen hate.

"I won't go in the train," he said, his voice trembling a little with anger. "We're going to the Barneses."

"I'm not!" she cried. "If you go I'm going home alone."

"Go on, then."

Without a word she turned toward the ticket office; simultaneously he remembered that she had some money with her and that this was not the sort of victory he wanted, the sort he must have. He took a step after her and seized her arm.

"See here!" he muttered, "you're *not* going alone!"

"I certainly am—why, Anthony!" This exclamation as she tried to pull away from him and he only tightened his grasp.

He looked at her with narrowed and malicious eyes.

"Let go!" Her cry had a quality of fierceness. "If you have *any* decency you'll let go."

"Why?" He knew why. But he took a confused and not quite confident pride in holding her there.

"I'm going home, do you understand? And you're going to let me go!"

"No, I'm not."

Her eyes were burning now.

"Are you going to make a scene here?"

"I say you're not going! I'm tired of your eternal self-ishness!"

"I only want to go home." Two wrathful tears started from her eyes.

"This time you're going to do what *I* say."

Slowly her body straightened: her head went back in a gesture of infinite scorn.

"I hate you!" Her low words were expelled like venom

through her clenched teeth. "Oh, *let* me go! Oh, I *hate* you!" She tried to jerk herself away but he only grasped the other arm. "I hate you! I hate you!"

At Gloria's fury his uncertainty returned, but he felt that now he had gone too far to give in. It seemed that he had always given in and that in her heart she had despised him for it. Ah, she might hate him now, but afterward she would admire him for his dominance.

The approaching train gave out a premonitory siren that tumbled melodramatically toward them down the glistening blue tracks. Gloria tugged and strained to free herself, and words older than the Book of Genesis came to her lips.

"Oh, you brute!" she sobbed. "Oh, you brute! Oh, I hate you! Oh, you brute! Oh—"

On the station platform other prospective passengers were beginning to turn and stare; the drone of the train was audible, it increased to a clamor. Gloria's efforts redoubled, then ceased altogether, and she stood there trembling and hot-eyed at this helpless humiliation, as the engine roared and thundered into the station.

Low, below the flood of steam and the grinding of the brakes came her voice:

"Oh, if there was one *man* here you couldn't do this! You couldn't do this! You coward! You coward, oh, you coward!"

Anthony, silent, trembling himself, gripped her rigidly, aware that faces, dozens of them, curiously unmoved, shadows of a dream, were regarding him. Then the bells distilled metallic crashes that were like physical pain, the smoke-stacks volleyed in slow acceleration at the sky, and in a moment of noise and gray gaseous turbulence the line of faces ran by, moved off, became indistinct—until suddenly there was only the sun slanting east across the tracks and a volume of sound decreasing far off like a train made out of tin thunder. He dropped her arms. He had won.

Now, if he wished, he might laugh. The test was done and he had sustained his will with violence. Let leniency walk in the wake of victory.

"We'll hire a car here and drive back to Marietta," he said with fine reserve.

For answer Gloria seized his hand with both of hers and raising it to her mouth bit deeply into his thumb. He scarcely noticed the pain; seeing the blood spurt he absent-mindedly drew out his handkerchief and wrapped the wound. That too was part of the triumph he supposed—it was inevitable that defeat should thus be resented—and as such was beneath notice.

She was sobbing, almost without tears, profoundly and bitterly.

"I won't go! I won't go! You—can't—make—me—go! You've—you've killed any love I ever had for you, and any respect. But all that's left in me would die before I'd move from this place. Oh, if I'd thought *you'd* lay your hands on me—"

"You're going with me," he said brutally, "if I have to carry you."

He turned, beckoned to a taxicab, told the driver to go to Marietta. The man dismounted and swung the door open. Anthony faced his wife and said between his clenched teeth:

"Will you get in?—or will I *put* you in?"

With a subdued cry of infinite pain and despair she yielded herself up and got into the car.

All the long ride, through the increasing dark of twilight, she sat huddled in her side of the car, her silence broken by an occasional dry and solitary sob. Anthony stared out the window, his mind working dully on the slowly changing significance of what had occurred. Something was wrong—that last cry of Gloria's had struck a chord which echoed posthumously and with incongruous disquiet in his heart. He must be right—yet, she seemed such a pathetic little thing now, broken and dispirited, humiliated beyond the measure of her lot to bear. The sleeves of her dress were torn; her parasol was gone, forgotten on the platform. It was a new costume, he remembered, and she had been so proud of it that very morning when they had left the house. . . . He began wondering if any one they knew had seen the incident. And persistently there recurred to him her cry:

"All that's left in me would die—"

This gave him a confused and increasing worry. It fitted so well with the Gloria who lay in the corner—no longer a proud Gloria, nor any Gloria he had known. He asked himself if it were possible. While he did not believe she would cease to love him—this, of course, was unthinkable—it was yet problematical whether Gloria without her arrogance, her independence, her virginal confidence and courage, would be the girl of his glory, the radiant woman who was precious and charming because she was ineffably, triumphantly herself.

He was very drunk even then, so drunk as not to realize his own drunkenness. When they reached the gray house he went to his own room and, his mind still wrestling helplessly and sombrely with what he had done, fell into a deep stupor on his bed.

It was after one o'clock and the hall seemed extraordinarily quiet when Gloria, wide-eyed and sleepless, traversed it and pushed open the door of his room. He had been too befuddled to open the windows and the air was stale and thick with whiskey. She stood for a moment by his bed, a slender, exquisitely graceful figure in her boyish silk pajamas— then with abandon she flung herself upon him, half waking him in the frantic emotion of her embrace, dropping her warm tears upon his throat.

"Oh, Anthony!" she cried passionately, "oh, my darling, you don't know what you did!"

Yet in the morning, coming early into her room, he knelt

down by her bed and cried like a little boy, as though it was his heart that had been broken.

"It seemed, last night," she said gravely, her fingers playing in his hair, "that all the part of me you loved, the part that was worth knowing, all the pride and fire, was gone. I knew that what was left of me would always love you, but never in quite the same way."

Nevertheless, she was aware even then that she would forget in time and that it is the manner of life seldom to strike but always to wear away. After that morning the incident was never mentioned and its deep wound healed with Anthony's hand—and if there was triumph some darker force than theirs possessed it, possessed the knowledge and the victory.

NIETZSCHEAN INCIDENT

Gloria's independence, like all sincere and profound qualities, had begun unconsciously, but, once brought to her attention by Anthony's fascinated discovery of it, it assumed more nearly the proportions of a formal code. From her conversation it might be assumed that all her energy and vitality went into a violent affirmation of the negative principle "Never give a damn."

"Not for anything or anybody," she said, "except myself and, by implication, for Anthony. That's the rule of all life and if it weren't I'd be that way anyhow. Nobody'd do anything for me if it didn't gratify them to, and I'd do as little for them."

She was on the front porch of the nicest lady in Marietta when she said this, and as she finished she gave a curious little cry and sank in a dead faint to the porch floor.

The lady brought her to and drove her home in her car. It had occurred to the estimable Gloria that she was probably with child.

She lay upon the long lounge down-stairs. Day was

slipping warmly out the window, touching the late roses on the porch pillars.

"All I think of ever is that I love you," she wailed. "I value my body because you think it's beautiful. And this body of mine—of yours—to have it grow ugly and shapeless? It's simply intolerable. Oh, Anthony, I'm not afraid of the pain."

He consoled her desperately—but in vain. She continued:

"And then afterward I might have wide hips and be pale, with all my freshness gone and no radiance in my hair."

He paced the floor with his hands in his pockets, asking:

"Is it certain?"

"I don't know anything. I've always hated obstrics, or whatever you call them. I thought I'd have a child some time. But not now."

"Well, for God's sake don't lie there and go to pieces."

Her sobs lapsed. She drew down a merciful silence from the twilight which filled the room. "Turn on the lights," she pleaded. "These days seem so short—June seemed—to—have—longer days when I was a little girl."

The lights snapped on and it was as though blue drapes of softest silk had been dropped behind the windows and the door. Her pallor, her immobility, without grief now, or joy, awoke his sympathy.

"Do you want me to have it?" she asked listlessly.

"I'm indifferent. That is, I'm neutral. If you have it I'll probably be glad. If you don't—well, that's all right too."

"I wish you'd make up your mind one way or the other!"

"Suppose you make up *your* mind."

She looked at him contemptuously, scorning to answer.

"You'd think you'd been singled out of all the women in the world for this crowning indignity."

"What if I do!" she cried angrily. "It isn't an indignity for them. It's their one excuse for living. It's the one thing they're good for. It *is* an indignity for *me.*

"See here, Gloria, I'm with you whatever you do, but for God's sake be a sport about it."

"Oh, don't *fuss* at me!" she wailed.

They exchanged a mute look of no particular significance but of much stress. Then Anthony took a book from the shelf and dropped into a chair.

Half an hour later her voice came out of the intense stillness that pervaded the room and hung like incense on the air.

"I'll drive over and see Constance Merriam to-morrow."

"All right. And I'll go to Tarrytown and see Grampa."

"—You see," she added, "it isn't that I'm afraid—of this or anything else. I'm being true to me, you know."

"I know," he agreed.

THE PRACTICAL MEN

Adam Patch, in a pious rage against the Germans, subsisted on the war news. Pin maps plastered his walls; atlases were piled deep on tables convenient to his hand together with "Photographic Histories of the World War," official Explain-alls, and the "Personal Impressions" of war correspondents and of Privates X, Y, and Z. Several times during Anthony's visit his grandfather's secretary, Edward Shuttleworth, the one-time "Accomplished Gin-physician" of "Pat's Place" in Hoboken, now shod with righteous indignation, would appear with an extra. The old man attacked each paper with untiring fury, tearing out those columns which appeared to him of sufficient pregnancy for preservation and thrusting them into one of his already bulging files.

"Well, what have you been doing?" he asked Anthony blandly. "Nothing? Well, I thought so. I've been intending to drive over and see you, all summer."

"I've been writing. Don't you remember the essay I sent you—the one I sold to The Florentine last winter?"

"Essay? You never sent *me* any essay."

"Oh, yes, I did. We talked about it."

Adam Patch shook his head mildly.

"Oh, no. You never sent *me* any essay. You may have thought you sent it but it never reached me."

"Why, you read it, Grampa," insisted Anthony, somewhat exasperated, "you read it and disagreed with it."

The old man suddenly remembered, but this was made apparent only by a partial falling open of his mouth, displaying rows of gray gums. Eying Anthony with a green and ancient stare he hesitated between confessing his error and covering it up.

"So you're writing," he said quickly. "Well, why don't you go over and write about these Germans? Write something real, something about what's going on, something people can read."

"Anybody can't be a war correspondent," objected Anthony. "You have to have some newspaper willing to buy your stuff. And I can't spare the money to go over as a free-lance."

"I'll send you over," suggested his grandfather surprisingly. "I'll get you over as an authorized correspondent of any newspaper you pick out."

Anthony recoiled from the idea—almost simultaneously he bounded toward it.

"I—don't—know—"

He would have to leave Gloria, whose whole life yearned toward him and enfolded him. Gloria was in trouble. Oh, the thing wasn't feasible—yet—he saw himself in khaki, leaning, as all war correspondents lean, upon a heavy stick, portfolio at shoulder—trying to look like an Englishman. "I'd like to think it over," he, confessed. "It's certainly very kind of you. I'll think it over and I'll let you know."

Thinking it over absorbed him on the journey to New York. He had had one of those sudden flashes of illumination vouchsafed to all men who are dominated by a strong and beloved woman, which show them a world of harder men, more fiercely trained and grappling with the abstractions of thought and war. In that world the arms of Gloria would exist only as the hot embrace of a chance mistress, coolly sought and quickly forgotten. . . .

These unfamiliar phantoms were crowding closely about him when he boarded his train for Marietta, in the Grand Central Station. The car was crowded; he secured the last vacant seat and it was only after several minutes that he gave even a casual glance to the man beside him. When he did he saw a heavy lay of jaw and nose, a curved chin and small, puffed-under eyes. In a moment he recognized Joseph Bloeckman.

Simultaneously they both half rose, were half embarrassed, and exchanged what amounted to a half handshake. Then, as though to complete the matter, they both half laughed.

"Well," remarked Anthony without inspiration, "I haven't seen you for a long time." Immediately he regretted his words and started to add: "I didn't know you lived out this way." But Bloeckman anticipated him by asking pleasantly:

"How's your wife? . . ."

"She's very well. How've you been?"

"Excellent." His tone amplified the grandeur of the word.

It seemed to Anthony that during the last year Bloeckman had grown tremendously in dignity. The boiled look was gone, he seemed "done" at last. In addition he was no longer overdressed. The inappropriate facetiousness he had affected in ties had given way to a sturdy dark pattern, and his right hand, which had formerly displayed two heavy rings, was now innocent of ornament and even without the raw glow of a manicure.

This dignity appeared also in his personality. The last

aura of the successful travelling-man had faded from him, that deliberate ingratiation of which the lowest form is the bawdy joke in the Pullman smoker. One imagined that, having been fawned upon financially, he had attained aloofness; having been snubbed socially, he had acquired reticence. But whatever had given him weight instead of bulk, Anthony no longer felt a correct superiority in his presence.

"D'you remember Caramel, Richard Caramel? I believe you met him one night."

"I remember. He was writing a book."

"Well, he sold it to the movies. Then they had some scenario man named Jordan work on it. Well, Dick subscribes to a clipping bureau and he's furious because about half the movie reviewers speak of the 'power and strength of William Jordan's "Demon Lover."' Didn't mention old Dick at all. You'd think this fellow Jordan had actually conceived and developed the thing."

Bloeckman nodded comprehensively.

"Most of the contracts state that the original writer's name goes into all the paid publicity. Is Caramel still writing?"

"Oh, yes. Writing hard. Short stories."

"Well, that's fine, that's fine. . . . You on this train often?"

"About once a week. We live in Marietta."

"Is that so? Well, well! I live near Cos Cob myself. Bought a place there only recently. We're only five miles apart."

"You'll have to come and see us." Anthony was surprised at his own courtesy. "I'm sure Gloria'd be delighted to see an old friend. Anybody'll tell you where the house is—it's our second season there."

"Thank you." Then, as though returning a complementary politeness: "How is your grandfather?"

"He's been well. I had lunch with him to-day."

"A great character," said Bloeckman severely. "A fine example of an American."

THE TRIUMPH OF LETHARGY

Anthony found his wife deep in the porch hammock voluptuously engaged with a lemonade and a tomato sandwich and carrying on an apparently cheery conversation with Tana upon one of Tana's complicated themes.

"In my countree," Anthony recognized his invariable preface, "all time—peoples—eat rice—because haven't got. Cannot eat what no have got." Had his nationality not been desperately apparent one would have thought he had acquired his knowledge of his native land from American primary-school geographies.

When the Oriental had been squelched and dismissed to the kitchen, Anthony turned questioningly to Gloria:

"It's all right," she announced, smiling broadly. "And it surprised me more than it does you."

"There's no doubt?"

"None! Couldn't be!"

They rejoiced happily, gay again with reborn irresponsibility. Then he told her of his opportunity to go abroad, and that he was almost ashamed to reject it.

"What do *you* think? Just tell me frankly."

"Why, Anthony!" Her eyes were startled. "Do you want to go? Without me?"

His face fell—yet he knew, with his wife's question, that it was too late. Her arms, sweet and strangling, were around him, for he had made all such choices back in that room in the Plaza the year before. This was an anachronism from an age of such dreams.

"Gloria," he lied, in a great burst of comprehension, "of course I don't. I was thinking you might go as a nurse or something." He wondered dully if his grandfather would consider this.

As she smiled he realized again how beautiful she was, a gorgeous girl of miraculous freshness and sheerly honorable eyes. She embraced his suggestion with luxurious intensity, holding it aloft like a sun of her own making and basking in its beams. She strung together an amazing synopsis for an extravaganza of martial adventure.

After supper, surfeited with the subject, she yawned. She wanted not to talk but only to read "Penrod," stretched upon the lounge until at midnight she fell asleep. But Anthony, after he had carried her romantically up the stairs, stayed awake to brood upon the day, vaguely angry with her, vaguely dissatisfied.

"What am I going to do?" he began at breakfast. "Here we've been married a year and we've just worried around without even being efficient people of leisure."

"Yes, you ought to do something," she admitted, being in an agreeable and loquacious humor. This was not the first of these discussions, but as they usually developed Anthony in the rôle of protagonist, she had come to avoid them.

"It's not that I have any moral compunctions about work," he continued, "but grampa may die to-morrow and he may live for ten years. Meanwhile we're living above our income and all we've got to show for it is a farmer's car and a few clothes. We keep an apartment that we've only lived in three months and a little old house way off in nowhere. We're frequently bored and yet we won't make any effort to know anyone except the same crowd who drift around California all summer wearing sport clothes and waiting for their families to die."

"How you've changed!" remarked Gloria. "Once you told me you didn't see why an American couldn't loaf gracefully."

"Well, damn it, I wasn't married. And the old mind was working at top speed and now it's going round and round like a cog-wheel with nothing to catch it. As a matter of fact I think that if I hadn't met you I *would* have done something. But you make leisure so subtly attractive—"

"Oh, it's all my fault—"

"I didn't mean that, and you know I didn't. But here I'm almost twenty-seven and—"

"Oh," she interrupted in vexation, "you make me tired! Talking as though I were objecting or hindering you!"

"I was just discussing it, Gloria. Can't I discuss—"

"I should think you'd be strong enough to settle—"

"—something with you without—"

"—your own problems without coming to me. You *talk* a lot about going to work. I could use more money very easily, but *I'm* not complaining. Whether you work or not I love you." Her last words were gentle as fine snow upon hard ground. But for the moment neither was attending to the other—they were each engaged in polishing and perfecting his own attitude.

"I have worked—some." This by Anthony was an imprudent bringing up of raw reserves. Gloria laughed, torn between delight and derision; she resented his sophistry as at the same time she admired his nonchalance. She would never blame him for being the ineffectual idler so long as he did it sincerely, from the attitude that nothing much was worth doing.

"Work!" she scoffed. "Oh, you sad bird! You bluffer! Work—that means a great arranging of the desk and the lights, a great sharpening of pencils, and 'Gloria, don't sing!' and 'Please keep that damn Tana away from me,' and 'Let me read you my opening sentence,' and 'I won't be through for a long time, Gloria, so don't stay up for me,' and a tremendous consumption of tea or coffee. And that's all. In just about an hour I hear the old pencil stop scratching and look over. You've got out a book and you're 'looking up' something. Then you're reading. Then yawns—then bed and a great tossing about because you're all full of caffeine and can't sleep. Two weeks later the whole performance over again."

With much difficulty Anthony retained a scanty breech-clout of dignity.

"Now that's a *slight* exaggeration. You know *darn well* I sold an essay to *The Florentine*—and it attracted a lot of attention considering the circulation of *The Florentine*. And what's more, Gloria, you know I sat up till five o'clock in the morning finishing it."

She lapsed into silence, giving him rope. And if he had not hanged himself he had certainly come to the end of it.

"At least," he concluded feebly, "I'm perfectly willing to be a war correspondent."

But so was Gloria. They were both willing—anxious; they assured each other of it. The evening ended on a note of tremendous sentiment, the majesty of leisure, the ill health of Adam Patch, love at any cost.

"Anthony!" she called over the banister one afternoon a week later, "there's some one at the door." Anthony, who had been lolling in the hammock on the sun-speckled south porch, strolled around to the front of the house. A foreign car, large and impressive, crouched like an immense and saturnine bug at the foot of the path. A man in a soft pongee suit, with cap to match, hailed him.

"Hello there, Patch. Ran over to call on you."

It was Bloeckman; as always, infinitesimally improved, of subtler intonation, of more convincing ease.

"I'm awfully glad you did." Anthony raised his voice to a vine-covered window: "Glor-i-*a*! We've got a visitor!"

"I'm in the tub," wailed Gloria politely.

With a smile the two men acknowledged the triumph of her alibi.

"She'll be down. Come round here on the side-porch. Like a drink? Gloria's always in the tub—good third of every day."

"Pity she doesn't live on the Sound."

"Can't afford it."

As coming from Adam Patch's grandson, Bloeckman took this as a form of pleasantry. After fifteen minutes filled with estimable brilliancies, Gloria appeared, fresh in starched yellow, bringing atmosphere and an increase of vitality.

"I want to be a successful sensation in the movies," she announced. "I hear that Mary Pickford makes a million dollars annually."

"You could, you know," said Bloeckman. "I think you'd film very well."

"Would you let me, Anthony? If I only play unsophisticated rôles?"

As the conversation continued in stilted commas, Anthony wondered that to him and Bloeckman both this girl had once been the most stimulating, the most tonic personality they had ever known—and now the three sat like overoiled machines, without conflict, without fear, without elation, heavily enamelled little figures secure beyond enjoyment in a world where death and war, dull emotion and noble savagery were covering a continent with the smoke of terror.

In a moment he would call Tana and they would pour into themselves a gay and delicate poison which would restore them momentarily to the pleasurable excitement of childhood, when every face in a crowd had carried its suggestion of splendid and significant transactions taking place somewhere to some magnificent and illimitable purpose. . . . Life was no more than this summer afternoon; a faint wind stirring the lace collar of Gloria's dress; the slow baking drowsiness of the veranda. . . . Intolerably unmoved they all seemed, removed from any romantic imminency of action. Even Gloria's beauty needed wild emotions, needed poignancy, needed death. . . .

". . . Any day next week," Bloeckman was saying to Gloria. "Here—take this card. What they do is to give you a test of about three hundred feet of film, and they can tell pretty accurately from that."

"How about Wednesday?"

"Wednesday's fine. Just phone me and I'll go around with you—"

F. SCOTT FITZGERALD

He was on his feet, shaking hands briskly—then his car was a wraith of dust down the road. Anthony turned to his wife in bewilderment.

"Why, Gloria!"

"You don't mind if I have a trial, Anthony. Just a trial? I've got to go to town Wednesday, *any*how."

"But it's so silly! You don't want to go into the movies—moon around a studio all day with a lot of cheap chorus people."

"Lot of mooning around Mary Pickford does!"

"Everybody isn't a Mary Pickford."

"Well, I can't see how you'd object to my *try*ing."

"I do, though. I hate actors."

"Oh, you make me tired. Do you imagine I have a very thrilling time dozing on this damn porch?"

"You wouldn't mind if you loved me."

"Of course I love you," she said impatiently, making out a quick case for herself. "It's just because I do that I hate to see you go to pieces by just lying around and saying you ought to work. Perhaps if I *did* go into this for a while it'd stir you up so you'd do something."

"It's just your craving for excitement, that's all it is."

"Maybe it is! It's a perfectly natural craving, isn't it?"

"Well, I'll tell you one thing. If you go to the movies I'm going to Europe."

"Well, go on then! *I'm* not stopping you!"

To show she was not stopping him she melted into melancholy tears. Together they marshalled the armies of sentiment—words, kisses, endearments, self-reproaches. They attained nothing. Inevitably they attained nothing. Finally, in a burst of gargantuan emotion each of them sat down and wrote a letter. Anthony's was to his grandfather; Gloria's was to Joseph Bloeckman. It was a triumph of lethargy.

One day early in July Anthony, returned from an afternoon in New York, called up-stairs to Gloria. Receiving no answer he guessed she was asleep and so went into the pantry for one of the little sandwiches that were always prepared for them. He found Tana seated at the kitchen table before a miscellaneous assortment of odds and ends—cigar-boxes, knives, pencils, the tops of cans, and some scraps of paper covered with elaborate figures and diagrams.

"What the devil you doing?" demanded Anthony curiously.

Tana politely grinned.

"I show you," he exclaimed enthusiastically. "I tell—"

"You making a dog-house?"

"No, sa." Tana grinned again. "Make typewutta."

"Typewriter?"

"Yes, sa. I think, oh all time I think, lie in bed think 'bout typewutta."

"So you thought you'd make one, eh?"

"Wait. I tell."

Anthony, munching a sandwich, leaned leisurely against the sink. Tana opened and closed his mouth several times as though testing its capacity for action. Then with a rush he began:

"I been think—typewutta—has, oh, many many many many *thing*. Oh many many many many."

"Many keys. I see."

"No-o? *Yes*-key! Many many many many lettah. Like so a-b-c."

"Yes, you're right."

"Wait. I tell." He screwed his face up in a tremendous effort to express himself: "I been think—many words—end same. Like i-n-g."

"You bet. A whole raft of them."

"So—I make—typewutta—quick. Not so many lettah—"

"That's a great idea, Tana. Save time. You'll make a fortune. Press one key and there's 'ing.' Hope you work it out."

Tana laughed disparagingly. "Wait. I tell—"

"Where's Mrs. Patch?"

"She out. Wait, I tell—" Again he screwed up his face for action. "*My* typewutta——"

"Where is she?"

"Here—I make." He pointed to the miscellany of junk on the table.

"I mean Mrs. Patch."

"She out." Tana reassured him. "She be back five o'clock, she say."

"Down in the village?"

"No. Went off before lunch. She go Mr. Bloeckman."

Anthony started.

"Went out with Mr. Bloeckman?"

"She be back five."

Without a word Anthony left the kitchen with Tana's disconsolate "I tell" trailing after him. So this was Gloria's idea of excitement, by God! His fists were clenched; within a moment he had worked himself up to a tremendous pitch of indignation. He went to the door and looked out; there was no car in sight and his watch stood at four minutes of five. With furious energy he dashed down to the end of the path—as far as the bend of the road a mile off he could see no car—except—but it was a farmer's flivver. Then, in an undignified pursuit of dignity, he rushed back to the shelter of the house as quickly as he had rushed out.

Pacing up and down the living room he began an angry rehearsal of the speech he would make to her when she came in—

"So this is love!" he would begin—or no, it sounded too much like the popular phrase "So this is Paris!" He must be dignified, hurt, grieved. Anyhow—"So this is what *you* do when I have to go up and trot all day around the hot city on business. No wonder I can't write! No wonder I don't dare let you out of my sight!" He was expanding now, warming to his subject. "I'll tell you," he continued, "I'll tell you—" He paused, catching a familiar ring in the words—then he realized—it was Tana's "I tell."

Yet Anthony neither laughed nor seemed absurd to himself. To his frantic imagination it was already six—seven—eight, and she was never coming! Bloeckman finding her bored and unhappy had persuaded her to go to California with him. . . .

—There was a great to-do out in front, a joyous "Yoho, Anthony!" and he rose trembling, weakly happy to see her fluttering up the path. Bloeckman was following, cap in hand.

"Dearest!" she cried.

"We've been for the best jaunt—all over New York State."

"I'll have to be starting home," said Bloeckman, almost immediately. "Wish you'd both been here when I came."

"I'm sorry I wasn't," answered Anthony dryly. When he had departed Anthony hesitated. The fear was gone from his heart, yet he felt that some protest was ethically apropos. Gloria resolved his uncertainty.

"I knew you wouldn't mind. He came just before lunch and said he had to go to Garrison on business and wouldn't I go with him. He looked so lonesome, Anthony. And I drove his car all the way."

Listlessly Anthony dropped into a chair, his mind tired—tired with nothing, tired with everything, with the world's weight he had never chosen to bear. He was ineffectual and vaguely helpless here as he had always been. One of those personalities who, in spite of all their words, are inarticulate, he seemed to have inherited only the vast tradition of human failure—that, and the sense of death.

"I suppose I don't care," he answered.

One must be broad about these things, and Gloria being young, being beautiful, must have reasonable privileges. Yet it wearied him that he failed to understand.

WINTER

She rolled over on her back and lay still for a moment in the great bed watching the February sun suffer one last attenuated refinement in its passage through the leaded panes into the room. For a time she had no accurate sense of her whereabouts or of the events of the day before, or the day before that; then, like a suspended pendulum, memory began to beat out its story, releasing with each swing a burdened quota of time until her life was given back to her.

She could hear, now, Anthony's troubled breathing beside her; she could smell whiskey and cigarette smoke. She noticed that she lacked complete muscular control; when she moved it was not a sinuous motion with the resultant strain distributed easily over her body—it was a tremendous effort of her nervous system as though each time she were hypnotizing herself into performing an impossible action. . . .

She was in the bathroom, brushing her teeth to get rid of that intolerable taste; then back by the bedside listening to the rattle of Bounds's key in the outer door.

"Wake up, Anthony!" she said sharply.

She climbed into bed beside him and closed her eyes. Almost the last thing she remembered was a conversation with Mr. and Mrs. Lacy. Mrs. Lacy had said, "Sure you don't want us to get you a taxi?" and Anthony had replied that he guessed they could walk over to Fifth all right. Then they had both attempted, imprudently, to bow—and collapsed absurdly into a battalion of empty milk bottles just outside the door. There must have been two dozen milk bottles standing open-mouthed in the dark. She could conceive of no plausible explanation of those milk bottles. Perhaps they had been attracted by the singing in the Lacy house and had hurried over agape with wonder to see the fun. Well, they'd had the worst of it—though it seemed that she and Anthony never would get up, the perverse things rolled so. . . .

Still, they had found a taxi. "My meter's broken and it'll cost you a dollar and a half to get home," said the taxi driver. "Well," said Anthony, "I'm young Packy McFarland and if you'll come down here I'll beat you till you can't stand up." . . . At that point the man had driven off without them. They must have found another taxi, for they were in the apartment. . . .

"What time is it?" Anthony was sitting up in bed, staring at her with owlish precision.

This was obviously a rhetorical question. Gloria could think of no reason why she should be expected to know the time.

"Golly, I feel like the devil!" muttered Anthony dispassionately. Relaxing, he tumbled back upon his pillow. "Bring on your grim reaper!"

"Anthony, how'd we finally get home last night?"

"Taxi."

"Oh!" Then, after a pause: "Did you put me to bed?"

"I don't know. Seems to me you put *me* to bed. What day is it?"

"Tuesday."

"Tuesday? I hope so. If it's Wednesday, I've got to start work at that idiotic place. Supposed to be down at nine or some such ungodly hour."

"Ask Bounds," suggested Gloria feebly.

"Bounds!" he called.

Sprightly, sober—a voice from a world that it seemed in the past two days they had left forever, Bounds sprang in short steps down the hall and appeared in the half darkness of the door.

"What day, Bounds?"

"February the twenty-second, I think, sir."

"I mean day of the week."

"Tuesday, sir." "Thanks." After a pause: "Are you ready for breakfast, sir?"

"Yes, and Bounds, before you get it, will you make a pitcher of water, and set it here beside the bed? I'm a little thirsty."

"Yes, sir."

Bounds retreated in sober dignity down the hallway.

"Lincoln's birthday," affirmed Anthony without enthusiasm, "or St. Valentine's or somebody's. When did we start on this insane party?"

"Sunday night."

"After prayers?" he suggested sardonically.

"We raced all over town in those hansoms and Maury sat up with his driver, don't you remember? Then we came home and he tried to cook some bacon—came out of the pantry with a few blackened remains, insisting it was 'fried to the proverbial crisp.'"

Both of them laughed, spontaneously but with some difficulty, and lying there side by side reviewed the chain of events that had ended in this rusty and chaotic dawn.

They had been in New York for almost four months, since the country had grown too cool in late October. They had given up California this year, partly because of lack of funds, partly with the idea of going abroad should this interminable war, persisting now into its second year, end during the winter. Of late their income had lost elasticity; no longer did it stretch to cover gay whims and pleasant extravagances, and Anthony had spent many puzzled and unsatisfactory hours over a densely figured pad, making remarkable budgets that left huge margins for "amusements, trips, etc.," and trying to apportion, even approximately, their past expenditures.

He remembered a time when in going on a "party" with his two best friends, he and Maury had invariably paid more than their share of the expenses. They would buy the tickets for the theatre or squabble between themselves for the dinner check. It had seemed fitting; Dick, with his naïveté and his astonishing fund of information about himself, had been a diverting, almost juvenile, figure—court jester to their royalty. But this was no longer true. It was Dick who always had money; it was Anthony who entertained within limitations—always excepting occasional wild, wine-inspired, check-cashing parties—and it was Anthony who was solemn about it next morning and told the scornful and disgusted Gloria that they'd have to be "more careful next time."

In the two years since the publication of "The Demon Lover," Dick had made over twenty-five thousand dollars, most of it lately, when the reward of the author of fiction had begun to swell unprecedentedly as a result of the voracious hunger of the motion pictures for plots. He received seven hundred dollars for every story, at that time a large emolument for such a young man—he was not quite thirty—and for every one that contained enough "action" (kissing, shooting, and sacrificing) for the movies, he obtained an additional thousand. His stories varied; there was a measure of vitality and a sort of instinctive in all of them, but none attained the personality of "The Demon Lover," and there were several that Anthony considered downright cheap. These, Dick explained severely, were to widen his audience. Wasn't it true that men who had attained real permanence from Shakespeare to Mark Twain had appealed to the many as well as to the elect?

Though Anthony and Maury disagreed, Gloria told him to go ahead and make as much money as he could—that was the only thing that counted anyhow. . . .

Maury, a little stouter, faintly mellower, and more complaisant, had gone to work in Philadelphia. He came to New York once or twice a month and on such occasions the four of them travelled the popular routes from dinner to the theatre, thence to the Frolic or, perhaps, at the urging of the ever-curious Gloria, to one of the cellars of Greenwich Village, notorious through the furious but short-lived vogue of the "new poetry movement."

In January, after many monologues directed at his reticent wife, Anthony determined to "get something to do," for the winter at any rate. He wanted to please his grandfather and even, in a measure, to see how he liked it himself. He discovered during several tentative semi-social calls that employers were not interested in a young man who was only going to "try it for a few months or so." As the grandson of Adam Patch he was received everywhere with marked courtesy, but the old man was a back number now—the heyday of his fame as first an "oppressor" and then an uplifter of the people had been during the twenty years preceding his retirement. Anthony even found several of the younger men who were under the impression that Adam Patch had been dead for some years.

Eventually Anthony went to his grandfather and asked his advice, which turned out to be that he should enter the bond business as a salesman, a tedious suggestion to Anthony, but one that in the end he determined to follow. Sheer money in deft manipulation had fascinations under all circumstances, while almost any side of manufacturing would be insufferably dull. He considered newspaper work but decided that the hours were not ordered for a married man. And he lingered over pleasant fancies of himself either as editor of a brilliant weekly of opinion, an American Mercure de France, or as scintillant producer of satiric comedy and Parisian musical revue. However, the approaches to these latter guilds seemed to be guarded by professional secrets. Men drifted into them by the devious highways of writing and acting. It was palpably impossible to get on a magazine unless you had been on one before.

So in the end he entered, by way of his grandfather's letter, that Sanctum Americanum where sat the president of Wilson, Hiemer and Hardy at his "cleared desk," and issued therefrom employed. He was to begin work on the twenty-third of February.

In tribute to the momentous occasion this two-day revel had been planned, since, he said, after he began working he'd have to get to bed early during the week. Maury Noble had arrived from Philadelphia on a trip that had to do with seeing some man in Wall Street (whom, incidentally, he failed to see), and Richard Caramel had been half persuaded, half tricked into joining them. They had condescended to a wet and fashionable wedding on Monday afternoon, and in the evening had occurred the dénouement: Gloria, going beyond her accustomed limit of four precisely timed cocktails, led them on as gay and joyous a bacchanal as they had ever known, disclosing an astonishing knowledge of ballet steps, and singing songs which she confessed had been taught her by her cook when she was innocent and seventeen. She repeated these by request at intervals throughout the evening with such frank conviviality that Anthony, far from being annoyed, was gratified at this fresh source of entertainment. The occasion was memorable in other ways—a long conversation between Maury and a defunct crab, which he was dragging around on the end of a string, as to whether the crab was fully conversant with the applications of the binomial theorem, and the aforementioned race in two hansom cabs with the sedate and impressive shadows of Fifth Avenue for audience, ending in a labyrinthine escape into the darkness of Central Park. Finally Anthony and Gloria had paid a call on some wild young married people—the Lacys—and collapsed in the empty milk bottles.

Morning now—theirs to add up the checks cashed here and there in clubs, stores, restaurants. Theirs to air the dank staleness of wine and cigarettes out of the tall blue front room, to pick up the broken glass and brush at the stained fabric of chairs and sofas; to give Bounds suits and dresses for the cleaners; finally, to take their smothery half-feverish bodies and faded depressed spirits out into the chill air of February, that life might go on and Wilson, Hiemer and Hardy obtain the services of a vigorous man at nine next morning.

"Do you remember," called Anthony from the bathroom, "when Maury got out at the corner of One Hundred and Tenth Street and acted as a traffic cop, beckoning cars forward and motioning them back? They must have thought he was a private detective."

After each reminiscence they both laughed inordinately, their overwrought nerves responding as acutely and janglingly to mirth as to depression.

Gloria at the mirror was wondering at the splendid color and freshness of her face—it seemed that she had never looked so well, though her stomach hurt her and her head was aching furiously.

The day passed slowly. Anthony, riding in a taxi to his broker's to borrow money on a bond, found that he had only two dollars in his pocket. The fare would cost all of that, but he felt that on this particular afternoon he could not have endured the subway. When the taximetre reached his limit he must get out and walk.

With this his mind drifted off into one of its characteristic day-dreams. . . . In this dream he discovered that the metre was going too fast—the driver had dishonestly adjusted it. Calmly he reached his destination and then nonchalantly handed the man what he justly owed him. The man showed fight, but almost before his hands were up Anthony had knocked him down with one terrific blow. And when he rose Anthony quickly sidestepped and floored him definitely with a crack in the temple.

. . . He was in court now. The judge had fined him five dollars and he had no money. Would the court take his check? Ah, but the court did not know him. Well, he could identify himself by having them call his apartment.

. . . They did so. Yes, it was Mrs. Anthony Patch speaking—but how did she know that this man was her husband? How could she know? Let the police sergeant ask her if she remembered the milk bottles . . .

He leaned forward hurriedly and tapped at the glass. The taxi was only at Brooklyn Bridge, but the metre showed a dollar and eighty cents, and Anthony would never have omitted the ten per cent tip.

Later in the afternoon he returned to the apartment. Gloria had also been out—shopping—and was asleep, curled in a corner of the sofa with her purchase locked securely in her arms. Her face was as untroubled as a little girl's, and the bundle that she pressed tightly to her bosom was a child's doll, a profound and infinitely healing balm to her disturbed and childish heart.

DESTINY

It was with this party, more especially with Gloria's part in it, that a decided change began to come over their way of living. The magnificent attitude of not giving a damn altered overnight; from being a mere tenet of Gloria's it became the entire solace and justification for what they chose to do and what consequence it brought. Not to be sorry, not to loose one cry of regret, to live according to a clear code of honor toward each other, and to seek the moment's happiness as fervently and persistently as possible.

"No one cares about us but ourselves, Anthony," she said one day. "It'd be ridiculous for me to go about pretending I felt any obligations toward the world, and as for worrying what people think about me, I simply *don't*, that's all. Since I was a little girl in dancing-school I've been criticised by the mothers of all the little girls who weren't as popular as I was, and I've always looked on criticism as a sort of envious tribute."

This was because of a party in the "Boul' Mich'" one night, where Constance Merriam had seen her as one of a highly stimulated party of four. Constance Merriam, "as an old school friend," had gone to the trouble of inviting her to lunch next day in order to inform her how terrible it was.

"I told her I couldn't see it," Gloria told Anthony. "Eric Merriam is a sort of sublimated Percy Wolcott—you remember that man in Hot Springs I told you about—his idea of respecting Constance is to leave her at home with her sewing and her baby and her book, and such innocuous amusements, whenever he's going on a party that promises to be anything but deathly dull."

"Did you tell her that?"

"I certainly did. And I told her that what she really objected to was that I was having a better time than she was."

Anthony applauded her. He was tremendously proud of Gloria, proud that she never failed to eclipse whatever other women might be in the party, proud that men were always glad to revel with her in great rowdy groups, without any attempt to do more than enjoy her beauty and the warmth of her vitality.

These "parties" gradually became their chief source of entertainment. Still in love, still enormously interested in each other, they yet found as spring drew near that staying at home in the evening palled on them; books were unreal; the old magic of being alone had long since vanished—instead they preferred to be bored by a stupid musical comedy, or to go to dinner with the most uninteresting of their acquaintances, so long as there would be enough cocktails to keep the conversation from becoming utterly intolerable. A scattering of younger married people who had been their friends in school or college, as well as a varied assortment of single men, began to think instinctively of them whenever color and excitement were needed, so there was scarcely a day without its phone call, its "Wondered what you were doing this evening." Wives, as a rule, were afraid of Gloria—her facile attainment of the centre of the stage, her innocent but nevertheless disturbing way of becoming a favorite with husbands—these things drove them instinctively into an attitude of profound distrust, heightened by the fact that Gloria was largely unresponsive to any intimacy shown her by a woman.

On the appointed Wednesday in February Anthony had gone to the imposing offices of Wilson, Hiemer and Hardy and listened to many vague instructions delivered by an energetic young man of about his own age, named Kahler, who wore a defiant yellow pompadour, and in announcing himself as an assistant secretary gave the impression that it was a tribute to exceptional ability.

"There's two kinds of men here, you'll find," he said. "There's the man who gets to be an assistant secretary or treasurer, gets his name on our folder here, before he's thirty, and there's the man who gets his name there at forty-five. The man who gets his name there at forty-five stays there the rest of his life."

"How about the man who gets it there at thirty?" inquired Anthony politely.

"Why, he gets up here, you see." He pointed to a list of assistant vice-presidents upon the folder. "Or maybe he gets to be president or secretary or treasurer."

"And what about these over here?"

"Those? Oh, those are the trustees—the men with capital."

"I see."

"Now some people," continued Kahler, "think that whether a man gets started early or late depends on whether he's got a college education. But they're wrong."

"I see."

"I had one; I was Buckleigh, class of nineteen-eleven, but when I came down to the Street I soon found that the things that would help me here weren't the fancy things I learned in college. In fact, I had to get a lot of fancy stuff out of my head."

Anthony could not help wondering what possible "fancy stuff" he had learned at Buckleigh in nineteen-eleven. An

irrepressible idea that it was some sort of needlework recurred
to him throughout the rest of the conversation.

"See that fellow over there?" Kahler pointed to a
youngish-looking man with handsome gray hair, sitting at a
desk inside a mahogany railing. "That's Mr. Ellinger, the first
vice-president. Been everywhere, seen everything; got a fine
education."

In vain did Anthony try to open his mind to the romance
of finance; he could think of Mr. Ellinger only as one of the
buyers of the handsome leather sets of Thackeray, Balzac,
Hugo, and Gibbon that lined the walls of the big bookstores.

Through the damp and uninspiring month of March he
was prepared for salesmanship. Lacking enthusiasm he was
capable of viewing the turmoil and bustle that surrounded
him only as a fruitless circumambient striving toward an
incomprehensible goal, tangibly evidenced only by the rival
mansions of Mr. Frick and Mr. Carnegie on Fifth Avenue.
That these portentous vice-presidents and trustees should be
actually the fathers of the "best men" he had known at
Harvard seemed to him incongruous.

He ate in an employees' lunch-room up-stairs with an
uneasy suspicion that he was being uplifted, wondering
through that first week if the dozens of young clerks, some
of them alert and immaculate, and just out of college, lived
in flamboyant hope of crowding onto that narrow slip of
cardboard before the catastrophic thirties. The conversation
that interwove with the pattern of the day's work was all
much of a piece. One discussed how Mr. Wilson had made
his money, what method Mr. Hiemer had employed, and the
means resorted to by Mr. Hardy. One related age-old but
eternally breathless anecdotes of the fortunes stumbled on
precipitously in the Street by a "butcher" or a "bartender,"
or "a darn messenger boy, by golly!" and then one talked of
the current gambles, and whether it was best to go out for a
hundred thousand a year or be content with twenty. During

the preceding year one of the assistant secretaries had invested all his savings in Bethlehem Steel. The story of his spectacular magnificence, of his haughty resignation in January, and of the triumphal palace he was now building in California, was the favorite office subject. The man's very name had acquired a magic significance, symbolizing as he did the aspirations of all good Americans. Anecdotes were told about him—how one of the vice-presidents had advised him to sell, by golly, but he had hung on, even bought on margin, "and *now* look where he is!"

Such, obviously, was the stuff of life—a dizzy triumph dazzling the eyes of all of them, a gypsy siren to content them with meagre wage and with the arithmetical improbability of their eventual success.

To Anthony the notion became appalling. He felt that to succeed here the idea of success must grasp and limit his mind. It seemed to him that the essential element in these men at the top was their faith that their affairs were the very core of life. All other things being equal, self-assurance and opportunism won out over technical knowledge; it was obvious that the more expert work went on near the bottom—so, with appropriate efficiency, the technical experts were kept there.

His determination to stay in at night during the week did not survive, and a good half of the time he came to work with a splitting, sickish headache and the crowded horror of the morning subway ringing in his ears like an echo of hell.

Then, abruptly, he quit. He had remained in bed all one Monday, and late in the evening, overcome by one of those attacks of moody despair to which he periodically succumbed, he wrote and mailed a letter to Mr. Wilson, confessing that he considered himself ill adapted to the work. Gloria, coming in from the theatre with Richard Caramel, found him on the lounge, silently staring at the high ceiling, more depressed and discouraged than he had been at any time since their marriage.

She wanted him to whine. If he had she would have reproached him bitterly, for she was not a little annoyed, but he only lay there so utterly miserable that she felt sorry for him, and kneeling down she stroked his head, saying how little it mattered, how little anything mattered so long as they loved each other. It was like their first year, and Anthony, reacting to her cool hand, to her voice that was soft as breath itself upon his ear, became almost cheerful, and talked with her of his future plans. He even regretted, silently, before he went to bed that he had so hastily mailed his resignation.

"Even when everything seems rotten you can't trust that judgment," Gloria had said. "It's the sum of all your judgments that counts."

In mid-April came a letter from the real-estate agent in Marietta, encouraging them to take the gray house for another year at a slightly increased rental, and enclosing a lease made out for their signatures. For a week lease and letter lay carelessly neglected on Anthony's desk. They had no intention of returning to Marietta. They were weary of the place, and had been bored most of the preceding summer. Besides, their car had deteriorated to a rattling mass of hypochondriacal metal, and a new one was financially inadvisable.

But because of another wild revel, enduring through four days and participated in, at one time or another, by more than a dozen people, they did sign the lease; to their utter horror they signed it and sent it, and immediately it seemed as though they heard the gray house, drably malevolent at last, licking its white chops and waiting to devour them.

"Anthony, where's that lease?" she called in high alarm one Sunday morning, sick and sober to reality. "Where did you leave it? It was here!"

Then she knew where it was. She remembered the house party they had planned on the crest of their exuberance; she remembered a room full of men to whose less exhilarated moments she and Anthony were of no importance, and Anthony's boast of the transcendent merit and seclusion of the gray house, that it was so isolated that it didn't matter how much noise went on there. Then Dick, who had visited them, cried enthusiastically that it was the best little house imaginable, and that they were idiotic not to take it for another summer. It had been easy to work themselves up to a sense of how hot and deserted the city was getting, of how cool and ambrosial were the charms of Marietta. Anthony had picked up the lease and waved it wildly, found Gloria happily acquiescent, and with one last burst of garrulous decision during which all the men agreed with solemn handshakes that they would come out for a visit . . .

"Anthony," she cried, "we've signed and sent it!"

"What?"

"The lease!"

"What the devil!"

"Oh, *An*thony!" There was utter misery in her voice. For the summer, for eternity, they had built themselves a prison. It seemed to strike at the last roots of their stability. Anthony thought they might arrange it with the real-estate agent. They could no longer afford the double rent, and going to Marietta meant giving up his apartment, his reproachless apartment with the exquisite bath and the rooms for which he had bought his furniture and hangings—it was the closest to a home that he had ever had—familiar with memories of four colorful years.

But it was not arranged with the real-estate agent, nor was it arranged at all. Dispiritedly, without even any talk of making the best of it, without even Gloria's all-sufficing "I don't care," they went back to the house that they now knew heeded neither youth nor love—only those austere and incommunicable memories that they could never share.

F. SCOTT FITZGERALD

THE SINISTER SUMMER

There was a horror in the house that summer. It came with them and settled itself over the place like a sombre pall, pervasive through the lower rooms, gradually spreading and climbing up the narrow stairs until it oppressed their very sleep. Anthony and Gloria grew to hate being there alone. Her bedroom, which had seemed so pink and young and delicate, appropriate to her pastel-shaded lingerie tossed here and there on chair and bed, seemed now to whisper with its rustling curtains:

"Ah, my beautiful young lady, yours is not the first daintiness and delicacy that has faded here under the summer suns . . . generations of unloved women have adorned themselves by that glass for rustic lovers who paid no heed. . . . Youth has come into this room in palest blue and left it in the gray cerements of despair, and through long nights many girls have lain awake where that bed stands pouring out waves of misery into the darkness."

Gloria finally tumbled all her clothes and unguents ingloriously out of it, declaring that she had come to live with Anthony, and making the excuse that one of her screens was rotten and admitted bugs. So her room was abandoned to insensitive guests, and they dressed and slept in her husband's chamber, which Gloria considered somehow "good," as though Anthony's presence there had acted as exterminator of any uneasy shadows of the past that might have hovered about its walls.

The distinction between "good" and "bad," ordered early and summarily out of both their lives, had been reinstated in another form. Gloria insisted that any one invited to the gray house must be "good," which, in the case of a girl, meant that she must be either simple and reproachless or, if otherwise, must possess a certain solidity and strength. Always intensely sceptical of her sex, her judgments were now concerned with the question of whether women were or were not clean. By uncleanliness she meant a variety of things, a lack of pride, a slackness in fiber and, most of all, the unmistakable aura of promiscuity.

"Women soil easily," she said, "far more easily than men. Unless a girl's very young and brave it's almost impossible for her to go down-hill without a certain hysterical animality, the cunning, dirty sort of animality. A man's different—and I suppose that's why one of the commonest characters of romance is a man going gallantly to the devil."

She was disposed to like many men, preferably those who gave her frank homage and unfailing entertainment—but often with a flash of insight she told Anthony that some one of his friends was merely using him, and consequently had best be left alone. Anthony customarily demurred, insisting that the accused was a "good one," but he found that his judgment was more fallible than hers, memorably when, as it happened on several occasions, he was left with a succession of restaurant checks for which to render a solitary account.

More from their fear of solitude than from any desire to go through the fuss and bother of entertaining, they filled the house with guests every week-end, and often on through the week. The week-end parties were much the same. When the three or four men invited had arrived, drinking was more or less in order, followed by a hilarious dinner and a ride to the Cradle Beach Country Club, which they had joined because it was inexpensive, lively if not fashionable, and almost a necessity for just such occasions as these. Moreover, it was of no great moment what one did there, and so long as the Patch party were reasonably inaudible, it mattered little whether or not the social dictators of Cradle Beach saw the gay Gloria imbibing cocktails in the supper room at frequent intervals during the evening.

Saturday ended, generally, in a glamourous confusion—it proving often necessary to assist a muddled guest to bed.

Sunday brought the New York papers and a quiet morning of recuperating on the porch—and Sunday afternoon meant good-by to the one or two guests who must return to the city, and a great revival of drinking among the one or two who remained until next day, concluding in a convivial if not hilarious evening.

The faithful Tana, pedagogue by nature and man of all work by profession, had returned with them. Among their more frequent guests a tradition had sprung up about him. Maury Noble remarked one afternoon that his real name was Tannenbaum, and that he was a German agent kept in this country to disseminate Teutonic propaganda through Westchester County, and, after that, mysterious letters began to arrive from Philadelphia addressed to the bewildered Oriental as "Lt. Emile Tannenbaum," containing a few cryptic messages signed "General Staff," and adorned with an atmospheric double column of facetious Japanese. Anthony always handed them to Tana without a smile; hours afterward the recipient could be found puzzling over them in the kitchen and declaring earnestly that the perpendicular symbols were not Japanese, nor anything resembling Japanese.

Gloria had taken a strong dislike to the man ever since the day when, returning unexpectedly from the village, she had discovered him reclining on Anthony's bed, puzzling out a newspaper. It was the instinct of all servants to be fond of Anthony and to detest Gloria, and Tana was no exception to the rule. But he was thoroughly afraid of her and made plain his aversion only in his moodier moments by subtly addressing Anthony with remarks intended for her ear:

"What Miz Pats want dinner?" he would say, looking at his master. Or else he would comment about the bitter selfishness of "'Merican peoples" in such manner that there was no doubt who were the "peoples" referred to.

But they dared not dismiss him. Such a step would have been abhorrent to their inertia. They endured Tana as they endured ill weather and sickness of the body and the estimable Will of God—as they endured all things, even themselves.

IN DARKNESS

One sultry afternoon late in July Richard Caramel telephoned from New York that he and Maury were coming out, bringing a friend with them. They arrived about five, a little drunk, accompanied by a small, stocky man of thirty-five, whom they introduced as Mr. Joe Hull, one of the best fellows that Anthony and Gloria had ever met.

Joe Hull had a yellow beard continually fighting through his skin and a low voice which varied between basso profundo and a husky whisper. Anthony, carrying Maury's suitcase up-stairs, followed into the room and carefully closed the door.

"Who is this fellow?" he demanded.

Maury chuckled enthusiastically.

"Who, Hull? Oh, *he's* all right. He's a good one."

"Yes, but who is he?"

"Hull? He's just a good fellow. He's a prince." His laughter redoubled, culminating in a succession of pleasant catlike grins. Anthony hesitated between a smile and a frown.

"He looks sort of funny to me. Weird-looking clothes"— he paused—"I've got a sneaking suspicion you two picked him up somewhere last night."

"Ridiculous," declared Maury. "Why, I've known him all my life." However, as he capped this statement with another series of chuckles, Anthony was impelled to remark: "The devil you have!"

Later, just before dinner, while Maury and Dick were conversing uproariously, with Joe Hull listening in silence as he sipped his drink, Gloria drew Anthony into the dining room:

"I don't like this man Hull," she said. "I wish he'd use Tana's bathtub."

"I can't very well ask him to."

"Well, I don't want him in ours."

"He seems to be a simple soul."

"He's got on white shoes that look like gloves. I can see his toes right through them. Uh! Who is he, anyway?"

"You've got me."

"Well, I think they've got their nerve to bring him out here. This isn't a Sailor's Rescue Home!"

"They were tight when they phoned. Maury said they've been on a party since yesterday afternoon."

Gloria shook her head angrily, and saying no more returned to the porch. Anthony saw that she was trying to forget her uncertainty and devote herself to enjoying the evening.

It had been a tropical day, and even into late twilight the heat-waves emanating from the dry road were quivering faintly like undulating panes of isinglass. The sky was cloudless, but far beyond the woods in the direction of the Sound a faint and persistent rolling had commenced. When Tana announced dinner the men, at a word from Gloria, remained coatless and went inside.

Maury began a song, which they accomplished in harmony during the first course. It had two lines and was sung to a popular air called Daisy Dear. The lines were:

"The—pan-ic—has—come—over us, So *ha-a-as*—the moral decline!"

Each rendition was greeted with bursts of enthusiasm and prolonged applause.

"Cheer up, Gloria!" suggested Maury. "You seem the least bit depressed."

"I'm not," she lied.

"Here, Tannenbaum!" he called over his shoulder. "I've filled you a drink. Come on!"

Gloria tried to stay his arm.

"Please don't, Maury!"

"Why not? Maybe he'll play the flute for us after dinner. Here, Tana."

Tana, grinning, bore the glass away to the kitchen. In a few moments Maury gave him another.

"Cheer up, Gloria!" he cried. "For Heaven's sakes everybody, cheer up Gloria."

"Dearest, have another drink," counselled Anthony.

"Do, please!"

"Cheer up, Gloria," said Joe Hull easily.

Gloria winced at this uncalled-for use of her first name, and glanced around to see if any one else had noticed it. The word coming so glibly from the lips of a man to whom she had taken an inordinate dislike repelled her. A moment later she noticed that Joe Hull had given Tana another drink, and her anger increased, heightened somewhat from the effects of the alcohol.

"—and once," Maury was saying, "Peter Granby and I went into a Turkish bath in Boston, about two o'clock at night. There was no one there but the proprietor, and we jammed him into a closet and locked the door. Then a fella came in and wanted a Turkish bath. Thought we were the rubbers, by golly! Well, we just picked him up and tossed him into the pool with all his clothes on. Then we dragged him out and laid him on a slab and slapped him until he was black and blue. 'Not so rough, fellows!' he'd say in a little squeaky voice, 'please! . . .'"

—Was this Maury? thought Gloria. From any one else the story would have amused her, but from Maury, the infinitely appreciative, the apotheosis of tact and consideration. . . .

"The—pan-ic—has—come—over us, So *ha-a-as—*"

A drum of thunder from outside drowned out the rest of the song; Gloria shivered and tried to empty her glass, but the first taste nauseated her, and she set it down. Dinner was over and they all marched into the big room, bearing several bottles and decanters. Some one had closed the porch door to keep out the wind, and in consequence circular tentacles of cigar smoke were twisting already upon the heavy air.

"Paging Lieutenant Tannenbaum!" Again it was the changeling Maury. "Bring us the flute!"

Anthony and Maury rushed into the kitchen; Richard Caramel started the phonograph and approached Gloria.

"Dance with your well-known cousin."

"I don't want to dance."

"Then I'm going to carry you around."

As though he were doing something of overpowering importance, he picked her up in his fat little arms and started trotting gravely about the room.

"Set me down, Dick! I'm dizzy!" she insisted.

He dumped her in a bouncing bundle on the couch, and rushed off to the kitchen, shouting "Tana! Tana!"

Then, without warning, she felt other arms around her, felt herself lifted from the lounge. Joe Hull had picked her up and was trying, drunkenly, to imitate Dick.

"Put me down!" she said sharply.

His maudlin laugh, and the sight of that prickly yellow jaw close to her face stirred her to intolerable disgust.

"At once!"

"The—pan-ic—" he began, but got no further, for Gloria's hand swung around swiftly and caught him in the cheek. At this he all at once let go of her, and she fell to the floor, her shoulder hitting the table a glancing blow in transit. . . .

Then the room seemed full of men and smoke. There was Tana in his white coat reeling about supported by Maury. Into his flute he was blowing a weird blend of sound that was known, cried Anthony, as the Japanese train-song. Joe Hull had found a box of candles and was juggling them, yelling "One down!" every time he missed, and Dick was dancing by himself in a fascinated whirl around and about the room. It appeared to her that everything in the room was staggering in grotesque fourth-dimensional gyrations through intersecting planes of hazy blue.

Outside, the storm had come up amazingly—the lulls within were filled with the scrape of the tall bushes against the house and the roaring of the rain on the tin roof of the kitchen. The lightning was interminable, letting down thick drips of thunder like pig iron from the heart of a white-hot furnace. Gloria could see that the rain was spitting in at three of the windows—but she could not move to shut them. . . .

. . . She was in the hall. She had said good night but no one had heard or heeded her. It seemed for an instant as though something had looked down over the head of the banister, but she could not have gone back into the living room—better madness than the madness of that clamor. . . . Up-stairs she fumbled for the electric switch and missed it in the darkness; a roomful of lightning showed her the button plainly on the wall. But when the impenetrable black shut down, it again eluded her fumbling fingers, so she slipped off her dress and petticoat and threw herself weakly on the dry side of the half-drenched bed.

She shut her eyes. From down-stairs arose the babel of the drinkers, punctured suddenly by a tinkling shiver of broken glass, and then another, and by a soaring fragment of unsteady, irregular song. . . .

She lay there for something over two hours—so she calculated afterward, sheerly by piecing together the bits of time. She was conscious, even aware, after a long while that the noise down-stairs had lessened, and that the storm was moving off westward, throwing back lingering showers of sound that fell, heavy and lifeless as her soul, into the soggy fields. This was succeeded by a slow, reluctant scattering of the rain and wind, until there was nothing outside her windows but a gentle dripping and the swishing play of a cluster of wet vine against the sill. She was in a state half-way between sleeping and waking, with neither condition predominant . . . and she was harassed by a desire to rid herself of a weight pressing down upon her breast. She felt that if she could cry the weight would be lifted, and forcing the lids of her eyes together she tried to raise a lump in her throat . . . to no avail. . . .

Drip! Drip! Drip! The sound was not unpleasant—like spring, like a cool rain of her childhood, that made cheerful mud in her back yard and watered the tiny garden she had dug with miniature rake and spade and hoe. Drip—dri-ip! It was like days when the rain came out of yellow skies that melted just before twilight and shot one radiant shaft of sunlight diagonally down the heavens into the damp green trees. So cool, so clear and clean—and her mother there at the centre of the world, at the centre of the rain, safe and dry and strong. She wanted her mother now, and her mother was dead, beyond sight and touch forever. And this weight was pressing on her, pressing on her—oh, it pressed on her so!

She became rigid. Some one had come to the door and was standing regarding her, very quiet except for a slight swaying motion. She could see the outline of his figure distinct against some indistinguishable light. There was no sound anywhere, only a great persuasive silence—even the dripping had ceased . . . only this figure, swaying, swaying in the doorway, an indiscernible and subtly menacing terror, a personality filthy under its varnish, like smallpox spots under a layer of powder. Yet her tired heart, beating until it shook her breasts, made her sure that there was still life in her, desperately shaken, threatened. . . .

The minute or succession of minutes prolonged itself interminably, and a swimming blur began to form before her eyes, which tried with childish persistence to pierce the gloom in the direction of the door. In another instant it seemed that some unimaginable force would shatter her out of existence . . . and then the figure in the doorway—it was Hull, she saw,

Hull—turned deliberately and, still slightly swaying, moved back and off, as if absorbed into that incomprehensible light that had given him dimension.

Blood rushed back into her limbs, blood and life together. With a start of energy she sat upright, shifting her body until her feet touched the floor over the side of the bed. She knew what she must do—now, now, before it was too late. She must go out into this cool damp, out, away, to feel the wet swish of the grass around her feet and the fresh moisture on her forehead. Mechanically she struggled into her clothes, groping in the dark of the closet for a hat. She must go from this house where the thing hovered that pressed upon her bosom, or else made itself into stray, swaying figures in the gloom.

In a panic she fumbled clumsily at her coat, found the sleeve just as she heard Anthony's footsteps on the lower stair. She dared not wait; he might not let her go, and even Anthony was part of this weight, part of this evil house and the sombre darkness that was growing up about it. . . .

Through the hall then . . . and down the back stairs, hearing Anthony's voice in the bedroom she had just left—

"Gloria! Gloria!"

But she had reached the kitchen now, passed out through the doorway into the night. A hundred drops, startled by a flare of wind from a dripping tree, scattered on her and she pressed them gladly to her face with hot hands.

"Gloria! Gloria!"

The voice was infinitely remote, muffled and made plaintive by the walls she had just left. She rounded the house and started down the front path toward the road, almost exultant as she turned into it, and followed the carpet of short grass alongside, moving with caution in the intense darkness.

"Gloria!"

She broke into a run, stumbled over the segment of a branch twisted off by the wind. The voice was outside the house now. Anthony, finding the bedroom deserted, had come onto the porch. But this thing was driving her forward; it was back there with Anthony, and she must go on in her flight under this dim and oppressive heaven, forcing herself through the silence ahead as though it were a tangible barrier before her.

She had gone some distance along the barely discernible road, probably half a mile, passed a single deserted barn that loomed up, black and foreboding, the only building of any sort between the gray house and Marietta; then she turned the fork, where the road entered the wood and ran between two high walls of leaves and branches that nearly touched overhead. She noticed suddenly a thin, longitudinal gleam of silver upon the road before her, like a bright sword half embedded in the mud. As she came closer she gave a little cry of satisfaction—it was a wagon-rut full of water, and glancing heavenward she saw a light rift of sky and knew that the moon was out.

"Gloria!"

She started violently. Anthony was not two hundred feet behind her.

"Gloria, wait for me!"

She shut her lips tightly to keep from screaming, and increased her gait. Before she had gone another hundred yards the woods disappeared, rolling back like a dark stocking from the leg of the road. Three minutes' walk ahead of her, suspended in the now high and limitless air, she saw a thin interlacing of attenuated gleams and glitters, centred in a regular undulation on some one invisible point. Abruptly she knew where she would go. That was the great cascade of wires that rose high over the river, like the legs of a gigantic spider whose eye was the little green light in the switch-house, and ran with the railroad bridge in the direction of the station. The station! There would be the train to take her away.

"Gloria, it's me! It's Anthony! Gloria, I won't try to stop you! For God's sake, where are you?"

She made no answer but began to run, keeping on the high side of the road and leaping the gleaming puddles—dimensionless pools of thin, unsubstantial gold. Turning sharply to the left, she followed a narrow wagon road, serving to avoid a dark body on the ground. She looked up as an owl hooted mournfully from a solitary tree. Just ahead of her she could see the trestle that led to the railroad bridge and the steps mounting up to it. The station lay across the river.

Another sounds startled her, the melancholy siren of an approaching train, and almost simultaneously, a repeated call, thin now and far away.

"Gloria! Gloria!"

Anthony must have followed the main road. She laughed with a sort of malicious cunning at having eluded him; she could spare the time to wait until the train went by.

The siren soared again, closer at hand, and then, with no anticipatory roar and clamor, a dark and sinuous body curved into view against the shadows far down the high-banked track, and with no sound but the rush of the cleft wind and the clocklike tick of the rails, moved toward the bridge—it was an electric train. Above the engine two vivid blurs of blue light formed incessantly a radiant crackling bar between them, which, like a spluttering flame in a lamp beside a corpse, lit for an instant the successive rows of trees and caused Gloria to draw back instinctively to the far side of the road. The light was tepid, the temperature of warm blood. . . . The clicking blended suddenly with itself in a rush of even sound, and then, elongating in sombre elasticity, the thing roared blindly by her and thundered onto the bridge, racing the lurid shaft of fire it cast into the solemn river alongside. Then it contracted swiftly, sucking in its sound until it left only a reverberant echo, which died upon the farther bank.

Silence crept down again over the wet country; the faint dripping resumed, and suddenly a great shower of drops tumbled upon Gloria stirring her out of the trance-like torpor

F. SCOTT FITZGERALD

which the passage of the train had wrought. She ran swiftly down a descending level to the bank and began climbing the iron stairway to the bridge, remembering that it was something she had always wanted to do, and that she would have the added excitement of traversing the yard-wide plank that ran beside the tracks over the river.

There! This was better. She was at the top now and could see the lands about her as successive sweeps of open country, cold under the moon, coarsely patched and seamed with thin rows and heavy clumps of trees. To her right, half a mile down the river, which trailed away behind the light like the shiny, slimy path of a snail, winked the scattered lights of Marietta. Not two hundred yards away at the end of the bridge squatted the station, marked by a sullen lantern. The oppression was lifted now—the tree-tops below her were rocking the young starlight to a haunted doze. She stretched out her arms with a gesture of freedom. This was what she had wanted, to stand alone where it was high and cool.

"Gloria!"

Like a startled child she scurried along the plank, hopping, skipping, jumping, with an ecstatic sense of her own physical lightness. Let him come now—she no longer feared that, only she must first reach the station, because that was part of the game. She was happy. Her hat, snatched off, was clutched tightly in her hand, and her short curled hair bobbed up and down about her ears. She had thought she would never feel so young again, but this was her night, her world. Triumphantly she laughed as she left the plank, and reaching the wooden platform flung herself down happily beside an iron roof-post.

"Here I am!" she called, gay as the dawn in her elation. "Here I am, Anthony, dear—old, worried Anthony."

"Gloria!" He reached the platform, ran toward her. "Are you all right?" Coming up he knelt and took her in his arms.

"Yes."

"What was the matter? Why did you leave?" he queried anxiously.

"I had to—there was something"—she paused and a flicker of uneasiness lashed at her mind—"there was something sitting on me—here." She put her hand on her breast. "I had to go out and get away from it."

"What do you mean by 'something'?"

"I don't know—that man Hull—"

"Did he bother you?"

"He came to my door, drunk. I think I'd gotten sort of crazy by that time."

"Gloria, dearest—"

Wearily she laid her head upon his shoulder.

"Let's go back," he suggested.

She shivered.

"Uh! No, I couldn't. It'd come and sit on me again." Her voice rose to a cry that hung plaintive on the darkness. "That thing—"

"There—there," he soothed her, pulling her close to him. "We won't do anything you don't want to do. What do you want to do? Just sit here?"

"I want—I want to go away."

"Where?"

"Oh—anywhere."

"By golly, Gloria," he cried, "you're still tight!"

"No, I'm not. I haven't been, all evening. I went up-stairs about, oh, I don't know, about half an hour after dinner . . . Ouch!"

He had inadvertently touched her right shoulder.

"It hurts me. I hurt it some way. I don't know—somebody picked me up and dropped me."

"Gloria, come home. It's late and damp."

"I can't," she wailed. "Oh, Anthony, don't ask me to! I will to-morrow. You go home and I'll wait here for a train. I'll go to a hotel—"

"I'll go with you."

"No, I don't want you with me. I want to be alone. I want to sleep—oh, I want to sleep. And then to-morrow, when you've got all the smell of whiskey and cigarettes out of the house, and everything straight, and Hull is gone, then I'll come home. If I went now, that thing—oh—!" She covered her eyes with her hand; Anthony saw the futility of trying to persuade her.

"I was all sober when you left," he said. "Dick was asleep on the lounge and Maury and I were having a discussion. That fellow Hull had wandered off somewhere. Then I began to realize I hadn't seen you for several hours, so I went up-stairs—"

He broke off as a salutatory "Hello, there!" boomed suddenly out of the darkness. Gloria sprang to her feet and he did likewise.

"It's Maury's voice," she cried excitedly. "If it's Hull with him, keep them away, keep them away!"

"Who's there?" Anthony called.

"Just Dick and Maury," returned two voices reassuringly.

"Where's Hull?"

"He's in bed. Passed out."

Their figures appeared dimly on the platform.

"What the devil are you and Gloria doing here?" inquired Richard Caramel with sleepy bewilderment.

"What are *you* two doing here?"

Maury laughed.

"Damned if I know. We followed you, and had the deuce of a time doing it. I heard you out on the porch yelling for Gloria, so I woke up the Caramel here and got it through his head, with some difficulty, that if there was a search-party we'd better be on it. He slowed me up by sitting down in the road at intervals and asking me what it was all about. We tracked you by the pleasant scent of Canadian Club."

There was a rattle of nervous laughter under the low train-shed.

"How did you track us, really?"

"Well, we followed along down the road and then we suddenly lost you. Seems you turned off at a wagontrail. After a while somebody hailed us and asked us if we were looking for a young girl. Well, we came up and found it was a little shivering old man, sitting on a fallen tree like somebody in a fairy tale. 'She turned down here,' he said, 'and most steppud on me, goin' somewhere in an awful hustle, and then a fella in short golfin' pants come runnin' along and went after her. He throwed me this.' The old fellow had a dollar bill he was waving around—"

"Oh, the poor old man!" ejaculated Gloria, moved.

"I threw him another and we went on, though he asked us to stay and tell him what it was all about."

"Poor old man," repeated Gloria dismally.

Dick sat down sleepily on a box.

"And now what?" he inquired in the tone of stoic resignation.

"Gloria's upset," explained Anthony. "She and I are going to the city by the next train."

Maury in the darkness had pulled a time-table from his pocket.

"Strike a match."

A tiny flare leaped out of the opaque background illuminating the four faces, grotesque and unfamiliar here in the open night.

"Let's see. Two, two-thirty—no, that's evening. By gad, you won't get a train till five-thirty."

Anthony hesitated.

"Well," he muttered uncertainly, "we've decided to stay here and wait for it. You two might as well go back and sleep."

"You go, too, Anthony," urged Gloria; "I want you to have some sleep, dear. You've been as pale as a ghost all day."

"Why, you little idiot!"

Dick yawned.

"Very well. You stay, we stay."

He walked out from under the shed and surveyed the heavens.

"Rather a nice night, after all. Stars are out and everything. Exceptionally tasty assortment of them."

"Let's see." Gloria moved after him and the other two followed her. "Let's sit out here," she suggested. "I like it much better."

Anthony and Dick converted a long box into a backrest and found a board dry enough for Gloria to sit on. Anthony dropped down beside her and with some effort Dick hoisted himself onto an apple-barrel near them.

"Tana went to sleep in the porch hammock," he remarked. "We carried him in and left him next to the kitchen stove to dry. He was drenched to the skin."

"That awful little man!" sighed Gloria.

"How do you do!" The voice, sonorous and funereal, had come from above, and they looked up startled to find that in some manner Maury had climbed to the roof of the shed, where he sat dangling his feet over the edge, outlined as a shadowy and fantastic gargoyle against the now brilliant sky.

"It must be for such occasions as this," he began softly, his words having the effect of floating down from an immense height and settling softly upon his auditors, "that the righteous of the land decorate the railroads with bill-boards asserting in red and yellow that 'Jesus Christ is God,' placing them, appropriately enough, next to announcements that 'Gunter's Whiskey is Good.'"

There was gentle laughter and the three below kept their heads tilted upward.

"I think I shall tell you the story of my education," continued Maury, "under these sardonic constellations."

"Do! Please!"

"Shall I, really?"

They waited expectantly while he directed a ruminative yawn toward the white smiling moon.

"Well," he began, "as an infant I prayed. I stored up prayers against future wickedness. One year I stored up nineteen hundred 'Now I lay me's.'"

"Throw down a cigarette," murmured some one.

A small package reached the platform simultaneously with the stentorian command:

"Silence! I am about to unburden myself of many memorable remarks reserved for the darkness of such earths and the brilliance of such skies."

Below, a lighted match was passed from cigarette to cigarette. The voice resumed:

"I was adept at fooling the deity. I prayed immediately after all crimes until eventually prayer and crime became indistinguishable to me. I believed that because a man cried out 'My God!' when a safe fell on him, it proved that belief was rooted deep in the human breast. Then I went to school. For fourteen years half a hundred earnest men pointed to ancient flint-locks and cried to me: 'There's the real thing. These new rifles are only shallow, superficial imitations.' They damned the books I read and the things I thought by calling them immoral; later the fashion changed, and they damned things by calling them 'clever'.

"And so I turned, canny for my years, from the professors to the poets, listening—to the lyric tenor of Swinburne and the tenor robusto of Shelley, to Shakespeare with his first bass and his fine range, to Tennyson with his second bass and his occasional falsetto, to Milton and Marlow, bassos profundo. I gave ear to Browning chatting, Byron declaiming, and Wordsworth droning. This, at least, did me no harm. I learned a little of beauty—enough to know that it had nothing to do with truth—and I found, moreover, that there was no great literary tradition; there was only the tradition of the eventful death of every literary tradition. . . .

"Then I grew up, and the beauty of succulent illusions fell away from me. The fibre of my mind coarsened and my eyes grew miserably keen. Life rose around my island like a sea, and presently I was swimming.

"The transition was subtle—the thing had lain in wait for me for some time. It has its insidious, seemingly innocuous trap for every one. With me? No—I didn't try to seduce the janitor's wife—nor did I run through the streets unclothed, proclaiming my virility. It is never quite passion that does the business—it is the dress that passion wears. I became bored— that was all. Boredom, which is another name and a frequent disguise for vitality, became the unconscious motive of all my acts. Beauty was behind me, do you understand?—I was grown." He paused. "End of school and college period. Opening of Part Two."

Three quietly active points of light showed the location of his listeners. Gloria was now half sitting, half lying, in Anthony's lap. His arm was around her so tightly that she could hear the beating of his heart. Richard Caramel, perched on the apple-barrel, from time to time stirred and gave off a faint grunt.

"I grew up then, into this land of jazz, and fell immediately into a state of almost audible confusion. Life stood over me like an immoral schoolmistress, editing my ordered thoughts. But, with a mistaken faith in intelligence, I plodded on. I read Smith, who laughed at charity and insisted that the sneer was the highest form of self-expression—but Smith himself replaced charity as an obscurer of the light. I read Jones, who neatly disposed of individualism—and behold! Jones was still in my way. I did not think—I was a battle-ground for the thoughts of many men; rather was I one of those desirable but impotent countries over which the great powers surge back and forth.

"I reached maturity under the impression that I was gathering the experience to order my life for happiness. Indeed, I accomplished the not unusual feat of solving each question in my mind long before it presented itself to me in life—and of being beaten and bewildered just the same.

"But after a few tastes of this latter dish I had had enough. Here! I said, Experience is not worth the getting. It's not a thing that happens pleasantly to a passive you—it's a wall that an active you runs up against. So I wrapped myself in what I thought was my invulnerable scepticism and decided that my education was complete. But it was too late. Protect myself as I might by making no new ties with tragic and predestined humanity, I was lost with the rest. I had traded the fight against love for the fight against loneliness, the fight against life for the fight against death."

He broke off to give emphasis to his last observation— after a moment he yawned and resumed.

"I suppose that the beginning of the second phase of my education was a ghastly dissatisfaction at being used in spite of myself for some inscrutable purpose of whose ultimate goal I was unaware—if, indeed, there *was* an ultimate goal. It was a difficult choice. The schoolmistress seemed to be saying, 'We're going to play football and nothing but football. If you don't want to play football you can't play at all—'

"What was I to do—the playtime was so short!

"You see, I felt that we were even denied what consolation there might have been in being a figment of a corporate man rising from his knees. Do you think that I leaped at this pessimism, grasped it as a sweetly smug superior thing, no more depressing really than, say, a gray autumn day before a fire?—I don't think I did that. I was a great deal too warm for that, and too alive.

"For it seemed to me that there was no ultimate goal for man. Man was beginning a grotesque and bewildered fight with nature—nature, that by the divine and magnificent accident had brought us to where we could fly in her face. She had invented ways to rid the race of the inferior and thus give the remainder strength to fill her higher—or, let us say, her more amusing—though still unconscious and accidental intentions. And, actuated by the highest gifts of the enlightenment, we were seeking to circumvent her. In this republic I saw the black beginning to mingle with the white—in Europe there was taking place an economic catastrophe to save three or four diseased and wretchedly governed races from the one mastery that might organize them for material prosperity.

"We produce a Christ who can raise up the leper—and presently the breed of the leper is the salt of the earth. If any one can find any lesson in that, let him stand forth."

"There's only one lesson to be learned from life, anyway," interrupted Gloria, not in contradiction but in a sort of melancholy agreement.

"What's that?" demanded Maury sharply.

"That there's no lesson to be learned from life."

After a short silence Maury said:

"Young Gloria, the beautiful and merciless lady, first looked at the world with the fundamental sophistication I have struggled to attain, that Anthony never will attain, that Dick will never fully understand."

There was a disgusted groan from the apple-barrel. Anthony, grown accustomed to the dark, could see plainly the flash of Richard Caramel's yellow eye and the look of resentment on his face as he cried:

"You're crazy! By your own statement I should have attained some experience by trying."

"Trying what?" cried Maury fiercely. "Trying to pierce the darkness of political idealism with some wild, despairing urge toward truth? Sitting day after day supine in a rigid chair and infinitely removed from life staring at the tip of a steeple through the trees, trying to separate, definitely and for all time, the knowable from the unknowable? Trying to take a piece of actuality and give it glamour from your own soul to make for that inexpressible quality it possessed in life and lost in transit to paper or canvas? Struggling in a laboratory through weary years for one iota of relative truth in a mass of wheels or a test tube—"

"Have you?"

Maury paused, and in his answer, when it came, there was a measure of weariness, a bitter overnote that lingered for a moment in those three minds before it floated up and off like a bubble bound for the moon.

"Not I," he said softly. "I was born tired—but with the quality of mother wit, the gift of women like Gloria—to that, for all my talking and listening, my waiting in vain for the eternal generality that seems to lie just beyond every argument and every speculation, to that I have added not one jot."

In the distance a deep sound that had been audible for some moments identified itself by a plaintive mooing like that of a gigantic cow and by the pearly spot of a headlight apparent half a mile away. It was a steam-driven train this time, rumbling and groaning, and as it tumbled by with a monstrous complaint it sent a shower of sparks and cinders over the platform.

"Not one jot!" Again Maury's voice dropped down to them as from a great height. "What a feeble thing intelligence is, with its short steps, its waverings, its pacings back and forth, its disastrous retreats! Intelligence is a mere instrument of circumstances. There are people who say that intelligence must have built the universe—why, intelligence never built a steam engine! Circumstances built a steam engine. Intelligence is little more than a short foot-rule by which we measure the infinite achievements of Circumstances.

"I could quote you the philosophy of the hour—but, for all we know, fifty years may see a complete reversal of this abnegation that's absorbing the intellectuals to-day, the triumph of Christ over Anatole France—" He hesitated, and then added: "But all I know—the tremendous importance of myself to me, and the necessity of acknowledging that importance to myself—these things the wise and lovely Gloria was born knowing these things and the painful futility of trying to know anything else.

"Well, I started to tell you of my education, didn't I? But I learned nothing, you see, very little even about myself. And if I had I should die with my lips shut and the guard on my fountain pen—as the wisest men have done since—oh, since the failure of a certain matter—a strange matter, by the way. It concerned some sceptics who thought they were far-sighted, just as you and I. Let me tell you about them by way of an evening prayer before you all drop off to sleep.

"Once upon a time all the men of mind and genius in the world became of one belief—that is to say, of no belief. But it wearied them to think that within a few years after their death many cults and systems and prognostications would be ascribed to them which they had never meditated nor intended. So they said to one another:

"'Let's join together and make a great book that will last forever to mock the credulity of man. Let's persuade our more erotic poets to write about the delights of the flesh, and induce some of our robust journalists to contribute stories of famous amours. We'll include all the most preposterous old wives' tales now current. We'll choose the keenest satirist alive to compile a deity from all the deities worshipped by mankind, a deity who will be more magnificent than any of them, and yet so weakly human that he'll become a byword for laughter the world over—and we'll ascribe to him all sorts of jokes and vanities and rages, in which he'll be supposed to indulge for his own diversion, so that the people will read our book and ponder it, and there'll be no more nonsense in the world.

"'Finally, let us take care that the book possesses all the virtues of style, so that it may last forever as a witness to our profound scepticism and our universal irony.'

"So the men did, and they died.

"But the book lived always, so beautifully had it been written, and so astounding the quality of imagination with which these men of mind and genius had endowed it. They had neglected to give it a name, but after they were dead it became known as the Bible."

When he concluded there was no comment. Some damp languor sleeping on the air of night seemed to have bewitched them all.

"As I said, I started on the story of my education. But my high-balls are dead and the night's almost over, and soon there'll be an awful jabbering going on everywhere, in the trees and the houses, and the two little stores over there behind the station, and there'll be a great running up and down upon the earth for a few hours—Well," he concluded with a laugh, "thank God we four can all pass to our eternal rest knowing we've left the world a little better for having lived in it."

A breeze sprang up, blowing with it faint wisps of life which flattened against the sky.

"Your remarks grow rambling and inconclusive," said Anthony sleepily. "You expected one of those miracles of illumination by which you say your most brilliant and pregnant things in exactly the setting that should provoke the ideal symposium. Meanwhile Gloria has shown her far-sighted detachment by falling asleep—I can tell that by the fact that she has managed to concentrate her entire weight upon my broken body."

"Have I bored you?" inquired Maury, looking down with some concern.

"No, you have disappointed us. You've shot a lot of arrows but did you shoot any birds?"

"I leave the birds to Dick," said Maury hurriedly. "I speak erratically, in disassociated fragments."

"You can get no rise from me," muttered Dick. "My mind is full of any number of material things. I want a warm bath too much to worry about the importance of my work or what proportion of us are pathetic figures."

Dawn made itself felt in a gathering whiteness eastward over the river and an intermittent cheeping in the near-by trees.

"Quarter to five," sighed Dick; "almost another hour to wait. Look! Two gone." He was pointing to Anthony, whose lids had sagged over his eyes. "Sleep of the Patch family—"

But in another five minutes, despite the amplifying cheeps and chirrups, his own head had fallen forward, nodded down twice, thrice. . . .

Only Maury Noble remained awake, seated upon the station roof, his eyes wide open and fixed with fatigued intensity upon the distant nucleus of morning. He was wondering at the unreality of ideas, at the fading radiance of existence, and at the little absorptions that were creeping avidly into his life, like rats into a ruined house. He was sorry for no one now—on Monday morning there would be his business, and later there would be a girl of another class whose whole life he was; these were the things nearest his heart. In the strangeness of the brightening day it seemed presumptuous that with this feeble, broken instrument of his mind he had ever tried to think.

There was the sun, letting down great glowing masses of heat; there was life, active and snarling, moving about them like a fly swarm—the dark pants of smoke from the engine, a crisp "all aboard!" and a bell ringing. Confusedly Maury saw eyes in the milk train staring curiously up at him, heard Gloria and Anthony in quick controversy as to whether he should go to the city with her, then another clamor and she was gone and the three men, pale as ghosts, were standing alone upon the platform while a grimy coal-heaver went down the road on top of a motor truck, carolling hoarsely at the summer morning.

CHAPTER 3

THE BROKEN LUTE

It is seven-thirty of an August evening. The windows in the living room of the gray house are wide open, patiently exchanging the tainted inner atmosphere of liquor and smoke for the fresh drowsiness of the late hot dusk. There are dying flower scents upon the air, so thin, so fragile, as to hint already of a summer laid away in time. But August is still proclaimed relentlessly by a thousand crickets around the side-porch, and by one who has broken into the house and concealed himself confidently behind a bookcase, from time to time shrieking of his cleverness and his indomitable will.

The room itself is in messy disorder. On the table is a dish of fruit, which is real but appears artificial. Around it are grouped an ominous assortment of decanters, glasses, and heaped ash-trays, the latter still raising wavy smoke-ladders into the stale air, the effect on the whole needing but a skull to resemble that venerable chromo, once a fixture in every "den," which presents the appendages to the life of pleasure with delightful and awe-inspiring sentiment.

After a while the sprightly solo of the supercricket is interrupted rather than joined by a new sound—the melancholy wail of an erratically fingered flute. It is obvious that the musician is practising rather than performing, for from time to time the gnarled strain breaks off and, after an interval of indistinct mutterings, recommences.

Just prior to the seventh false start a third sound contributes to the subdued discord. It is a taxi outside. A minute's silence, then the taxi again, its boisterous retreat almost obliterating the scrape of footsteps on the cinder walk. The door-bell shrieks alarmingly through the house.

From the kitchen enters a small, fatigued Japanese, hastily buttoning a servant's coat of white duck. He opens the front screen-door and admits a handsome young man of thirty, clad in the sort of well-intentioned clothes peculiar to those who serve mankind. To his whole personality clings a well-intentioned air: his glance about the room is compounded of curiosity and a determined optimism; when he looks at Tana the entire burden of uplifting the godless Oriental is in his eyes. His name is FREDERICK E. PARAMORE. *He was at Harvard with* ANTHONY, *where because of the initials of their surnames they were constantly placed next to each other in classes. A fragmentary acquaintance developed—but since that time they have never met.*

Nevertheless, PARAMORE *enters the room with a certain air of arriving for the evening.*

Tana is answering a question.

TANA: (*Grinning with ingratiation*) Gone to Inn for dinnah. Be back half-hour. Gone since ha' past six.

PARAMORE: (*Regarding the glasses on the table*) Have they company?

TANA: Yes. Company. Mistah Caramel, Mistah and Missays Barnes, Miss Kane, all stay here.

PARAMORE: I see. (*Kindly*) They've been having a spree, I see.

TANA: I no un'stan'.

PARAMORE: They've been having a fling.

TANA: Yes, they have drink. Oh, many, many, many drink.

PARAMORE: (*Receding delicately from the subject*) "Didn't I hear the sounds of music as I approached the house"?

TANA: (*With a spasmodic giggle*) Yes, I play.

PARAMORE: One of the Japanese instruments.

(*He is quite obviously a subscriber to the "National Geographic Magazine."*)

TANA: I play flu-u-ute, Japanese flu-u-ute.

PARAMORE: What song were you playing? One of your Japanese melodies?

TANA: (*His brow undergoing preposterous contraction*) I play train song. How you call?—railroad song. So call in my countree. Like train. It go so-o-o; that mean whistle; train start. Then go so-o-o; that mean train go. Go like that. Vera nice song in my countree. Children song.

PARAMORE: It sounded very nice. (*It is apparent at this point that only a gigantic effort at control restrains Tana from rushing up-stairs for his post cards, including the six made in America.*)

TANA: I fix high-ball for gentleman?

PARAMORE: "No, thanks. I don't use it". (*He smiles.*)

(TANA *withdraws into the kitchen, leaving the intervening door slightly ajar. From the crevice there suddenly issues again the melody of the Japanese train song—this time not a practice, surely, but a performance, a lusty, spirited performance.*

The phone rings. TANA, *absorbed in his harmonics, gives no heed, so* PARAMORE *takes up the receiver.*)

PARAMORE: Hello. . . . Yes. . . . No, he's not here now, but he'll be back any moment. . . . Butterworth? Hello, I didn't quite catch the name. . . . Hello, hello, hello. Hello! . . . Huh!

(*The phone obstinately refuses to yield up any more sound. Paramore replaces the receiver.*

At this point the taxi motif re-enters, wafting with it a second young man; he carries a suitcase and opens the front door without ringing the bell.)

MAURY: (*In the hall*) "Oh, Anthony! Yoho"! (*He comes into the large room and sees* PARAMORE) How do?

PARAMORE: (*Gazing at him with gathering intensity*) Is this—is this Maury Noble?

MAURY: "That's it". (*He advances, smiling, and holding out his hand*) How are you, old boy? Haven't seen you for years.

(*He has vaguely associated the face with Harvard, but is not even positive about that. The name, if he ever knew it, he has long since forgotten. However, with a fine sensitiveness and an equally commendable charity* PARAMORE *recognizes the fact and tactfully relieves the situation.*)

PARAMORE: You've forgotten Fred Paramore? We were both in old Unc Robert's history class.

MAURY: No, I haven't, Unc—I mean Fred. Fred was—I mean Unc was a great old fellow, wasn't he?

PARAMORE: (*Nodding his head humorously several times*) Great old character. Great old character.

MAURY: (*After a short pause*) Yes—he was. Where's Anthony?

PARAMORE: The Japanese servant told me he was at some inn. Having dinner, I suppose.

MAURY: (*Looking at his watch*) Gone long?

PARAMORE: I guess so. The Japanese told me they'd be back shortly.

MAURY: Suppose we have a drink.

PARAMORE: No, thanks. I don't use it. (*He smiles.*)

MAURY: Mind if I do? (*Yawning as he helps himself from a bottle*) What have you been doing since you left college?

PARAMORE: Oh, many things. I've led a very active life. Knocked about here and there. (*His tone implies anything front lion-stalking to organized crime.*)

MAURY: Oh, been over to Europe?

PARAMORE: No, I haven't—unfortunately.

MAURY: I guess we'll all go over before long.

PARAMORE: Do you really think so?

MAURY: Sure! Country's been fed on sensationalism for more than two years. Everybody getting restless. Want to have some fun.

PARAMORE: Then you don't believe any ideals are at stake?

MAURY: Nothing of much importance. People want excitement every so often.

PARAMORE: (*Intently*) It's very interesting to hear you say that. Now I was talking to a man who'd been over there——

(*During the ensuing testament, left to be filled in by the reader with such phrases as "Saw with his own eyes," "Splendid spirit of France," and "Salvation of civilization," MAURY sits with lowered eyelids, dispassionately bored.*)

MAURY: (*At the first available opportunity*) By the way, do you happen to know that there's a German agent in this very house?

PARAMORE: (*Smiling cautiously*) Are you serious?

MAURY: Absolutely. Feel it my duty to warn you.

PARAMORE: (*Convinced*) A governess?

MAURY: (*In a whisper, indicating the kitchen with his thumb*) Tana! That's not his real name. I understand he constantly gets mail addressed to Lieutenant Emile Tannenbaum.

PARAMORE: (*Laughing with hearty tolerance*) You were kidding me.

MAURY: I may be accusing him falsely. But, you haven't told me what you've been doing.

PARAMORE: For one thing—writing.

MAURY: Fiction?

PARAMORE: No. Non-fiction.

MAURY: What's that? A sort of literature that's half fiction and half fact?

PARAMORE: Oh, I've confined myself to fact. I've been doing a good deal of social-service work.

MAURY: Oh!

(*An immediate glow of suspicion leaps into his eyes. It is as though* PARAMORE *had announced himself as an amateur pickpocket.*)

PARAMORE: At present I'm doing service work in Stamford. Only last week some one told me that Anthony Patch lived so near.

(*They are interrupted by a clamor outside, unmistakable as that of two sexes in conversation and laughter. Then there enter the room in a body* ANTHONY, GLORIA, RICHARD CARAMEL, MURIEL KANE, RACHAEL BARNES *and* RODMAN BARNES, *her husband. They surge about* MAURY, *illogically replying* "Fine!" *to his general* "Hello." . . . ANTHONY, *meanwhile, approaches his other guest.*)

ANTHONY: Well, I'll be darned. How are you? Mighty glad to see you.

PARAMORE: It's good to see you, Anthony. I'm stationed in Stamford, so I thought I'd run over. (*Roguishly*) We have to work to beat the devil most of the time, so we're entitled to a few hours' vacation.

(*In an agony of concentration* ANTHONY *tries to recall the name. After a struggle of parturition his memory gives up the fragment "Fred," around which he hastily builds the sentence "Glad you did, Fred!" Meanwhile the slight hush prefatory to an introduction has fallen upon the company.* MAURY, *who could help, prefers to look on in malicious enjoyment.*)

ANTHONY: (*In desperation*) Ladies and gentlemen, this is— this is Fred.

MURIEL: (*With obliging levity*) Hello, Fred!

(RICHARD CARAMEL *and* PARAMORE *greet each other intimately by their first names, the latter recollecting that*

DICK *was one of the men in his class who had never before troubled to speak to him.* DICK *fatuously imagines that* PARAMORE *is some one he has previously met in* ANTHONY'S *house.*

The three young women go up-stairs.)

MAURY: (*In an undertone to* DICK) Haven't seen Muriel since Anthony's wedding.

DICK: She's now in her prime. Her latest is "I'll say so!"

(ANTHONY *struggles for a while with* PARAMORE *and at length attempts to make the conversation general by asking every one to have a drink.*)

MAURY: I've done pretty well on this bottle. I've gone from "Proof" down to "Distillery." (*He indicates the words on the label.*)

ANTHONY: (*To* PARAMORE) Never can tell when these two will turn up. Said good-by to them one afternoon at five and darned if they didn't appear about two in the morning. A big hired touring-car from New York drove up to the door and out they stepped, drunk as lords, of course.

(*In an ecstasy of consideration* PARAMORE *regards the cover of a book which he holds in his hand.* MAURY *and* DICK *exchange a glance.*)

DICK: (*Innocently, to* PARAMORE) You work here in town?

PARAMORE: No, I'm in the Laird Street Settlement in Stamford. (*To* ANTHONY) You have no idea of the amount of poverty in these small Connecticut towns. Italians and other immigrants. Catholics mostly, you know, so it's very hard to reach them.

ANTHONY: (*Politely*) Lot of crime?

PARAMORE: Not so much crime as ignorance and dirt.

MAURY: That's my theory: immediate electrocution of all ignorant and dirty people. I'm all for the criminals—give color to life. Trouble is if you started to punish ignorance you'd have to begin in the first families, then you could take up the moving picture people, and finally Congress and the clergy.

PARAMORE: (*Smiling uneasily*) I was speaking of the more fundamental ignorance—of even our language.

MAURY: (*Thoughtfully*) I suppose it is rather hard. Can't even keep up with the new poetry.

PARAMORE: It's only when the settlement work has gone on for months that one realizes how bad things are. As our secretary said to me, your finger-nails never seem dirty until you wash your hands. Of course we're already attracting much attention.

MAURY: (*Rudely*) As your secretary might say, if you stuff paper into a grate it'll burn brightly for a moment.

(*At this point* GLORIA, *freshly tinted and lustful of admiration and entertainment, rejoins the party, followed by her two friends. For several moments the conversation becomes entirely fragmentary.* GLORIA *calls* ANTHONY *aside.*)

GLORIA: Please don't drink much, Anthony.

ANTHONY: Why?

GLORIA: Because you're so simple when you're drunk.

ANTHONY: Good Lord! What's the matter now?

GLORIA: (*After a pause during which her eyes gaze coolly into his*) Several things. In the first place, why do you insist on paying for everything? Both those men have more money than you!

ANTHONY: Why, Gloria! They're my guests!

GLORIA: That's no reason why you should pay for a bottle of champagne Rachael Barnes smashed. Dick tried to fix that second taxi bill, and you wouldn't let him.

ANTHONY: Why, Gloria—

GLORIA: When we have to keep selling bonds to even pay our bills, it's time to cut down on excess generosities. Moreover, I wouldn't be quite so attentive to Rachael Barnes. Her husband doesn't like it any more than I do!

ANTHONY: Why, Gloria—

GLORIA: (*Mimicking him sharply*) "Why, Gloria!" But that's
    happened a little too often this summer—with every
    pretty woman you meet. It's grown to be a sort of habit,
    and I'm *not* going to stand it! If you can play around, I
    can, too. (*Then, as an afterthought*) By the way, this Fred
    person isn't a second Joe Hull, is he?

ANTHONY: Heavens, no! He probably came up to get me to
    wheedle some money out of grandfather for his flock.

(GLORIA *turns away from a very depressed* ANTHONY *and
    returns to her guests.*

*By nine o'clock these can be divided into two classes—those who
    have been drinking consistently and those who have taken
    little or nothing. In the second group are the* BARNESES,
    MURIEL, *and* FREDERICK E. PARAMORE.)

MURIEL: I wish I could write. I get these ideas but I never
    seem to be able to put them in words.

DICK: As Goliath said, he understood how David felt, but he
    couldn't express himself. The remark was immediately
    adopted for a motto by the Philistines.

MURIEL: I don't get you. I must be getting stupid in my old
    age.

GLORIA: (*Weaving unsteadily among the company like an
    exhilarated angel*) If anyone's hungry there's some
    French pastry on the dining room table.

MAURY: Can't tolerate those Victorian designs it comes in.

MURIEL: (*Violently amused*) I'll say you're tight, Maury.

(*Her bosom is still a pavement that she offers to the hoofs of
    many passing stallions, hoping that their iron shoes may
    strike even a spark of romance in the darkness . . .*

Messrs. BARNES *and* PARAMORE *have been engaged in
    conversation upon some wholesome subject, a subject so
    wholesome that* MR. BARNES *has been trying for several
    moments to creep into the more tainted air around the
    central lounge. Whether* PARAMORE *is lingering in the
    gray house out of politeness or curiosity, or in order at*

some future time to make a sociological report on the decadence of American life, is problematical.)

MAURY: Fred, I imagined you were very broad-minded.

PARAMORE: I am.

MURIEL: Me, too. I believe one religion's as good as another and everything.

PARAMORE: There's some good in all religions.

MURIEL: I'm a Catholic but, as I always say, I'm not working at it.

PARAMORE: (*With a tremendous burst of tolerance*) The Catholic religion is a very—a very powerful religion.

MAURY: Well, such a broad-minded man should consider the raised plane of sensation and the stimulated optimism contained in this cocktail.

PARAMORE: (*Taking the drink, rather defiantly*) Thanks, I'll try—one.

MAURY: One? Outrageous! Here we have a class of nineteen ten reunion, and you refuse to be even a little pickled. Come on!

"*Here's a health to King Charles, Here's a health to King Charles, Bring the bowl that you boast——*"

(PARAMORE *joins in with a hearty voice.*)

MAURY: Fill the cup, Frederick. You know everything's subordinated to nature's purposes with us, and her purpose with you is to make you a rip-roaring tippler.

PARAMORE: If a fellow can drink like a gentleman—

MAURY: What is a gentleman, anyway?

ANTHONY: A man who never has pins under his coat lapel.

MAURY: Nonsense! A man's social rank is determined by the amount of bread he eats in a sandwich.

DICK: He's a man who prefers the first edition of a book to the last edition of a newspaper.

RACHAEL: A man who never gives an impersonation of a dope-fiend.

MAURY: An American who can fool an English butler into thinking he's one.

MURIEL: A man who comes from a good family and went to Yale or Harvard or Princeton, and has money and dances well, and all that.

MAURY: At last—the perfect definition! Cardinal Newman's is now a back number.

PARAMORE: I think we ought to look on the question more broad-mindedly. Was it Abraham Lincoln who said that a gentleman is one who never inflicts pain?

MAURY: It's attributed, I believe, to General Ludendorff.

PARAMORE: Surely you're joking.

MAURY: Have another drink.

PARAMORE: I oughtn't to. (*Lowering his voice for* MAURY'S *ear alone*) What if I were to tell you this is the third drink I've ever taken in my life?

(DICK *starts the phonograph, which provokes* MURIEL *to rise and sway from side to side, her elbows against her ribs, her forearms perpendicular to her body and out like fins.*)

MURIEL: Oh, let's take up the rugs and dance!

(*This suggestion is received by* ANTHONY *and* GLORIA *with interior groans and sickly smiles of acquiescence.*)

MURIEL: Come on, you lazy-bones. Get up and move the furniture back.

DICK: Wait till I finish my drink.

MAURY: (*Intent on his purpose toward* PARAMORE) I'll tell you what. Let's each fill one glass, drink it off and then we'll dance.

(*A wave of protest which breaks against the rock of* MAURY'S *insistence.*)

MURIEL: My head is simply going *round* now.

RACHAEL: (*In an undertone to* ANTHONY) Did Gloria tell you to stay away from me?

ANTHONY: (*Confused*) Why, certainly not. Of course not.

(RACHAEL *smiles at him inscrutably. Two years have given her a sort of hard, well-groomed beauty.*)

MAURY: (*Holding up his glass*) Here's to the defeat of democracy and the fall of Christianity.

MURIEL: Now really!

(*She flashes a mock-reproachful glance at MAURY and then drinks.*

They all drink, with varying degrees of difficulty.)

MURIEL: Clear the floor!

(*It seems inevitable that this process is to be gone through, so ANTHONY and GLORIA join in the great moving of tables, piling of chairs, rolling of carpets, and breaking of lamps. When the furniture has been stacked in ugly masses at the sides, there appears a space about eight feet square.*)

MURIEL: Oh, let's have music!

MAURY: Tana will render the love song of an eye, ear, nose, and throat specialist.

(*Amid some confusion due to the fact that TANA has retired for the night, preparations are made for the performance. The pajamaed Japanese, flute in hand, is wrapped in a comforter and placed in a chair atop one of the tables, where he makes a ludicrous and grotesque spectacle. PARAMORE is perceptibly drunk and so enraptured with the notion that he increases the effect by simulating funny-paper staggers and even venturing on an occasional hiccough.*)

PARAMORE: (*To GLORIA*) Want to dance with me?

GLORIA: No, sir! Want to do the swan dance. Can you do it?

PARAMORE: Sure. Do them all.

GLORIA: All right. You start from that side of the room and I'll start from this.

MURIEL: Let's go!

(*Then Bedlam creeps screaming out of the bottles: TANA plunges into the recondite mazes of the train song, the plaintive "tootle toot-toot" blending its melancholy cadences with the* "Poor Butter-fly (tink-atink), by the blossoms wait-ing" *of the phonograph.* MURIEL *is too weak with laughter to do more than cling desperately to* BARNES, *who, dancing with the ominous rigidity of an army officer, tramps without humor around the small space.* ANTHONY *is trying to hear* RACHAEL'S *whisper—without attracting* GLORIA's *attention. . . .*

But the grotesque, the unbelievable, the histrionic incident is about to occur, one of those incidents in which life seems set upon the passionate imitation of the lowest forms of literature. PARAMORE *has been trying to emulate* GLORIA, *and as the commotion reaches its height he begins to spin round and round, more and more dizzily—he staggers, recovers, staggers again and then falls in the direction of the hall . . . almost into the arms of old* ADAM PATCH, *whose approach has been rendered inaudible by the pandemonium in the room.*

ADAM PATCH *is very white. He leans upon a stick. The man with him is* EDWARD SHUTTLEWORTH, *and it is he who seizes* PARAMORE *by the shoulder and deflects the course of his fall away from the venerable philanthropist.*

The time required for quiet to descend upon the room like a monstrous pall may be estimated at two minutes, though for a short period after that the phonograph gags and the notes of the Japanese train song dribble from the end of TANA'S flute. Of the nine people only BARNES, PARAMORE, and TANA are unaware of the late-comer's identity. Of the nine not one is aware that ADAM PATCH has that morning made a contribution of fifty thousand dollars to the cause of national prohibition.

It is given to PARAMORE to break the gathering silence; the high tide of his life's depravity is reached in his incredible remark.)

PARAMORE: (*Crawling rapidly toward the kitchen on his hands and knees*) I'm not a guest here—I work here.

(*Again silence falls—so deep now, so weighted with intolerably*

F. SCOTT FITZGERALD

> *contagious apprehension, that* RACHAEL *gives a nervous
> little giggle, and* DICK *finds himself telling over and over
> a line from Swinburne, grotesquely appropriate to the scene:*
> "One gaunt bleak blossom of scentless breath."
> *. . . Out of the hush the voice of* ANTHONY, *sober and strained,
> saying something to* ADAM PATCH; *then this, too, dies
> away.*)

SHUTTLEWORTH: (*Passionately*) Your grandfather thought
he would motor over to see your house. I phoned from
Rye and left a message.

(*A series of little gasps, emanating, apparently, from nowhere,
from no one, fall into the next pause.* ANTHONY *is the
color of chalk.* GLORIA'S *lips are parted and her level
gaze at the old man is tense and frightened. There is not
one smile in the room. Not one? Or does* CROSS PATCH'S
*drawn mouth tremble slightly open, to expose the even rows
of his thin teeth? He speaks—five mild and simple words.*)

ADAM PATCH: We'll go back now, Shuttleworth—(*And that
is all. He turns, and assisted by his cane goes out through
the hall, through the front door, and with hellish porten-
tousness his uncertain footsteps crunch on the gravel path
under the August moon.*)

RETROSPECT

In this extremity they were like two goldfish in a bowl from
which all the water had been drawn; they could not even
swim across to each other.

Gloria would be twenty-six in May. There was nothing,
she had said, that she wanted, except to be young and beautiful
for a long time, to be gay and happy, and to have money and
love. She wanted what most women want, but she wanted it
much more fiercely and passionately. She had been married over
two years. At first there had been days of serene understanding,
rising to ecstasies of proprietorship and pride. Alternating with

these periods had occurred sporadic hates, enduring a short hour, and forgetfulnesses lasting no longer than an afternoon. That had been for half a year.

Then the serenity, the content, had become less jubilant, had become, gray—very rarely, with the spur of jealousy or forced separation, the ancient ecstasies returned, the apparent communion of soul and soul, the emotional excitement. It was possible for her to hate Anthony for as much as a full day, to be carelessly incensed at him for as long as a week. Recrimination had displaced affection as an indulgence, almost as an entertainment, and there were nights when they would go to sleep trying to remember who was angry and who should be reserved next morning. And as the second year waned there had entered two new elements. Gloria realized that Anthony had become capable of utter indifference toward her, a temporary indifference, more than half lethargic, but one from which she could no longer stir him by a whispered word, or a certain intimate smile. There were days when her caresses affected him as a sort of suffocation. She was conscious of these things; she never entirely admitted them to herself.

It was only recently that she perceived that in spite of her adoration of him, her jealousy, her servitude, her pride, she fundamentally despised him—and her contempt blended indistinguishably with her other emotions. . . . All this was her love—the vital and feminine illusion that had directed itself toward him one April night, many months before.

On Anthony's part she was, in spite of these qualifications, his sole preoccupation. Had he lost her he would have been a broken man, wretchedly and sentimentally absorbed in her memory for the remainder of life. He seldom took pleasure in an entire day spent alone with her—except on occasions he preferred to have a third person with them. There were times when he felt that if he were not left absolutely alone he would go mad—there were a few times when he definitely hated her. In his cups he was capable of short attractions toward other women, the hitherto-suppressed outcroppings of an experimental temperament.

That spring, that summer, they had speculated upon future happiness—how they were to travel from summer land to summer land, returning eventually to a gorgeous estate and possible idyllic children, then entering diplomacy or politics, to accomplish, for a while, beautiful and important things, until finally as a white-haired (beautifully, silkily, white-haired) couple they were to loll about in serene glory, worshipped by the bourgeoisie of the land. . . . These times were to begin "when we get our money"; it was on such dreams rather than on any satisfaction with their increasingly irregular, increasingly dissipated life that their hope rested. On gray mornings when the jests of the night before had shrunk to ribaldries without wit or dignity, they could, after a fashion, bring out this batch of common hopes and count them over, then smile at each other and repeat, by way of clinching the matter, the terse yet sincere Nietzscheanism of Gloria's defiant "I don't care!"

Things had been slipping perceptibly. There was the money question, increasingly annoying, increasingly ominous; there was the realization that liquor had become a practical necessity to their amusement—not an uncommon phenomenon in the British aristocracy of a hundred years ago, but a somewhat alarming one in a civilization steadily becoming more temperate and more circumspect. Moreover, both of them seemed vaguely weaker in fibre, not so much in what they did as in their subtle reactions to the civilization about them. In Gloria had been born something that she had hitherto never needed—the skeleton, incomplete but nevertheless unmistakable, of her ancient abhorrence, a conscience. This admission to herself was coincidental with the slow decline of her physical courage.

Then, on the August morning after Adam Patch's unexpected call, they awoke, nauseated and tired, dispirited with life, capable only of one pervasive emotion—fear.

PANIC

"Well?" Anthony sat up in bed and looked down at her. The corners of his lips were drooping with depression, his voice was strained and hollow.

Her reply was to raise her hand to her mouth and begin a slow, precise nibbling at her finger.

"We've done it," he said after a pause; then, as she was still silent, he became exasperated. "Why don't you say something?"

"What on earth do you want me to say?"

"What are you thinking?"

"Nothing."

"Then stop biting your finger!"

Ensued a short confused discussion of whether or not she had been thinking. It seemed essential to Anthony that she should muse aloud upon last night's disaster. Her silence was a method of settling the responsibility on him. For her part she saw no necessity for speech—the moment required that she should gnaw at her finger like a nervous child.

"I've got to fix up this damn mess with my grandfather," he said with uneasy conviction. A faint newborn respect was indicated by his use of "my grandfather" instead of "grampa."

"You can't," she affirmed abruptly. "You can't—*ever*. He'll never forgive you as long as he lives."

"Perhaps not," agreed Anthony miserably. "Still—I might possibly square myself by some sort of reformation and all that sort of thing—"

"He looked sick," she interrupted, "pale as flour."

"He *is* sick. I told you that three months ago."

"I wish he'd died last week!" she said petulantly. "Inconsiderate old fool!"

Neither of them laughed.

"But just let me say," she added quietly, "the next time I see you acting with any woman like you did with Rachael

Barnes last night, I'll leave you—*just—like—that!* I'm simply *not* going to stand it!"

Anthony quailed.

"Oh, don't be absurd," he protested. "You know there's no woman in the world for me except you—none, dearest."

His attempt at a tender note failed miserably—the more imminent danger stalked back into the foreground.

"If I went to him," suggested Anthony, "and said with appropriate biblical quotations that I'd walked too long in the way of unrighteousness and at last seen the light—" He broke off and glanced with a whimsical expression at his wife. "I wonder what he'd do?"

"I don't know."

She was speculating as to whether or not their guests would have the acumen to leave directly after breakfast.

Not for a week did Anthony muster the courage to go to Tarrytown. The prospect was revolting and left alone he would have been incapable of making the trip—but if his will had deteriorated in these past three years, so had his power to resist urging. Gloria compelled him to go. It was all very well to wait a week, she said, for that would give his grandfather's violent animosity time to cool—but to wait longer would be an error—it would give it a chance to harden.

He went, in trepidation . . . and vainly. Adam Patch was not well, said Shuttleworth indignantly. Positive instructions had been given that no one was to see him. Before the ex-"gin-physician's" vindictive eye Anthony's front wilted. He walked out to his taxicab with what was almost a slink—recovering only a little of his self-respect as he boarded the train; glad to escape, boylike, to the wonder palaces of consolation that still rose and glittered in his own mind.

Gloria was scornful when he returned to Marietta. Why had he not forced his way in? That was what she would have done!

Between them they drafted a letter to the old man, and

after considerable revision sent it off. It was half an apology, half a manufactured explanation. The letter was not answered.

Came a day in September, a day slashed with alternate sun and rain, sun without warmth, rain without freshness. On that day they left the gray house, which had seen the flower of their love. Four trunks and three monstrous crates were piled in the dismantled room where, two years before, they had sprawled lazily, thinking in terms of dreams, remote, languorous, content. The room echoed with emptiness. Gloria, in a new brown dress edged with fur, sat upon a trunk in silence, and Anthony walked nervously to and fro smoking, as they waited for the truck that would take their things to the city.

"What are those?" she demanded, pointing to some books piled upon one of the crates.

"That's my old stamp collection," he confessed sheepishly. "I forgot to pack it."

"Anthony, it's so silly to carry it around."

"Well, I was looking through it the day we left the apartment last spring, and I decided not to store it."

"Can't you sell it? Haven't we enough junk?"

"I'm sorry," he said humbly.

With a thunderous rattling the truck rolled up to the door. Gloria shook her fist defiantly at the four walls.

"I'm so glad to go!" she cried, "so glad. Oh, my God, how I hate this house!"

So the brilliant and beautiful lady went up with her husband to New York. On the very train that bore them away they quarrelled—her bitter words had the frequency, the regularity, the inevitability of the stations they passed.

"Don't be cross," begged Anthony piteously. "We've got nothing but each other, after all."

"We haven't even that, most of the time," cried Gloria.

"When haven't we?"

"A lot of times—beginning with one occasion on the station platform at Redgate."

"You don't mean to say that—"

"No," she interrupted coolly, "I don't brood over it. It came and went—and when it went it took something with it."

She finished abruptly. Anthony sat in silence, confused, depressed. The drab visions of train-side Mamaroneck, Larchmont, Rye, Pelham Manor, succeeded each other with intervals of bleak and shoddy wastes posing ineffectually as country. He found himself remembering how on one summer morning they two had started from New York in search of happiness. They had never expected to find it, perhaps, yet in itself that quest had been happier than anything he expected forevermore. Life, it seemed, must be a setting up of props around one—otherwise it was disaster. There was no rest, no quiet. He had been futile in longing to drift and dream; no one drifted except to maelstroms, no one dreamed, without his dreams becoming fantastic nightmares of indecision and regret.

Pelham! They had quarrelled in Pelham because Gloria must drive. And when she set her little foot on the accelerator the car had jumped off spunkily, and their two heads had jerked back like marionettes worked by a single string.

The Bronx—the houses gathering and gleaming in the sun, which was falling now through wide refulgent skies and tumbling caravans of light down into the streets. New York, he supposed, was home—the city of luxury and mystery, of preposterous hopes and exotic dreams. Here on the outskirts absurd stucco palaces reared themselves in the cool sunset, poised for an instant in cool unreality, glided off far away, succeeded by the mazed confusion of the Harlem River. The train moved in through the deepening twilight, above and past half a hundred cheerful sweating streets of the upper East Side, each one passing the car window like the space between the spokes of a gigantic wheel, each one with its vigorous colorful revelation of poor children swarming in feverish activity like vivid ants in alleys of red sand. From the tenement windows leaned rotund, moon-shaped mothers, as constellations of this sordid heaven; women like dark imperfect jewels, women like vegetables, women like great bags of abominably dirty laundry.

"I like these streets," observed Anthony aloud. "I always feel as though it's a performance being staged for me; as though the second I've passed they'll all stop leaping and laughing and, instead, grow very sad, remembering how poor they are, and retreat with bowed heads into their houses. You often get that effect abroad, but seldom in this country."

Down in a tall busy street he read a dozen Jewish names on a line of stores; in the door of each stood a dark little man watching the passers from intent eyes—eyes gleaming with suspicion, with pride, with clarity, with cupidity, with comprehension. New York—he could not dissociate it now from the slow, upward creep of this people—the little stores, growing, expanding, consolidating, moving, watched over with hawk's eyes and a bee's attention to detail—they slathered out on all sides. It was impressive—in perspective it was tremendous.

Gloria's voice broke in with strange appropriateness upon his thoughts.

"I wonder where Bloeckman's been this summer."

THE APARTMENT

After the sureties of youth there sets in a period of intense and intolerable complexity. With the soda-jerker this period is so short as to be almost negligible. Men higher in the scale hold out longer in the attempt to preserve the ultimate niceties of relationship, to retain "impractical" ideas of integrity. But by the late twenties the business has grown too intricate, and what has hitherto been imminent and confusing has become gradually remote and dim. Routine comes down like twilight on a harsh landscape, softening it until it is tolerable. The complexity is too subtle, too varied; the values are changing utterly with each lesion of vitality; it has begun to appear that we can learn nothing from the past with which to face the future—so we cease to be impulsive, convincible men, interested in what is ethically true by fine margins, we substitute rules of conduct for ideas of integrity, we value safety above romance, we become, quite unconsciously, pragmatic. It is left to the few to be persistently concerned with the nuances of relationships—and even this few only in certain hours especially set aside for the task.

Anthony Patch had ceased to be an individual of mental adventure, of curiosity, and had become an individual of bias and prejudice, with a longing to be emotionally undisturbed. This gradual change had taken place through the past several years, accelerated by a succession of anxieties preying on his mind. There was, first of all, the sense of waste, always dormant in his heart, now awakened by the circumstances of his position. In his moments of insecurity he was haunted by the suggestion that life might be, after all, significant. In his early twenties the conviction of the futility of effort, of the wisdom of abnegation, had been confirmed by the philosophies he had admired as well as by his association with Maury Noble, and later with his wife. Yet there had been occasions—just before his first meeting with Gloria, for example, and when his grandfather had suggested that he should go abroad as a war correspondent—upon which his dissatisfaction had driven him almost to a positive step.

One day just before they left Marietta for the last time, in carelessly turning over the pages of a Harvard Alumni Bulletin, he had found a column which told him what his contemporaries had been about in this six years since graduation. Most of them were in business, it was true, and several were converting the heathen of China or America to a nebulous protestantism; but a few, he found, were working constructively at jobs that were neither sinecures nor routines. There was Calvin Boyd, for instance, who, though barely out of medical school, had discovered a new treatment for typhus, had shipped abroad and was mitigating some of the civilization that the Great Powers had brought to Servia; there was Eugene Bronson, whose articles in The New Democracy were stamping him as a man with ideas transcending both vulgar timeliness and popular hysteria; there was a man named Daly who had been suspended from the faculty of a righteous university for preaching Marxian doctrines in the classroom: in art, science, politics, he saw the authentic personalities of his time emerging—there was even Severance, the quarter-back, who had given up his life rather neatly and gracefully with the Foreign Legion on the Aisne.

He laid down the magazine and thought for a while about these diverse men. In the days of his integrity he would have defended his attitude to the last—an Epicurus in Nirvana, he would have cried that to struggle was to believe, to believe was to limit. He would as soon have become a churchgoer because the prospect of immortality gratified him as he would have considered entering the leather business because the intensity of the competition would have kept him from unhappiness. But at present he had no such delicate scruples. This autumn, as his twenty-ninth year began, he was inclined to close his mind to many things, to avoid prying deeply into motive and first causes, and mostly to long passionately for security from the world and from himself. He hated to be alone, as has been said he often dreaded being alone with Gloria.

Because of the chasm which his grandfather's visit had opened before him, and the consequent revulsion from his late mode of life, it was inevitable that he should look around in this suddenly hostile city for the friends and environments that had once seemed the warmest and most secure. His first step was a desperate attempt to get back his old apartment.

In the spring of 1912 he had signed a four-year lease at seventeen hundred a year, with an option of renewal. This lease had expired the previous May. When he had first rented the rooms they had been mere potentialities, scarcely to be discerned as that, but Anthony had seen into these potentialities and arranged in the lease that he and the landlord should each spend a certain amount in improvements. Rents had gone up in the past four years, and last spring when Anthony had waived his option the landlord, a Mr. Sohenberg, had realized that he could get a much bigger price for what was now a prepossessing apartment. Accordingly, when Anthony approached him on the subject in September he was met with Sohenberg's offer of a three-year lease at twenty-five hundred a year. This, it seemed to Anthony, was outrageous. It meant that well over a third of their income would be consumed in rent. In vain he argued that his own money, his own ideas on the repartitioning, had made the rooms attractive.

In vain he offered two thousand dollars—twenty-two hundred, though they could ill afford it: Mr. Sohenberg was obdurate. It seemed that two other gentlemen were considering it; just that sort of an apartment was in demand for the moment, and it would scarcely be business to *give* it to Mr. Patch. Besides, though he had never mentioned it before, several of the other tenants had complained of noise during the previous winter— singing and dancing late at night, that sort of thing.

Internally raging Anthony hurried back to the Ritz to report his discomfiture to Gloria.

"I can just see you," she stormed, "letting him back you down!"

"What could I say?"

"You could have told him what he *was*. I wouldn't have *stood* it. No other man in the world would have stood it! You just let people order you around and cheat you and bully you and take advantage of you as if you were a silly little boy. It's absurd!"

"Oh, for Heaven's sake, don't lose your temper."

"I know, Anthony, but you *are* such an ass!"

"Well, possibly. Anyway, we can't afford that apartment. But we can afford it better than living here at the Ritz."

"You were the one who insisted on coming here."

"Yes, because I knew you'd be miserable in a cheap hotel."

"Of course I would!"

"At any rate we've got to find a place to live."

"How much can we pay?" she demanded.

"Well, we can pay even his price if we sell more bonds, but we agreed last night that until I had gotten something definite to do we—"

"Oh, I know all that. I asked you how much we can pay out of just our income."

"They say you ought not to pay more than a fourth."

"How much is a fourth?"

"One hundred and fifty a month."

"Do you mean to say we've got only six hundred dollars coming in every month?" A subdued note crept into her voice.

"Of course!" he answered angrily. "Do you think we've gone on spending more than twelve thousand a year without cutting way into our capital?"

"I knew we'd sold bonds, but—have we spent that much a year? How did we?" Her awe increased.

"Oh, I'll look in those careful account-books we kept," he remarked ironically, and then added: "Two rents a good part of the time, clothes, travel—why, each of those springs in California cost about four thousand dollars. That darn car was an expense from start to finish. And parties and amusements and—oh, one thing or another."

They were both excited now and inordinately depressed. The situation seemed worse in the actual telling Gloria than it had when he had first made the discovery himself.

"You've got to make some money," she said suddenly.

"I know it."

"And you've got to make another attempt to see your grandfather."

"I will."

"When?"

"When we get settled."

This eventuality occurred a week later. They rented a

small apartment on Fifty-seventh Street at one hundred and fifty a month. It included bedroom, living-room, kitchenette, and bath, in a thin, white-stone apartment house, and though the rooms were too small to display Anthony's best furniture, they were clean, new, and, in a blonde and sanitary way, not unattractive. Bounds had gone abroad to enlist in the British army, and in his place they tolerated rather than enjoyed the services of a gaunt, big-boned Irishwoman, whom Gloria loathed because she discussed the glories of Sinn Fein as she served breakfast. But they vowed they would have no more Japanese, and English servants were for the present hard to obtain. Like Bounds, the woman prepared only breakfast. Their other meals they took at restaurants and hotels.

What finally drove Anthony post-haste up to Tarrytown was an announcement in several New York papers that Adam Patch, the multimillionaire, the philanthropist, the venerable uplifter, was seriously ill and not expected to recover.

THE KITTEN

Anthony could not see him. The doctors' instructions were that he was to talk to no one, said Mr. Shuttleworth—who offered kindly to take any message that Anthony might care to intrust with him, and deliver it to Adam Patch when his condition permitted. But by obvious innuendo he confirmed Anthony's melancholy inference that the prodigal grandson would be particularly unwelcome at the bedside. At one point in the conversation Anthony, with Gloria's positive instructions in mind, made a move as though to brush by the secretary, but Shuttleworth with a smile squared his brawny shoulders, and Anthony saw how futile such an attempt would be.

Miserably intimidated, he returned to New York, where husband and wife passed a restless week. A little incident that occurred one evening indicated to what tension their nerves were drawn.

Walking home along a cross-street after dinner, Anthony noticed a night-bound cat prowling near a railing.

"I always have an instinct to kick a cat," he said idly.

"I like them."

"I yielded to it once."

"When?"

"Oh, years ago; before I met you. One night between the acts of a show. Cold night, like this, and I was a little tight—one of the first times I was ever tight," he added. "The poor little beggar was looking for a place to sleep, I guess, and I was in a mean mood, so it took my fancy to kick it—"

"Oh, the poor kitty!" cried Gloria, sincerely moved. Inspired with the narrative instinct, Anthony enlarged on the theme.

"It was pretty bad," he admitted. "The poor little beast turned around and looked at me rather plaintively as though hoping I'd pick him up and be kind to him—he was really just a kitten—and before he knew it a big foot launched out at him and caught his little back."

"Oh!" Gloria's cry was full of anguish.

"It was such a cold night," he continued, perversely, keeping his voice upon a melancholy note. "I guess it expected kindness from somebody, and it got only pain—"

He broke off suddenly—Gloria was sobbing. They had reached home, and when they entered the apartment she threw herself upon the lounge, crying as though he had struck at her very soul.

"Oh, the poor little kitty!" she repeated piteously, "the poor little kitty. So cold—"

"Gloria."

"Don't come near me! Please, don't come near me. You killed the soft little kitty."

Touched, Anthony knelt beside her.

"Dear," he said. "Oh, Gloria, darling. It isn't true. I invented it—every word of it."

But she would not believe him. There had been something in the details he had chosen to describe that made her cry herself asleep that night, for the kitten, for Anthony for herself, for the pain and bitterness and cruelty of all the world.

THE PASSING OF AN AMERICAN MORALIST

Old Adam died on a midnight of late November with a pious compliment to his God on his thin lips. He, who had been flattered so much, faded out flattering the Omnipotent Abstraction which he fancied he might have angered in the more lascivious moments of his youth. It was announced that he had arranged some sort of an armistice with the deity, the terms of which were not made public, though they were thought to have included a large cash payment. All the newspapers printed his biography, and two of them ran short editorials on his sterling worth, and his part in the drama of industrialism, with which he had grown up. They referred guardedly to the reforms he had sponsored and financed. The memories of Comstock and Cato the Censor were resuscitated and paraded like gaunt ghosts through the columns.

Every newspaper remarked that he was survived by a single grandson, Anthony Comstock Patch, of New York.

The burial took place in the family plot at Tarrytown. Anthony and Gloria rode in the first carriage, too worried to feel grotesque, both trying desperately to glean presage of fortune from the faces of retainers who had been with him at the end.

They waited a frantic week for decency, and then, having received no notification of any kind, Anthony called up his grandfather's lawyer. Mr. Brett was not he was expected back in an hour. Anthony left his telephone number.

It was the last day of November, cool and crackling outside, with a lustreless sun peering bleakly in at the windows. While they waited for the call, ostensibly engaged in reading, the atmosphere, within and without, seemed pervaded with a deliberate rendition of the pathetic fallacy. After an interminable while, the bell jingled, and Anthony, starting violently, took up the receiver.

"Hello . . ." His voice was strained and hollow. "Yes—I did leave word. Who is this, please? . . . Yes. . . . Why, it was about the estate. Naturally I'm interested, and I've received no word about the reading of the will—I thought you might not have my address. . . . What? . . . Yes . . ."

Gloria fell on her knees. The intervals between Anthony's speeches were like tourniquets winding on her heart. She found herself helplessly twisting the large buttons from a velvet cushion. Then:

"That's—that's very, very odd—that's very odd—that's very odd. Not even any—ah—mention or any—ah—reason?"

His voice sounded faint and far away. She uttered a little sound, half gasp, half cry.

"Yes, I'll see. . . . All right, thanks . . . thanks. . . ."

The phone clicked. Her eyes looking along the floor saw his feet cut the pattern of a patch of sunlight on the carpet. She arose and faced him with a gray, level glance just as his arms folded about her.

"My dearest," he whispered huskily. "He did it, God damn him!"

NEXT DAY

"Who are the heirs?" asked Mr. Haight. "You see when you can tell me so little about it—"

Mr. Haight was tall and bent and beetle-browed. He had been recommended to Anthony as an astute and tenacious lawyer.

"I only know vaguely," answered Anthony. "A man named Shuttleworth, who was a sort of pet of his, has the whole thing in charge as administrator or trustee or something—all except

271

the direct bequests to charity and the provisions for servants and for those two cousins in Idaho."

"How distant are the cousins?"

"Oh, third or fourth, anyway. I never even heard of them."

Mr. Haight nodded comprehensively.

"And you want to contest a provision of the will?"

"I guess so," admitted Anthony helplessly. "I want to do what sounds most hopeful—that's what I want you to tell me."

"You want them to refuse probate to the will?"

Anthony shook his head.

"You've got me. I haven't any idea what 'probate' is. I want a share of the estate."

"Suppose you tell me some more details. For instance, do you know why the testator disinherited you?"

"Why—yes," began Anthony. "You see he was always a sucker for moral reform, and all that—"

"I know," interjected Mr. Haight humorlessly.

"—and I don't suppose he ever thought I was much good. I didn't go into business, you see. But I feel certain that up to last summer I was one of the beneficiaries. We had a house out in Marietta, and one night grandfather got the notion he'd come over and see us. It just happened that there was a rather gay party going on and he arrived without any warning. Well, he took one look, he and this fellow Shuttleworth, and then turned around and tore right back to Tarrytown. After that he never answered my letters or even let me see him."

"He was a prohibitionist, wasn't he?"

"He was everything—regular religious maniac."

"How long before his death was the will made that disinherited you?"

"Recently—I mean since August."

"And you think that the direct reason for his not leaving you the majority of the estate was his displeasure with your recent actions?"

"Yes."

Mr. Haight considered. Upon what grounds was Anthony thinking of contesting the will?

"Why, isn't there something about evil influence?"

"Undue influence is one ground—but it's the most difficult. You would have to show that such pressure was brought to bear so that the deceased was in a condition where he disposed of his property contrary to his intentions—"

"Well, suppose this fellow Shuttleworth dragged him over to Marietta just when he thought some sort of a celebration was probably going on?"

"That wouldn't have any bearing on the case. There's a strong division between advice and influence. You'd have to prove that the secretary had a sinister intention. I'd suggest some other grounds. A will is automatically refused probate in case of insanity, drunkenness"—here Anthony smiled—"or feeble-mindedness through premature old age."

"But," objected Anthony, "his private physician, being one of the beneficiaries, would testify that he wasn't feeble-minded. And he wasn't. As a matter of fact he probably did just what he intended to with his money—it was perfectly consistent with everything he'd ever done in his life—"

"Well, you see, feeble-mindedness is a great deal like undue influence—it implies that the property wasn't disposed of as originally intended. The most common ground is duress—physical pressure."

Anthony shook his head.

"Not much chance on that, I'm afraid. Undue influence sounds best to me."

After more discussion, so technical as to be largely unintelligible to Anthony, he retained Mr. Haight as counsel. The lawyer proposed an interview with Shuttleworth, who, jointly with Wilson, Hiemer and Hardy, was executor of the will. Anthony was to come back later in the week.

It transpired that the estate consisted of approximately

forty million dollars. The largest bequest to an individual was of one million, to Edward Shuttleworth, who received in addition thirty thousand a year salary as administrator of the thirty-million-dollar trust fund, left to be doled out to various charities and reform societies practically at his own discretion. The remaining nine millions were proportioned among the two cousins in Idaho and about twenty-five other beneficiaries: friends, secretaries, servants, and employees, who had, at one time or another, earned the seal of Adam Patch's approval.

At the end of another fortnight Mr. Haight, on a retainer's fee of fifteen thousand dollars, had begun preparations for contesting the will.

THE WINTER OF DISCONTENT

Before they had been two months in the little apartment on Fifty-seventh Street, it had assumed for both of them the same indefinable but almost material taint that had impregnated the gray house in Marietta. There was the odor of tobacco always—both of them smoked incessantly; it was in their clothes, their blankets, the curtains, and the ash-littered carpets. Added to this was the wretched aura of stale wine, with its inevitable suggestion of beauty gone foul and revelry remembered in disgust. About a particular set of glass goblets on the sideboard the odor was particularly noticeable, and in the main room the mahogany table was ringed with white circles where glasses had been set down upon it. There had been many parties—people broke things; people became sick in Gloria's bathroom; people spilled wine; people made unbelievable messes of the kitchenette.

These things were a regular part of their existence. Despite the resolutions of many Mondays it was tacitly understood as the week end approached that it should be observed with some sort of unholy excitement. When Saturday came they would not discuss the matter, but would call up this person or that from among their circle of sufficiently irresponsible friends, and suggest a rendezvous. Only after the friends had gathered and Anthony had set out decanters, would he murmur casually "I guess I'll have just one high-ball myself—"

Then they were off for two days—realizing on a wintry dawn that they had been the noisiest and most conspicuous members of the noisiest and most conspicuous party at the Boul' Mich', or the Club Ramée, or at other resorts much less particular about the hilarity of their clientèle. They would find that they had, somehow, squandered eighty or ninety dollars, how, they never knew; they customarily attributed it to the general penury of the "friends" who had accompanied them.

It began to be not unusual for the more sincere of their friends to remonstrate with them, in the very course of a party, and to predict a sombre end for them in the loss of Gloria's "looks" and Anthony's "constitution."

The story of the summarily interrupted revel in Marietta had, of course, leaked out in detail—"Muriel doesn't mean to tell every one she knows," said Gloria to Anthony, "but she thinks every one she tells is the only one she's going to tell"— and, diaphanously veiled, the tale had been given a conspicuous place in Town Tattle. When the terms of Adam Patch's will were made public and the newspapers printed items concerning Anthony's suit, the story was beautifully rounded out—to Anthony's infinite disparagement. They began to hear rumors about themselves from all quarters, rumors founded usually on a soupcon of truth, but overlaid with preposterous and sinister detail.

Outwardly they showed no signs of deterioration. Gloria at twenty-six was still the Gloria of twenty; her complexion a fresh damp setting for her candid eyes; her hair still a childish glory, darkening slowly from corn color to a deep russet gold; her slender body suggesting ever a nymph running and dancing through Orphic groves. Masculine eyes, dozens of them, followed her with a fascinated stare when she walked through a hotel lobby or down the aisle of a theatre. Men asked to be introduced to her, fell into prolonged states of sincere admiration, made definite love to her—for she was still a thing of exquisite and unbelievable beauty. And for his part Anthony had rather gained than lost in appearance; his face had taken on a certain intangible air of tragedy, romantically contrasted with his trim and immaculate person.

Early in the winter, when all conversation turned on the probability of America's going into the war, when Anthony was making a desperate and sincere attempt to write, Muriel Kane arrived in New York and came immediately to see them. Like Gloria, she seemed never to change. She knew the latest slang, danced the latest dances, and talked of the latest songs and plays with all the fervor of her first season as a New York drifter. Her coyness was eternally new, eternally ineffectual; her clothes were extreme; her black hair was bobbed, now, like Gloria's.

"I've come up for the midwinter prom at New Haven," she announced, imparting her delightful secret. Though she must have been older then than any of the boys in college, she managed always to secure some sort of invitation, imagining vaguely that at the next party would occur the flirtation which was to end at the romantic altar.

"Where've you been?" inquired Anthony, unfailingly amused.

"I've been at Hot Springs. It's been slick and peppy this fall—more *men!*"

"Are you in love, Muriel?"

"What do you mean 'love'?" This was the rhetorical question of the year. "I'm going to tell you something," she said, switching the subject abruptly. "I suppose it's none of my business, but I think it's time for you two to settle down."

"Why, we are settled down."

"Yes, you are!" she scoffed archly. "Everywhere I go I hear stories of your escapades. Let me tell you, I have an awful time sticking up for you."

"You needn't bother," said Gloria coldly.

"Now, Gloria," she protested, "you know I'm one of your best friends."

Gloria was silent. Muriel continued:

"It's not so much the idea of a woman drinking, but Gloria's so pretty, and so many people know her by sight all around, that it's naturally conspicuous—"

"What have you heard recently?" demanded Gloria, her dignity going down before her curiosity.

"Well, for instance, that that party in Marietta *killed* Anthony's grandfather."

Instantly husband and wife were tense with annoyance.

"Why, I think that's outrageous."

"That's what they say," persisted Muriel stubbornly.

Anthony paced the room. "It's preposterous!" he declared. "The very people we take on parties shout the story around as a great joke—and eventually it gets back to us in some such form as this."

Gloria began running her finger through a stray red-dish curl. Muriel licked her veil as she considered her next remark.

"You ought to have a baby."

Gloria looked up wearily.

"We can't afford it."

"All the people in the slums have them," said Muriel triumphantly.

Anthony and Gloria exchanged a smile. They had reached the stage of violent quarrels that were never made up, quarrels that smouldered and broke out again at intervals or died away from sheer indifference—but this visit of Muriel's drew them temporarily together. When the discomfort under which they were living was remarked upon by a third party, it gave them the impetus to face this hostile world together. It was very seldom, now, that the impulse toward reunion sprang from within.

Anthony found himself associating his own existence

with that of the apartment's night elevator man, a pale, scraggly bearded person of about sixty, with an air of being somewhat above his station. It was probably because of this quality that he had secured the position; it made him a pathetic and memorable figure of failure. Anthony recollected, without humor, a hoary jest about the elevator man's career being a matter of ups and downs—it was, at any rate, an enclosed life of infinite dreariness. Each time Anthony stepped into the car he waited breathlessly for the old man's "Well, I guess we're going to have some sunshine to-day." Anthony thought how little rain or sunshine he would enjoy shut into that close little cage in the smoke-colored, windowless hall.

A darkling figure, he attained tragedy in leaving the life that had used him so shabbily. Three young gunmen came in one night, tied him up and left him on a pile of coal in the cellar while they went through the trunk room. When the janitor found him next morning he had collapsed from chill. He died of pneumonia four days later.

He was replaced by a glib Martinique negro, with an incongruous British accent and a tendency to be surly, whom Anthony detested. The passing of the old man had approximately the same effect on him that the kitten story had had on Gloria. He was reminded of the cruelty of all life and, in consequence, of the increasing bitterness of his own.

He was writing—and in earnest at last. He had gone to Dick and listened for a tense hour to an elucidation of those minutiae of procedure which hitherto he had rather scornfully looked down upon. He needed money immediately—he was selling bonds every month to pay their bills. Dick was frank and explicit:

"So far as articles on literary subjects in these obscure magazines go, you couldn't make enough to pay your rent. Of course if a man has the gift of humor, or a chance at a big biography, or some specialized knowledge, he may strike it rich. But for you, fiction's the only thing. You say you need money right away?"

"I certainly do."

"Well, it'd be a year and a half before you'd make any money out of a novel. Try some popular short stories. And, by the way, unless they're exceptionally brilliant they have to be cheerful and on the side of the heaviest artillery to make you any money."

Anthony thought of Dick's recent output, which had been appearing in a well-known monthly. It was concerned chiefly with the preposterous actions of a class of sawdust effigies who, one was assured, were New York society people, and it turned, as a rule, upon questions of the heroine's technical purity, with mock-sociological overtones about the "mad antics of the four hundred."

"But your stories—" exclaimed Anthony aloud, almost involuntarily.

"Oh, that's different," Dick asserted astoundingly. "I have a reputation, you see, so I'm expected to deal with strong themes."

Anthony gave an interior start, realizing with this remark how much Richard Caramel had fallen off. Did he actually think that these amazing latter productions were as good as his first novel?

Anthony went back to the apartment and set to work. He found that the business of optimism was no mean task. After half a dozen futile starts he went to the public library and for a week investigated the files of a popular magazine. Then, better equipped, he accomplished his first story, "The Dictaphone of Fate." It was founded upon one of his few remaining impressions of that six weeks in Wall Street the year before. It purported to be the sunny tale of an office boy who, quite by accident, hummed a wonderful melody into the dictaphone. The cylinder was discovered by the boss's brother, a well-known producer of musical comedy—and then immediately lost. The body of the story was concerned with the pursuit of the missing cylinder and the eventual marriage of the noble office boy (now a successful composer) to Miss Rooney, the virtuous stenographer, who was half Joan of Arc and half Florence Nightingale.

He had gathered that this was what the magazines wanted. He offered, in his protagonists, the customary denizens of the pink-and-blue literary world, immersing them in a saccharine plot that would offend not a single stomach in Marietta. He had it typed in double space—this last as advised by a booklet, "Success as a Writer Made Easy," by R. Meggs Widdlestien, which assured the ambitious plumber of the futility of perspiration, since after a six-lesson course he could make at least a thousand dollars a month.

After reading it to a bored Gloria and coaxing from her the immemorial remark that it was "better than a lot of stuff that gets published," he satirically affixed the nom de plume of "Gilles de Sade," enclosed the proper return envelope, and sent it off.

Following the gigantic labor of conception he decided to wait until he heard from the first story before beginning another. Dick had told him that he might get as much as two hundred dollars. If by any chance it did happen to be unsuited, the editor's letter would, no doubt, give him an idea of what changes should be made.

"It is, without question, the most abominable piece of writing in existence," said Anthony.

The editor quite conceivably agreed with him. He returned the manuscript with a rejection slip. Anthony sent it off elsewhere and began another story. The second one was called "The Little Open Doors"; it was written in three days. It concerned the occult: an estranged couple were brought together by a medium in a vaudeville show.

There were six altogether, six wretched and pitiable efforts to "write down" by a man who had never before made a consistent effort to write at all. Not one of them contained a spark of vitality, and their total yield of grace and felicity was less than that of an average newspaper column. During their circulation they collected, all told, thirty-one rejection slips, headstones for the packages that he would find lying like dead bodies at his door.

In mid-January Gloria's father died, and they went again to Kansas City—a miserable trip, for Gloria brooded interminably, not upon her father's death, but on her mother's. Russel Gilbert's affairs having been cleared up they came into possession of about three thousand dollars, and a great amount of furniture. This was in storage, for he had spent his last days in a small hotel. It was due to his death that Anthony made a new discovery concerning Gloria. On the journey East she disclosed herself, astonishingly, as a Bilphist.

"Why, Gloria," he cried, "you don't mean to tell me you believe that stuff."

"Well," she said defiantly, "why not?"

"Because it's—it's fantastic. You know that in every sense of the word you're an agnostic. You'd laugh at any orthodox form of Christianity—and then you come out with the statement that you believe in some silly rule of reincarnation."

"What if I do? I've heard you and Maury, and every one else for whose intellect I have the slightest respect, agree that life as it appears is utterly meaningless. But it's always seemed to me that if I were unconsciously learning something here it might not be so meaningless."

"You're not learning anything—you're just getting tired. And if you must have a faith to soften things, take up one that appeals to the reason of some one beside a lot of hysterical women. A person like you oughtn't to accept anything unless it's decently demonstrable."

"I don't care about truth. I want some happiness."

"Well, if you've got a decent mind the second has got

to be qualified by the first. Any simple soul can delude himself with mental garbage."

"I don't care," she held out stoutly, "and, what's more, I'm not propounding any doctrine."

The argument faded off, but reoccurred to Anthony several times thereafter. It was disturbing to find this old belief, evidently assimilated from her mother, inserting itself again under its immemorial disguise as an innate idea.

They reached New York in March after an expensive and ill-advised week spent in Hot Springs, and Anthony resumed his abortive attempts at fiction. As it became plainer to both of them that escape did not lie in the way of popular literature, there was a further slipping of their mutual confidence and courage. A complicated struggle went on incessantly between them. All efforts to keep down expenses died away from sheer inertia, and by March they were again using any pretext as an excuse for a "party." With an assumption of recklessness Gloria tossed out the suggestion that they should take all their money and go on a real spree while it lasted—anything seemed better than to see it go in unsatisfactory driblets.

"Gloria, you want parties as much as I do."

"It doesn't matter about me. Everything I do is in accordance with my ideas: to use every minute of these years, when I'm young, in having the best time I possibly can."

"How about after that?"

"After that I won't care."

"Yes, you will."

"Well, I may—but I won't be able to do anything about it. And I'll have had my good time."

"You'll be the same then. After a fashion, we *have* had our good time, raised the devil, and we're in the state of paying for it."

Nevertheless, the money kept going. There would be two days of gaiety, two days of moroseness—an endless, almost invariable round. The sharp pull-ups, when they occurred, resulted usually in a spurt of work for Anthony, while Gloria, nervous and bored, remained in bed or else chewed abstractedly at her fingers. After a day or so of this, they would make an engagement, and then—Oh, what did it matter? This night, this glow, the cessation of anxiety and the sense that if living was not purposeful it was, at any rate, essentially romantic! Wine gave a sort of gallantry to their own failure.

Meanwhile the suit progressed slowly, with interminable examinations of witnesses and marshallings of evidence. The preliminary proceedings of settling the estate were finished. Mr. Haight saw no reason why the case should not come up for trial before summer.

Bloeckman appeared in New York late in March; he had been in England for nearly a year on matters concerned with "Films Par Excellence." The process of general refinement was still in progress—always he dressed a little better, his intonation was mellower, and in his manner there was perceptibly more assurance that the fine things of the world were his by a natural and inalienable right. He called at the apartment, remained only an hour, during which he talked chiefly of the war, and left telling them he was coming again. On his second visit Anthony was not at home, but an absorbed and excited Gloria greeted her husband later in the afternoon.

"Anthony," she began, "would you still object if I went in the movies?"

His whole heart hardened against the idea. As she seemed to recede from him, if only in threat, her presence became again not so much precious as desperately necessary.

"Oh, Gloria—!"

"Blockhead said he'd put me in—only if I'm ever going to do anything I'll have to start now. They only want young women. Think of the money, Anthony!"

"For you—yes. But how about me?"

"Don't you know that anything I have is yours too?"

"It's such a hell of a career!" he burst out, the moral,

the infinitely circumspect Anthony, "and such a hell of a bunch. And I'm so utterly tired of that fellow Bloeckman coming here and interfering. I hate theatrical things."

"It isn't theatrical! It's utterly different."

"What am I supposed to do? Chase you all over the country? Live on your money?"

"Then make some yourself."

The conversation developed into one of the most violent quarrels they had ever had. After the ensuing reconciliation and the inevitable period of moral inertia, she realized that he had taken the life out of the project. Neither of them ever mentioned the probability that Bloeckman was by no means disinterested, but they both knew that it lay back of Anthony's objection.

In April war was declared with Germany. Wilson and his cabinet—a cabinet that in its lack of distinction was strangely reminiscent of the twelve apostles—let loose the carefully starved dogs of war, and the press began to whoop hysterically against the sinister morals, sinister philosophy, and sinister music produced by the Teutonic temperament. Those who fancied themselves particularly broad-minded made the exquisite distinction that it was only the German Government which aroused them to hysteria; the rest were worked up to a condition of retching indecency. Any song which contained the word "mother" and the word "kaiser" was assured of a tremendous success. At last every one had something to talk about—and almost every one fully enjoyed it, as though they had been cast for parts in a sombre and romantic play.

Anthony, Maury, and Dick sent in their applications for officers' training-camps and the two latter went about feeling strangely exalted and reproachless; they chattered to each other, like college boys, of war's being the one excuse for, and justification of, the aristocrat, and conjured up an impossible caste of officers, to be composed, it appeared, chiefly of the more attractive alumni of three or four Eastern colleges. It seemed to Gloria that in this huge red light streaming across the nation even Anthony took on a new glamour.

The Tenth Infantry, arriving in New York from Panama, were escorted from saloon to saloon by patriotic citizens, to their great bewilderment. West Pointers began to be noticed for the first time in years, and the general impression was that everything was glorious, but not half so glorious as it was going to be pretty soon, and that everybody was a fine fellow, and every race a great race—always excepting the Germans— and in every strata of society outcasts and scapegoats had but to appear in uniform to be forgiven, cheered, and wept over by relatives, ex-friends, and utter strangers.

Unfortunately, a small and precise doctor decided that there was something the matter with Anthony's blood-pressure. He could not conscientiously pass him for an officers' training-camp.

THE BROKEN LUTE

Their third anniversary passed, uncelebrated, unnoticed. The season warmed in thaw, melted into hotter summer, simmered and boiled away. In July the will was offered for probate, and upon the contestation was assigned by the surrogate to trial term for trial. The matter was prolonged into September— there was difficulty in empanelling an unbiassed jury because of the moral sentiments involved. To Anthony's disappointment a verdict was finally returned in favor of the testator, whereupon Mr. Haight caused a notice of appeal to be served upon Edward Shuttleworth.

As the summer waned Anthony and Gloria talked of the things they were to do when the money was theirs, and of the places they were to go to after the war, when they would "agree on things again," for both of them looked forward to a time when love, springing like the phoenix from its own ashes, should be born again in its mysterious and unfathomable haunts.

He was drafted early in the fall, and the examining doctor made no mention of low blood-pressure. It was all very purposeless and sad when Anthony told Gloria one night that he wanted, above all things, to be killed. But, as always, they were sorry for each other for the wrong things at the wrong times. . . .

They decided that for the present she was not to go with him to the Southern camp where his contingent was ordered. She would remain in New York to "use the apartment," to save money, and to watch the progress of the case—which was pending now in the Appellate Division, of which the calendar, Mr. Haight told them, was far behind.

Almost their last conversation was a senseless quarrel about the proper division of the income—at a word either would have given it all to the other. It was typical of the muddle and confusion of their lives that on the October night when Anthony reported at the Grand Central Station for the journey to camp, she arrived only in time to catch his eye over the anxious heads of a gathered crowd. Through the dark light of the enclosed train-sheds their glances stretched across a hysterical area, foul with yellow sobbing and the smells of poor women. They must have pondered upon what they had done to one another, and each must have accused himself of drawing this sombre pattern through which they were tracing tragically and obscurely. At the last they were too far away for either to see the other's tears.

BOOK THREE

CHAPTER 1

A MATTER OF CIVILIZATION

At a frantic command from some invisible source, Anthony groped his way inside. He was thinking that for the first time in more than three years he was to remain longer than a night away from Gloria. The finality of it appealed to him drearily. It was his clean and lovely girl that he was leaving.

They had arrived, he thought, at the most practical financial settlement: she was to have three hundred and seventy-five dollars a month—not too much considering that over half of that would go in rent—and he was taking fifty to supplement his pay. He saw no need for more: food, clothes, and quarters would be provided—there were no social obligations for a private.

The car was crowded and already thick with breath. It was one of the type known as "tourist" cars, a sort of brummagem Pullman, with a bare floor, and straw seats that needed cleaning. Nevertheless, Anthony greeted it with relief. He had vaguely expected that the trip South would be made in a freight-car, in one end of which would stand eight horses and in the other forty men. He had heard the "hommes 40, chevaux 8" story so often that it had become confused and ominous.

As he rocked down the aisle with his barrack-bag slung at his shoulder like a monstrous blue sausage, he saw no vacant seats, but after a moment his eye fell on a single space at present occupied by the feet of a short swarthy Sicilian, who, with his hat drawn over his eyes, hunched defiantly in the corner. As Anthony stopped beside him he stared up with a scowl, evidently intended to be intimidating; he must have adopted it as a defense against this entire gigantic equation. At Anthony's sharp "That seat taken?" he very slowly lifted the feet as though they were a breakable package, and placed them with some care upon the floor. His eyes remained on Anthony, who meanwhile sat down and unbuttoned the uniform coat issued him at Camp Upton the day before. It chafed him under the arms.

Before Anthony could scrutinize the other occupants of the section a young second lieutenant blew in at the upper end of the car and wafted airily down the aisle, announcing in a voice of appalling acerbity:

"There will be no smoking in this car! No smoking! Don't smoke, men, in this car!"

As he sailed out at the other end a dozen little clouds of expostulation arose on all sides.

"Oh, cripe!"

"Jeese!"

"No *smokin'*?"

"Hey, come back here, fella!"

"What's 'ee idea?"

Two or three cigarettes were shot out through the open windows. Others were retained inside, though kept sketchily away from view. From here and there in accents of bravado, of mockery, of submissive humor, a few remarks were dropped that soon melted into the listless and pervasive silence.

The fourth occupant of Anthony's section spoke up suddenly.

"G'by, liberty," he said sullenly. "G'by, everything except bein' an officer's dog."

Anthony looked at him. He was a tall Irishman with an expression moulded of indifference and utter disdain. His eyes fell on Anthony, as though he expected an answer, and then upon the others. Receiving only a defiant stare from the Italian he groaned and spat noisily on the floor by way of a dignified transition back into taciturnity.

A few minutes later the door opened again and the second lieutenant was borne in upon his customary official zephyr, this time singing out a different tiding:

"All right, men, smoke if you want to! My mistake, men! It's all right, men! Go on and smoke—my mistake!"

This time Anthony had a good look at him. He was young, thin, already faded; he was like his own mustache; he was like a great piece of shiny straw. His chin receded, faintly; this was offset by a magnificent and unconvincing scowl, a scowl that Anthony was to connect with the faces of many young officers during the ensuing year.

Immediately every one smoked—whether they had previously desired to or not. Anthony's cigarette contributed to the hazy oxidation which seemed to roll back and forth in opalescent clouds with every motion of the train. The conversation, which had lapsed between the two impressive visits of the young officer, now revived tepidly; the men across the aisle began making clumsy experiments with their straw seats' capacity for comparative comfort; two card games, half-heartedly begun, soon drew several spectators to sitting positions on the arms of seats. In a few minutes Anthony became aware of a persistently obnoxious sound—the small, defiant Sicilian had fallen audibly asleep. It was wearisome to contemplate that animate protoplasm, reasonable by courtesy only, shut up in a car by an incomprehensible civilization, taken somewhere, to do a vague something without aim or significance or consequence. Anthony sighed, opened a newspaper which he had no recollection of buying, and began to read by the dim yellow light.

Ten o'clock bumped stuffily into eleven; the hours clogged and caught and slowed down. Amazingly the train halted along the dark countryside, from time to time indulging in short, deceitful movements backward or forward, and whistling harsh paeans into the high October night. Having read his newspaper through, editorials, cartoons, and war-poems, his eye fell on a half-column headed *Shakespeareville, Kansas.* It seemed that the Shakespeareville Chamber of Commerce had recently held an enthusiastic debate as to whether the American soldiers should be known as "Sammies" or "Battling Christians." The thought gagged him. He dropped the newspaper, yawned, and let his mind drift off at a tangent. He wondered why Gloria had been late. It seemed so long ago already—he had a pang of illusive loneliness. He tried to imagine from what angle she would regard her new position, what place in her considerations he would continue to hold. The thought acted as a further depressant—he opened his paper and began to read again.

The members of the Chamber of Commerce in Shakespeareville had decided upon "Liberty Lads."

For two nights and two days they rattled southward, making mysterious inexplicable stops in what were apparently arid wastes, and then rushing through large cities with a pompous air of hurry. The whimsicalities of this train foreshadowed for Anthony the whimsicalities of all army administration.

In the arid wastes they were served from the baggage-car with beans and bacon that at first he was unable to eat—he dined scantily on some milk chocolate distributed by a village canteen. But on the second day the baggage-car's output began to appear surprisingly palatable. On the third morning the rumor was passed along that within the hour they would arrive at their destination, Camp Hooker.

It had become intolerably hot in the car, and the men were all in shirt sleeves. The sun came in through the windows, a tired and ancient sun, yellow as parchment and stretched out of shape in transit. It tried to enter in triumphant squares and produced only warped splotches—but it was appallingly steady; so much so that it disturbed Anthony not to be the pivot of all the inconsequential sawmills and trees and telegraph poles that were turning around him so fast. Outside it played its heavy tremolo over olive roads and fallow cotton-fields, back of which ran a ragged line of woods broken with eminences of gray rock. The foreground was dotted sparsely with wretched, ill-patched shanties, among which there would flash by, now and then, a specimen of the languid yokelry of South Carolina, or else a strolling darky with sullen and bewildered eyes.

Then the woods moved off and they rolled into a broad space like the baked top of a gigantic cake, sugared with an infinity of tents arranged in geometric figures over its surface. The train came to an uncertain stop, and the sun and the poles and the trees faded, and his universe rocked itself slowly back to its old usualness, with Anthony Patch in the centre. As the men, weary and perspiring, crowded out of the car, he smelt that unforgetable aroma that impregnates all permanent camps—the odor of garbage.

Camp Hooker was an astonishing and spectacular growth, suggesting "A Mining Town in 1870—The Second Week." It was a thing of wooden shacks and whitish-gray tents, connected by a pattern of roads, with hard tan drill-grounds fringed with trees. Here and there stood green Y.M.C.A. houses, unpromising oases, with their muggy odor of wet flannels and closed telephone-booths—and across from each of them there was usually a canteen, swarming with life, presided over indolently by an officer who, with the aid of a side-car, usually managed to make his detail a pleasant and chatty sinecure.

Up and down the dusty roads sped the soldiers of the quartermaster corps, also in side-cars. Up and down drove the generals in their government automobiles, stopping now and then to bring unalert details to attention, to frown heavily upon captains marching at the heads of companies, to set the pompous pace in that gorgeous game of showing off which was taking place triumphantly over the entire area.

The first week after the arrival of Anthony's draft was filled with a series of interminable inoculations and physical examinations, and with the preliminary drilling. The days left him desperately tired. He had been issued the wrong size shoes by a popular, easy-going supply-sergeant, and in consequence his feet were so swollen that the last hours of the afternoon were an acute torture. For the first time in his life he could throw himself down on his cot between dinner and afternoon drill-call, and seeming to sink with each moment deeper into a bottomless bed, drop off immediately to sleep, while the noise and laughter around him faded to a pleasant drone of drowsy summer sound. In the morning he awoke stiff and aching, hollow as a ghost, and hurried forth to meet the other ghostly figures who swarmed in the wan company streets, while a harsh bugle shrieked and spluttered at the gray heavens.

He was in a skeleton infantry company of about a hundred men. After the invariable breakfast of fatty bacon, cold toast, and cereal, the entire hundred would rush for the latrines, which, however well-policed, seemed always intolerable, like the lavatories in cheap hotels. Out on the field, then, in ragged order—the lame man on his left grotesquely marring Anthony's listless efforts to keep in step, the platoon sergeants either showing off violently to impress the officers and recruits, or else quietly lurking in close to the line of march, avoiding both labor and unnecessary visibility.

When they reached the field, work began immediately— they peeled off their shirts for calisthenics. This was the only part of the day that Anthony enjoyed. Lieutenant Kretching, who presided at the antics, was sinewy and muscular, and

Anthony, followed his movements faithfully, with a feeling that he was doing something of positive value to himself. The other officers and sergeants walked about among the men with the malice of schoolboys, grouping here and there around some unfortunate who lacked muscular control, giving him confused instructions and commands. When they discovered a particularly forlorn, ill-nourished specimen, they would linger the full half-hour making cutting remarks and snickering among themselves.

One little officer named Hopkins, who had been a sergeant in the regular army, was particularly annoying. He took the war as a gift of revenge from the high gods to himself, and the constant burden of his harangues was that these rookies did not appreciate the full gravity and responsibility of "the service." He considered that by a combination of foresight and dauntless efficiency he had raised himself to his current magnificence. He aped the particular tyrannies of every officer under whom he had served in times gone by. His frown was frozen on his brow—before giving a private a pass to go to town he would ponderously weigh the effect of such an absence upon the company, the army, and the welfare of the military profession the world over.

Lieutenant Kretching, blond, dull and phlegmatic, introduced Anthony ponderously to the problems of attention, right face, about face, and at ease. His principal defect was his forgetfulness. He often kept the company straining and aching at attention for five minutes while he stood out in front and explained a new movement—as a result only the men in the centre knew what it was all about—those on both flanks had been too emphatically impressed with the necessity of staring straight ahead.

The drill continued until noon. It consisted of stressing a succession of infinitely remote details, and though Anthony perceived that this was consistent with the logic of war, it none the less irritated him. That the same faulty blood-pressure which would have been indecent in an officer did not interfere with the duties of a private was a preposterous incongruity. Sometimes, after listening to a sustained invective concerned with a dull and, on the face of it, absurd subject known as military "courtesy," he suspected that the dim purpose of the war was to let the regular army officers—men with the mentality and aspirations of schoolboys—have their fling with some real slaughter. He was being grotesquely sacrificed to the twenty-year patience of a Hopkins!

Of his three tent-mates—a flat-faced, conscientious objector from Tennessee, a big, scared Pole, and the disdainful Celt whom he had sat beside on the train—the two former spent the evenings in writing eternal letters home, while the Irishman sat in the tent door whistling over and over to himself half a dozen shrill and monotonous bird-calls. It was rather to avoid an hour of their company than with any hope of diversion that, when the quarantine was lifted at the end of the week, he went into town. He caught one of the swarm of jitneys that overran the camp each evening, and in half an hour was set down in front of the Stonewall Hotel on the hot and drowsy main street.

Under the gathering twilight the town was unexpectedly attractive. The sidewalks were peopled by vividly dressed, overpainted girls, who chattered volubly in low, lazy voices, by dozens of taxi-drivers who assailed passing officers with "Take y' anywheh, Lieutenant," and by an intermittent procession of ragged, shuffling, subservient negroes. Anthony, loitering along through the warm dusk, felt for the first time in years the slow, erotic breath of the South, imminent in the hot softness of the air, in the pervasive lull, of thought and time.

He had gone about a block when he was arrested suddenly by a harsh command at his elbow.

"Haven't you been taught to salute officers?"

He looked dumbly at the man who addressed him, a

stout, black-haired captain, who fixed him menacingly with brown pop-eyes.

"*Come to attention!*" The words were literally thundered. A few pedestrians near by stopped and stared. A soft-eyed girl in a lilac dress tittered to her companion.

Anthony came to attention.

"What's your regiment and company?"

Anthony told him.

"After this when you pass an officer on the street you straighten up and salute!"

"All right!"

"Say 'Yes, sir!'"

"Yes, sir."

The stout officer grunted, turned sharply, and marched down the street. After a moment Anthony moved on; the town was no longer indolent and exotic; the magic was suddenly gone out of the dusk. His eyes were turned precipitately inward upon the indignity of his position. He hated that officer, every officer—life was unendurable.

After he had gone half a block he realized that the girl in the lilac dress who had giggled at his discomfiture was walking with her friend about ten paces ahead of him. Several times she had turned and stared at Anthony, with cheerful laughter in the large eyes that seemed the same color as her gown.

At the corner she and her companion visibly slackened their pace—he must make his choice between joining them and passing obliviously by. He passed, hesitated, then slowed down. In a moment the pair were abreast of him again, dissolved in laughter now—not such strident mirth as he would have expected in the North from actresses in this familiar comedy, but a soft, low rippling, like the overflow from some subtle joke, into which he had inadvertently blundered.

"How do you do?" he said.

Her eyes were soft as shadows. Were they violet, or was it their blue darkness mingling with the gray hues of dusk?

"Pleasant evening," ventured Anthony uncertainly.

"Sure is," said the second girl.

"Hasn't been a very pleasant evening for you," sighed the girl in lilac. Her voice seemed as much a part of the night as the drowsy breeze stirring the wide brim of her hat.

"He had to have a chance to show off," said Anthony with a scornful laugh.

"Reckon so," she agreed.

They turned the corner and moved lackadaisically up a side street, as if following a drifting cable to which they were attached. In this town it seemed entirely natural to turn corners like that, it seemed natural to be bound nowhere in particular, to be thinking nothing. . . . The side street was dark, a sudden offshoot into a district of wild rose hedges and little quiet houses set far back from the street.

"Where're you going?" he inquired politely.

"Just goin'." The answer was an apology, a question, an explanation.

"Can I stroll along with you?"

"Reckon so."

It was an advantage that her accent was different. He could not have determined the social status of a Southerner from her talk—in New York a girl of a lower class would have been raucous, unendurable—except through the rosy spectacles of intoxication.

Dark was creeping down. Talking little—Anthony in careless, casual questions, the other two with provincial economy of phrase and burden—they sauntered past another corner, and another. In the middle of a block they stopped beneath a lamp-post.

"I live near here," explained the other girl.

"I live around the block," said the girl in lilac.

"Can I see you home?"

"To the corner, if you want to."

The other girl took a few steps backward. Anthony removed his hat.

"You're supposed to salute," said the girl in lilac with a laugh. "All the soldiers salute."

"I'll learn," he responded soberly.

The other girl said, "Well—" hesitated, then added, "call me up to-morrow, Dot," and retreated from the yellow circle of the street-lamp. Then, in silence, Anthony and the girl in lilac walked the three blocks to the small rickety house which was her home. Outside the wooden gate she hesitated.

"Well—thanks."

"Must you go in so soon?"

"I ought to."

"Can't you stroll around a little longer?" She regarded him dispassionately.

"I don't even know you."

Anthony laughed.

"It's not too late."

"I reckon I better go in."

"I thought we might walk down and see a movie."

"I'd like to."

"Then I could bring you home. I'd have just enough time. I've got to be in camp by eleven."

It was so dark that he could scarcely see her now. She was a dress swayed infinitesimally by the wind, two limpid, reckless eyes . . .

"Why don't you come—Dot? Don't you like movies? Better come."

She shook her head.

"I oughtn't to."

He liked her, realizing that she was temporizing for the effect on him. He came closer and took her hand.

"If we get back by ten, can't you? just to the movies?"

"Well—I reckon so—"

Hand in hand they walked back toward down-town,

along a hazy, dusky street where a negro newsboy was calling an extra in the cadence of the local venders' tradition, a cadence that was as musical as song.

DOT

Anthony's affair with Dorothy Raycroft was an inevitable result of his increasing carelessness about himself. He did not go to her desiring to possess the desirable, nor did he fall before a personality more vital, more compelling than his own, as he had done with Gloria four years before. He merely slid into the matter through his inability to make definite judgments. He could say "No!" neither to man nor woman; borrower and temptress alike found him tender-minded and pliable. Indeed he seldom made decisions at all, and when he did they were but half-hysterical resolves formed in the panic of some aghast and irreparable awakening.

The particular weakness he indulged on this occasion was his need of excitement and stimulus from without. He felt that for the first time in four years he could express and interpret himself anew. The girl promised rest; the hours in her company each evening alleviated the morbid and inevitably futile poundings of his imagination. He had become a coward in earnest—completely the slave of a hundred disordered and prowling thoughts which were released by the collapse of the authentic devotion to Gloria that had been the chief jailer of his insufficiency.

On that first night, as they stood by the gate, he kissed Dorothy and made an engagement to meet her the following Saturday. Then he went out to camp, and with the light burning lawlessly in his tent, he wrote a long letter to Gloria, a glowing letter, full of the sentimental dark, full of the remembered breath of flowers, full of a true and exceeding tenderness—these things he had learned again for a moment in a kiss given and taken under a rich warm moonlight just an hour before.

When Saturday night came he found Dot waiting at the entrance of the Bijou Moving Picture Theatre. She was dressed as on the preceding Wednesday in her lilac gown of frailest organdy, but it had evidently been washed and starched since then, for it was fresh and unrumpled. Daylight confirmed the impression he had received that in a sketchy, faulty way she was lovely. She was clean, her features were small, irregular, but eloquent and appropriate to each other. She was a dark, unenduring little flower—yet he thought he detected in her some quality of spiritual reticence, of strength drawn from her passive acceptance of all things. In this he was mistaken.

Dorothy Raycroft was nineteen. Her father had kept a small, unprosperous corner store, and she had graduated from high school in the lowest fourth of her class two days before he died. At high school she had enjoyed a rather unsavory reputation. As a matter of fact her behavior at the class picnic, where the rumors started, had been merely indiscreet—she had retained her technical purity until over a year later. The boy had been a clerk in a store on Jackson Street, and on the day after the incident he departed unexpectedly to New York. He had been intending to leave for some time, but had tarried for the consummation of his amorous enterprise.

After a while she confided the adventure to a girl friend, and later, as she watched her friend disappear down the sleepy street of dusty sunshine she knew in a flash of intuition that her story was going out into the world. Yet after telling it she felt much better, and a little bitter, and made as near an approach to character as she was capable of by walking in another direction and meeting another man with the honest intention of gratifying herself again. As a rule things happened to Dot. She was not weak, because there was nothing in her to tell her she was being weak. She was not strong, because she never knew that some of the things she did were brave. She neither defied nor conformed nor compromised.

She had no sense of humor, but, to take its place, a happy

disposition that made her laugh at the proper times when she was with men. She had no definite intentions—sometimes she regretted vaguely that her reputation precluded what chance she had ever had for security. There had been no open discovery: her mother was interested only in starting her off on time each morning for the jewelry store where she earned fourteen dollars a week. But some of the boys she had known in high school now looked the other way when they were walking with "nice girls," and these incidents hurt her feelings. When they occurred she went home and cried.

Besides the Jackson Street clerk there had been two other men, of whom the first was a naval officer, who passed through town during the early days of the war. He had stayed over a night to make a connection, and was leaning idly against one of the pillars of the Stonewall Hotel when she passed by. He remained in town four days. She thought she loved him—lavished on him that first hysteria of passion that would have gone to the pusillanimous clerk. The naval officer's uniform—there were few of them in those days—had made the magic. He left with vague promises on his lips, and, once on the train, rejoiced that he had not told her his real name.

Her resultant depression had thrown her into the arms of Cyrus Fielding, the son of a local clothier, who had hailed her from his roadster one day as she passed along the sidewalk. She had always known him by name. Had she been born to a higher stratum he would have known her before. She had descended a little lower—so he met her after all. After a month he had gone away to training-camp, a little afraid of the intimacy, a little relieved in perceiving that she had not cared deeply for him, and that she was not the sort who would ever make trouble. Dot romanticized this affair and conceded to her vanity that the war had taken these men away from her. She told herself that she could have married the naval officer. Nevertheless, it worried her that within eight months there had been three men in her life. She thought with more fear than wonder in her heart that she would soon be like those "bad girls" on Jackson Street at whom she and her gum-chewing, giggling friends had stared with fascinated glances three years before.

For a while she attempted to be more careful. She let men "pick her up"; she let them kiss her, and even allowed certain other liberties to be forced upon her, but she did not add to her trio. After several months the strength of her resolution—or rather the poignant expediency of her fears—was worn away. She grew restless drowsing there out of life and time while the summer months faded. The soldiers she met were either obviously below her or, less obviously, above her—in which case they desired only to use her; they were Yankees, harsh and ungracious; they swarmed in large crowds. . . . And then she met Anthony.

On that first evening he had been little more than a pleasantly unhappy face, a voice, the means with which to pass an hour, but when she kept her engagement with him on Saturday she regarded him with consideration. She liked him. Unknowingly she saw her own tragedies mirrored in his face.

Again they went to the movies, again they wandered along the shadowy, scented streets, hand in hand this time, speaking a little in hushed voices. They passed through the gate—up toward the little porch—

"I can stay a while, can't I?"

"Sh!" she whispered, "we've got to be very quiet. Mother sits up reading Snappy Stories." In confirmation he heard the faint crackling inside as a page was turned. The open-shutter slits emitted horizontal rods of light that fell in thin parallels across Dorothy's skirt. The street was silent save for a group on the steps of a house across the way, who, from time to time, raised their voices in a soft, bantering song.

"—*When you wa-ake You shall ha-ave All the pretty little hawsiz—*"

Then, as though it had been waiting on a near-by roof

for their arrival, the moon came slanting suddenly through the vines and turned the girl's face to the color of white roses.

Anthony had a start of memory, so vivid that before his closed eyes there formed a picture, distinct as a flashback on a screen—a spring night of thaw set out of time in a half-forgotten winter five years before—another face, radiant, flower-like, upturned to lights as transforming as the stars—

Ah, *la belle dame sans merci* who lived in his heart, made known to him in transitory fading splendor by dark eyes in the Ritz-Carlton, by a shadowy glance from a passing carriage in the Bois de Boulogne! But those nights were only part of a song, a remembered glory—here again were the faint winds, the illusions, the eternal present with its promise of romance.

"Oh," she whispered, "do you love me? Do you love me?"

The spell was broken—the drifted fragments of the stars became only light, the singing down the street diminished to a monotone, to the whimper of locusts in the grass. With almost a sigh he kissed her fervent mouth, while her arms crept up about his shoulders.

THE MAN-AT-ARMS

As the weeks dried up and blew away, the range of Anthony's travels extended until he grew to comprehend the camp and its environment. For the first time in his life he was in constant personal contact with the waiters to whom he had given tips, the chauffeurs who had touched their hats to him, the carpenters, plumbers, barbers, and farmers who had previously been remarkable only in the subservice of their professional genuflections. During his first two months in camp he did not hold ten minutes' consecutive conversation with a single man.

On the service record his occupation stood as "student"; on the original questionnaire he had prematurely written "author"; but when men in his company asked his business he commonly gave it as bank clerk—had he told the truth, that he did no work, they would have been suspicious of him as a member of the leisure class.

His platoon sergeant, Pop Donnelly, was a scraggly "old soldier," worn thin with drink. In the past he had spent unnumbered weeks in the guard-house, but recently, thanks to the drill-master famine, he had been elevated to his present pinnacle. His complexion was full of shell-holes—it bore an unmistakable resemblance to those aerial photographs of "the battle-field at Blank." Once a week he got drunk down-town on white liquor, returned quietly to camp and collapsed upon his bunk, joining the company at reveille looking more than ever like a white mask of death.

He nursed the astounding delusion that he was astutely "slipping it over" on the government—he had spent eighteen years in its service at a minute wage, and he was soon to retire (here he usually winked) on the impressive income of fifty-five dollars a month. He looked upon it as a gorgeous joke that he had played upon the dozens who had bullied and scorned him since he was a Georgia country boy of nineteen.

At present there were but two lieutenants—Hopkins and the popular Kretching. The latter was considered a good fellow and a fine leader, until a year later, when he disappeared with a mess fund of eleven hundred dollars and, like so many leaders, proved exceedingly difficult to follow.

Eventually there was Captain Dunning, god of this brief but self-sufficing microcosm. He was a reserve officer, nervous, energetic, and enthusiastic. This latter quality, indeed, often took material form and was visible as fine froth in the corners of his mouth. Like most executives he saw his charges strictly from the front, and to his hopeful eyes his command seemed just such an excellent unit as such an excellent war deserved. For all his anxiety and absorption he was having the time of his life.

Baptiste, the little Sicilian of the train, fell foul of him the second week of drill. The captain had several times ordered the men to be clean-shaven when they fell in each morning. One day there was disclosed an alarming breech of this rule, surely a case of Teutonic connivance—during the night four men had grown hair upon their faces. The fact that three of the four understood a minimum of English made a practical object-lesson only the more necessary, so Captain Dunning resolutely sent a volunteer barber back to the company street for a razor. Whereupon for the safety of democracy a half-ounce of hair was scraped dry from the cheeks of three Italians and one Pole.

Outside the world of the company there appeared, from time to time, the colonel, a heavy man with snarling teeth, who circumnavigated the battalion drill-field upon a handsome black horse. He was a West Pointer, and, mimetically, a gentleman. He had a dowdy wife and a dowdy mind, and spent much of his time in town taking advantage of the army's lately exalted social position. Last of all was the general, who traversed the roads of the camp preceded by his flag—a figure so austere, so removed, so magnificent, as to be scarcely comprehensible.

December. Cool winds at night now, and damp, chilly mornings on the drill-grounds. As the heat faded, Anthony found himself increasingly glad to be alive. Renewed strangely through his body, he worried little and existed in the present with a sort of animal content. It was not that Gloria or the life that Gloria represented was less often in his thoughts—it was simply that she became, day by day, less real, less vivid. For a week they had corresponded passionately, almost hysterically—then by an unwritten agreement they had ceased to write more than twice, and then once, a week. She was bored, she said; if his brigade was to be there a long time she was coming down to join him. Mr. Haight was going to be able to submit a stronger brief than he had expected, but doubted that the appealed case would come up until late spring. Muriel was in the city doing

Red Cross work, and they went out together rather often. What would Anthony think if *she* went into the Red Cross? Trouble was she had heard that she might have to bathe negroes in alcohol, and after that she hadn't felt so patriotic. The city was full of soldiers and she'd seen a lot of boys she hadn't laid eyes on for years. . . .

Anthony did not want her to come South. He told himself that this was for many reasons—he needed a rest from her and she from him. She would be bored beyond measure in town, and she would be able to see Anthony for only a few hours each day. But in his heart he feared that it was because he was attracted to Dorothy. As a matter of fact he lived in terror that Gloria should learn by some chance or intention of the relation he had formed. By the end of a fortnight the entanglement began to give him moments of misery at his own faithlessness. Nevertheless, as each day ended he was unable to withstand the lure that would draw him irresistibly out of his tent and over to the telephone at the Y.M.C.A.

"Dot."

"Yes?"

"I may be able to get in to-night."

"I'm so glad."

"Do you want to listen to my splendid eloquence for a few starry hours?"

"Oh, you funny—" For an instant he had a memory of five years before—of Geraldine. Then—

"I'll arrive about eight."

At seven he would be in a jitney bound for the city, where hundreds of little Southern girls were waiting on moonlit porches for their lovers. He would be excited already for her warm retarded kisses, for the amazed quietude of the glances she gave him—glances nearer to worship than any he had ever inspired. Gloria and he had been equals, giving without thought of thanks or obligation. To this girl his very caresses were an inestimable boon. Crying quietly she had confessed to him that he was not the first man in her life; there had been one other—he gathered that the affair had no sooner commenced than it had been over.

Indeed, so far as she was concerned, she spoke the truth. She had forgotten the clerk, the naval officer, the clothier's son, forgotten her vividness of emotion, which is true forgetting. She knew that in some opaque and shadowy existence some one had taken her—it was as though it had occurred in sleep.

Almost every night Anthony came to town. It was too cool now for the porch, so her mother surrendered to them the tiny sitting room, with its dozens of cheaply framed chromos, its yard upon yard of decorative fringe, and its thick atmosphere of several decades in the proximity of the kitchen. They would build a fire—then, happily, inexhaustibly, she would go about the business of love. Each evening at ten she would walk with him to the door, her black hair in disarray, her face pale without cosmetics, paler still under the whiteness of the moon. As a rule it would be bright and silver outside; now and then there was a slow warm rain, too indolent, almost, to reach the ground.

"Say you love me," she would whisper.

"Why, of course, you sweet baby."

"Am I a baby?" This almost wistfully.

"Just a little baby."

She knew vaguely of Gloria. It gave her pain to think of it, so she imagined her to be haughty and proud and cold. She had decided that Gloria must be older than Anthony, and that there was no love between husband and wife. Sometimes she let herself dream that after the war Anthony would get a divorce and they would be married—but she never mentioned this to Anthony, she scarcely knew why. She shared his company's idea that he was a sort of bank clerk—she thought that he was respectable and poor. She would say:

"If I had some money, darlin', I'd give ev'y bit of it to you. . . . I'd like to have about fifty thousand dollars."

"I suppose that'd be plenty," agreed Anthony.

—In her letter that day Gloria had written: "I suppose if we *could* settle for a million it would be better to tell Mr. Haight to go ahead and settle. But it'd seem a pity. . . ."

. . . "We could have an automobile," exclaimed Dot, in a final burst of triumph.

AN IMPRESSIVE OCCASION

Captain Dunning prided himself on being a great reader of character. Half an hour after meeting a man he was accustomed to place him in one of a number of astonishing categories—fine man, good man, smart fellow, theorizer, poet, and "worthless." One day early in February he caused Anthony to be summoned to his presence in the orderly tent.

"Patch," he said sententiously, "I've had my eye on you for several weeks."

Anthony stood erect and motionless.

"And I think you've got the makings of a good soldier."

He waited for the warm glow, which this would naturally arouse, to cool—and then continued:

"This is no child's play," he said, narrowing his brows.

Anthony agreed with a melancholy "No, sir."

"It's a man's game—and we need leaders." Then the climax, swift, sure, and electric: "Patch, I'm going to make you a corporal."

At this point Anthony should have staggered slightly backward, overwhelmed. He was to be one of the quarter million selected for that consummate trust. He was going to be able to shout the technical phrase, "Follow me!" to seven other frightened men.

"You seem to be a man of some education," said Captain Dunning.

"Yes, Sir."

"That's good, that's good. Education's a great thing, but

don't let it go to your head. Keep on the way you're doing and you'll be a good soldier."

With these parting words lingering in his ears, Corporal Patch saluted, executed a right about face, and left the tent.

Though the conversation amused Anthony, it did generate the idea that life would be more amusing as a sergeant or, should he find a less exacting medical examiner, as an officer. He was little interested in the work, which seemed to belie the army's boasted gallantry. At the inspections one did not dress up to look well, one dressed up to keep from looking badly.

But as winter wore away—the short, snowless winter marked by damp nights and cool, rainy days—he marvelled at how quickly the system had grasped him. He was a soldier—all who were not soldiers were civilians. The world was divided primarily into those two classifications.

It occurred to him that all strongly accentuated classes, such as the military, divided men into two kinds: their own kind—and those without. To the clergyman there were clergy and laity, to the Catholic there were Catholics and non-Catholics, to the negro there were blacks and whites, to the prisoner there were the imprisoned and the free, and to the sick man there were the sick and the well. . . . So, without thinking of it once in his lifetime, he had been a civilian, a layman, a non-Catholic, a Gentile, white, free, and well. . . .

As the American troops were poured into the French and British trenches he began to find the names of many Harvard men among the casualties recorded in the Army and Navy Journal. But for all the sweat and blood the situation appeared unchanged, and he saw no prospect of the war's ending in the perceptible future. In the old chronicles the right wing of one army always defeated the left wing of the other, the left wing being, meanwhile, vanquished by the enemy's right. After that the mercenaries fled. It had been so simple, in those days, almost as if prearranged. . . .

Gloria wrote that she was reading a great deal. What a mess they had made of their affairs, she said. She had so little to do now that she spent her time imagining how differently things might have turned out. Her whole environment appeared insecure—and a few years back she had seemed to hold all the strings in her own little hand. . . .

In June her letters grew hurried and less frequent. She suddenly ceased to write about coming South.

DEFEAT

March in the country around was rare with jasmine and jonquils and patches of violets in the warming grass. Afterward he remembered especially one afternoon of such a fresh and magic glamour that as he stood in the rifle-pit marking targets he recited "Atalanta in Calydon" to an uncomprehending Pole, his voice mingling with the rip, sing, and splatter of the bullets overhead.

"When the hounds of spring . . ."

Spang!

"Are on winter's traces . . ."

Whirr-r-r-r! . . .

"The mother of months . . ."

"Hey! Come to! Mark three-e-e! . . ."

In town the streets were in a sleepy dream again, and together Anthony and Dot idled in their own tracks of the previous autumn until he began to feel a drowsy attachment for this South—a South, it seemed, more of Algiers than of Italy, with faded aspirations pointing back over innumerable generations to some warm, primitive Nirvana, without hope or care. Here there was an inflection of cordiality, of comprehension, in every voice. "Life plays the same lovely and agonizing joke on all of us," they seemed to say in their plaintive pleasant cadence, in the rising inflection terminating on an unresolved minor.

He liked his barber shop where he was "Hi, corporal!" to a pale, emaciated young man, who shaved him and pushed a cool vibrating machine endlessly over his insatiable head. He liked "Johnston's Gardens" where they danced, where a tragic negro made yearning, aching music on a saxophone until the garish hall became an enchanted jungle of barbaric rhythms and smoky laughter, where to forget the uneventful passage of time upon Dorothy's soft sighs and tender whisperings was the consummation of all aspiration, of all content.

There was an undertone of sadness in her character, a conscious evasion of all except the pleasurable minutiae of life. Her violet eyes would remain for hours apparently insensate as, thoughtless and reckless, she basked like a cat in the sun. He wondered what the tired, spiritless mother thought of them, and whether in her moments of uttermost cynicism she ever guessed at their relationship.

On Sunday afternoons they walked along the countryside, resting at intervals on the dry moss in the outskirts of a wood. Here the birds had gathered and the clusters of violets and white dogwood; here the hoar trees shone crystalline and cool, oblivious to the intoxicating heat that waited outside; here he would talk, intermittently, in a sleepy monologue, in a conversation of no significance, of no replies.

July came scorching down. Captain Dunning was ordered to detail one of his men to learn blacksmithing. The regiment was filling up to war strength, and he needed most of his veterans for drill-masters, so he selected the little Italian, Baptiste, whom he could most easily spare. Little Baptiste had never had anything to do with horses. His fear made matters worse. He reappeared in the orderly room one day and told Captain Dunning that he wanted to die if he couldn't be relieved. The horses kicked at him, he said; he was no good at the work. Finally he fell on his knees and besought Captain Dunning, in a mixture of broken English and scriptural Italian, to get him out of it. He had not slept for three days; monstrous stallions reared and cavorted through his dreams.

Captain Dunning reproved the company clerk (who had burst out laughing), and told Baptiste he would do what he could. But when he thought it over he decided that he couldn't spare a better man. Little Baptiste went from bad to worse. The horses seemed to divine his fear and take every advantage of it. Two weeks later a great black mare crushed his skull in with her hoofs while he was trying to lead her from her stall.

In mid-July came rumors, and then orders, that concerned a change of camp. The brigade was to move to an empty cantonment, a hundred miles farther south, there to be expanded into a division. At first the men thought they were departing for the trenches, and all evening little groups jabbered in the company street, shouting to each other in swaggering exclamations: "Su-u-ure we are!" When the truth leaked out, it was rejected indignantly as a blind to conceal their real destination. They revelled in their own importance. That night they told their girls in town that they were "going to get the Germans." Anthony circulated for a while among the groups—then, stopping a jitney, rode down to tell Dot that he was going away.

She was waiting on the dark veranda in a cheap white dress that accentuated the youth and softness of her face.

"Oh," she whispered, "I've wanted you so, honey. All this day."

"I have something to tell you."

She drew him down beside her on the swinging seat, not noticing his ominous tone.

"Tell me."

"We're leaving next week."

Her arms seeking his shoulders remained poised upon

the dark air, her chin tipped up. When she spoke the softness was gone from her voice.

"Leaving for France?"

"No. Less luck than that. Leaving for some darn camp in Mississippi."

She shut her eyes and he could see that the lids were trembling.

"Dear little Dot, life is so damned hard."

She was crying upon his shoulder.

"So damned hard, so damned hard," he repeated aimlessly; "it just hurts people and hurts people, until finally it hurts them so that they can't be hurt ever any more. That's the last and worst thing it does."

Frantic, wild with anguish, she strained him to her breast.

"Oh, God!" she whispered brokenly, "you can't go way from me. I'd die."

He was finding it impossible to pass off his departure as a common, impersonal blow. He was too near to her to do more than repeat "Poor little Dot. Poor little Dot."

"And then what?" she demanded wearily.

"What do you mean?"

"You're my whole life, that's all. I'd die for you right now if you said so. I'd get a knife and kill myself. You can't leave me here."

Her tone frightened him.

"These things happen," he said evenly.

"Then I'm going with you." Tears were streaming down her checks. Her mouth was trembling in an ecstasy of grief and fear.

"Sweet," he muttered sentimentally, "sweet little girl. Don't you see we'd just be putting off what's bound to happen? I'll be going to France in a few months—"

She leaned away from him and clinching her fists lifted her face toward the sky.

"I want to die," she said, as if moulding each word carefully in her heart.

"Dot," he whispered uncomfortably, "you'll forget. Things are sweeter when they're lost. I know—because once I wanted something and got it. It was the only thing I ever wanted badly, Dot. And when I got it it turned to dust in my hands."

"All right."

Absorbed in himself, he continued:

"I've often thought that if I hadn't got what I wanted things might have been different with me. I might have found something in my mind and enjoyed putting it in circulation. I might have been content with the work of it, and had some sweet vanity out of the success. I suppose that at one time I could have had anything I wanted, within reason, but that was the only thing I ever wanted with any fervor. God! And that taught me you can't have *any*thing, you can't have anything at *all*. Because desire just cheats you. It's like a sunbeam skipping here and there about a room. It stops and gilds some inconsequential object, and we poor fools try to grasp it—but when we do the sunbeam moves on to something else, and you've got the inconsequential part, but the glitter that made you want it is gone—" He broke off uneasily. She had risen and was standing, dry-eyed, picking little leaves from a dark vine.

"Dot—"

"Go way," she said coldly. "What? Why?"

"I don't want just words. If that's all you have for me you'd better go."

"Why, Dot—"

"What's death to me is just a lot of words to you. You put 'em together so pretty."

"I'm sorry. I was talking about you, Dot."

"Go way from here."

He approached her with arms outstretched, but she held him away.

"You don't want me to go with you," she said evenly; "maybe you're going to meet that—that girl—" She could not bring herself to say wife. "How do I know? Well, then, I reckon you're not my fellow any more. So go way."

For a moment, while conflicting warnings and desires prompted Anthony, it seemed one of those rare times when he would take a step prompted from within. He hesitated. Then a wave of weariness broke against him. It was too late—everything was too late. For years now he had dreamed the world away, basing his decisions upon emotions unstable as water. The little girl in the white dress dominated him, as she approached beauty in the hard symmetry of her desire. The fire blazing in her dark and injured heart seemed to glow around her like a flame. With some profound and uncharted pride she had made herself remote and so achieved her purpose.

"I didn't—mean to seem so callous, Dot."

"It don't matter."

The fire rolled over Anthony. Something wrenched at his bowels, and he stood there helpless and beaten.

"Come with me, Dot—little loving Dot. Oh, come with me. I couldn't leave you now—"

With a sob she wound her arms around him and let him support her weight while the moon, at its perennial labor of covering the bad complexion of the world, showered its illicit honey over the drowsy street.

THE CATASTROPHE

Early September in Camp Boone, Mississippi. The darkness, alive with insects, beat in upon the mosquito-netting, beneath the shelter of which Anthony was trying to write a letter. An intermittent chatter over a poker game was going on in the next tent, and outside a man was strolling up the company street singing a current bit of doggerel about "K-K-K-Katy."

With an effort Anthony hoisted himself to his elbow and, pencil in hand, looked down at his blank sheet of paper. Then, omitting any heading, he began:

I can't imagine what the matter is, Gloria. I haven't had a line from you for two weeks and it's only natural to be worried—

He threw this away with a disturbed grunt and began again:

I don't know what to think, Gloria. Your last letter, short, cold, without a word of affection or even a decent account of what you've been doing, came two weeks ago. It's only natural that I should wonder. If your love for me isn't absolutely dead it seems that you'd at least keep me from worry—

Again he crumpled the page and tossed it angrily through a tear in the tent wall, realizing simultaneously that he would have to pick it up in the morning. He felt disinclined to try again. He could get no warmth into the lines—only a persistent jealousy and suspicion. Since midsummer these discrepancies in Gloria's correspondence had grown more and more noticeable. At first he had scarcely perceived them. He was so inured to the perfunctory "dearest" and "darlings" scattered through her letters that he was oblivious to their presence or absence. But in this last fortnight he had become increasingly aware that there was something amiss.

He had sent her a night-letter saying that he had passed his examinations for an officers' training-camp, and expected to leave for Georgia shortly. She had not answered. He had wired again—when he received no word he imagined that she might be out of town. But it occurred and recurred to him that she was not out of town, and a series of distraught imaginings began to plague him. Supposing Gloria, bored and restless, had found some one, even as he had. The thought terrified him with its possibility—it was chiefly because he had been so sure of her personal integrity that he had considered her so sparingly during the year. And now, as a doubt was born, the old angers, the rages of possession, swarmed back a thousandfold. What more natural than that she should be in love again?

He remembered the Gloria who promised that should she ever want anything, she would take it, insisting that since she would act entirely for her own satisfaction she could go through such an affair unsmirched—it was only the effect on a person's mind that counted, anyhow, she said, and her reaction would be the masculine one, of satiation and faint dislike.

But that had been when they were first married. Later, with the discovery that she could be jealous of Anthony, she had, outwardly at least, changed her mind. There were no other men in the world for her. This he had known only too surely. Perceiving that a certain fastidiousness would restrain her, he had grown lax in preserving the completeness of her love—which, after all, was the keystone of the entire structure.

Meanwhile all through the summer he had been maintaining Dot in a boarding-house down-town. To do this it had been necessary to write to his broker for money. Dot had covered her journey south by leaving her house a day before the brigade broke camp, informing her mother in a note that she had gone to New York. On the evening following Anthony had called as though to see her. Mrs. Raycroft was in a state of collapse and there was a policeman in the parlor. A questionnaire had ensued, from which Anthony had extricated himself with some difficulty.

In September, with his suspicions of Gloria, the company of Dot had become tedious, then almost intolerable. He was nervous and irritable from lack of sleep; his heart was sick and afraid. Three days ago he had gone to Captain Dunning and asked for a furlough, only to be met with benignant procrastination. The division was starting overseas, while

Anthony was going to an officers' training-camp; what furloughs could be given must go to the men who were leaving the country.

Upon this refusal Anthony had started to the telegraph office intending to wire Gloria to come South—he reached the door and receded despairingly, seeing the utter impracticability of such a move. Then he had spent the evening quarrelling irritably with Dot, and returned to camp morose and angry with the world. There had been a disagreeable scene, in the midst of which he had precipitately departed. What was to be done with her did not seem to concern him vitally at present—he was completely absorbed in the disheartening silence of his wife. . . .

The flap of the tent made a sudden triangle back upon itself, and a dark head appeared against the night.

"Sergeant Patch?" The accent was Italian, and Anthony saw by the belt that the man was a headquarters orderly.

"Want me?"

"Lady call up headquarters ten minutes ago. Say she have speak with you. Ver' important."

Anthony swept aside the mosquito-netting and stood up. It might be a wire from Gloria telephoned over.

"She say to get you. She call again ten o'clock."

"All right, thanks." He picked up his hat and in a moment was striding beside the orderly through the hot, almost suffocating, darkness. Over in the headquarters shack he saluted a dozing night-service officer.

"Sit down and wait," suggested the lieutenant nonchalantly. "Girl seemed awful anxious to speak to you."

Anthony's hopes fell away.

"Thank you very much, sir." And as the phone squeaked on the side-wall he knew who was calling.

"This is Dot," came an unsteady voice, "I've got to see you."

"Dot, I told you I couldn't get down for several days."

"I've got to see you to-night. It's important."

"It's too late," he said coldly; "it's ten o'clock, and I have to be in camp at eleven."

"All right." There was so much wretchedness compressed into the two words that Anthony felt a measure of compunction.

"What's the matter?"

"I want to tell you good-by.

"Oh, don't be a little idiot!" he exclaimed. But his spirits rose. What luck if she should leave town this very night! What a burden from his soul. But he said: "You can't possibly leave before to-morrow."

Out of the corner of his eye he saw the night-service officer regarding him quizzically. Then, startlingly, came Dot's next words:

"I don't mean 'leave' that way."

Anthony's hand clutched the receiver fiercely. He felt his nerves turning cold as if the heat was leaving his body.

"What?"

Then quickly in a wild broken voice he heard:

"Good-by—oh, good-by!"

Cul-*lup!* She had hung up the receiver. With a sound that was half a gasp, half a cry, Anthony hurried from the headquarters building. Outside, under the stars that dripped like silver tassels through the trees of the little grove, he stood motionless, hesitating. Had she meant to kill herself?—oh, the little fool! He was filled with bitter hate toward her. In this dénouement he found it impossible to realize that he had ever begun such an entanglement, such a mess, a sordid mélange of worry and pain.

He found himself walking slowly away, repeating over and over that it was futile to worry. He had best go back to his tent and sleep. He needed sleep. God! Would he ever sleep again? His mind was in a vast clamor and confusion; as he reached the road he turned around in a panic and began running, not toward his company but away from it. Men were returning now—he could find a taxicab. After a minute two yellow eyes appeared around a bend. Desperately he ran toward them.

"Jitney! Jitney!" . . . It was an empty Ford. . . . "I want to go to town."

"Cost you a dollar."

"All right. If you'll just hurry—"

After an interminable time he ran up the steps of a dark ramshackle little house, and through the door, almost knocking over an immense negress who was walking, candle in hand, along the hall.

"Where's my wife?" he cried wildly.

"She gone to bed."

Up the stairs three at a time, down the creaking passage. The room was dark and silent, and with trembling fingers he struck a match. Two wide eyes looked up at him from a wretched ball of clothes on the bed.

"Ah, I knew you'd come," she murmured brokenly.

Anthony grew cold with anger.

"So it was just a plan to get me down here, get me in trouble!" he said. "God damn it, you've shouted 'wolf' once too often!"

She regarded him pitifully.

"I had to see you. I couldn't have lived. Oh, I had to see you—"

He sat down on the side of the bed and slowly shook his head.

"You're no good," he said decisively, talking unconsciously as Gloria might have talked to him. "This sort of thing isn't fair to me, you know."

"Come closer." Whatever he might say Dot was happy now. He cared for her. She had brought him to her side.

"Oh, God," said Anthony hopelessly. As weariness rolled along its inevitable wave his anger subsided, receded, vanished. He collapsed suddenly, fell sobbing beside her on the bed.

"Oh, my darling," she begged him, "don't cry! Oh, don't cry!"

She took his head upon her breast and soothed him, mingled her happy tears with the bitterness of his. Her hand played gently with his dark hair.

"I'm such a little fool," she murmured brokenly, "but I love you, and when you're cold to me it seems as if it isn't worth while to go on livin'."

After all, this was peace—the quiet room with the mingled scent of women's powder and perfume, Dot's hand soft as a warm wind upon his hair, the rise and fall of her bosom as she took breath—for a moment it was as though it were Gloria there, as though he were at rest in some sweeter and safer home than he had ever known.

An hour passed. A clock began to chime in the hall. He jumped to his feet and looked at the phosphorescent hands of his wrist watch. It was twelve o'clock.

He had trouble in finding a taxi that would take him out at that hour. As he urged the driver faster along the road he speculated on the best method of entering camp. He had been late several times recently, and he knew that were he caught again his name would probably be stricken from the list of officer candidates. He wondered if he had not better dismiss the taxi and take a chance on passing the sentry in the dark. Still, officers often rode past the sentries after midnight. . . .

"Halt!" The monosyllable came from the yellow glare that the headlights dropped upon the changing road. The taxi-driver threw out his clutch and a sentry walked up, carrying his rifle at the port. With him, by an ill chance, was the officer of the guard.

"Out late, sergeant."

"Yes, sir. Got delayed."

"Too bad. Have to take your name."

As the officer waited, note-book and pencil in hand,

something not fully intended crowded to Anthony's lips, something born of panic, of muddle, of despair.

"Sergeant R.A. Foley," he answered breathlessly.

"And the outfit?"

"Company Q, Eighty-third Infantry."

"All right. You'll have to walk from here, sergeant."

Anthony saluted, quickly paid his taxi-driver, and set off for a run toward the regiment he had named. When he was out of sight he changed his course, and with his heart beating wildly, hurried to his company, feeling that he had made a fatal error of judgment.

Two days later the officer who had been in command of the guard recognized him in a barber shop down-town. In charge of a military policeman he was taken back to the camp, where he was reduced to the ranks without trial, and confined for a month to the limits of his company street.

With this blow a spell of utter depression overtook him, and within a week he was again caught down-town, wandering around in a drunken daze, with a pint of bootleg whiskey in his hip pocket. It was because of a sort of craziness in his behavior at the trial that his sentence to the guard-house was for only three weeks.

NIGHTMARE

Early in his confinement the conviction took root in him that he was going mad. It was as though there were a quantity of dark yet vivid personalities in his mind, some of them familiar, some of them strange and terrible, held in check by a little monitor, who sat aloft somewhere and looked on. The thing that worried him was that the monitor was sick, and holding out with difficulty. Should he give up, should he falter for a moment, out would rush these intolerable things—only Anthony could know what a state of blackness there would be if the worst of him could roam his consciousness unchecked.

The heat of the day had changed, somehow, until it was a burnished darkness crushing down upon a devastated land. Over his head the blue circles of ominous uncharted suns, of unnumbered centres of fire, revolved interminably before his eyes as though he were lying constantly exposed to the hot light and in a state of feverish coma. At seven in the morning something phantasmal, something almost absurdly unreal that he knew was his mortal body, went out with seven other prisoners and two guards to work on the camp roads. One day they loaded and unloaded quantities of gravel, spread it, raked it—the next day they worked with huge barrels of red-hot tar, flooding the gravel with black, shining pools of molten heat. At night, locked up in the guard-house, he would lie without thought, without courage to compass thought, staring at the irregular beams of the ceiling overhead until about three o'clock, when he would slip into a broken, troubled sleep.

During the work hours he labored with uneasy haste, attempting, as the day bore toward the sultry Mississippi sunset, to tire himself physically so that in the evening he might sleep deeply from utter exhaustion. . . . Then one afternoon in the second week he had a feeling that two eyes were watching him from a place a few feet beyond one of the guards. This aroused him to a sort of terror. He turned his back on the eyes and shovelled feverishly, until it became necessary for him to face about and go for more gravel. Then they entered his vision again, and his already taut nerves tightened up to the breaking-point. The eyes were leering at him. Out of a hot silence he heard his name called in a tragic voice, and the earth tipped absurdly back and forth to a babel of shouting and confusion.

When next he became conscious he was back in the guard-house, and the other prisoners were throwing him curious glances. The eyes returned no more. It was many days before he realized that the voice must have been Dot's, that she had called out to him and made some sort of disturbance. He decided this just previous to the expiration of his sentence, when the cloud that oppressed him had lifted, leaving him in a deep, dispirited lethargy. As the conscious mediator, the monitor who kept that fearsome ménage of horror, grew stronger, Anthony became physically weaker. He was scarcely able to get through the two days of toil, and when he was released, one rainy afternoon, and returned to his company, he reached his tent only to fall into a heavy doze, from which he awoke before dawn, aching and unrefreshed. Beside his cot were two letters that had been awaiting him in the orderly tent for some time. The first was from Gloria; it was short and cool:

> *The case is coming to trial late in November. Can you possibly get leave?*
> *I've tried to write you again and again but it just seems to make things worse. I want to see you about several matters, but you know that you have once prevented me from coming and I am disinclined to try again. In view of a number of things it seems necessary that we have a conference. I'm very glad about your appointment.*

GLORIA.

He was too tired to try to understand—or to care. Her phrases, her intentions, were all very far away in an incomprehensible past. At the second letter he scarcely glanced; it was from Dot—an incoherent, tear-swollen scrawl, a flood of protest, endearment, and grief. After a page he let it slip from his inert hand and drowsed back into a nebulous hinterland of his own. At drill-call he awoke with a high fever and fainted when he tried to leave his tent—at noon he was sent to the base hospital with influenza.

He was aware that this sickness was providential. It saved

him from a hysterical relapse—and he recovered in time to entrain on a damp November day for New York, and for the interminable massacre beyond.

When the regiment reached Camp Mills, Long Island, Anthony's single idea was to get into the city and see Gloria as soon as possible. It was now evident that an armistice would be signed within the week, but rumor had it that in any case troops would continue to be shipped to France until the last moment. Anthony was appalled at the notion of the long voyage, of a tedious debarkation at a French port, and of being kept abroad for a year, possibly, to replace the troops who had seen actual fighting.

His intention had been to obtain a two-day furlough, but Camp Mills proved to be under a strict influenza quarantine—it was impossible for even an officer to leave except on official business. For a private it was out of the question.

The camp itself was a dreary muddle, cold, wind-swept, and filthy, with the accumulated dirt incident to the passage through of many divisions. Their train came in at seven one night, and they waited in line until one while a military tangle was straightened out somewhere ahead. Officers ran up and down ceaselessly, calling orders and making a great uproar. It turned out that the trouble was due to the colonel, who was in a righteous temper because he was a West Pointer, and the war was going to stop before he could get overseas. Had the militant governments realized the number of broken hearts among the older West Pointers during that week, they would indubitably have prolonged the slaughter another month. The thing was pitiable!

Gazing out at the bleak expanse of tents extending for miles over a trodden welter of slush and snow, Anthony saw the impracticability of trudging to a telephone that night. He would call her at the first opportunity in the morning.

Aroused in the chill and bitter dawn he stood at reveille and listened to a passionate harangue from Captain Dunning:

"You men may think the war is over. Well, let me tell you, it isn't! Those fellows aren't going to sign the armistice. It's another trick, and we'd be crazy to let anything slacken up here in the company, because, let me tell you, we're going to sail from here within a week, and when we do we're going to see some real fighting." He paused that they might get the full effect of his pronouncement. And then: "If you think the war's over, just talk to any one who's been in it and see if *they* think the Germans are all in. They don't. Nobody does. I've talked to the people that *know*, and they say there'll be, anyways, a year longer of war. *They* don't think it's over. So you men better not get any foolish ideas that it is."

Doubly stressing this final admonition, he ordered the company dismissed.

At noon Anthony set off at a run for the nearest canteen telephone. As he approached what corresponded to the downtown of the camp, he noticed that many other soldiers were running also, that a man near him had suddenly leaped into the air and clicked his heels together. The tendency to run became general, and from little excited groups here and there came the sounds of cheering. He stopped and listened—over the cold country whistles were blowing and the chimes of the Garden City churches broke suddenly into reverberatory sound.

Anthony began to run again. The cries were clear and distinct now as they rose with clouds of frosted breath into the chilly air:

"Germany's surrendered! Germany's surrendered!"

THE FALSE ARMISTICE

That evening in the opaque gloom of six o'clock Anthony slipped between two freight-cars, and once over the railroad, followed the track along to Garden City, where he caught an

electric train for New York. He stood some chance of appre-
hension—he knew that the military police were often sent
through the cars to ask for passes, but he imagined that
to-night the vigilance would be relaxed. But, in any event,
he would have tried to slip through, for he had been unable
to locate Gloria by telephone, and another day of suspense
would have been intolerable.

After inexplicable stops and waits that reminded him of
the night he had left New York, over a year before, they drew
into the Pennsylvania Station, and he followed the familiar
way to the taxi-stand, finding it grotesque and oddly stimulating to give his own address.

Broadway was a riot of light, thronged as he had never
seen it with a carnival crowd which swept its glittering way
through scraps of paper, piled ankle-deep on the sidewalks.
Here and there, elevated upon benches and boxes, soldiers
addressed the heedless mass, each face in which was clear cut
and distinct under the white glare overhead. Anthony picked
out half a dozen figures—a drunken sailor, tipped backward
and supported by two other gobs, was waving his hat and
emitting a wild series of roars; a wounded soldier, crutch in
hand, was borne along in an eddy on the shoulders of some
shrieking civilians; a dark-haired girl sat cross-legged and
meditative on top of a parked taxicab. Here surely the victory
had come in time, the climax had been scheduled with the
uttermost celestial foresight. The great rich nation had made
triumphant war, suffered enough for poignancy but not
enough for bitterness—hence the carnival, the feasting, the
triumph. Under these bright lights glittered the faces of
peoples whose glory had long since passed away, whose very
civilizations were dead-men whose ancestors had heard the
news of victory in Babylon, in Nineveh, in Bagdad, in Tyre,
a hundred generations before; men whose ancestors had seen
a flower-decked, slave-adorned cortege drift with its wake of
captives down the avenues of Imperial Rome. . . .

Past the Rialto, the glittering front of the Astor, the jewelled magnificence of Times Square . . . a gorgeous alley of incandescence ahead. . . . Then—was it years later?—he was paying the taxi-driver in front of a white building on Fifty-seventh Street. He was in the hall—ah, there was the negro boy from Martinique, lazy, indolent, unchanged.

"Is Mrs. Patch in?"

"I have just came on, sah," the man announced with his incongruous British accent.

"Take me up—"

Then the slow drone of the elevator, the three steps to the door, which swung open at the impetus of his knock.

"Gloria!" His voice was trembling. No answer. A faint string of smoke was rising from a cigarette-tray—a number of Vanity Fair sat astraddle on the table.

"Gloria!"

He ran into the bedroom, the bath. She was not there. A negligée of robin's-egg blue laid out upon the bed diffused a faint perfume, illusive and familiar. On a chair were a pair of stockings and a street dress; an open powder box yawned upon the bureau. She must just have gone out.

The telephone rang abruptly and he started—answered it with all the sensations of an impostor.

"Hello. Is Mrs. Patch there?"

"No, I'm looking for her myself. Who is this?"

"This is Mr. Crawford."

"This is Mr. Patch speaking. I've just arrived unexpect-edly, and I don't know where to find her."

"Oh." Mr. Crawford sounded a bit taken aback. "Why, I imagine she's at the Armistice Ball. I know she intended going, but I didn't think she'd leave so early."

"Where's the Armistice Ball?"

"At the Astor."

"Thanks."

Anthony hung up sharply and rose. Who was Mr. Crawford?

And who was it that was taking her to the ball? How long had this been going on? All these questions asked and answered themselves a dozen times, a dozen ways. His very proximity to her drove him half frantic.

In a frenzy of suspicion he rushed here and there about the apartment, hunting for some sign of masculine occupation, opening the bathroom cupboard, searching feverishly through the bureau drawers. Then he found something that made him stop suddenly and sit down on one of the twin beds, the corners of his mouth drooping as though he were about to weep. There in a corner of her drawer, tied with a frail blue ribbon, were all the letters and telegrams he had written her during the year past. He was suffused with happy and sentimental shame.

"I'm not fit to touch her," he cried aloud to the four walls. "I'm not fit to touch her little hand."

Nevertheless, he went out to look for her.

In the Astor lobby he was engulfed immediately in a crowd so thick as to make progress almost impossible. He asked the direction of the ballroom from half a dozen people before he could get a sober and intelligible answer. Eventually, after a last long wait, he checked his military overcoat in the hall.

It was only nine but the dance was in full blast. The panorama was incredible. Women, women everywhere—girls gay with wine singing shrilly above the clamor of the dazzling confetti-covered throng; girls set off by the uniforms of a dozen nations; fat females collapsing without dignity upon the floor and retaining self-respect by shouting "Hurraw for the Allies!"; three women with white hair dancing hand in hand around a sailor, who revolved in a dizzying spin upon the floor, clasping to his heart an empty bottle of champagne.

Breathlessly Anthony scanned the dancers, scanned the muddled lines trailing in single file in and out among the tables, scanned the horn-blowing, kissing, coughing, laughing, drinking parties under the great full-bosomed flags which leaned in glowing color over the pageantry and the sound.

Then he saw Gloria. She was sitting at a table for two directly across the room. Her dress was black, and above it her animated face, tinted with the most glamorous rose, made, he thought, a spot of poignant beauty on the room. His heart leaped as though to a new music. He jostled his way toward her and called her name just as the gray eyes looked up and found him. For that instant as their bodies met and melted, the world, the revel, the tumbling whimper of the music faded to an ecstatic monotone hushed as a song of bees.

"Oh, my Gloria!" he cried.

Her kiss was a cool rill flowing from her heart.

CHAPTER 2

A MATTER OF AESTHETICS

On the night when Anthony had left for Camp Hooker one year before, all that was left of the beautiful Gloria Gilbert—her shell, her young and lovely body—moved up the broad marble steps of the Grand Central Station with the rhythm of the engine beating in her ears like a dream, and out onto Vanderbilt Avenue, where the huge bulk of the Biltmore overhung, the street and, down at its low, gleaming entrance, sucked in the many-colored opera-cloaks of gorgeously dressed girls. For a moment she paused by the taxi-stand and watched them—wondering that but a few years before she had been of their number, ever setting out for a radiant Somewhere, always just about to have that ultimate passionate adventure for which the girls' cloaks were delicate and beautifully furred, for which their cheeks were painted and their hearts higher than the transitory dome of pleasure that would engulf them, coiffure, cloak, and all.

It was growing colder and the men passing had flipped up the collars of their overcoats. This change was kind to her. It would have been kinder still had everything changed, weather, streets, and people, and had she been whisked away, to wake in some high, fresh-scented room, alone, and statuesque within and without, as in her virginal and colorful past.

Inside the taxicab she wept impotent tears. That she had not been happy with Anthony for over a year mattered little. Recently his presence had been no more than what it would awake in her of that memorable June. The Anthony of late, irritable, weak, and poor, could do no less than make her irritable in turn—and bored with everything except the fact that in a highly imaginative and eloquent youth they had come together in an ecstatic revel of emotion. Because of this mutually vivid memory she would have done more for Anthony than for any other human—so when she got into the taxicab she wept passionately, and wanted to call his name aloud.

Miserable, lonesome as a forgotten child, she sat in the quiet apartment and wrote him a letter full of confused sentiment:

> . . . I can almost look down the tracks and see
> you going but without you, dearest, dearest, I can't
> see or hear or feel or think. Being apart—whatever
> has happened or will happen to us—is like begging
> for mercy from a storm, Anthony; it's like growing
> old. I want to kiss you so—in the back of your neck
> where your old black hair starts. Because I love
> you and whatever we do or say to each other, or
> have done, or have said, you've got to feel how
> much I do, how inanimate I am when you're gone.
> I can't even hate the damnable presence of
> PEOPLE, those people in the station who haven't
> any right to live—I can't resent them even though
> they're dirtying up our world, because I'm
> engrossed in wanting you so.
>
> If you hated me, if you were covered with

sores like a leper, if you ran away with another
woman or starved me or beat me—how absurd this
sounds—I'd still want you, I'd still love you. I
KNOW, my darling.

It's late—I have all the windows open and the
air outside, is just as soft as spring, yet, somehow,
much more young and frail than spring. Why do
they make spring a young girl, why does that illusion dance and yodel its way for three months
through the world's preposterous barrenness. Spring
is a lean old plough horse with its ribs showing—it's
a pile of refuse in a field, parched by the sun and
the rain to an ominous cleanliness.

In a few hours you'll wake up, my darling—
and you'll be miserable, and disgusted with life.
You'll be in Delaware or Carolina or somewhere
and so unimportant. I don't believe there's any
one alive who can contemplate themselves as an
impermanent institution, as a luxury or an
unnecessary evil. Very few of the people who accentuate the futility of life remark the futility of
themselves. Perhaps they think that in proclaiming
the evil of living they somehow salvage their own
worth from the ruin—but they don't, even you and
I. . . .

. . . Still I can see you. There's blue haze
about the trees where you'll be passing, too beautiful to be predominant. No, the fallow squares of
earth will be most frequent—they'll be along beside
the track like dirty coarse brown sheets drying in
the sun, alive, mechanical, abominable. Nature,
slovenly old hag, has been sleeping in them with
every old farmer or negro or immigrant who
happened to covet her. . . .

So you see that now you're gone I've written a

letter all full of contempt and despair. And that
just means that I love you, Anthony, with all there
is to love with in your
GLORIA.

When she had addressed the letter she went to her twin bed and lay down upon it, clasping Anthony's pillow in her arms as though by sheer force of emotion she could metamorphize it into his warm and living body. Two o'clock saw her dry-eyed, staring with steady persistent grief into the darkness, remembering, remembering unmercifully, blaming herself for a hundred fancied unkindnesses, making a likeness of Anthony akin to some martyred and transfigured Christ. For a time she thought of him as he, in his more sentimental moments, probably thought of himself.

At five she was still awake. A mysterious grinding noise that went on every morning across the areaway told her the hour. She heard an alarm clock ring, and saw a light make a yellow square on an illusory blank wall opposite. With the half-formed resolution of following him South immediately, her sorrow grew remote and unreal, and moved off from her as the dark moved westward. She fell asleep.

When she awoke the sight of the empty bed beside her brought a renewal of misery, dispelled shortly, however, by the inevitable callousness of the bright morning. Though she was not conscious of it, there was relief in eating breakfast without Anthony's tired and worried face opposite her. Now that she was alone she lost all desire to complain about the food. She would change her breakfasts, she thought—have a lemonade and a tomato sandwich instead of the sempiternal bacon and eggs and toast.

Nevertheless, at noon when she had called up several of her acquaintances, including the martial Muriel, and found each one engaged for lunch, she gave way to a quiet pity for herself and her loneliness. Curled on the bed with pencil and paper she wrote Anthony another letter.

Late in the afternoon arrived a special delivery, mailed from some small New Jersey town, and the familiarity of the phrasing, the almost audible undertone of worry and discontent, were so familiar that they comforted her. Who knew? Perhaps army discipline would harden Anthony and accustom him to the idea of work. She had immutable faith that the war would be over before he was called upon to fight, and meanwhile the suit would be won, and they could begin again, this time on a different basis. The first thing different would be that she would have a child. It was unbearable that she should be so utterly alone.

It was a week before she could stay in the apartment with the probability of remaining dry-eyed. There seemed little in the city that was amusing. Muriel had been shifted to a hospital in New Jersey, from which she took a metropolitan holiday only every other week, and with this defection Gloria grew to realize how few were the friends she had made in all these years of New York. The men she knew were in the army. "Men she knew"?—she had conceded vaguely to herself that all the men who had ever been in love with her were her friends. Each one of them had at a certain considerable time professed to value her favor above anything in life. But now—where were they? At least two were dead, half a dozen or more were married, the rest scattered from France to the Philippines. She wondered whether any of them thought of her, and how often, and in what respect. Most of them must still picture the little girl of seventeen or so, the adolescent siren of nine years before.

The girls, too, were gone far afield. She had never been popular in school. She had been too beautiful, too lazy, not sufficiently conscious of being a Farmover girl and a "Future Wife and Mother" in perpetual capital letters. And girls who had never been kissed hinted, with shocked expressions on their plain but not particularly wholesome faces, that Gloria had. Then these girls had gone east or west or south, married and become "people," prophesying, if they prophesied about Gloria, that she would come to a bad end—not knowing that no endings were bad, and that they, like her, were by no means the mistresses of their destinies.

Gloria told over to herself the people who had visited them in the gray house at Marietta. It had seemed at the time that they were always having company—she had indulged in an unspoken conviction that each guest was ever afterward slightly indebted to her. They owed her a sort of moral ten dollars apiece, and should she ever be in need she might, so to speak, borrow from them this visionary currency. But they were gone, scattered like chaff, mysteriously and subtly vanished in essence or in fact.

By Christmas, Gloria's conviction that she should join Anthony had returned, no longer as a sudden emotion, but as a recurrent need. She decided to write him word of her coming, but postponed the announcement upon the advice of Mr. Haight, who expected almost weekly that the case was coming up for trial.

One day, early in January, as she was walking on Fifth Avenue, bright now with uniforms and hung with the flags of the virtuous nations, she met Rachael Barnes, whom she had not seen for nearly a year. Even Rachael, whom she had grown to dislike, was a relief from ennui, and together they went to the Ritz for tea.

After a second cocktail they became enthusiastic. They liked each other. They talked about their husbands, Rachael in that tone of public vainglory, with private reservations, in which wives are wont to speak.

"Rodman's abroad in the Quartermaster Corps. He's a captain. He was bound he would go, and he didn't think he could get into anything else."

"Anthony's in the Infantry." The words in their relation

to the cocktail gave Gloria a sort of glow. With each sip she approached a warm and comforting patriotism.

"By the way," said Rachael half an hour later, as they were leaving, "can't you come up to dinner to-morrow night? I'm having two awfully sweet officers who are just going overseas. I think we ought to do all we can to make it attractive for them."

Gloria accepted gladly. She took down the address—recognizing by its number a fashionable apartment building on Park Avenue.

"It's been awfully good to have seen you, Rachael."

"It's been wonderful. I've wanted to."

With these three sentences a certain night in Marietta two summers before, when Anthony and Rachael had been unnecessarily attentive to each other, was forgiven—Gloria forgave Rachael, Rachael forgave Gloria. Also it was forgiven that Rachael had been witness to the greatest disaster in the lives of Mr. and Mrs. Anthony Patch—

Compromising with events time moves along.

THE WILES OF CAPTAIN COLLINS

The two officers were captains of the popular craft, machine gunnery. At dinner they referred to themselves with conscious boredom as members of the "Suicide Club"—in those days every recondite branch of the service referred to itself as the Suicide Club. One of the captains—Rachael's captain, Gloria observed—was a tall horsy man of thirty with a pleasant mustache and ugly teeth. The other, Captain Collins, was chubby, pink-faced, and inclined to laugh with abandon every time he caught Gloria's eye. He took an immediate fancy to her, and throughout dinner showered her with inane compliments. With her second glass of champagne Gloria decided that for the first time in months she was thoroughly enjoying herself.

After dinner it was suggested that they all go somewhere and dance. The two officers supplied themselves with bottles of liquor from Rachael's sideboard—a law forbade service to the military—and so equipped they went through innumerable fox trots in several glittering caravanseries along Broadway, faithfully alternating partners—while Gloria became more and more uproarious and more and more amusing to the pink-faced captain, who seldom bothered to remove his genial smile at all.

At eleven o'clock to her great surprise she was in the minority for staying out. The others wanted to return to Rachael's apartment—to get some more liquor, they said. Gloria argued persistently that Captain Collins's flask was half full—she had just seen it—then catching Rachael's eye she received an unmistakable wink. She deduced, confusedly, that her hostess wanted to get rid of the officers and assented to being bundled into a taxicab outside.

Captain Wolf sat on the left with Rachael on his knees. Captain Collins sat in the middle, and as he settled himself he slipped his arm about Gloria's shoulder. It rested there lifelessly for a moment and then tightened like a vise. He leaned over her.

"You're awfully pretty," he whispered.

"Thank you kindly, sir." She was neither pleased nor annoyed. Before Anthony came so many arms had done like-wise that it had become little more than a gesture, sentimental but without significance.

Up in Rachael's long front room a low fire and two lamps shaded with orange silk gave all the light, so that the corners were full of deep and somnolent shadows. The hostess, moving about in a dark-figured gown of loose chiffon, seemed to accentuate the already sensuous atmosphere. For a while they were all four together, tasting the sandwiches that waited on the tea table—then Gloria found herself alone with Captain Collins on the fireside lounge; Rachael and Captain Wolf had withdrawn to the other side of the room, where they were conversing in subdued voices.

"I wish you weren't married," said Collins, his face a ludicrous travesty of "in all seriousness."

"Why?" She held out her glass to be filled with a high-ball.

"Don't drink any more," he urged her, frowning.

"Why not?"

"You'd be nicer—if you didn't."

Gloria caught suddenly the intended suggestion of the remark, the atmosphere he was attempting to create. She wanted to laugh—yet she realized that there was nothing to laugh at. She had been enjoying the evening, and she had no desire to go home—at the same time it hurt her pride to be flirted with on just that level.

"Pour me another drink," she insisted.

"Please—"

"Oh, don't be ridiculous!" she cried in exasperation.

"Very well." He yielded with ill grace.

Then his arm was about her again, and again she made no protest. But when his pink cheek came close she leaned away.

"You're awfully sweet," he said with an aimless air.

She began to sing softly, wishing now that he would take down his arm. Suddenly her eye fell on an intimate scene across the room—Rachael and Captain Wolf were engrossed in a long kiss. Gloria shivered slightly—she knew not why. . . . Pink face approached again.

"You shouldn't look at them," he whispered. Almost immediately his other arm was around her . . . his breath was on her cheek. Again absurdity triumphed over disgust, and her laugh was a weapon that needed no edge of words.

"Oh, I thought you were a sport," he was saying.

"What's a sport?"

"Why, a person that likes to—to enjoy life."

"Is kissing you generally considered a joyful affair?"

They were interrupted as Rachael and Captain Wolf appeared suddenly before them.

"It's late, Gloria," said Rachael—she was flushed and her hair was dishevelled. "You'd better stay here all night."

For an instant Gloria thought the officers were being dismissed. Then she understood, and, understanding, got to her feet as casually as she was able.

Uncomprehendingly Rachael continued:

"You can have the room just off this one. I can lend you everything you need."

Collins's eyes implored her like a dog's; Captain Wolf's arm had settled familiarly around Rachael's waist; they were waiting.

But the lure of promiscuity, colorful, various, labyrinthine, and ever a little odorous and stale, had no call or promise for Gloria. Had she so desired she would have remained, without hesitation, without regret; as it was she could face coolly the six hostile and offended eyes that followed her out into the hall with forced politeness and hollow words.

"*He* wasn't even sport, enough to try to take me home," she thought in the taxi, and then with a quick surge of resentment: "How *utterly* common!"

GALLANTRY

In February she had an experience of quite a different sort. Tudor Baird, an ancient flame, a young man whom at one time she had fully intended to marry, came to New York by way of the Aviation Corps, and called upon her. They went several times to the theatre, and within a week, to her great enjoyment, he was as much in love with her as ever. Quite deliberately she brought it about, realizing too late that she had done a mischief. He reached the point of sitting with her in miserable silence whenever they went out together.

A Scroll and Keys man at Yale, he possessed the correct reticences of a "good egg," the correct notions of chivalry and *noblesse oblige*—and, of course but unfortunately, the correct biases and the correct lack of ideas—all those traits which Anthony had taught her to despise, but which, nevertheless, she rather admired. Unlike the majority of his type, she found that he was not a bore. He was handsome, witty in a light way, and when she was with him she felt that because of some quality he possessed—call it stupidity, loyalty, sentimentality, or something not quite as definite as any of the three— he would have done anything in his power to please her.

He told her this among other things, very correctly and with a ponderous manliness that masked a real suffering. Loving him not at all she grew sorry for him and kissed him sentimentally one night because he was so charming, a relic of a vanishing generation which lived a priggish and graceful illusion and was being replaced by less gallant fools. Afterward she was glad she had kissed him, for next day when his plane fell fifteen hundred feet at Mineola a piece of a gasolene engine smashed through his heart.

GLORIA ALONE

When Mr. Haight told her that the trial would not take place until autumn she decided that without telling Anthony she would go into the movies. When he saw her successful, both histrionically and financially, when he saw that she could have her will of Joseph Bloeckman, yielding nothing in return, he would lose his silly prejudices. She lay awake half one night planning her career and enjoying her successes in anticipation, and the next morning she called up "Films Par Excellence." Mr. Bloeckman was in Europe.

But the idea had gripped her so strongly this time that she decided to go the rounds of the moving picture employment agencies. As so often had been the case, her sense of smell worked against her good intentions. The employment agency smelt as though it had been dead a very long time. She waited five minutes inspecting her unprepossessing competitors—then she walked briskly out into the farthest recesses of Central Park and remained so long that she caught a cold. She was trying to air the employment agency out of her walking suit.

In the spring she began to gather from Anthony's letters— not from any one in particular but from their culminative effect—that he did not want her to come South. Curiously repeated excuses that seemed to haunt him by their very insufficiency occurred with Freudian regularity. He set them down in each letter as though he feared he had forgotten them the last time, as though it were desperately necessary to impress her with them. And the dilutions of his letters with affectionate diminutives began to be mechanical and unspontaneous—almost as though, having completed the letter, he had looked it over and literally stuck them in, like epigrams in an Oscar Wilde play. She jumped to the solution, rejected it, was angry and depressed by turns—finally she shut her mind to it proudly, and allowed an increasing coolness to creep into her end of the correspondence.

Of late she had found a good deal to occupy her attention. Several aviators whom she had met through Tudor Baird came into New York to see her and two other ancient beaux turned up, stationed at Camp Dix. As these men were ordered overseas they, so to speak, handed her down to their friends. But after another rather disagreeable experience with a potential Captain Collins she made it plain that when any one was introduced to her he should be under no misapprehensions as to her status and personal intentions.

When summer came she learned, like Anthony, to watch the officers' casualty list, taking a sort of melancholy pleasure in hearing of the death of some one with whom she had once danced a german and in identifying by name the younger brothers of former suitors—thinking, as the drive toward Paris progressed, that here at length went the world to inevitable and well-merited destruction.

She was twenty-seven. Her birthday fled by scarcely noticed. Years before it had frightened her when she became twenty, to some extent when she reached twenty-six—but now she looked in the glass with calm self-approval seeing the British freshness of her complexion and her figure boyish and slim as of old.

She tried not to think of Anthony. It was as though she were writing to a stranger. She told her friends that he had been made a corporal and was annoyed when they were politely unimpressed. One night she wept because she was sorry for him—had he been even slightly responsive she would have gone to him without hesitation on the first train—whatever he was doing he needed to be taken care of spiritually, and she felt that now she would be able to do even that. Recently, without his continual drain upon her moral strength she found herself wonderfully revived. Before he left she had been inclined through sheer association to brood on her wasted opportunities—now she returned to her normal state of mind, strong, disdainful, existing each day for each day's worth. She bought a doll and dressed it; one week she wept over "Ethan Frome"; the next she revelled in some novels of Galsworthy's, whom she liked for his power of recreating, by spring in darkness, that illusion of young romantic love to which women look forever forward and forever back.

In October Anthony's letters multiplied, became almost frantic—then suddenly ceased. For a worried month it needed all her powers of control to refrain from leaving immediately for Mississippi. Then a telegram told her that he had been in the hospital and that she could expect him in New York within ten days. Like a figure in a dream he came back into her life across the ballroom on that November evening—and all through long hours that held familiar gladness she took him close to her breast, nursing an illusion of happiness and security she had not thought that she would know again.

DISCOMFITURE OF THE GENERALS

After a week Anthony's regiment went back to the Mississippi camp to be discharged. The officers shut themselves up in the compartments on the Pullman cars and drank the whiskey they had bought in New York, and in the coaches the soldiers got as drunk as possible also—and pretended whenever the train stopped at a village that they were just returned from France, where they had practically put an end to the German army. As they all wore overseas caps and claimed that they had not had time to have their gold service stripes sewed on, the yokelry of the seaboard were much impressed and asked them how they liked the trenches—to which they replied "Oh, *boy!*" with great smacking of tongues and shaking of heads. Some one took a piece of chalk and scrawled on the side of the train, "We won the war—now we're going home," and the officers laughed and let it stay. They were all getting what swagger they could out of this ignominious return.

As they rumbled on toward camp, Anthony was uneasy lest he should find Dot awaiting him patiently at the station. To his relief he neither saw nor heard anything of her and thinking that were she still in town she would certainly attempt to communicate with him, he concluded that she had gone—whither he neither knew nor cared. He wanted only to return to Gloria—Gloria reborn and wonderfully alive. When eventually he was discharged he left his company on the rear of a great truck with a crowd who had given tolerant, almost sentimental, cheers for their officers, especially for Captain Dunning. The captain, on his part, had addressed them with tears in his eyes as to the pleasure, etc., and the work, etc., and time not wasted, etc., and duty, etc. It was very dull and human; having given ear to it Anthony, whose mind was freshened by his week in New York, renewed his deep loathing for the military profession and all it connoted. In their childish hearts two out of every three professional officers considered that wars were made for armies and not armies for wars. He rejoiced to see general and field-officers riding desolately about the barren camp deprived of their commands. He rejoiced to hear the men in his company laugh scornfully at the inducements tendered them to remain in the army. They were to attend "schools." He knew what these "schools" were.

Two days later he was with Gloria in New York.

ANOTHER WINTER

Late one February afternoon Anthony came into the apartment and groping through the little hall, pitch-dark in the winter dusk, found Gloria sitting by the window. She turned as he came in.

"What did Mr. Haight have to say?" she asked listlessly.

"Nothing," he answered, "usual thing. Next month, perhaps."

She looked at him closely; her ear attuned to his voice caught the slightest thickness in the dissyllable.

"You've been drinking," she remarked dispassionately.

"Couple glasses."

"Oh."

He yawned in the armchair and there was a moment's silence between them. Then she demanded suddenly:

"Did you go to Mr. Haight? Tell me the truth."

"No." He smiled weakly. "As a matter of fact I didn't have time."

"I thought you didn't go. . . . He sent for you."

"I don't give a damn. I'm sick of waiting around his office. You'd think he was doing *me* a favor." He glanced at Gloria as though expecting moral support, but she had turned back to her contemplation of the dubious and unprepossessing out-of-doors.

"I feel rather weary of life to-day," he offered tentatively. Still she was silent. "I met a fellow and we talked in the Biltmore bar."

The dusk had suddenly deepened but neither of them made any move to turn on the lights. Lost in heaven knew what contemplation, they sat there until a flurry of snow drew a languid sigh from Gloria.

"What've you been doing?" he asked, finding the silence oppressive.

"Reading a magazine—all full of idiotic articles by prosperous authors about how terrible it is for poor people to buy silk shirts. And while I was reading it I could think of nothing except how I wanted a gray squirrel coat—and how we can't afford one."

"Yes, we can."

"Oh, no."

"Oh, yes! If you want a fur coat you can have one."

Her voice coming through the dark held an implication of scorn.

"You mean we can sell another bond?"

"If necessary. I don't want to go without things. We have spent a lot, though, since I've been back."

"Oh, shut up!" she said in irritation.

"Why?"

"Because I'm sick and tired of hearing you talk about what we've spent or what we've done. You came back two months ago and we've been on some sort of a party practically every night since. We've both wanted to go out, and we've gone. Well, you haven't heard me complain, have you? But all you do is whine, whine, whine. I don't care any more what we do or what becomes of us and at least I'm consistent. But I will *not* tolerate your complaining and calamity-howling——"

"You're not very pleasant yourself sometimes, you know."

"I'm under no obligations to be. You're not making any attempt to make things different."

"But I am—"

"Huh! Seems to me I've heard that before. This morning you weren't going to touch another thing to drink until you'd gotten a position. And you didn't even have the spunk to go to Mr. Haight when he sent for you about the suit."

Anthony got to his feet and switched on the lights.

"See here!" he cried, blinking, "I'm getting sick of that sharp tongue of yours."

"Well, what are you going to do about it?"

"Do you think *I'm* particularly happy?" he continued, ignoring her question. "Do you think I don't know we're not living as we ought to?"

In an instant Gloria stood trembling beside him.

"I won't *stand* it!" she burst out. "I won't be lectured to. You and your suffering! You're just a pitiful weakling and you always have been!"

They faced one another idiotically, each of them unable to impress the other, each of them tremendously, achingly, bored. Then she went into the bedroom and shut the door behind her.

His return had brought into the foreground all their pre-bellum exasperations. Prices had risen alarmingly and in perverse ratio their income had shrunk to a little over half of its original size. There had been the large retainer's fee to Mr. Haight; there were stocks bought at one hundred, now down to thirty and forty and other investments that were not paying at all. During the previous spring Gloria had been given the alternative of leaving the apartment or of signing a year's lease at two hundred and twenty-five a month. She had signed it. Inevitably as the necessity for economy had increased they found themselves as a pair quite unable to save. The old policy of prevarication was resorted to. Weary of their incapabilities they chattered of what they would do—oh—to-morrow, of how they would "stop going on parties" and of how Anthony would go to work. But when dark came down Gloria, accustomed to an engagement every night, would feel the ancient restlessness creeping over her. She would stand in the doorway of the bedroom, chewing furiously at her fingers and sometimes meeting Anthony's eyes as he glanced up from his book. Then the telephone, and her nerves would relax, she would answer it with ill-concealed eagerness. Some one was coming up "for just a few minutes"—and oh, the weariness of pretense, the appearance of the wine table, the revival of their jaded spirits—and the awakening, like the mid-point of a sleepless night in which they moved.

As the winter passed with the march of the returning troops along Fifth Avenue they became more and more aware that since Anthony's return their relations had entirely changed. After that reflowering of tenderness and passion each of them had returned into some solitary dream unshared by the other and what endearments passed between them passed, it seemed, from empty heart to empty heart, echoing hollowly the departure of what they knew at last was gone.

Anthony had again made the rounds of the metropolitan newspapers and had again been refused encouragement by a motley of office boys, telephone girls, and city editors. The word was: "We're keeping any vacancies open for our own men who are still in France." Then, late in March, his eye fell on an advertisement in the morning paper and in consequence he found at last the semblance of an occupation.

YOU CAN SELL!!!
Why not earn while you learn?
Our salesmen make $50-$200 weekly.

There followed an address on Madison Avenue, and instructions to appear at one o'clock that afternoon. Gloria, glancing over his shoulder after one of their usual late breakfasts, saw him regarding it idly.

"Why don't you try it?" she suggested.

"Oh—it's one of these crazy schemes."

"It might not be. At least it'd be experience."

At her urging he went at one o'clock to the appointed address, where he found himself one of a dense miscellany of men waiting in front of the door. They ranged from a messenger-boy evidently misusing his company's time to an immemorial individual with a gnarled body and a gnarled cane. Some of the men were seedy, with sunken cheeks and puffy pink eyes—others were young; possibly still in high school. After a jostled fifteen minutes during which they all eyed one another with apathetic suspicion there appeared a smart young shepherd clad in a "waist-line" suit and wearing the manner of an assistant rector who herded them up-stairs into a large room, which resembled a school-room and contained innumerable desks. Here the prospective salesmen sat down—and again waited. After an interval a platform at the end of the hall was clouded with half a dozen sober but sprightly men who, with one exception, took seats in a semi-circle facing the audience.

The exception was the man who seemed the soberest, the most sprightly and the youngest of the lot, and who advanced to the front of the platform. The audience scrutinized him hopefully. He was rather small and rather pretty, with the commercial rather than the thespian sort of prettiness. He had straight blond bushy brows and eyes that were almost preposterously honest, and as he reached the edge of his rostrum he seemed to throw these eyes out into the audience, simultaneously extending his arm with two fingers outstretched. Then while he rocked himself to a state of balance an expectant silence settled over the hall. With perfect assurance the young man had taken his listeners in hand and his words when they came were steady and confident and of the school of "straight from the shoulder."

"Men!"—he began, and paused. The word died with a

prolonged echo at the end of the hall, the faces regarding him, hopefully, cynically, wearily, were alike arrested, engrossed. Six hundred eyes were turned slightly upward. With an even graceless flow that reminded Anthony of the rolling of bowling balls he launched himself into the sea of exposition.

"This bright and sunny morning you picked up your favorite newspaper and you found an advertisement which made the plain, unadorned statement that *you* could sell. That was all it said—it didn't say 'what,' it didn't say 'how,' it didn't say 'why.' It just made one single solitary assertion that *you* and *you* and *you*"—business of pointing—"could sell. Now my job isn't to make a success of you, because every man is born a success, he makes himself a failure; it's not to teach you how to talk, because each man is a natural orator and only makes himself a clam; my business is to tell you one thing in a way that will make you *know* it—it's to tell you that *you* and *you* and *you* have the heritage of money and prosperity waiting for you to come and claim it."

At this point an Irishman of saturnine appearance rose from his desk near the rear of the hall and went out.

"That man thinks he'll go look for it in the beer parlor around the corner. (Laughter.) He won't find it there. Once upon a time I looked for it there myself (laughter), but that was before I did what every one of you men no matter how young or how old, how poor or how rich (a faint ripple of satirical laughter), can do. It was before I found—*myself*!

"Now I wonder if any of you men know what a 'Heart Talk' is. A 'Heart Talk' is a little book in which I started, about five years ago, to write down what I had discovered were the principal reasons for a man's failure and the principal reasons for a man's success—from John D. Rockerfeller back to John D. Napoleon (laughter), and before that, back in the days when Abel sold his birthright for a mess of pottage. There are now one hundred of these 'Heart Talks.' Those of you who are sincere, who are interested in our proposition, above all who are dissatisfied with the way things are breaking for you at present will be handed one to take home with you as you go out yonder door this afternoon.

"Now in my own pocket I have four letters just received concerning 'Heart Talks.' These letters have names signed to them that are familiar in every house-hold in the U.S.A. Listen to this one from Detroit:

> "DEAR MR. CARLETON:
> "I want to order three thousand more copies of 'Heart Talks' for distribution among my salesmen. They have done more for getting work out of the men than any bonus proposition ever considered. I read them myself constantly, and I desire to heartily congratulate you on getting at the roots of the biggest problem that faces our generation to-day—the problem of salesmanship. The rock bottom on which the country is founded is the problem of salesmanship. With many felicitations I am
>
> > "Yours very cordially,
> > "HENRY W. TERRAL."

He brought the name out in three long booming triumphancies—pausing for it to produce its magical effect. Then he read two more letters, one from a manufacturer of vacuum cleaners and one from the president of the Great Northern Doily Company.

"And now," he continued, "I'm going to tell you in a few words what the proposition is that's going to *make* those of you who go into it in the right spirit. Simply put, it's this: 'Heart Talks' have been incorporated as a company. We're going to put these little pamphlets into the hands of every big business organization, every salesman, and every man who *knows*—I don't say 'thinks,' I say *'knows'*—that he can sell! We are offering some of the stock of the 'Heart Talks' concern upon the market, and in order that the distribution may be as wide as possible, and in order also that we can furnish a living, concrete, flesh-and-blood example of what salesmanship is, or rather what it may be, we're going to give those of you who are the real thing a chance to sell that stock. Now, I don't care what you've tried to sell before or how you've tried to sell it. It don't matter how old you are or how young you are. I only want to know two things—first, do you *want* success, and, second, will you work for it?

"My name is Sammy Carleton. Not 'Mr.' Carleton, but just plain Sammy. I'm a regular no-nonsense man with no fancy frills about me. I want you to call me Sammy.

"Now this is all I'm going to say to you to-day. To-morrow I want those of you who have thought it over and have read the copy of 'Heart Talks' which will be given to you at the door, to come back to this same room at this same time, then we'll, go into the proposition further and I'll explain to you what I've found the principles of success to be. I'm going to make you *feel* that *you* and *you* and *you* can sell!"

Mr. Carleton's voice echoed for a moment through the hall and then died away. To the stamping of many feet Anthony was pushed and jostled with the crowd out of the room.

FURTHER ADVENTURES WITH "HEART TALKS"

With an accompaniment of ironic laughter Anthony told Gloria the story of his commercial adventure. But she listened without amusement.

"You're going to give up again?" she demanded coldly.

"Why—you don't expect me to—"

"I never expected anything of you."

He hesitated.

"Well—I can't see the slightest benefit in laughing myself

F. SCOTT FITZGERALD

sick over this sort of affair. If there's anything older than the old story, it's the new twist."

It required an astonishing amount of moral energy on Gloria's part to intimidate him into returning, and when he reported next day, somewhat depressed from his perusal of the senile bromides skittishly set forth in "Heart Talks on Ambition," he found only fifty of the original three hundred awaiting the appearance of the vital and compelling Sammy Carleton. Mr. Carleton's powers of vitality and compulsion were this time exercised in elucidating that magnificent piece of speculation—how to sell. It seemed that the approved method was to state one's proposition and then to say not "And now, will you buy?"—this was not the way—oh, no!—the way was to state one's proposition and then, having reduced one's adversary to a state of exhaustion, to deliver oneself of the categorical imperative: "Now see here! You've taken up my time explaining this matter to you. You've admitted my points—all I want to ask is how many do you want?"

As Mr. Carleton piled assertion upon assertion Anthony began to feel a sort of disgusted confidence in him. The man appeared to know what he was talking about. Obviously prosperous, he had risen to the position of instructing others. It did not occur to Anthony that the type of man who attains commercial success seldom knows how or why, and, as in his grandfather's case, when he ascribes reasons, the reasons are generally inaccurate and absurd.

Anthony noted that of the numerous old men who had answered the original advertisement, only two had returned, and that among the thirty odd who assembled on the third day to get actual selling instructions from Mr. Carleton, only one gray head was in evidence. These thirty were eager converts; with their mouths they followed the working of Mr. Carleton's mouth; they swayed in their seats with enthusiasm, and in the intervals of his talk they spoke to each other in tense approving whispers. Yet of the chosen few who, in the words of Mr. Carleton, "were determined to get those deserts that rightly and truly belonged to them," less than half a dozen combined even a modicum of personal appearance with that great gift of being a "pusher." But they were told that they were all natural pushers—it was merely necessary that they should believe with a sort of savage passion in what they were selling. He even urged each one to buy some stock himself, if possible, in order to increase his own sincerity.

On the fifth day then, Anthony sallied into the street with all the sensations of a man wanted by the police. Acting according to instructions he selected a tall office building in order that he might ride to the top story and work downward, stopping in every office that had a name on the door. But at the last minute he hesitated. Perhaps it would be more practicable to acclimate himself to the chilly atmosphere which he felt was awaiting him by trying a few offices on, say, Madison Avenue. He went into an arcade that seemed only semi-prosperous, and seeing a sign which read Percy B. Weatherbee, Architect, he opened the door heroically and entered. A starchy young woman looked up questioningly.

"Can I see Mr. Weatherbee?" He wondered if his voice sounded tremulous.

She laid her hand tentatively on the telephone-receiver.

"What's the name, please?"

"He wouldn't—ah—know me. He wouldn't know my name."

"What's your business with him? You an insurance agent?"

"Oh, no, nothing like that!" denied Anthony hurriedly. "Oh, no. It's a—it's a personal matter." He wondered if he should have said this. It had all sounded so simple when Mr. Carleton had enjoined his flock:

"Don't allow yourself to be kept out! Show them you've made up your mind to talk to them, and they'll listen."

The girl succumbed to Anthony's pleasant, melancholy

face, and in a moment the door to the inner room opened and admitted a tall, splay-footed man with slicked hair. He approached Anthony with ill-concealed impatience.

"You wanted to see me on a personal matter?"

Anthony quailed.

"I wanted to talk to you," he said defiantly.

"About what?"

"It'll take some time to explain."

"Well, what's it about?" Mr. Weatherbee's voice indicated rising irritation.

Then Anthony, straining at each word, each syllable, began:

"I don't know whether or not you've ever heard of a series of pamphlets called 'Heart Talks'—"

"Good grief!" cried Percy B. Weatherbee, Architect, "are you trying to touch my heart?"

"No, it's business. 'Heart Talks' have been incorporated and we're putting some shares on the market—"

His voice faded slowly off, harassed by a fixed and contemptuous stare from his unwilling prey. For another minute he struggled on, increasingly sensitive, entangled in his own words. His confidence oozed from him in great retching emanations that seemed to be sections of his own body. Almost mercifully Percy B. Weatherbee, Architect, terminated the interview:

"Good grief!" he exploded in disgust, "and you call that a *personal* matter!" He whipped about and strode into his private office, banging the door behind him. Not daring to look at the stenographer, Anthony in some shameful and mysterious way got himself from the room. Perspiring profusely he stood in the hall wondering why they didn't come and arrest him; in every hurried look he discerned infallibly a glance of scorn.

After an hour and with the help of two strong whiskies he brought himself up to another attempt. He walked into a plumber's shop, but when he mentioned his business the plumber began pulling on his coat in a great hurry, gruffly announcing that he had to go to lunch. Anthony remarked politely that it was futile to try to sell a man anything when he was hungry, and the plumber heartily agreed.

This episode encouraged Anthony; he tried to think that had the plumber not been bound for lunch he would at least have listened.

Passing by a few glittering and formidable bazaars he entered a grocery store. A talkative proprietor told him that before buying any stocks he was going to see how the armistice affected the market. To Anthony this seemed almost unfair. In Mr. Carleton's salesman's Utopia the only reason prospective buyers ever gave for not purchasing stock was that they doubted it to be a promising investment. Obviously a man in that state was almost ludicrously easy game, to be brought down merely by the judicious application of the correct selling points. But these men—why, actually they weren't considering buying anything at all.

Anthony took several more drinks before he approached his fourth man, a real-estate agent; nevertheless, he was floored with a coup as decisive as a syllogism. The real-estate agent said that he had three brothers in the investment business. Viewing himself as a breaker-up of homes Anthony apologized and went out.

After another drink he conceived the brilliant plan of selling the stock to the bartenders along Lexington Avenue. This occupied several hours, for it was necessary to take a few drinks in each place in order to get the proprietor in the proper frame of mind to talk business. But the bartenders one and all contended that if they had any money to buy bonds they would not be bartenders. It was as though they had all convened and decided upon that rejoinder. As he approached a dark and soggy five o'clock he found that they were developing a still more annoying tendency to turn him off with a jest.

At five, then, with a tremendous effort at concentration he decided that he must put more variety into his canvassing. He selected a medium-sized delicatessen store, and went in. He felt, illuminatingly, that the thing to do was to cast a spell not only over the storekeeper but over all the customers as well—and perhaps through the psychology of the herd instinct they would buy as an astounded and immediately convinced whole.

"Af'ernoon," he began in a loud thick voice. "Ga l'il prop'sition."

If he had wanted silence he obtained it. A sort of awe descended upon the half-dozen women marketing and upon the gray-haired ancient who in cap and apron was slicing chicken.

Anthony pulled a batch of papers from his flapping brief-case and waved them cheerfully.

"Buy a bon'," he suggested, "good as liberty bon'!" The phrase pleased him and he elaborated upon it. "Better'n liberty bon'. Every one these bon's worth *two* liberty bon's." His mind made a hiatus and skipped to his peroration, which he delivered with appropriate gestures, these being somewhat marred by the necessity of clinging to the counter with one or both hands.

"Now see here. You taken up my time. I don't want know *why* you won't buy. I just want you say *why*. Want you say *how many!*"

At this point they should have approached him with check-books and fountain pens in hand. Realizing that they must have missed a cue Anthony, with the instincts of an actor, went back and repeated his finale.

"Now see here! You taken up my time. You followed prop'sition. You agreed 'th reasonin'? Now, all I want from *you* is, how many lib'ty bon's?"

"See here!" broke in a new voice. A portly man whose face was adorned with symmetrical scrolls of yellow hair had come out of a glass cage in the rear of the store and was bearing down upon Anthony. "See here, you!"

"How many?" repeated the salesman sternly. "You taken up my time—"

"Hey, you!" cried the proprietor, "I'll have you taken up by the police."

"You mos' cert'nly won't!" returned Anthony with fine defiance. "All I want know is how many."

From here and there in the store went up little clouds of comment and expostulation.

"How terrible!"

"He's a raving maniac."

"He's disgracefully drunk."

The proprietor grasped Anthony's arm sharply.

"Get out, or I'll call a policeman."

Some relics of rationality moved Anthony to nod and replace his bonds clumsily in the case.

"How many?" he reiterated doubtfully.

"The whole force if necessary!" thundered his adversary, his yellow mustache trembling fiercely.

"Sell 'em all a bon'."

With this Anthony turned, bowed gravely to his late auditors, and wabbled from the store. He found a taxicab at the corner and rode home to the apartment. There he fell sound asleep on the sofa, and so Gloria found him, his breath filling the air with an unpleasant pungency, his hand still clutching his open brief case.

Except when Anthony was drinking, his range of sensation had become less than that of a healthy old man and when prohibition came in July he found that, among those who could afford it, there was more drinking than ever before. One's host now brought out a bottle upon the slightest pretext. The tendency to display liquor was a manifestation of the same instinct that led a man to deck his wife with jewels. To have liquor was a boast, almost a badge of respectability.

In the mornings Anthony awoke tired, nervous, and worried. Halcyon summer twilights and the purple chill of morning alike left him unresponsive. Only for a brief moment every day in the warmth and renewed life of a first high-ball did his mind turn to those opalescent dreams of future pleasure—the mutual heritage of the happy and the damned. But this was only for a little while. As he grew drunker the dreams faded and he became a confused spectre, moving in odd crannies of his own mind, full of unexpected devices, harshly contemptuous at best and reaching sodden and dispirited depths. One night in June he had quarrelled violently with Maury over a matter of the utmost triviality. He remembered dimly next morning that it had been about a broken pint bottle of champagne. Maury had told him to sober up and Anthony's feelings had been hurt, so with an attempted gesture of dignity he had risen from the table and seizing Gloria's arm half led, half shamed her into a taxicab outside, leaving Maury with three dinners ordered and tickets for the opera.

This sort of semi-tragic fiasco had become so usual that when they occurred he was no longer stirred into making amends. If Gloria protested—and of late she was more likely to sink into contemptuous silence—he would either engage in a bitter defense of himself or else stalk dismally from the apartment. Never since the incident on the station platform at Redgate had he laid his hands on her in anger—though he was withheld often only by some instinct that itself made him tremble with rage. Just as he still cared more for her than for any other creature, so did he more intensely and frequently hate her.

So far, the judges of the Appellate Division had failed to hand down a decision, but after another postponement they finally affirmed the decree of the lower court—two justices dissenting. A notice of appeal was served upon Edward Shuttleworth. The case was going to the court of last resort, and they were in for another interminable wait. Six months, perhaps a year. It had grown enormously unreal to them, remote and uncertain as heaven.

Throughout the previous winter one small matter had been a subtle and omnipresent irritant—the question of Gloria's gray fur coat. At that time women enveloped in long squirrel wraps could be seen every few yards along Fifth Avenue. The women were converted to the shape of tops. They seemed porcine and obscene; they resembled kept women in the concealing richness, the feminine animality of the garment. Yet—Gloria wanted a gray squirrel coat.

Discussing the matter—or, rather, arguing it, for even more than in the first year of their marriage did every discussion take the form of bitter debate full of such phrases as "most certainly," "utterly outrageous," "it's so, nevertheless," and the ultra-emphatic "regardless"—they concluded that they could not afford it. And so gradually it began to stand as a symbol of their growing financial anxiety.

To Gloria the shrinkage of their income was a remarkable phenomenon, without explanation or precedent—that it could happen at all within the space of five years seemed almost an intended cruelty, conceived and executed by a sardonic God. When they were married seventy-five hundred a year had seemed ample for a young couple, especially when augmented by the expectation of many millions. Gloria had failed to realize that it was decreasing not only in amount but in purchasing power until the payment of Mr. Haight's retaining fee of fifteen thousand dollars made the fact suddenly and startlingly obvious. When Anthony was drafted they had calculated their income at over four hundred a month, with the dollar even then decreasing in value, but on his return to New York they discovered an even more alarming condition of affairs. They were receiving only forty-five hundred a year from their investments. And though the suit over the will moved ahead of them like a persistent mirage and the financial danger-mark loomed up in the near distance they found, nevertheless, that living within their income was impossible.

So Gloria went without the squirrel coat and every day upon Fifth Avenue she was a little conscious of her well-worn, half-length leopard skin, now hopelessly old-fashioned. Every other month they sold a bond, yet when the bills were paid it left only enough to be gulped down hungrily by their current expenses. Anthony's calculations showed that their capital would last about seven years longer. So Gloria's heart was very bitter, for in one week, on a prolonged hysterical party during which Anthony whimsically divested himself of coat, vest, and shirt in a theatre and was assisted out by a posse of ushers, they spent twice what the gray squirrel coat would have cost.

It was November, Indian summer rather, and a warm, warm night—which was unnecessary, for the work of the summer was done. Babe Ruth had smashed the home-run record for the first time and Jack Dempsey had broken Jess Willard's cheek-bone out in Ohio. Over in Europe the usual number of children had swollen stomachs from starvation, and the diplomats were at their customary business of making the world safe for new wars. In New York City the proletariat were being "disciplined," and the odds on Harvard were generally quoted at five to three. Peace had come down in earnest, the beginning of new days.

Up in the bedroom of the apartment on Fifty-seventh Street Gloria lay upon her bed and tossed from side to side, sitting up at intervals to throw off a superfluous cover and once asking Anthony, who was lying awake beside her, to bring her a glass of ice-water. "Be sure and put ice in it," she said with insistence; "it isn't cold enough the way it comes from the faucet."

Looking through the frail curtains she could see the rounded moon over the roofs and beyond it on the sky the yellow glow from Times Square—and watching the two incongruous lights, her mind worked over an emotion, or rather an interwoven complex of emotions, that had occupied it through the day, and the day before that and back to the last time when she could remember having thought clearly and consecutively about anything—which must have been while Anthony was in the army.

She would be twenty-nine in February. The month assumed an ominous and inescapable significance—making her wonder, through these nebulous half-fevered hours whether after all she had not wasted her faintly tired beauty, whether there was such a thing as use for any quality bounded by a harsh and inevitable mortality.

Years before, when she was twenty-one, she had written in her diary: "Beauty is only to be admired, only to be loved—to be harvested carefully and then flung at a chosen lover like a gift of roses. It seems to me, so far as I can judge clearly at all, that my beauty should be used like that. . . ."

And now, all this November day, all this desolate day, under a sky dirty and white, Gloria had been thinking that perhaps she had been wrong. To preserve the integrity of her first gift she had looked no more for love. When the first flame and ecstasy had grown dim, sunk down, departed, she had begun preserving—what? It puzzled her that she no longer knew just what she was preserving—a sentimental memory or some profound and fundamental concept of honor. She was doubting now whether there had been any moral issue involved in her way of life—to walk unworried and unregretful along the gayest of all possible lanes and to keep her pride by being always herself and doing what it seemed beautiful that she should do. From the first little boy in an Eton collar whose "girl" she had been, down to the latest casual man whose eyes had grown alert and appreciative as they rested upon her, there was needed only that matchless candor she could throw into a look or clothe with an inconsequent clause—for she had talked always in broken clauses—to weave about her immeasurable illusions, immeasurable distances, immeasurable light. To create souls in men, to create fine happiness and fine despair she must remain deeply proud—proud to be inviolate, proud also to be melting, to be passionate and possessed.

She knew that in her breast she had never wanted children. The reality, the earthiness, the intolerable sentiment of child-bearing, the menace to her beauty—had appalled her. She wanted to exist only as a conscious flower, prolonging and preserving itself. Her sentimentality could cling fiercely to her own illusions, but her ironic soul whispered that motherhood was also the privilege of the female baboon. So her dreams were of ghostly children only—the early, the perfect symbols of her early and perfect love for Anthony.

In the end then, her beauty was all that never failed her. She had never seen beauty like her own. What it meant ethically or aesthetically faded before the gorgeous concreteness of her pink-and-white feet, the clean perfectness of her body, and the baby mouth that was like the material symbol of a kiss.

She would be twenty-nine in February. As the long night waned she grew supremely conscious that she and beauty were going to make use of these next three months. At first she was not sure for what, but the problem resolved itself gradually into the old lure of the screen. She was in earnest now. No material want could have moved her as this fear moved her. No matter for Anthony, Anthony the poor in spirit, the weak and broken man with bloodshot eyes, for whom she still had moments of tenderness. No matter. She would be twenty-nine in February—a hundred days, so many days; she would go to Bloeckman to-morrow.

With the decision came relief. It cheered her that in some manner the illusion of beauty could be sustained, or preserved perhaps in celluloid after the reality had vanished. Well—to-morrow.

The next day she felt weak and ill. She tried to go out, and saved herself from collapse only by clinging to a mail box near the front door. The Martinique elevator boy helped her up-stairs, and she waited on the bed for Anthony's return without energy to unhook her brassiere.

For five days she was down with influenza, which, just as the month turned the corner into winter, ripened into double pneumonia. In the feverish perambulations of her mind she prowled through a house of bleak unlighted rooms hunting for her mother. All she wanted was to be a little girl, to be efficiently taken care of by some yielding yet superior power, stupider and steadier than herself. It seemed that the only lover she had ever wanted was a lover in a dream.

"ODI PROFANUM VULGUS"

One day in the midst of Gloria's illness there occurred a curious incident that puzzled Miss McGovern, the trained nurse, for some time afterward. It was noon, but the room in which the patient lay was dark and quiet. Miss McGovern was standing near the bed mixing some medicine, when Mrs. Patch, who had apparently been sound asleep, sat up and began to speak vehemently:

"Millions of people," she said, "swarming like rats, chattering like apes, smelling like all hell . . . monkeys! Or lice, I suppose. For one really exquisite palace . . . on Long Island, say—or even in Greenwich . . . for one palace full of pictures from the Old World and exquisite things—with avenues of trees and green lawns and a view of the blue sea, and lovely people about in slick dresses . . . I'd sacrifice a hundred thousand of them, a million of them." She raised her hand feebly and snapped her fingers. "I care nothing for them—understand me?"

The look she bent upon Miss McGovern at the conclusion of this speech was curiously elfin, curiously intent. Then she gave a short little laugh polished with scorn, and tumbling backward fell off again to sleep.

Miss McGovern was bewildered. She wondered what were the hundred thousand things that Mrs. Patch would sacrifice for her palace. Dollars, she supposed—yet it had not sounded exactly like dollars.

THE MOVIES

It was February, seven days before her birthday, and the great snow that had filled up the cross-streets as dirt fills the cracks in a floor had turned to slush and was being escorted to the gutters by the hoses of the street-cleaning department. The wind, none the less bitter for being casual, whipped in through the open windows of the living room bearing with it the dismal secrets of the areaway and clearing the Patch apartment of stale smoke in its cheerless circulation.

Gloria, wrapped in a warm kimona, came into the chilly room and taking up the telephone receiver called Joseph Bloeckman.

"Do you mean Mr. Joseph *Black*?" demanded the telephone girl at "Films Par Excellence."

"Bloeckman, Joseph Bloeckman. B-l-o—"

"Mr. Joseph Bloeckman has changed his name to Black. Do you want him?"

"Why—yes." She remembered nervously that she had once called him "Blockhead" to his face.

His office was reached by courtesy of two additional female voices; the last was a secretary who took her name. Only with the flow through the transmitter of his own familiar but faintly impersonal tone did she realize that it had been three years since they had met. And he had changed his name to Black.

"Can you see me?" she suggested lightly. "It's on a business matter, really. I'm going into the movies at last—if I can."

"I'm awfully glad. I've always thought you'd like it."

"Do you think you can get me a trial?" she demanded with the arrogance peculiar to all beautiful women, to all women who have ever at any time considered themselves beautiful.

He assured her that it was merely a question of when she wanted the trial. Any time? Well, he'd phone later in the day and let her know a convenient hour. The conversation closed with conventional padding on both sides. Then from three o'clock to five she sat close to the telephone—with no result.

But next morning came a note that contented and excited her:

> *My dear Gloria:*
>
> *Just by luck a matter came to my attention that I think will be just suited to you. I would like to see you start with something that would bring you notice. At the same time if a very beautiful girl of your sort is put directly into a picture next to one of the rather shop-worn stars with which every company is afflicted, tongues would very likely wag. But there is a "flapper" part in a Percy B. Debris production that I think would be just suited to you and would bring you notice. Willa Sable plays opposite Gaston Mears in a sort of character part and your part I believe would be her younger sister.*
>
> *Anyway Percy B. Debris who is directing the picture says if you'll come to the studios day after to-morrow (Thursday) he will run off a test. If ten o'clock is suited to you I will meet you there at that time.*
>
> *With all good wishes*
> *Ever Faithfully*
> *JOSEPH BLACK.*

Gloria had decided that Anthony was to know nothing of this until she had obtained a definite position, and accordingly she was dressed and out of the apartment next morning before he awoke. Her mirror had given her, she thought, much the same account as ever. She wondered if there were any lingering traces of her sickness. She was still slightly under weight, and she had fancied, a few days before, that her cheeks were a trifle thinner—but she felt that those were merely transitory conditions and that on this particular day she looked as fresh as ever. She had bought and charged a new hat, and as the day was warm she had left the leopard skin coat at home.

At the "Films Par Excellence" studios she was announced over the telephone and told that Mr. Black would be down directly. She looked around her. Two girls were being shown about by a little fat man in a slash-pocket coat, and one of them had indicated a stack of thin parcels, piled breast-high against the wall, and extending along for twenty feet.

"That's studio mail," explained the fat man. "Pictures of the stars who are with 'Films Par Excellence.'"

"Oh."

"Each one's autographed by Florence Kelley or Gaston Mears or Mack Dodge—" He winked confidentially. "At least when Minnie McGlook out in Sauk Center gets the picture she wrote for, she *thinks* it's autographed."

"Just a stamp?"

"Sure. It'd take 'em a good eight-hour day to autograph half of 'em. They say Mary Pickford's studio mail costs her fifty thousand a year."

"Say!"

"Sure. Fifty thousand. But it's the best kinda advertising there is—"

They drifted out of earshot and almost immediately Bloeckman appeared—Bloeckman, a dark suave gentleman, gracefully engaged in the middle forties, who greeted her with courteous warmth and told her she had not changed a bit in three years. He led the way into a great hall, as large as an armory and broken intermittently with busy sets and blinding rows of unfamiliar light. Each piece of scenery was marked in large white letters "Gaston Mears Company," "Mack Dodge Company," or simply "Films Par Excellence."

"Ever been in a studio before?"

"Never have."

She liked it. There was no heavy closeness of greasepaint, no scent of soiled and tawdry costumes which years before had revolted her behind the scenes of a musical comedy. This work was done in the clean mornings; the appurtenances seemed rich and gorgeous and new. On a set that was joyous with Manchu hangings a perfect Chinaman was going through a scene according to megaphone directions as the great glittering machine ground out its ancient moral tale for the edification of the national mind.

A red-headed man approached them and spoke with familiar deference to Bloeckman, who answered:

"Hello, Debris. Want you to meet Mrs. Patch. . . . Mrs. Patch wants to go into pictures, as I explained to you. . . . All right, now, where do we go?"

Mr. Debris—the great Percy B. Debris, thought Gloria—showed them to a set which represented the interior of an office. Some chairs were drawn up around the camera, which stood in front of it, and the three of them sat down.

"Ever been in a studio before?" asked Mr. Debris, giving her a glance that was surely the quintessence of keenness. "No? Well, I'll explain exactly what's going to happen. We're going to take what we call a test in order to see how your features photograph and whether you've got natural stage presence and how you respond to coaching. There's no need to be nervous over it. I'll just have the camera-man take a few hundred feet in an episode I've got marked here in the scenario. We can tell pretty much what we want to from that."

He produced a typewritten continuity and explained to her the episode she was to enact. It developed that one Barbara Wainwright had been secretly married to the junior partner of the firm whose office was there represented. Entering the deserted office one day by accident she was naturally interested in seeing where her husband worked. The telephone rang and after some hesitation she answered it. She learned that her husband had been struck by an automobile and instantly killed. She was overcome. At first she was unable to realize the truth, but finally she succeeded in comprehending it, and went into a dead faint on the floor.

"Now that's all we want," concluded Mr. Debris. "I'm going to stand here and tell you approximately what to do, and you're to act as though I wasn't here, and just go on do it your own way. You needn't be afraid we're going to judge this too severely. We simply want to get a general idea of your screen personality."

"I see."

"You'll find make-up in the room in back of the set. Go light on it. Very little red."

"I see," repeated Gloria, nodding. She touched her lips nervously with the tip of her tongue.

THE TEST

As she came into the set through the real wooden door and closed it carefully behind her, she found herself inconveniently dissatisfied with her clothes. She should have bought a "misses'" dress for the occasion—she could still wear them, and it might have been a good investment if it had accentuated her airy youth.

Her mind snapped sharply into the momentous present as Mr. Debris's voice came from the glare of the white lights in front.

"You look around for your husband. . . . Now—you don't see him . . . you're curious about the office. . . ."

She became conscious of the regular sound of the camera. It worried her. She glanced toward it involuntarily and wondered if she had made up her face correctly. Then, with a definite effort she forced herself to act—and she had never felt that the gestures of her body were so banal, so awkward, so bereft of grace or distinction. She strolled around the office, picking up articles here and there and looking at them inanely. Then she scrutinized the ceiling, the floor, and thoroughly inspected an inconsequential lead pencil on the desk. Finally, because she could think of nothing else to do, and less than nothing to express, she forced a smile.

"All right. Now the phone rings. Ting-a-ling-a-ling! Hesitate, and then answer it."

She hesitated—and then, too quickly, she thought, picked up the receiver.

"Hello."

Her voice was hollow and unreal. The words rang in the empty set like the ineffectualities of a ghost. The absurdities of their requirements appalled her—Did they expect that on an instant's notice she could put herself in the place of this preposterous and unexplained character?

". . . No . . . no. . . . Not yet! Now listen: 'John Sumner has just been knocked over by an automobile and instantly killed!'"

Gloria let her baby mouth drop slowly open. Then:

"Now hang up! With a bang!"

She obeyed, clung to the table with her eyes wide and staring. At length she was feeling slightly encouraged and her confidence increased.

"My God!" she cried. Her voice was good, she thought. "Oh, my God!"

"Now faint."

She collapsed forward to her knees and throwing her body outward on the ground lay without breathing.

"All right!" called Mr. Debris. "That's enough, thank you. That's plenty. Get up—that's enough."

Gloria arose, mustering her dignity and brushing off her skirt.

"Awful!" she remarked with a cool laugh, though her heart was bumping tumultuously. "Terrible, wasn't it?"

"Did you mind it?" said Mr. Debris, smiling blandly. "Did it seem hard? I can't tell anything about it until I have it run off."

"Of course not," she agreed, trying to attach some sort of meaning to his remark—and failing. It was just the sort of thing he would have said had he been trying not to encourage her.

A few moments later she left the studio. Bloeckman had promised that she should hear the result of the test within the next few days. Too proud to force any definite comment she felt a baffling uncertainty and only now when the step had at last been taken did she realize how the possibility of a successful screen career had played in the back of her mind for the past three years. That night she tried to tell over to herself the elements that might decide for or against her. Whether or not she had used enough make-up worried her, and as the part was that of a girl of twenty, she wondered if she had not been just a little too grave. About her acting she was least of all satisfied. Her entrance had been abominable—in fact not until she reached the phone had she displayed a shred of poise—and then the test had been over. If they had only realized! She wished that she could try it again. A mad plan to call up in the morning and ask for a new trial took possession of her, and as suddenly faded. It seemed neither politic nor polite to ask another favor of Bloeckman.

The third day of waiting found her in a highly nervous condition. She had bitten the insides of her mouth until they were raw and smarting, and burnt unbearably when she washed them with listerine. She had quarrelled so persistently with Anthony that he had left the apartment in a cold fury. But because he was intimidated by her exceptional frigidity, he called up an hour afterward, apologized and said he was having dinner at the Amsterdam Club, the only one in which he still retained membership.

It was after one o'clock and she had breakfasted at eleven, so, deciding to forego luncheon, she started for a walk in the Park. At three there would be a mail. She would be back by three.

It was an afternoon of premature spring. Water was drying on the walks and in the Park little girls were gravely wheeling white doll-buggies up and down under the thin trees while behind them followed bored nursery-maids in two's, discussing with each other those tremendous secrets that are peculiar to nursery-maids.

Two o'clock by her little gold watch. She should have a new watch, one made in a platinum oblong and incrusted with diamonds—but those cost even more than squirrel coats and of course they were out of her reach now, like everything else—unless perhaps the right letter was awaiting her . . . in about an hour . . . fifty-eight minutes exactly. Ten to get there left forty-eight . . . forty-seven now . . .

Little girls soberly wheeling their buggies along the damp sunny walks. The nursery-maids chattering in pairs about their inscrutable secrets. Here and there a raggedy man seated upon newspapers spread on a drying bench, related not to the radiant and delightful afternoon but to the dirty snow that slept exhausted in obscure corners, waiting for extermination. . . .

Ages later, coming into the dim hall she saw the Martinique elevator boy standing incongruously in the light of the stained-glass window.

"Is there any mail for us?" she asked.

"Up-stays, madame."

The switchboard squawked abominably and Gloria waited while he ministered to the telephone. She sickened as the elevator groaned its way up—the floors passed like the slow lapse of centuries, each one ominous, accusing, significant. The letter, a white leprous spot, lay upon the dirty tiles of the hall. . . .

> *My dear Gloria:*
>
> *We had the test run off yesterday afternoon, and Mr. Debris seemed to think that for the part he had in mind he needed a younger woman. He said that the acting was not bad, and that there was a small character part supposed to be a very haughty rich widow that he thought you might——*

Desolately Gloria raised her glance until it fell out across the areaway. But she found she could not see the opposite wall, for her gray eyes were full of tears. She walked into the bedroom, the letter crinkled tightly in her hand, and sank down upon her knees before the long mirror on the wardrobe floor. This was her twenty-ninth birthday, and the world was melting away before her eyes. She tried to think that it had been the make-up, but her emotions were too profound, too overwhelming for any consolation that the thought conveyed.

She strained to see until she could feel the flesh on her temples pull forward. Yes—the cheeks were ever so faintly thin, the corners of the eyes were lined with tiny wrinkles. The eyes were different. Why, they were different! . . . And then suddenly she knew how tired her eyes were.

"Oh, my pretty face," she whispered, passionately

grieving. "Oh, my pretty face! Oh, I don't want to live without my pretty face! Oh, what's *happened?*"

Then she slid toward the mirror and, as in the test, sprawled face downward upon the floor—and lay there sobbing. It was the first awkward movement she had ever made.

CHAPTER 3

NO MATTER!

Within another year Anthony and Gloria had become like players who had lost their costumes, lacking the pride to continue on the note of tragedy—so that when Mrs. and Miss Hulme of Kansas City cut them dead in the Plaza one evening, it was only that Mrs. and Miss Hulme, like most people, abominated mirrors of their atavistic selves.

Their new apartment, for which they paid eighty-five dollars a month, was situated on Claremont Avenue, which is two blocks from the Hudson in the dim hundreds. They had lived there a month when Muriel Kane came to see them late one afternoon.

It was a reproachless twilight on the summer side of spring. Anthony lay upon the lounge looking up One Hundred and Twenty-seventh Street toward the river, near which he could just see a single patch of vivid green trees that guaranteed the brummagem umbrageousness of Riverside Drive. Across the water were the Palisades, crowned by the ugly framework of the amusement park—yet soon it would be dusk and those same iron cobwebs would be a glory against the heavens, an enchanted palace set over the smooth radiance of a tropical canal.

The streets near the apartment, Anthony had found, were streets where children played—streets a little nicer than those he had been used to pass on his way to Marietta, but of the same general sort, with an occasional hand organ or hurdy-gurdy, and in the cool of the evening many pairs of young girls walking down to the corner drug-store for ice cream soda and dreaming unlimited dreams under the low heavens.

Dusk in the streets now, and children playing, shouting up incoherent ecstatic words that faded out close to the open window—and Muriel, who had come to find Gloria, chattering to him from an opaque gloom over across the room.

"Light the lamp, why don't we?" she suggested. "It's getting *ghostly* in here."

With a tired movement he arose and obeyed; the gray window-panes vanished. He stretched himself. He was heavier now, his stomach was a limp weight against his belt; his flesh had softened and expanded. He was thirty-two and his mind was a bleak and disordered wreck.

"Have a little drink, Muriel?"

"Not me, thanks. I don't use it anymore. What're you doing these days, Anthony?" she asked curiously.

"Well, I've been pretty busy with this lawsuit," he answered indifferently. "It's gone to the Court of Appeals—ought to be settled up one way or another by autumn. There's been some objection as to whether the Court of Appeals has jurisdiction over the matter."

Muriel made a clicking sound with her tongue and cocked her head on one side.

"Well, you tell 'em! I never heard of anything taking so long."

"Oh, they all do," he replied listlessly; "all will cases.

They say it's exceptional to have one settled under four or five years."

"Oh . . ." Muriel daringly changed her tack, "why don't you go to work, you la-azy!"

"At what?" he demanded abruptly.

"Why, at anything, I suppose. You're still a young man."

"If that's encouragement, I'm much obliged," he answered dryly—and then with sudden weariness: "Does it bother you particularly that I don't want to work?"

"It doesn't bother me—but, it does bother a lot of people who claim—"

"Oh, God!" he said brokenly, "it seems to me that for three years I've heard nothing about myself but wild stories and virtuous admonitions. I'm tired of it. If you don't want to see us, let us alone. I don't bother my former friends.' But I need no charity calls, and no criticism disguised as good advice—" Then he added apologetically: "I'm sorry—but really, Muriel, you mustn't talk like a lady slum-worker even if you are visiting the lower middle classes." He turned his bloodshot eyes on her reproachfully—eyes that had once been a deep, clear blue, that were weak now, strained, and half-ruined from reading when he was drunk.

"Why do you say such awful things?" she protested. You talk as if you and Gloria were in the middle classes."

"Why pretend we're not? I hate people who claim to be great aristocrats when they can't even keep up the appearances of it."

"Do you think a person has to have money to be aristocratic?"

Muriel . . . the horrified democrat . . .!

"Why, of course. Aristocracy's only an admission that certain traits which we call fine—courage and honor and beauty and all that sort of thing—can best be developed in a favorable environment, where you don't have the warpings of ignorance and necessity."

Muriel bit her lower lip and waved her head from side to side.

"Well, all *I* say is that if a person comes from a good family they're always nice people. That's the trouble with you and Gloria. You think that just because things aren't going your way right now all your old friends are trying to avoid you. You're too sensitive—"

"As a matter of fact," said Anthony, "you know nothing at all about it. With me it's simply a matter of pride, and for once Gloria's reasonable enough to agree that we oughtn't go where we're not wanted. And people don't want us. We're too much the ideal bad examples."

"Nonsense! You can't park your pessimism in my little sun parlor. I think you ought to forget all those morbid speculations and go to work."

"Here I am, thirty-two. Suppose I did start in at some idiotic business. Perhaps in two years I might rise to fifty dollars a week—with luck. That's *if* I could get a job at all; there's an awful lot of unemployment. Well, suppose I made fifty a week. Do you think I'd be any happier? Do you think that if I don't get this money of my grandfather's life will be *endurable?*"

Muriel smiled complacently.

"Well," she said, "that may be clever but it isn't common sense."

A few minutes later Gloria came in seeming to bring with her into the room some dark color, indeterminate and rare. In a taciturn way she was happy to see Muriel. She greeted Anthony with a casual "Hi!"

"I've been talking philosophy with your husband," cried the irrepressible Miss Kane.

"We took up some fundamental concepts," said Anthony, a faint smile disturbing his pale cheeks, paler still under two days' growth of beard.

Oblivious to his irony Muriel rehashed her contention. When she had done, Gloria said quietly:

"Anthony's right. It's no fun to go around when you have the sense that people are looking at you in a certain way."

He broke in plaintively:

"Don't you think that when even Maury Noble, who was my best friend, won't come to see us it's high time to stop calling people up?" Tears were standing in his eyes.

"That was your fault about Maury Noble," said Gloria coolly.

"It wasn't."

"It most certainly was."

Muriel intervened quickly:

"I met a girl who knew Maury, the other day, and she says he doesn't drink any more. He's getting pretty cagey."

"Doesn't?"

"Practically not at all. He's making *piles* of money. He's sort of changed since the war. He's going to marry a girl in Philadelphia who has millions, Ceci Larrabee—anyhow, that's what Town Tattle said."

"He's thirty-three," said Anthony, thinking aloud. But it's odd to imagine his getting married. I used to think he was so brilliant."

"He was," murmured Gloria, "in a way."

"But brilliant people don't settle down in business—or do they? Or what do they do? Or what becomes of everybody you used to know and have so much in common with?"

"You drift apart," suggested Muriel with the appropriate dreamy look.

"They change," said Gloria. "All the qualities that they don't use in their daily lives get cobwebbed up."

"The last thing he said to me," recollected Anthony, "was that he was going to work so as to forget that there was nothing worth working for."

Muriel caught at this quickly.

"That's what *you* ought to do," she exclaimed triumphantly. "Of course I shouldn't think anybody would want to work for nothing. But it'd give you something to do. What do you do with yourselves, anyway? Nobody ever sees you at Montmartre or—or anywhere. Are you economizing?"

Gloria laughed scornfully, glancing at Anthony from the corners of her eyes.

"Well," he demanded, "what are you laughing at?" "You know what I'm laughing at," she answered coldly.

"At that case of whiskey?"

"Yes"—she turned to Muriel—"he paid seventy-five dollars for a case of whiskey yesterday."

"What if I did? It's cheaper that way than if you get it by the bottle. You needn't pretend that you won't drink any of it."

"At least I don't drink in the daytime."

"That's a fine distinction!" he cried, springing to his feet in a weak rage. "What's more, I'll be damned if you can hurl that at me every few minutes!"

"It's true."

"It is *not!* And I'm getting sick of this eternal business of criticising me before visitors!" He had worked himself up to such a state that his arms and shoulders were visibly trembling. "You'd think everything was my fault. You'd think you hadn't encouraged me to spend money—and spent a lot more on yourself than I ever did by a long shot."

Now Gloria rose to her feet.

"I *won't* let you talk to me that way!"

"All right, then; by Heaven, you don't have to!"

In a sort of rush he left the room. The two women heard his steps in the hall and then the front door banged. Gloria sank back into her chair. Her face was lovely in the lamplight, composed, inscrutable.

"Oh—!" cried Muriel in distress. "Oh, what *is* the matter?"

"Nothing particularly. He's just drunk."

"Drunk? Why, he's perfectly sober. He talked——"

Gloria shook her head.

"Oh, no, he doesn't show it any more unless he can hardly stand up, and he talks all right until he gets excited. He talks much better than he does when he's sober. But he's been sitting here all day drinking—except for the time it took him to walk to the corner for a newspaper."

"Oh, how terrible!" Muriel was sincerely moved. Her eyes filled with tears. "Has this happened much?"

"Drinking, you mean?"

"No, this—leaving you?"

"Oh, yes. Frequently. He'll come in about midnight—and weep and ask me to forgive him."

"And do you?"

"I don't know. We just go on."

The two women sat there in the lamplight and looked at each other, each in a different way helpless before this thing. Gloria was still pretty, as pretty as she would ever be again—her cheeks were flushed and she was wearing a new dress that she had bought—imprudently—for fifty dollars. She had hoped she could persuade Anthony to take her out to-night, to a restaurant or even to one of the great, gorgeous moving picture palaces where there would be a few people to look at her, at whom she could bear to look in turn. She wanted this because she knew her cheeks were flushed and because her dress was new and becomingly fragile. Only very occasionally, now, did they receive any invitations. But she did not tell these things to Muriel.

"Gloria, dear, I wish we could have dinner together, but I promised a man and it's seven-thirty already. I've got to *tear*."

"Oh, I couldn't, anyway. In the first place I've been ill all day. I couldn't eat a thing."

After she had walked with Muriel to the door, Gloria came back into the room, turned out the lamp, and leaning her elbows on the window sill looked out at Palisades Park, where the brilliant revolving circle of the Ferris wheel was like a trembling mirror catching the yellow reflection of the moon. The street was quiet now; the children had gone in—over the way she could see a family at dinner. Pointlessly, ridiculously, they rose and walked about the table; seen thus, all that they did appeared incongruous—it was as though they were being jiggled carelessly and to no purpose by invisible overhead wires.

She looked at her watch—it was eight o'clock. She had been pleased for a part of the day—the early afternoon—in walking along that Broadway of Harlem, One Hundred and Twenty-fifth Street, with her nostrils alert to many odors, and her mind excited by the extraordinary beauty of some Italian children. It affected her curiously—as Fifth Avenue had affected her once, in the days when, with the placid confidence of beauty, she had known that it was all hers, every shop and all it held, every adult toy glittering in a window, all hers for the asking. Here on One Hundred and Twenty-fifth Street there were Salvation Army bands and spectrum-shawled old ladies on door-steps and sugary, sticky candy in the grimy hands of shiny-haired children—and the late sun striking down on the sides of the tall tenements. All very rich and racy and savory, like a dish by a provident French chef that one could not help enjoying, even though one knew that the ingredients were probably left-overs. . . .

Gloria shuddered suddenly as a river siren came moaning over the dusky roofs, and leaning back in till the ghostly curtains fell from her shoulder, she turned on the electric lamp. It was growing late. She knew there was some change in her purse, and she considered whether she would go down and have some coffee and rolls where the liberated subway made a roaring cave of Manhattan Street or eat the devilled ham and bread in the kitchen. Her purse decided for her. It contained a nickel and two pennies.

After an hour the silence of the room had grown unbearable, and she found that her eyes were wandering from her magazine to the ceiling, toward which she stared without thought. Suddenly she stood up, hesitated for a moment, biting at her finger—then she went to the pantry, took down a bottle of whiskey from the shelf and poured herself a drink. She filled up the glass with ginger ale, and returning to her chair finished an article in the magazine. It concerned the last revolutionary widow, who, when a young girl, had married an ancient veteran of the Continental Army and who had died in 1906. It seemed strange and oddly romantic to Gloria that she and this woman had been contemporaries.

She turned a page and learned that a candidate for Congress was being accused of atheism by an opponent. Gloria's surprise vanished when she found that the charges were false. The candidate had merely denied the miracle of the loaves and fishes. He admitted, under pressure, that he gave full credence to the stroll upon the water.

Finishing her first drink, Gloria got herself a second. After slipping on a negligée and making herself comfortable on the lounge, she became conscious that she was miserable and that the tears were rolling down her cheeks. She wondered if they were tears of self-pity, and tried resolutely not to cry, but this existence without hope, without happiness, oppressed her, and she kept shaking her head from side to side, her mouth drawn down tremulously in the corners, as though she were denying an assertion made by some one, somewhere. She did not know that this gesture of hers was years older than history, that, for a hundred generations of men, intolerable and persistent grief has offered that gesture, of denial, of protest, of bewilderment, to something more profound, more powerful than the God made in the image of man, and before which that God, did he exist, would be equally impotent. It is a truth set at the heart of tragedy that this force never explains, never answers—this force intangible as air, more definite than death.

RICHARD CARAMEL

Early in the summer Anthony resigned from his last club, the Amsterdam. He had come to visit it hardly twice a year, and the dues were a recurrent burden. He had joined it on his return from Italy because it had been his grandfather's club and his father's, and because it was a club that, given the opportunity, one indisputably joined—but as a matter of fact he had preferred the Harvard Club, largely because of Dick and Maury. However, with the decline of his fortunes, it had seemed an increasingly desirable bauble to cling to. . . . It was relinquished at the last, with some regret. . . .

His companions numbered now a curious dozen. Several of them he had met in a place called "Sammy's," on Forty-third Street, where, if one knocked on the door and were favorably passed on from behind a grating, one could sit around a great round table drinking fairly good whiskey. It was here that he encountered a man named Parker Allison, who had been exactly the wrong sort of rounder at Harvard, and who was running through a large "yeast" fortune as rapidly as possible. Parker Allison's notion of distinction consisted in driving a noisy red-and-yellow racing-car up Broadway with two glittering, hard-eyed girls beside him. He was the sort who dined with two girls rather than with one—his imagination was almost incapable of sustaining a dialogue.

Besides Allison there was Pete Lytell, who wore a gray derby on the side of his head. He always had money and he was customarily cheerful, so Anthony held aimless, long-winded conversation with him through many afternoons of the summer and fall. Lytell, he found, not only talked but reasoned in phrases. His philosophy was a series of them, assimilated here and there through an active, thoughtless life. He had phrases about Socialism—the immemorial ones; he had phrases pertaining to the existence of a personal deity—something about one time when he had been in a railroad accident; and he had phrases about the Irish problem, the sort of woman he respected, and the futility of prohibition. The only time his conversation ever rose superior to these muddled clauses, with which he interpreted the most rococo happenings in a life that had been more than usually eventful, was when he got down to the detailed discussion of his most animal existence: he knew, to a subtlety, the foods, the liquor, and the women that he preferred.

He was at once the commonest and the most remarkable product of civilization. He was nine out of ten people that one passes on a city street—and he was a hairless ape with two dozen tricks. He was the hero of a thousand romances of life and art—and he was a virtual moron, performing staidly yet absurdly a series of complicated and infinitely astounding epics over a span of threescore years.

With such men as these two Anthony Patch drank and discussed and drank and argued. He liked them because they knew nothing about him, because they lived in the obvious and had not the faintest conception of the inevitable continuity of life. They sat not before a motion picture with consecutive reels, but at a musty old-fashioned travelogue with all values stark and hence all implications confused. Yet they themselves were not confused, because there was nothing in them to be confused—they changed phrases from month to month as they changed neckties.

Anthony, the courteous, the subtle, the perspicacious, was drunk each day—in Sammy's with these men, in the apartment over a book, some book he knew, and, very rarely, with Gloria, who, in his eyes, had begun to develop the unmistakable outlines of a quarrelsome and unreasonable woman. She was not the Gloria of old, certainly—the Gloria who, had she been sick, would have preferred to inflict misery upon every one around her, rather than confess that she needed sympathy or assistance. She was not above whining now; she was not above being sorry for herself. Each night when she prepared for bed she smeared her face with some new unguent which she hoped illogically would give back the glow and freshness to her vanishing beauty. When Anthony was drunk he taunted her about this. When he was sober he was polite to her, on occasions even tender; he seemed to show for short hours a trace of that old quality of understanding too well to blame— that quality which was the best of him and had worked swiftly and ceaselessly toward his ruin.

But he hated to be sober. It made him conscious of the people around him, of that air of struggle, of greedy ambition, of hope more sordid than despair, of incessant passage up or down, which in every metropolis is most in evidence through the unstable middle class. Unable to live with the rich he thought that his next choice would have been to live with the very poor. Anything was better than this cup of perspiration and tears.

The sense of the enormous panorama of life, never strong in Anthony, had become dim almost to extinction. At long intervals now some incident, some gesture of Gloria's, would take his fancy—but the gray veils had come down in earnest upon him. As he grew older those things faded—after that there was wine.

There was a kindliness about intoxication—there was that indescribable gloss and glamor it gave, like the memories of ephemeral and faded evenings. After a few high-balls there was magic in the tall glowing Arabian night of the Bush Terminal Building—its summit a peak of sheer grandeur, gold and dreaming against the inaccessible sky. And Wall Street, the crass, the banal—again it was the triumph of gold, a gorgeous sentient spectacle; it was where the great kings kept the money for their wars. . . .

. . . The fruit of youth or of the grape, the transitory magic of the brief passage from darkness to darkness—the old illusion that truth and beauty were in some way entwined.

As he stood in front of Delmonico's lighting a cigarette one night he saw two hansoms drawn up close to the curb, waiting for a chance drunken fare. The outmoded cabs were worn and dirty—the cracked patent leather wrinkled like an old man's face, the cushions faded to a brownish lavender; the very horses were ancient and weary, and so were the white-haired men who sat aloft, cracking their whips with a grotesque affectation of gallantry. A relic of vanished gaiety!

Anthony Patch walked away in a sudden fit of depression, pondering the bitterness of such survivals. There was nothing, it seemed, that grew stale so soon as pleasure.

On Forty-second Street one afternoon he met Richard Caramel for the first time in many months, a prosperous, fattening Richard Caramel, whose face was filling out to match the Bostonian brow.

"Just got in this week from the coast. Was going to call you up, but I didn't know your new address."

"We've moved."

Richard Caramel noticed that Anthony was wearing a soiled shirt, that his cuffs were slightly but perceptibly frayed, that his eyes were set in half-moons the color of cigar smoke.

"So I gathered," he said, fixing his friend with his bright-yellow eye. "But where and how is Gloria? My God, Anthony, I've been hearing the dog-gonedest stories about you two even out in California—and when I get back to New York I find you've sunk absolutely out of sight. Why don't you pull yourself together?"

"Now, listen," chattered Anthony unsteadily, "I can't stand a long lecture. We've lost money in a dozen ways, and naturally people have talked—on account of the lawsuit, but the thing's coming to a final decision this winter, surely—"

"You're talking so fast that I can't understand you," interrupted Dick calmly.

"Well, I've said all I'm going to say," snapped Anthony. "Come and see us if you like—or don't!"

With this he turned and started to walk off in the crowd, but Dick overtook him immediately and grasped his arm.

"Say, Anthony, don't fly off the handle so easily! You know Gloria's my cousin, and you're one of my oldest friends, so it's natural for me to be interested when I hear that you're going to the dogs—and taking her with you."

"I don't want to be preached to."

"Well, then, all right—How about coming up to my apartment and having a drink? I've just got settled. I've bought three cases of Gordon gin from a revenue officer."

As they walked along he continued in a burst of exasperation:

"And how about your grandfather's money—you going to get it?"

"Well," answered Anthony resentfully, "that old fool Haight seems hopeful, especially because people are tired of reformers right now—you know it might make a slight difference, for instance, if some judge thought that Adam Patch made it harder for him to get liquor."

"You can't do without money," said Dick sententiously. "Have you tried to write any—lately?"

Anthony shook his head silently.

"That's funny," said Dick. "I always thought that you and Maury would write some day, and now he's grown to be a sort of tight-fisted aristocrat, and you're—"

"I'm the bad example."

"I wonder why?"

"You probably think you know," suggested Anthony, with an effort at concentration. "The failure and the success both believe in their hearts that they have accurately balanced points of view, the success because he's succeeded, and the failure because he's failed. The successful man tells his son to profit by his father's good fortune, and the failure tells *his* son to profit by his father's mistakes."

"I don't agree with you," said the author of "A Shave-tail in France." "I used to listen to you and Maury when we were young, and I used to be impressed because you were so consistently cynical, but now—well, after all, by God, which of us three has taken to the—to the intellectual life? I don't want to sound vainglorious, but—it's me, and I've always believed that moral values existed, and I always will."

"Well," objected Anthony, who was rather enjoying himself, "even granting that, you know that in practice life never presents problems as clear cut, does it?"

"It does to me. There's nothing I'd violate certain principles for."

"But how do you know when you're violating them? You have to guess at things just like most people do. You have to apportion the values when you look back. You finish up the portrait then—paint in the details and shadows."

Dick shook his head with a lofty stubbornness. "Same old futile cynic," he said. "It's just a mode of being sorry for yourself. You don't do anything—so nothing matters."

"Oh, I'm quite capable of self-pity," admitted Anthony, "nor am I claiming that I'm getting as much fun out of life as you are."

"You say—at least you used to—that happiness is the only thing worth while in life. Do you think you're any happier for being a pessimist?"

Anthony grunted savagely. His pleasure in the conversation began to wane. He was nervous and craving for a drink.

"My golly!" he cried, "where do you live? I can't keep walking forever."

"Your endurance is all mental, eh?" returned Dick sharply. "Well, I live right here."

He turned in at the apartment house on Forty-ninth Street, and a few minutes later they were in a large new room with an open fireplace and four walls lined with books. A colored butler served them gin rickeys, and an hour vanished politely with the mellow shortening of their drinks and the glow of a light mid-autumn fire.

"The arts are very old," said Anthony after a while. With

a few glasses the tension of his nerves relaxed and he found that he could think again.

"Which art?"

"All of them. Poetry is dying first. It'll be absorbed into prose sooner or later. For instance, the beautiful word, the colored and glittering word, and the beautiful simile belong in prose now. To get attention poetry has got to strain for the unusual word, the harsh, earthy word that's never been beautiful before. Beauty, as the sum of several beautiful parts, reached its apotheosis in Swinburne. It can't go any further—except in the novel, perhaps."

Dick interrupted him impatiently:

"You know these new novels make me tired. My God! Everywhere I go some silly girl asks me if I've read 'This Side of Paradise.' Are our girls really like that? If it's true to life, which I don't believe, the next generation is going to the dogs. I'm sick of all this shoddy realism. I think there's a place for the romanticist in literature."

Anthony tried to remember what he had read lately of Richard Caramel's. There was "A Shave-tail in France," a novel called "The Land of Strong Men," and several dozen short stories, which were even worse. It had become the custom among young and clever reviewers to mention Richard Caramel with a smile of scorn. "Mr." Richard Caramel, they called him. His corpse was dragged obscenely through every literary supplement. He was accused of making a great fortune by writing trash for the movies. As the fashion in books shifted he was becoming almost a byword of contempt.

While Anthony was thinking this, Dick had got to his feet and seemed to be hesitating at an avowal.

"I've gathered quite a few books," he said suddenly.

"So I see."

"I've made an exhaustive collection of good American stuff, old and new. I don't mean the usual Longfellow-Whittier thing—in fact, most of it's modern."

He stepped to one of the walls and, seeing that it was expected of him, Anthony arose and followed.

"Look!"

Under a printed tag *Americana* he displayed six long rows of books, beautifully bound and, obviously, carefully chosen.

"And here are the contemporary novelists."

Then Anthony saw the joker. Wedged in between Mark Twain and Dreiser were eight strange and inappropriate volumes, the works of Richard Caramel—"The Demon Lover," true enough . . . but also seven others that were execrably awful, without sincerity or grace.

Unwillingly Anthony glanced at Dick's face and caught a slight uncertainty there.

"I've put my own books in, of course," said Richard Caramel hastily, "though one or two of them are uneven—I'm afraid I wrote a little too fast when I had that magazine contract. But I don't believe in false modesty. Of course some of the critics haven't paid so much attention to me since I've been established—but, after all, it's not the critics that count. They're just sheep."

For the first time in so long that he could scarcely remember, Anthony felt a touch of the old pleasant contempt for his friend. Richard Caramel continued:

"My publishers, you know, have been advertising me as the Thackeray of America—because of my New York novel."

"Yes," Anthony managed to muster, "I suppose there's a good deal in what you say."

He knew that his contempt was unreasonable. He knew that he would have changed places with Dick unhesitatingly. He himself had tried his best to write with his tongue in his cheek. Ah, well, then—can a man disparage his life-work so readily? . . .

—And that night while Richard Caramel was hard at toil, with great hittings of the wrong keys and screwings up of his weary, unmatched eyes, laboring over his trash far into those cheerless hours when the fire dies down, and the head is swimming from the effect of prolonged concentration—Anthony, abominably drunk, was sprawled across the back seat of a taxi on his way to the flat on Claremont Avenue.

THE BEATING

As winter approached it seemed that a sort of madness seized upon Anthony. He awoke in the morning so nervous that Gloria could feel him trembling in the bed before he could muster enough vitality to stumble into the pantry for a drink. He was intolerable now except under the influence of liquor, and as he seemed to decay and coarsen under her eyes, Gloria's soul and body shrank away from him; when he stayed out all night, as he did several times, she not only failed to be sorry but even felt a measure of relief. Next day he would be faintly repentant, and would remark in a gruff, hang-dog fashion that he guessed he was drinking a little too much.

For hours at a time he would sit in the great armchair that had been in his apartment, lost in a sort of stupor—even his interest in reading his favorite books seemed to have departed, and though an incessant bickering went on between husband and wife, the one subject upon which they ever really conversed was the progress of the will case. What Gloria hoped in the tenebrous depths of her soul, what she expected that great gift of money to bring about, is difficult to imagine. She was being bent by her environment into a grotesque similitude of a housewife. She who until three years before had never made coffee, prepared sometimes three meals a day. She walked a great deal in the afternoons, and in the evenings she read—books, magazines, anything she found at hand. If now she wished for a child, even a child of the Anthony who sought her bed blind drunk, she neither said so nor gave any show or sign of interest in children. It is doubtful if she could have made it clear to any one what it was she wanted, or indeed what there was to want—a lonely, lovely woman, thirty now, retrenched behind some impregnable inhibition born and coexistent with her beauty.

One afternoon when the snow was dirty again along Riverside Drive, Gloria, who had been to the grocer's, entered the apartment to find Anthony pacing the floor in a state of aggravated nervousness. The feverish eyes he turned on her were traced with tiny pink lines that reminded her of rivers on a map. For a moment she received the impression that he was suddenly and definitely old.

"Have you any money?" he inquired of her precipitately.

"What? What do you mean?"

"Just what I said. Money! Money! Can't you speak English?"

She paid no attention but brushed by him and into the pantry to put the bacon and eggs in the ice-box. When his drinking had been unusually excessive he was invariably in a whining mood. This time he followed her and, standing in the pantry door, persisted in his question.

"You heard what I said. Have you any money?"

She turned about from the ice-box and faced him.

"Why, Anthony, you must be crazy! You know I haven't any money—except a dollar in change."

He executed an abrupt about-face and returned to the living room, where he renewed his pacing. It was evident that he had something portentous on his mind—he quite obviously wanted to be asked what was the matter. Joining him a moment later she sat upon the long lounge and began taking down her hair. It was no longer bobbed, and it had changed in the last year from a rich gold dusted with red to an unresplendent light brown. She had bought some shampoo soap and meant to wash it now; she had considered putting a bottle of peroxide into the rinsing water.

"—Well?" she implied silently.

"That darn bank!" he quavered. "They've had my account for over ten years—ten *years*. Well, it seems they've got some autocratic rule that you have to keep over five hundred dollars there or they won't carry you. They wrote me a letter a few months ago and told me I'd been running too low. Once I gave out two bum checks—remember? that night in Reisenweber's?—but I made them good the very next day. Well, I promised old Halloran—he's the manager, the greedy Mick—that I'd watch out. And I thought I was going all right; I kept up the stubs in my check-book pretty regular. Well, I went in there to-day to cash a check, and Halloran came up and told me they'd have to close my account. Too many bad checks, he said, and I never had more than five hundred to my credit—and that only for a day or so at a time. And by God! What do you think he said then?"

"What?"

"He said this was a good time to do it because I didn't have a damn penny in there!"

"You didn't?"

"That's what he told me. Seems I'd given these Bedros people a check for sixty for that last case of liquor—and I only had forty-five dollars in the bank. Well, the Bedros people deposited fifteen dollars to my account and drew the whole thing out."

In her ignorance Gloria conjured up a spectre of imprisonment and disgrace.

"Oh, they won't do anything," he assured her. "Bootlegging's too risky a business. They'll send me a bill for fifteen dollars and I'll pay it."

"Oh." She considered a moment. "—Well, we can sell another bond."

He laughed sarcastically.

"Oh, yes, that's always easy. When the few bonds we

have that are paying any interest at all are only worth between fifty and eighty cents on the dollar. We lose about half the bond every time we sell."

"What else can we do?"

"Oh, we'll sell something—as usual. We've got paper worth eighty thousand dollars at par." Again he laughed unpleasantly. "Bring about thirty thousand on the open market."

"I distrusted those ten per cent investments."

"The deuce you did!" he said. "You pretended you did, so you could claw at me if they went to pieces, but you wanted to take a chance as much as I did."

She was silent for a moment as if considering, then:

"Anthony," she cried suddenly, "two hundred a month is worse than nothing. Let's sell all the bonds and put the thirty thousand dollars in the bank—and if we lose the case we can live in Italy for three years, and then just die." In her excitement as she talked she was aware of a faint flush of sentiment, the first she had felt in many days.

"Three years," he said nervously, "three years! You're crazy. Mr. Haight'll take more than that if we lose. Do you think he's working for charity?"

"I forgot that."

"—And here it is Saturday," he continued, "and I've only got a dollar and some change, and we've got to live till Monday, when I can get to my broker's. . . . And not a drink in the house," he added as a significant afterthought.

"Can't you call up Dick?"

"I did. His man says he's gone down to Princeton to address a literary club or some such thing. Won't be back till Monday."

"Well, let's see—Don't you know some friend you might go to?"

"I tried a couple of fellows. Couldn't find anybody in. I wish I'd sold that Keats letter like I started to last week."

"How about those men you play cards with in that Sammy place?"

"Do you think I'd ask *them?*" His voice rang with righteous horror. Gloria winced. He would rather contemplate her active discomfort than feel his own skin crawl at asking an inappropriate favor. "I thought of Muriel," he suggested.

"She's in California."

"Well, how about some of those men who gave you such a good time while I was in the army? You'd think they might be glad to do a little favor for you."

She looked at him contemptuously, but he took no notice.

"Or how about your old friend Rachael—or Constance Merriam?"

"Constance Merriam's been dead a year, and I wouldn't ask Rachael."

"Well, how about that gentleman who was so anxious to help you once that he could hardly restrain himself, Bloeckman?"

"Oh—!" He had hurt her at last, and he was not too obtuse or too careless to perceive it.

"Why not him?" he insisted callously.

"Because—he doesn't like me any more," she said with difficulty, and then as he did not answer but only regarded her cynically: "If you want to know why, I'll tell you. A year ago I went to Bloeckman—he's changed his name to Black—and asked him to put me into pictures."

"You went to Bloeckman?"

"Yes."

"Why didn't you tell me?" he demanded incredulously, the smile fading from his face.

"Because you were probably off drinking somewhere. He had them give me a test, and they decided that I wasn't young enough for anything except a character part."

"A character part?"

"The 'woman of thirty' sort of thing. I wasn't thirty, and I didn't think I—looked thirty."

"Why, damn him!" cried Anthony, championing her violently with a curious perverseness of emotion, "why—"

"Well, that's why I can't go to him."

"Why, the insolence!" insisted Anthony nervously, "the insolence!"

"Anthony, that doesn't matter now; the thing is we've got to live over Sunday and there's nothing in the house but a loaf of bread and a half-pound of bacon and two eggs for breakfast." She handed him the contents of her purse. "There's seventy, eighty, a dollar fifteen. With what you have that makes about two and a half altogether, doesn't it? Anthony, we can get along on that. We can buy lots of food with that—more than we can possibly eat."

Jingling the change in his hand he shook his head. "No. I've got to have a drink. I'm so darn nervous that I'm shivering." A thought struck him. "Perhaps Sammy'd cash a check. And then Monday I could rush down to the bank with the money."

"But they've closed your account."

"That's right, that's right—I'd forgotten. I'll tell you what: I'll go down to Sammy's and I'll find somebody there who'll lend me something. I hate like the devil to ask them, though. . . ." He snapped his fingers suddenly. "I know what I'll do. I'll hock my watch. I can get twenty dollars on it, and get it back Monday for sixty cents extra. It's been hocked before—when I was at Cambridge."

He had put on his overcoat, and with a brief good-by he started down the hall toward the outer door.

Gloria got to her feet. It had suddenly occurred to her where he would probably go first.

"Anthony!" she called after him, "hadn't you better leave two dollars with me? You'll only need car-fare."

The outer door slammed—he had pretended not to hear

her. She stood for a moment looking after him; then she went into the bathroom among her tragic unguents and began preparations for washing her hair.

Down at Sammy's he found Parker Allison and Pete Lytell sitting alone at a table, drinking whiskey sours. It was just after six o'clock, and Sammy, or Samuele Bendiri, as he had been christened, was sweeping an accumulation of cigarette butts and broken glass into a corner.

"Hi, Tony!" called Parker Allison to Anthony. Sometimes he addressed him as Tony, at other times it was Dan. To him all Anthonys must sail under one of these diminutives.

"Sit down. What'll you have?"

On the subway Anthony had counted his money and found that he had almost four dollars. He could pay for two rounds at fifty cents a drink—which meant that he would have six drinks. Then he would go over to Sixth Avenue and get twenty dollars and a pawn ticket in exchange for his watch.

"Well, roughnecks," he said jovially, "how's the life of crime?"

"Pretty good," said Allison. He winked at Pete Lytell. "Too bad you're a married man. We've got some pretty good stuff lined up for about eleven o'clock, when the shows let out. Oh, boy! Yes, sir—too bad he's married—isn't it, Pete?"

"'Sa shame."

At half past seven, when they had completed the six rounds, Anthony found that his intentions were giving audience to his desires. He was happy and cheerful now—thoroughly enjoying himself. It seemed to him that the story which Pete had just finished telling was unusually and profoundly humorous—and he decided, as he did every day at about this point, that they were "damn good fellows, by golly!" who would do a lot more for him than any one else he knew. The pawnshops would remain open until late Saturday nights, and he felt that if he took just one more drink he would attain a gorgeous rose-colored exhilaration.

Artfully, he fished in his vest pockets, brought up his two quarters, and stared at them as though in surprise.

"Well, I'll be darned," he protested in an aggrieved tone, "here I've come out without my pocketbook."

"Need some cash?" asked Lytell easily.

"I left my money on the dresser at home. And I wanted to buy you another drink."

"Oh—knock it." Lytell waved the suggestion away disparagingly. "I guess we can blow a good fella to all the drinks he wants. What'll you have—same?"

"I tell you," suggested Parker Allison, "suppose we send Sammy across the street for some sandwiches and eat dinner here."

The other two agreed.

"Good idea."

"Hey, Sammy, wantcha do somep'm for us. . . ."

Just after nine o'clock Anthony staggered to his feet and, bidding them a thick good night, walked unsteadily to the door, handing Sammy one of his two quarters as he passed out. Once in the street he hesitated uncertainly and then started in the direction of Sixth Avenue, where he remembered to have frequently passed several loan offices. He went by a news-stand and two drug-stores—and then he realized that he was standing in front of the place which he sought, and that it was shut and barred. Unperturbed he continued; another one, half a block down, was also closed—so were two more across the street, and a fifth in the square below. Seeing a faint light in the last one, he began to knock on the glass door; he desisted only when a watchman appeared in the back of the shop and motioned him angrily to move on. With growing discouragement, with growing befuddlement, he crossed the street and walked back toward Forty-third. On the corner near Sammy's he paused undecided—if he went back to the apartment, as he felt his body required, he would lay himself open to bitter reproach; yet, now that the pawn-shops were closed, he had no notion where to get the money. He decided finally that he might ask Parker Allison, after all—but he approached Sammy's only to find the door locked and the lights out. He looked at his watch; nine-thirty. He began walking.

Ten minutes later he stopped aimlessly at the corner of Forty-third Street and Madison Avenue, diagonally across from the bright but nearly deserted entrance to the Biltmore Hotel. Here he stood for a moment, and then sat down heavily on a damp board amid some debris of construction work. He rested there for almost half an hour, his mind a shifting pattern of surface thoughts, chiefest among which were that he must obtain some money and get home before he became too sodden to find his way.

Then, glancing over toward the Biltmore, he saw a man standing directly under the overhead glow of the porte-cochère lamps beside a woman in an ermine coat. As Anthony watched, the couple moved forward and signalled to a taxi. Anthony perceived by the infallible identification that lurks in the walk of a friend that it was Maury Noble.

He rose to his feet.

"Maury!" he shouted.

Maury looked in his direction, then turned back to the girl just as the taxi came up into place. With the chaotic idea of borrowing ten dollars, Anthony began to run as fast as he could across Madison Avenue and along Forty-third Street.

As he came up Maury was standing beside the yawning door of the taxicab. His companion turned and looked curiously at Anthony.

"Hello, Maury!" he said, holding out his hand. "How are you?"

"Fine, thank you."

Their hands dropped and Anthony hesitated. Maury made no move to introduce him, but only stood there regarding him with an inscrutable feline silence.

"I wanted to see you—" began Anthony uncertainly. He did not feel that he could ask for a loan with the girl not four feet away, so he broke off and made a perceptible motion of his head as if to beckon Maury to one side.

"I'm in rather a big hurry, Anthony."

"I know—but can you, can you—" Again he hesitated.

"I'll see you some other time," said Maury. "It's important."

"I'm sorry, Anthony."

Before Anthony could make up his mind to blurt out his request, Maury had turned coolly to the girl, helped her into the car and, with a polite "good evening," stepped in after her. As he nodded from the window it seemed to Anthony that his expression had not changed by a shade or a hair. Then with a fretful clatter the taxi moved off, and Anthony was left standing there alone under the lights.

Anthony went on into the Biltmore, for no reason in particular except that the entrance was at hand, and ascending the wide stair found a seat in an alcove. He was furiously aware that he had been snubbed; he was as hurt and angry as it was possible for him to be when in that condition. Nevertheless, he was stubbornly preoccupied with the necessity of obtaining some money before he went home, and once again he told over on his fingers the acquaintances he might conceivably call on in this emergency. He thought, eventually, that he might approach Mr. Howland, his broker, at his home.

After a long wait he found that Mr. Howland was out. He returned to the operator, leaning over her desk and fingering his quarter as though loath to leave unsatisfied.

"Call Mr. Bloeckman," he said suddenly. His own words

surprised him. The name had come from some crossing of two suggestions in his mind.

"What's the number, please?"

Scarcely conscious of what he did, Anthony looked up Joseph Bloeckman in the telephone directory. He could find no such person, and was about to close the book when it flashed into his mind that Gloria had mentioned a change of name. It was the matter of a minute to find Joseph Black—then he waited in the booth while central called the number.

"Hello-o. Mr. Bloeckman—I mean Mr. Black in?"

"No, he's out this evening. Is there any message?" The intonation was cockney; it reminded him of the rich vocal deferences of Bounds.

"Where is he?"

"Why, ah, who is this, please, sir?"

"This Mr. Patch. Matter of vi'al importance."

"Why, he's with a party at the Boul' Mich', sir."

"Thanks."

Anthony got his five cents change and started for the Boul' Mich', a popular dancing resort on Forty-fifth Street. It was nearly ten but the streets were dark and sparsely peopled until the theatres should eject their spawn an hour later. Anthony knew the Boul' Mich', for he had been there with Gloria during the year before, and he remembered the existence of a rule that patrons must be in evening dress. Well, he would not go up-stairs—he would send a boy up for Bloeckman and wait for him in the lower hall. For a moment he did not doubt that the whole project was entirely natural and graceful. To his distorted imagination Bloeckman had become simply one of his old friends.

The entrance hall of the Boul' Mich' was warm. There were high yellow lights over a thick green carpet, from the centre of which a white stairway rose to the dancing floor.

Anthony spoke to the hallboy:

"I want to see Mr. Bloeckman—Mr. Black," he said. "He's up-stairs—have him paged."

The boy shook his head.

"'Sagainsa rules to have him paged. You know what table he's at?"

"No. But I've got see him."

"Wait an' I'll getcha waiter."

After a short interval a head waiter appeared, bearing a card on which were charted the table reservations. He darted a cynical look at Anthony—which, however, failed of its target. Together they bent over the cardboard and found the table without difficulty—a party of eight, Mr. Black's own.

"Tell him Mr. Patch. Very, very important."

Again he waited, leaning against the banister and listening to the confused harmonies of "Jazz-mad" which came floating down the stairs. A check-girl near him was singing:

> *"Out in—the shimmee sanitarium*
> *The jazz-mad nuts reside.*
> *Out in—the shimmee sanitarium*
> *I left my blushing bride.*
> *She went and shook herself insane,*
> *So let her shiver back again—"*

Then he saw Bloeckman descending the staircase, and took a step forward to meet him and shake hands.

"You wanted to see me?" said the older man coolly.

"Yes," answered Anthony, nodding, "personal matter. Can you jus' step over here?"

Regarding him narrowly Bloeckman followed Anthony to a half bend made by the staircase where they were beyond observation or earshot of any one entering or leaving the restaurant.

"Well?" he inquired.

"Wanted talk to you."

"What about?"

Anthony only laughed—a silly laugh; he intended it to sound casual.

"What do you want to talk to me about?" repeated Bloeckman.

"Wha's hurry, old man?" He tried to lay his hand in a friendly gesture upon Bloeckman's shoulder, but the latter drew away slightly. "How've been?"

"Very well, thanks. . . . See here, Mr. Patch, I've got a party up-stairs. They'll think it's rude if I stay away too long. What was it you wanted to see me about?"

For the second time that evening Anthony's mind made an abrupt jump, and what he said was not at all what he had intended to say.

"Un'erstand you kep' my wife out of the movies."

"What?" Bloeckman's ruddy face darkened in parallel planes of shadows.

"You heard me."

"Look here, Mr. Patch," said Bloeckman, evenly and without changing his expression, "you're drunk. You're disgustingly and insultingly drunk."

"Not too drunk talk to you," insisted Anthony with a leer. "Firs' place, my wife wants nothin' whatever do with you. Never did. Un'erstand me?"

"Be quiet!" said the older man angrily. "I should think you'd respect your wife enough not to bring her into the conversation under these circumstances."

"Never you min' how I expect my wife. One thing—you leave her alone. You go to hell!"

"See here—I think you're a little crazy!" exclaimed Bloeckman. He took two paces forward as though to pass by, but Anthony stepped in his way.

"Not so fas', you Goddam Jew."

For a moment they stood regarding each other, Anthony

swaying gently from side to side, Bloeckman almost trembling with fury.

"Be careful!" he cried in a strained voice.

Anthony might have remembered then a certain look Bloeckman had given him in the Biltmore Hotel years before. But he remembered nothing, nothing——

"I'll say it again, you God——"

Then Bloeckman struck out, with all the strength in the arm of a well-conditioned man of forty-five, struck out and caught Anthony squarely in the mouth. Anthony cracked up against the staircase, recovered himself and made a wild drunken swing at his opponent, but Bloeckman, who took exercise every day and knew something of sparring, blocked it with ease and struck him twice in the face with two swift smashing jabs. Anthony gave a little grunt and toppled over onto the green plush carpet, finding, as he fell, that his mouth was full of blood and seemed oddly loose in front. He struggled to his feet, panting and spitting, and then as he started toward Bloeckman, who stood a few feet away, his fists clenched but not up, two waiters who had appeared from nowhere seized his arms and held him, helpless. In back of them a dozen people had miraculously gathered.

"I'll kill him," cried Anthony, pitching and straining from side to side. "Let me kill——"

"Throw him out!" ordered Bloeckman excitedly, just as a small man with a pockmarked face pushed his way hurriedly through the spectators.

"Any trouble, Mr. Black?"

"This bum tried to blackmail me!" said Bloeckman, and then, his voice rising to a faintly shrill note of pride: "He got what was coming to him!"

The little man turned to a waiter.

"Call a policeman!" he commanded.

"Oh, no," said Bloeckman quickly. "I can't be bothered. Just throw him out in the street. . . . Ugh! What an outrage!"

He turned and with conscious dignity walked toward the wash-room just as six brawny hands seized upon Anthony and dragged him toward the door. The "bum" was propelled violently to the sidewalk, where he landed on his hands and knees with a grotesque slapping sound and rolled over slowly onto his side.

The shock stunned him. He lay there for a moment in acute distributed pain. Then his discomfort became centralized in his stomach, and he regained consciousness to discover that a large foot was prodding him.

"You've got to move on, y' bum! Move on!"

It was the bulky doorman speaking. A town car had stopped at the curb and its occupants had disembarked—that is, two of the women were standing on the dashboard, waiting in offended delicacy until this obscene obstacle should be removed from their path.

"Move on! Or else I'll *throw* y'on!"

"Here—I'll get him."

This was a new voice; Anthony imagined that it was somehow more tolerant, better disposed than the first. Again arms were about him, half lifting, half dragging him into a welcome shadow four doors up the street and propping him against the stone front of a millinery shop.

"Much obliged," muttered Anthony feebly. Some one pushed his soft hat down upon his head and he winced.

"Just sit still, buddy, and you'll feel better. Those guys sure give you a bump."

"I'm going back and kill that dirty—" He tried to get to his feet but collapsed backward against the wall.

"You can't do nothin' now," came the voice. "Get 'em some other time. I'm tellin' you straight, ain't I? I'm helpin' you."

Anthony nodded.

"An' you better go home. You dropped a tooth to-night, buddy. You know that?"

Anthony explored his mouth with his tongue, verifying the statement. Then with an effort he raised his hand and located the gap.

"I'm agoin' to get you home, friend. Whereabouts do you live—"

"Oh, by God! By God!" interrupted Anthony, clenching his fists passionately. "I'll show the dirty bunch. You help me show 'em and I'll fix it with you. My grandfather's Adam Patch, of Tarrytown"—

"Who?"

"Adam Patch, by God!"

"You wanna go all the way to Tarrytown?"

"No."

"Well, you tell me where to go, friend, and I'll get a cab."

Anthony made out that his Samaritan was a short, broad-shouldered individual, somewhat the worse for wear.

"Where d'you live, hey?"

Sodden and shaken as he was, Anthony felt that his address would be poor collateral for his wild boast about his grandfather.

"Get me a cab," he commanded, feeling in his pockets.

A taxi drove up. Again Anthony essayed to rise, but his ankle swung loose, as though it were in two sections. The Samaritan must needs help him in—and climb in after him.

"See here, fella," said he, "you're soused and you're bunged up, and you won't be able to get in your house 'less somebody carries you in, so I'm going with you, and I know you'll make it all right with me. Where d'you live?"

With some reluctance Anthony gave his address. Then, as the cab moved off, he leaned his head against the man's shoulder and went into a shadowy, painful torpor. When he awoke, the man had lifted him from the cab in front of the apartment on Claremont Avenue and was trying to set him on his feet.

"Can y' walk?"

"Yes—sort of. You better not come in with me." Again he felt helplessly in his pockets. "Say," he continued, apologetically, swaying dangerously on his feet, "I'm afraid I haven't got a cent."

"Huh?"

"I'm cleaned out."

"Sa-a-ay! Didn't I hear you promise you'd fix it with me? Who's goin' to pay the taxi bill?" He turned to the driver for confirmation. "Didn't you hear him say he'd fix it? All that about his grandfather?"

"Matter of fact," muttered Anthony imprudently, "it was you did all the talking; however, if you come round, to-morrow—"

At this point the taxi-driver leaned from his cab and said ferociously:

"Ah, poke him one, the dirty cheap skate. If he wasn't a bum they wouldn'ta throwed him out."

In answer to this suggestion the fist of the Samaritan shot out like a battering-ram and sent Anthony crashing down against the stone steps of the apartment-house, where he lay without movement, while the tall buildings rocked to and fro above him. . . .

After a long while he awoke and was conscious that it had grown much colder. He tried to move himself but his muscles refused to function. He was curiously anxious to know the time, but he reached for his watch, only to find the pocket empty. Involuntarily his lips formed an immemorial phrase:

"What a night!"

Strangely enough, he was almost sober. Without moving his head he looked up to where the moon was anchored in mid-sky, shedding light down into Claremont Avenue as into the bottom of a deep and uncharted abyss. There was no sign or sound of life save for the continuous buzzing in his own ears, but after a moment Anthony himself broke the silence with a distinct and peculiar murmur. It was the sound that he had consistently attempted to make back there in the Boul' Mich', when he had been face to face with Bloeckman—the unmistakable sound of ironic laughter. And on his torn and bleeding lips it was like a pitiful retching of the soul.

Three weeks later the trial came to an end. The seemingly endless spool of legal red tape having unrolled over a period of four and a half years, suddenly snapped off. Anthony and Gloria and, on the other side, Edward Shuttleworth and a platoon of beneficiaries testified and lied and ill-behaved generally in varying degrees of greed and desperation. Anthony awoke one morning in March realizing that the verdict was to be given at four that afternoon, and at the thought he got up out of his bed and began to dress. With his extreme nervousness there was mingled an unjustified optimism as to the outcome. He believed that the decision of the lower court would be reversed, if only because of the reaction, due to excessive prohibition, that had recently set in against reforms and reformers. He counted more on the personal attacks that they had levelled at Shuttleworth than on the more sheerly legal aspects of the proceedings.

Dressed, he poured himself a drink of whiskey and then went into Gloria's room, where he found her already wide awake. She had been in bed for a week, humoring herself, Anthony fancied, though the doctor had said that she had best not be disturbed.

"Good morning," she murmured, without smiling. Her eyes seemed unusually large and dark.

"How do you feel?" he asked grudgingly. "Better?"

"Yes."

"Much?"

"Yes."

"Do you feel well enough to go down to court with me this afternoon?"

She nodded.

"Yes. I want to. Dick said yesterday that if the weather

was nice he was coming up in his car and take me for a ride in Central Park—and look, the room's all full of sunshine."

Anthony glanced mechanically out the window and then sat down upon the bed.

"God, I'm nervous!" he exclaimed.

"Please don't sit there," she said quickly.

"Why not?"

"You smell of whiskey. I can't stand it."

He got up absent-mindedly and left the room. A little later she called to him and he went out and brought her some potato salad and cold chicken from the delicatessen.

At two o'clock Richard Caramel's car arrived at the door and, when he phoned up, Anthony took Gloria down in the elevator and walked with her to the curb.

She told her cousin that it was sweet of him to take her riding. "Don't be simple," Dick replied disparagingly. "It's nothing."

But he did not mean that it was nothing and this was a curious thing. Richard Caramel had forgiven many people for many offenses. But he had never forgiven his cousin, Gloria Gilbert, for a statement she had made just prior to her wedding, seven years before. She had said that she did not intend to read his book.

Richard Caramel remembered this—he had remembered it well for seven years.

"What time will I expect you back?" asked Anthony.

"We won't come back," she answered, "we'll meet you down there at four."

"All right," he muttered, "I'll meet you."

Up-stairs he found a letter waiting for him. It was a mimeographed notice urging "the boys" in condescendingly colloquial language to pay the dues of the American Legion. He threw it impatiently into the waste-basket and sat down with his elbows on the window sill, looking down blindly into the sunny street.

Italy—if the verdict was in their favor it meant Italy. The word had become a sort of talisman to him, a land where the intolerable anxieties of life would fall away like an old garment. They would go to the watering-places first and among the bright and colorful crowds forget the gray appendages of despair. Marvellously renewed, he would walk again in the Piazza di Spanga at twilight, moving in that drifting flotsam of dark women and ragged beggars, of austere, barefooted friars. The thought of Italian women stirred him faintly—when his purse hung heavy again even romance might fly back to perch upon it—the romance of blue canals in Venice, of the golden green hills of Fiesole after rain, and of women, women who changed, dissolved, melted into other women and receded from his life, but who were always beautiful and always young.

But it seemed to him that there should be a difference in his attitude. All the distress that he had ever known, the sorrow and the pain, had been because of women. It was something that in different ways they did to him, unconsciously, almost casually—perhaps finding him tender-minded and afraid, they killed the things in him that menaced their absolute sway.

Turning about from the window he faced his reflection in the mirror, contemplating dejectedly the wan, pasty face, the eyes with their crisscross of lines like shreds of dried blood, the stooped and flabby figure whose very sag was a document in lethargy. He was thirty three—he looked forty. Well, things would be different.

The door-bell rang abruptly and he started as though he had been dealt a blow. Recovering himself, he went into the hall and opened the outer door. It was Dot.

THE ENCOUNTER

He retreated before her into the living room, comprehending only a word here and there in the slow flood of sentences that poured from her steadily, one after the other, in a persistent monotone. She was decently and shabbily dressed—a somehow pitiable little hat adorned with pink and blue flowers covered and hid her dark hair. He gathered from her words that several days before she had seen an item in the paper concerning the lawsuit, and had obtained his address from the clerk of the Appellate Division. She had called up the apartment and had been told that Anthony was out by a woman to whom she had refused to give her name.

In a living room he stood by the door regarding her with a sort of stupefied horror as she rattled on. . . . His predominant sensation was that all the civilization and convention around him was curiously unreal. . . . She was in a milliner's shop on Sixth Avenue, she said. It was a lonesome life. She had been sick for a long while after he left for Camp Mills; her mother had come down and taken her home again to Carolina. . . . She had come to New York with the idea of finding Anthony.

She was appallingly in earnest. Her violet eyes were red with tears; her soft intonation was ragged with little gasping sobs.

That was all. She had never changed. She wanted him now, and if she couldn't have him she must die. . . .

"You'll have to get out," he said at length, speaking with tortuous intensity. "Haven't I enough to worry me now without you coming here? My *God*! You'll have to get *out!*"

Sobbing, she sat down in a chair.

"I love you," she cried; "I don't care what you say to me! I love you."

"I don't care!" he almost shrieked; "get out—oh, get out! Haven't you done me harm enough? Haven't—you—done—*enough?*"

"Hit me!" she implored him—wildly, stupidly. "Oh, hit me, and I'll kiss the hand you hit me with!"

His voice rose until it was pitched almost at a scream.

"I'll kill you!" he cried. "If you don't get out I'll kill you, I'll kill you!"

There was madness in his eyes now, but, unintimidated, Dot rose and took a step toward him.

"Anthony! Anthony!—"

He made a little clicking sound with his teeth and drew back as though to spring at her—then, changing his purpose, he looked wildly about him on the floor and wall.

"I'll kill you!" he was muttering in short, broken gasps. "I'll *kill* you!" He seemed to bite at the word as though to force it into materialization. Alarmed at last she made no further movement forward, but meeting his frantic eyes took a step back toward the door. Anthony began to race here and there on his side of the room, still giving out his single cursing cry. Then he found what he had been seeking—a stiff oaken chair that stood beside the table. Uttering a harsh, broken shout, he seized it, swung it above his head and let it go with all his raging strength straight at the white, frightened face across the room . . . then a thick, impenetrable darkness came down upon him and blotted out thought, rage, and madness together—with almost a tangible snapping sound the face of the world changed before his eyes. . . .

Gloria and Dick came in at five and called his name. There was no answer—they went into the living room and found a chair with its back smashed lying in the doorway, and they noticed that all about the room there was a sort of disorder—the rugs had slid, the pictures and bric-à-brac were upset upon the centre table. The air was sickly sweet with cheap perfume.

They found Anthony sitting in a patch of sunshine on the floor of his bedroom. Before him, open, were spread his three big stamp-books, and when they entered he was running his hands through a great pile of stamps that he had dumped from the back of one of them. Looking up and seeing Dick and Gloria he put his head critically on one side and motioned them back.

"Anthony!" cried Gloria tensely, "we've won! They reversed the decision!"

"Don't come in," he murmured wanly, "you'll muss them. I'm sorting, and I know you'll step in them. Everything always gets mussed."

"What are you doing?" demanded Dick in astonishment. "Going back to childhood? Don't you realize you've won the suit? They've reversed the decision of the lower courts. You're worth thirty millions!"

Anthony only looked at him reproachfully.

"Shut the door when you go out." He spoke like a pert child.

With a faint horror dawning in her eyes, Gloria gazed at him—

"Anthony!" she cried, "what is it? What's the matter? Why didn't you come—why, what *is* it?"

"See here," said Anthony softly, "you two get out—now, both of you. Or else I'll tell my grandfather."

He held up a handful of stamps and let them come drifting down about him like leaves, varicolored and bright, turning and fluttering gaudily upon the sunny air: stamps of England and Ecuador, Venezuela and Spain—Italy. . . .

TOGETHER WITH THE SPARROWS

That exquisite heavenly irony which has tabulated the demise of so many generations of sparrows doubtless records the subtlest verbal inflections of the passengers of such ships as *The Berengaria*. And doubtless it was listening when the young man in the plaid cap crossed the deck quickly and spoke to the pretty girl in yellow.

"That's him," he said, pointing to a bundled figure seated

in a wheel chair near the rail. "That's Anthony Patch. First time he's been on deck."

"Oh—that's him?"

"Yes. He's been a little crazy, they say, ever since he got his money, four or five months ago. You see, the other fellow, Shuttleworth, the religious fellow, the one that didn't get the money, he locked himself up in a room in a hotel and shot himself—"

"Oh, he did—"

"But I guess Anthony Patch don't care much. He got his thirty million. And he's got his private physician along in case he doesn't feel just right about it. Has *she* been on deck?" he asked.

The pretty girl in yellow looked around cautiously.

"She was here a minute ago. She had on a Russian-sable coat that must have cost a small fortune." She frowned and then added decisively: "I can't stand her, you know. She seems sort of—sort of dyed and *unclean*, if you know what I mean. Some people just have that look about them whether they are or not."

"Sure, I know," agreed the man with the plaid cap. "She's not bad-looking, though." He paused. "Wonder what he's thinking about—his money, I guess, or maybe he's got remorse about that fellow Shuttleworth."

"Probably. . . ."

But the man in the plaid cap was quite wrong. Anthony Patch, sitting near the rail and looking out at the sea, was not thinking of his money, for he had seldom in his life been really preoccupied with material vainglory, nor of Edward Shuttleworth, for it is best to look on the sunny side of these things. No—he was concerned with a series of reminiscences, much as a general might look back upon a successful campaign and analyze his victories. He was thinking of the hardships, the insufferable tribulations he had gone through. They had tried to penalize him for the mistakes of his youth.

He had been exposed to ruthless misery, his very craving for romance had been punished, his friends had deserted him—even Gloria had turned against him. He had been alone, alone—facing it all.

Only a few months before people had been urging him to give in, to submit to mediocrity, to go to work. But he had known that he was justified in his way of life—and he had stuck it out stanchly. Why, the very friends who had been most unkind had come to respect him, to know he had been right all along. Had not the Lacys and the Merediths and the Cartwright-Smiths called on Gloria and him at the Ritz-Carlton just a week before they sailed?

Great tears stood in his eyes, and his voice was tremulous as he whispered to himself.

"I showed them," he was saying. "It was a hard fight, but I didn't give up and I came through!"

CLASSIC LITERATURE: WORDS AND PHRASES
adapted from the Collins English Dictionary

Accoucheur NOUN a male midwife or doctor ❏ *I think my sister must have had some general idea that I was a young offender whom an Accoucheur Policemen had taken up (on my birthday) and delivered over to her* (*Great Expectations* by Charles Dickens)

addled ADJ confused and unable to think properly ❏ *But she counted and counted till she got that addled* (*The Adventures of Huckleberry Finn* by Mark Twain)

admiration NOUN amazement or wonder ❏ *lifting up his hands and eyes by way of admiration* (*Gulliver's Travels* by Jonathan Swift)

afeard ADJ afeard means afraid ❏ *shake it—and don't be afeard* (*The Adventures of Huckleberry Finn* by Mark Twain)

affected VERB affected means followed ❏ *Hadst thou affected sweet divinity* (*Doctor Faustus 5.2* by Christopher Marlowe)

aground ADV when a boat runs aground, it touches the ground in a shallow part of the water and gets stuck ❏ *what kep' you?—boat get aground?* (*The Adventures of Huckleberry Finn* by Mark Twain)

ague NOUN a fever in which the patient has alternate hot and cold shivering fits ❏ *his exposure to the wet and cold had brought on fever and ague* (*Oliver Twist* by Charles Dickens)

alchemy ADJ false or worthless ❏ *all wealth alchemy* (*The Sun Rising* by John Donne)

all alike PHRASE the same all the time ❏ *Love, all alike* (*The Sun Rising* by John Donne)

alow and aloft PHRASE alow means in the lower part or bottom, and aloft means on the top, so alow and aloft means on the top and in the bottom or throughout ❏ *Someone's turned the chest out alow and aloft* (*Treasure Island* by Robert Louis Stevenson)

ambuscade NOUN ambuscade is not a proper word. Tom means an ambush, which is when a group of people attack their enemies, after hiding and waiting for them ❏ *and so we would lie in ambuscade, as he called it* (*The Adventures of Huckleberry Finn* by Mark Twain)

amiable ADJ likeable or pleasant ❏ *Such amiable qualities must speak for themselves* (*Pride and Prejudice* by Jane Austen)

amulet NOUN an amulet is a charm thought to drive away evil spirits. ❏ *uttered phrases at once occult and familiar, like the amulet worn on the heart* (*Silas Marner* by George Eliot)

amusement NOUN here amusement means a strange and disturbing puzzle ❏ *this was an amusement the other way* (*Robinson Crusoe* by Daniel Defoe)

ancient NOUN an ancient was the flag displayed on a ship to show which country it belongs to. It is also called the ensign ❏ *her ancient and pendants out* (*Robinson Crusoe* by Daniel Defoe)

antic ADJ here antic means horrible or grotesque ❏ *armed and dressed after a very antic manner* (*Gulliver's Travels* by Jonathan Swift)

antics NOUN antics is an old word meaning clowns, or people who do silly things to make other people laugh ❏ *And point like antics at his triple crown* (*Doctor Faustus 3.2* by Christopher Marlowe)

appanage NOUN an appanage is a living allowance ❑ *As if loveliness were not the special prerogative of woman–her legitimate appanage and heritage! (Jane Eyre* by Charlotte Brontë)

appended VERB appended means attached or added to ❑ *and these words appended (Treasure Island* by Robert Louis Stevenson)

approver NOUN an approver is someone who gives evidence against someone he used to work with ❑ *Mr. Noah Claypole: receiving a free pardon from the Crown in consequence of being admitted approver against Fagin (Oliver Twist* by Charles Dickens)

areas NOUN the areas is the space, below street level, in front of the basement of a house ❑ *The Dodger had a vicious propensity, too, of pulling the caps from the heads of small boys and tossing them down areas (Oliver Twist* by Charles Dickens)

argument NOUN theme or important idea or subject which runs through a piece of writing ❑ *Thrice needful to the argument which now (The Prelude* by William Wordsworth)

artificially ADJ artfully or cleverly ❑ *and he with a sharp flint sharpened very artificially (Gulliver's Travels* by Jonathan Swift)

artist NOUN here artist means a skilled workman ❑ *This man was a most ingenious artist (Gulliver's Travels* by Jonathan Swift)

assizes NOUN assizes were regular court sessions which a visiting judge was in charge of ❑ *you shall hang at the next assizes (Treasure Island* by Robert Louis Stevenson)

attraction NOUN gravitation, or Newton's theory of gravitation ❑ *he predicted the same fate to attraction (Gulliver's Travels* by Jonathan Swift)

aver VERB to aver is to claim something strongly ❑ *for Jem Rodney, the mole catcher, averred that one evening as he was returning homeward (Silas Marner* by George Eliot)

baby NOUN here baby means doll, which is a child's toy that looks like a small person ❑ *and skilful dressing her baby (Gulliver's Travels* by Jonathan Swift)

bagatelle NOUN bagatelle is a game rather like billiards and pool ❑ *Breakfast had been ordered at a pleasant little tavern, a mile or so away upon the rising ground beyond the green; and there was a bagatelle board in the room, in case we should desire to unbend our minds after the solemnity. (Great Expectations* by Charles Dickens)

bah EXCLAM Bah is an exclamation of frustration or anger ❑ *"Bah," said Scrooge. (A Christmas Carol* by Charles Dickens)

bairn NOUN a northern word for child ❑ *Who has taught you those fine words, my bairn? (Wuthering Heights* by Emily Brontë)

bait VERB to bait means to stop on a journey to take refreshment ❑ *So, when they stopped to bait the horse, and ate and drank and enjoyed themselves, I could touch nothing that they touched, but kept my fast unbroken. (David Copperfield* by Charles Dickens)

balustrade NOUN a balustrade is a row of vertical columns that form railings ❑ *but I mean to say you might have got a hearse up that staircase, and taken it broadwise, with the splinter-bar towards the wall, and the door towards the balustrades: and done it easy (A Christmas Carol* by Charles Dickens)

bandbox NOUN a large lightweight box for carrying bonnets or hats ❑ *I am glad I bought my bonnet, if it is only for the fun of having another bandbox (Pride and Prejudice* by Jane Austen)

barren NOUN a barren here is a stretch or expanse of barren land ❑ *a line* *of upright stones, continued the length of the barren* (Wuthering Heights *by Emily Brontë)*

basin NOUN a basin was a cup without a handle ❏ *who is drinking his tea out of a basin* (Wuthering Heights *by Emily Brontë)*

battalia NOUN the order of battle ❏ *till I saw part of his army in battalia* (Gulliver's Travels *by Jonathan Swift)*

battery NOUN a Battery is a fort or a place where guns are positioned ❏ *You bring the lot to me, at that old Battery over yonder* (Great Expectations *by Charles Dickens)*

battledore and shuttlecock NOUN The game battledore and shuttlecock was an early version of the game now known as badminton. The aim of the early game was simply to keep the shuttlecock from hitting the ground. ❏ *Battledore and shuttlecock's a wery good game vhen you an't the shuttlecock and two lawyers the battledores, in which case it gets too excitin' to be pleasant* (Pickwick Papers *by Charles Dickens)*

beadle NOUN a beadle was a local official who had power over the poor ❏ *But these impertinences were speedily checked by the evidence of the surgeon, and the testimony of the beadle* (Oliver Twist *by Charles Dickens)*

bearings NOUN the bearings of a place are the measurements or directions that are used to find or locate it ❏ *the bearings of the island* (Treasure Island *by Robert Louis Stevenson)*

beaufet NOUN a beaufet was a sideboard ❏ *and sweet-cake from the beaufet* (Emma *by Jane Austen)*

beck NOUN a beck is a small stream ❏ *a beck which follows the bend of the glen* (Wuthering Heights *by Emily Brontë)*

bedight VERB decorated ❏ *and bedight with Christmas holly stuck into the top.* (A Christmas Carol *by Charles Dickens)*

Bedlam NOUN Bedlam was a lunatic asylum in London which had statues carved by Caius Gabriel Cibber at its entrance ❏ *Bedlam, and those carved maniacs at the gates* (The Prelude *by William Wordsworth)*

beeves NOUN oxen or castrated bulls which are animals used for pulling vehicles or carrying things ❏ *to deliver in every morning six beeves* (Gulliver's Travels *by Jonathan Swift)*

begot VERB created or caused ❏ *Begot in thee* (On His Mistress *by John Donne)*

behoof NOUN behoof means benefit ❏ *"Yes, young man," said he, releasing the handle of the article in question, retiring a step or two from my table, and speaking for the behoof of the landlord and waiter at the door* (Great Expectations *by Charles Dickens)*

berth NOUN a berth is a bed on a boat ❏ *this is the berth for me* (Treasure Island *by Robert Louis Stevenson)*

bevers NOUN a bever was a snack, or small portion of food, eaten between main meals ❏ *that buys me thirty meals a day and ten bevers* (Doctor Faustus 2.1 *by Christopher Marlowe)*

bilge water NOUN the bilge is the widest part of a ship's bottom, and the bilge water is the dirty water that collects there ❏ *no gush of bilge-water had turned it to fetid puddle* (Jane Eyre *by Charlotte Brontë)*

bills NOUN bills is an old term meaning prescription. A prescription is the piece of paper on which your doctor writes an order for medicine and which you give to a chemist to get the medicine ❏ *Are not thy bills hung up as monuments* (Doctor Faustus 1.1 *by Christopher Marlowe)*

black cap NOUN a judge wore a black cap when he was about to sentence a prisoner to death ❏ *The judge* assumed the black cap, and the prisoner still stood with the same air and gesture. (*Oliver Twist* by Charles Dickens)

black gentleman NOUN this was another word for the devil ❑ *for she is as impatient as the black gentleman* (*Emma* by Jane Austen)

boot-jack NOUN a wooden device to help take boots off ❑ *The speaker appeared to throw a boot-jack, or some such article, at the person he addressed* (*Oliver Twist* by Charles Dickens)

booty NOUN booty means treasure or prizes ❑ *would be inclined to give up their booty in payment of the dead man's debts* (*Treasure Island* by Robert Louis Stevenson)

Bow Street runner PHRASE Bow Street runners were the first British police force, set up by the author Henry Fielding in the eighteenth century ❑ *as would have convinced a judge or a Bow Street runner* (*Treasure Island* by Robert Louis Stevenson)

brawn NOUN brawn is a dish of meat which is set in jelly ❑ *Heaped up upon the floor, to form a kind of throne, were turkeys, geese, game, poultry, brawn, great joints of meat, sucking-pigs* (*A Christmas Carol* by Charles Dickens)

bray VERB when a donkey brays, it makes a loud, harsh sound ❑ *and she doesn't bray like a jackass* (*The Adventures of Huckleberry Finn* by Mark Twain)

break VERB in order to train a horse you first have to break it ❑ *"If a high-mettled creature like this," said he, "can't be broken by fair means, she will never be good for anything"* (*Black Beauty* by Anna Sewell)

bullyragging VERB bullyragging is an old word which means bullying. To bullyrag someone is to threaten or force someone to do something they don't want to do ❑ *and a lot of loafers bullyragging him for sport* (*The Adventures of Huckleberry Finn* by Mark Twain)

but PREP except for (this) ❑ *but this, all pleasures fancies be* (*The Good-Morrow* by John Donne)

by hand PHRASE by hand was a common expression of the time meaning that baby had been fed either using a spoon or a bottle rather than by breast-feeding ❑ *My sister, Mrs. Joe Gargery, was more than twenty years older than I, and had established a great reputation with herself . . . because she had bought me up 'by hand'* (*Great Expectations* by Charles Dickens)

bye-spots NOUN bye-spots are lonely places ❑ *and bye-spots of tales rich with indigenous produce* (*The Prelude* by William Wordsworth)

calico NOUN calico is plain white fabric made from cotton ❑ *There was two old dirty calico dresses* (*The Adventures of Huckleberry Finn* by Mark Twain)

camp-fever NOUN camp-fever was another word for the disease typhus ❑ *during a severe camp-fever* (*Emma* by Jane Austen)

cant NOUN cant is insincere or empty talk ❑ *"Man," said the Ghost, "if man you be in heart, not adamant, forbear that wicked cant until you have discovered What the surplus is, and Where it is."* (*A Christmas Carol* by Charles Dickens)

canty ADJ canty means lively, full of life ❑ *My mother lived til eighty, a canty dame to the last* (*Wuthering Heights* by Emily Brontë)

canvas VERB to canvas is to discuss ❑ *We think so very differently on this point Mr Knightley, that there can be no use in canvassing it* (*Emma* by Jane Austen)

capital ADJ capital means excellent or extremely good ❑ *for it's capital, so shady, light, and big* (*Little Women* by Louisa May Alcott)

capstan NOUN a capstan is a device used on a ship to lift sails and anchors ❑ *capstans going, ships going out to sea, and unintelligible* *sea creatures roaring curses over the bulwarks at respondent lightermen* (*Great Expectations* by Charles Dickens)

case-bottle NOUN a square bottle designed to fit with others into a case ❑ *The spirit being set before him in a huge case-bottle, which had originally come out of some ship's locker* (*The Old Curiosity Shop* by Charles Dickens)

casement NOUN casement is a word meaning window. The teacher in Nicholas Nickleby misspells window showing what a bad teacher he is ❑ *W-i-n, win, d-e-r, der, winder, a casement.'* (*Nicholas Nickleby* by Charles Dickens)

cataleptic ADJ a cataleptic fit is one in which the victim goes into a trance-like state and remains still for a long time ❑ *It was at this point in their history that Silas's cataleptic fit occurred during the prayer-meeting* (*Silas Marner* by George Eliot)

cauldron NOUN a cauldron is a large cooking pot made of metal ❑ *stirring a large cauldron which seemed to be full of soup* (*Alice's Adventures in Wonderland* by Lewis Carroll)

cephalic ADJ cephalic means to do with the head ❑ *with ink composed of a cephalic tincture* (*Gulliver's Travels* by Jonathan Swift)

chaise and four NOUN a closed four-wheel carriage pulled by four horses ❑ *he came down on Monday in a chaise and four to see the place* (*Pride and Prejudice* by Jane Austen)

chamberlain NOUN the main servant in a household ❑ *In those times a bed was always to be got there at any hour of the night, and the chamberlain, letting me in at his ready wicket, lighted the candle next in order on his shelf* (*Great Expectations* by Charles Dickens)

characters NOUN distinguishing marks ❑ *Impressed upon all forms the characters* (*The Prelude* by William Wordsworth)

chary ADJ cautious ❑ *I should have been chary of discussing my guardian too freely even with her* (*Great Expectations* by Charles Dickens)

cherishes VERB here cherishes means cheers or brightens ❑ *some philosophic song of Truth that cherishes our daily life* (*The Prelude* by William Wordsworth)

chickens' meat PHRASE chickens' meat is an old term which means chickens' feed or food ❑ *I had shook a bag of chickens' meat out in that place* (*Robinson Crusoe* by Daniel Defoe)

chimeras NOUN a chimera is an unrealistic idea or a wish which is unlikely to be fulfilled ❑ *with many other wild impossible chimeras* (*Gulliver's Travels* by Jonathan Swift)

chines NOUN chine is a cut of meat that includes part or all of the backbone of the animal ❑ *and they found hams and chines uncut* (*Silas Marner* by George Eliot)

chits NOUN chits is a slang word which means girls ❑ *I hate affected, niminy-piminy chits!* (*Little Women* by Louisa May Alcott)

chopped VERB chopped means come suddenly or accidentally ❑ *if I had chopped upon them* (*Robinson Crusoe* by Daniel Defoe)

chute NOUN a narrow channel ❑ *One morning about day-break, I found a canoe and crossed over a chute to the main shore* (*The Adventures of Huckleberry Finn* by Mark Twain)

circumspection NOUN careful observation of events and circumstances; caution ❑ *I honour your circumspection* (*Pride and Prejudice* by Jane Austen)

clambered VERB clambered means to climb somewhere with difficulty, usually using your hands and your feet ❑ *he clambered up and down stairs* (*Treasure Island* by Robert Louis Stevenson)

clime NOUN climate ❏ *no season knows nor clime* (*The Sun Rising* by John Donne)

clinched VERB clenched ❏ *the tops whereof I could but just reach with my fist clinched* (*Gulliver's Travels* by Jonathan Swift)

close chair NOUN a close chair is a sedan chair, which is an covered chair which has room for one person. The sedan chair is carried on two poles by two men, one in front and one behind ❏ *persuaded even the Empress herself to let me hold her in her close chair* (*Gulliver's Travels* by Jonathan Swift)

clown NOUN clown here means peasant or person who lives off the land ❏ *In ancient days by emperor and clown* (*Ode on a Nightingale* by John Keats)

coalheaver NOUN a coalheaver loaded coal onto ships using a spade ❏ *Good, strong, wholesome medicine, as was given with great success to two Irish labourers and a coalheaver* (*Oliver Twist* by Charles Dickens)

coal-whippers NOUN men who worked at docks using machines to load coal onto ships ❏ *here, were colliers by the score and score, with the coal-whippers plunging off stages on deck* (*Great Expectations* by Charles Dickens)

cobweb NOUN a cobweb is the net which a spider makes for catching insects ❏ *the walls and ceilings were all hung round with cobwebs* (*Gulliver's Travels* by Jonathan Swift)

coddling VERB coddling means to treat someone too kindly or protect them too much ❏ *and I've been coddling the fellow as if I'd been his grandmother* (*Little Women* by Louisa May Alcott)

coil NOUN coil means noise or fuss or disturbance ❏ *What a coil is there?* (*Doctor Faustus 4.7* by Christopher Marlowe)

collared VERB to collar something is a slang term which means to capture.

In this sentence, it means he stole it [the money] ❏ *he collared it* (*The Adventures of Huckleberry Finn* by Mark Twain)

colling VERB colling is an old word which means to embrace and kiss ❏ *and no clasping and colling at all* (*Tess of the D'Urbervilles* by Thomas Hardy)

colloquies NOUN colloquy is a formal conversation or dialogue ❏ *Such colloquies have occupied many a pair of pale-faced weavers* (*Silas Marner* by George Eliot)

comfit NOUN sugar-covered pieces of fruit or nut eaten as sweets ❏ *and pulled out a box of comfits* (*Alice's Adventures in Wonderland* by Lewis Carroll)

coming out VERB when a girl came out in society it meant she was of marriageable age. In order to 'come out' girls were expecting to attend balls and other parties during a season ❏ *The younger girls formed hopes of coming out a year or two sooner than they might otherwise have done* (*Pride and Prejudice* by Jane Austen)

commit VERB commit means arrest or stop ❏ *Commit the rascals* (*Doctor Faustus 4.7* by Christopher Marlowe)

commodious ADJ commodious means convenient ❏ *the most commodious and effectual ways* (*Gulliver's Travels* by Jonathan Swift)

commons NOUN commons is an old term meaning food shared with others ❏ *his pauper assistants ranged themselves behind him; the gruel was served out; and a long grace was said over the short commons.* (*Oliver Twist* by Charles Dickens)

complacency NOUN here complacency means a desire to please others. To-day complacency means feeling pleased with oneself without good reason. ❏ *Twas thy power that raised the first complacency in me* (*The Prelude* by William Wordsworth)

complaisance NOUN complaisance was eagerness to please ❑ *we cannot wonder at his complaisance* (*Pride and Prejudice* by Jane Austen)

complaisant ADJ complaisant means polite ❑ *extremely cheerful and complaisant to their guest* (*Gulliver's Travels* by Jonathan Swift)

conning VERB conning means learning by heart ❑ *Or conning more* (*The Prelude* by William Wordsworth)

consequent NOUN consequence ❑ *as avarice is the necessary consequent of old age* (*Gulliver's Travels* by Jonathan Swift)

consorts NOUN concerts ❑ *The King, who delighted in music, had frequent consorts at Court* (*Gulliver's Travels* by Jonathan Swift)

conversible ADJ conversible meant easy to talk to, companionable ❑ *He can be a conversible companion* (*Pride and Prejudice* by Jane Austen)

copper NOUN a copper is a large pot that can be heated directly over a fire ❑ *He gazed in stupefied astonishment on the small rebel for some seconds, and then clung for support to the copper* (*Oliver Twist* by Charles Dickens)

copper-stick NOUN a copper-stick is the long piece of wood used to stir washing in the copper (or boiler) which was usually the biggest cooking pot in the house ❑ *It was Christmas Eve, and I had to stir the pudding for next day, with a copper-stick, from seven to eight by the Dutch clock* (*Great Expectations* by Charles Dickens)

counting-house NOUN a counting house is a place where accountants work ❑ *Once upon a time–of all the good days in the year, on Christmas Eve–old Scrooge sat busy in his countinghouse* (*A Christmas Carol* by Charles Dickens)

courtier NOUN a courtier is someone who attends the king or queen–a member of the court ❑ *next the ten courtiers;* (*Alice's Adventures in Wonderland* by Lewis Carroll)

covies NOUN covies were flocks of partridges ❑ *and will save all of the best covies for you* (*Pride and Prejudice* by Jane Austen)

cowed VERB cowed means frightened or intimidated ❑ *it cowed me more than the pain* (*Treasure Island* by Robert Louis Stevenson)

cozened VERB cozened means tricked or deceived ❑ *Do you remember, sir, how you cozened me* (*Doctor Faustus 4.7* by Christopher Marlowe)

cravats NOUN a cravat is a folded cloth that a man wears wrapped around his neck as a decorative item of clothing ❑ *we'd'a' slept in our cravats to-night* (*The Adventures of Huckleberry Finn* by Mark Twain)

crock and dirt PHRASE crock and dirt is an old expression meaning soot and dirt ❑ *and the mare catching cold at the door, and the boy grimed with crock and dirt* (*Great Expectations* by Charles Dickens)

crockery NOUN here crockery means pottery ❑ *By one of the parrots was a cat made of crockery* (*The Adventures of Huckleberry Finn* by Mark Twain)

crooked sixpence PHRASE it was considered unlucky to have a bent sixpence ❑ *You've got the beauty, you see, and I've got the luck, so you must keep me by you for your crooked sixpence* (*Silas Marner* by George Eliot)

croquet NOUN croquet is a traditional English summer game in which players try to hit wooden balls through hoops ❑ *and once she remembered trying to box her own ears for having cheated herself in a game of croquet* (*Alice's Adventures in Wonderland* by Lewis Carroll)

cross PREP across ❑ *The two great streets, which run cross and divide it into four quarters* (*Gulliver's Travels* by Jonathan Swift)

culpable ADJ if you are culpable for something it means you are to blame ❑ *deep are the sorrows that spring from false ideas for which no man is culpable.* (*Silas Marner* by George Eliot)

cultured ADJ cultivated ❑ *Nor less when spring had warmed the cultured Vale* (*The Prelude* by William Wordsworth)

cupidity NOUN cupidity is greed ❑ *These people hated me with the hatred of cupidity and disappointment.* (*Great Expectations* by Charles Dickens)

curricle NOUN an open two-wheeled carriage with one seat for the driver and space for a single passenger ❑ *and they saw a lady and a gentleman in a curricle* (*Pride and Prejudice* by Jane Austen)

cynosure NOUN a cynosure is something that strongly attracts attention or admiration ❑ *Then I thought of Eliza and Georgiana; I beheld one the cynosure of a ballroom, the other the inmate of a convent cell* (*Jane Eyre* by Charlotte Brontë)

dalliance NOUN someone's dalliance with something is a brief involvement with it ❑ *nor sporting in the dalliance of love* (*Doctor Faustus Chorus* by Christopher Marlowe)

darkling ADV darkling is an archaic way of saying in the dark ❑ *Darkling I listen* (*Ode on a Nightingale* by John Keats)

delf-case NOUN a sideboard for holding dishes and crockery ❑ *at the pewter dishes and delf-case* (*Wuthering Heights* by Emily Brontë)

determined ■ VERB here determined means ended ❑ *and be out of vogue when that was determined* (*Gulliver's Travels* by Jonathan Swift) ■ VERB determined can mean to have been learned or found especially by investigation or experience ❑ *All the sensitive feelings it wounded so cruelly, all the shame and misery it kept alive within my breast, became more poignant as I*

thought of this; and I determined that the life was unendurable (*David Copperfield* by Charles Dickens)

Deuce NOUN a slang term for the Devil ❑ *Ah, I dare say I did. Deuce take me, he added suddenly, I know I did. I find I am not quite unscrewed yet.* (*Great Expectations* by Charles Dickens)

diabolical ADJ diabolical means devilish or evil ❑ *and with a thousand diabolical expressions* (*Treasure Island* by Robert Louis Stevenson)

direction NOUN here direction means address ❑ *Elizabeth was not surprised at it, as Jane had written the direction remarkably ill* (*Pride and Prejudice* by Jane Austen)

discover VERB to make known or announce ❑ *the Emperor would discover the secret while I was out of his power* (*Gulliver's Travels* by Jonathan Swift)

dissemble VERB hide or conceal ❑ *Dissemble nothing* (*On His Mistress* by John Donne)

dissolve VERB dissolve here means to release from life, to die ❑ *Fade far away, dissolve, and quite forget* (*Ode on a Nightingale* by John Keats)

distrain VERB to distrain is to seize the property of someone who is in debt in compensation for the money owed ❑ *for he's threatening to distrain for it* (*Silas Marner* by George Eliot)

Divan NOUN a Divan was originally a Turkish council of state–the name was transferred to the couches they sat on and is used to mean this in English ❑ *Mr Brass applauded this picture very much, and the bed being soft and comfortable, Mr Quilp determined to use it, both as a sleeping place by night and as a kind of Divan by day.* (*The Old Curiosity Shop* by Charles Dickens)

divorcement NOUN separation ❑ *By all pains which want and divorcement* hath (*On His Mistress* by John Donne)

dog in the manger, PHRASE this phrase describes someone who prevents you from enjoying something that they themselves have no need for ❏ *You are a dog in the manger, Cathy, and desire no one to be loved but yourself* (*Wuthering Heights* by Emily Brontë)

dolorifuge NOUN dolorifuge is a word which Thomas Hardy invented. It means pain-killer or comfort ❏ *as a species of dolorifuge* (*Tess of the D'Urbervilles* by Thomas Hardy)

dome NOUN building ❏ *that river and that mouldering dome* (*The Prelude* by William Wordsworth)

domestic PHRASE here domestic means a person's management of the house ❏ *to give some account of my domestic* (*Gulliver's Travels* by Jonathan Swift)

dunce NOUN a dunce is another word for idiot ❏ *Do you take me for a dunce? Go on?* (*Alice's Adventures in Wonderland* by Lewis Carroll)

Ecod EXCLAM a slang exclamation meaning 'oh God!' ❏ *"Ecod,"* replied Wemmick, shaking his head, *"that's not my trade."* (*Great Expectations* by Charles Dickens)

egg-hot NOUN an egg-hot (see also 'flip' and 'negus') was a hot drink made from beer and eggs, sweetened with nutmeg ❏ *She fainted when she saw me return, and made a little jug of egg-hot afterwards to console us while we talked it over.* (*David Copperfield* by Charles Dickens)

encores NOUN an encore is a short extra performance at the end of a longer one, which the entertainer gives because the audience has enthusiastically asked for it ❏ *we want a little something to answer encores with, anyway* (*The Adventures of Huckleberry Finn* by Mark Twain)

equipage NOUN an elegant and impressive carriage ❏ *and besides, the equipage did not answer to any of*

their *neighbours* (*Pride and Prejudice* by Jane Austen)

exordium NOUN an exordium is the opening part of a speech ❏ *"Now, Handel,"* as if it were the grave beginning of a portentous business exordium, he had suddenly given up that tone (*Great Expectations* by Charles Dickens)

expect VERB here expect means to wait for ❏ *to expect his farther commands* (*Gulliver's Travels* by Jonathan Swift)

familiars NOUN familiars means spirits or devils who come to someone when they are called ❏ *I'll turn all the lice about thee into familiars* (*Doctor Faustus 1.4* by Christopher Marlowe)

fantods NOUN a fantod is a person who fidgets or can't stop moving nervously ❏ *It most give me the fantods* (*The Adventures of Huckleberry Finn* by Mark Twain)

farthing NOUN a farthing is an old unit of British currency which was worth a quarter of a penny ❏ *Not a farthing less. A great many back-payments are included in it, I assure you.* (*A Christmas Carol* by Charles Dickens)

farthingale NOUN a hoop worn under a skirt to extend it ❏ *A bell with an old voice–which I dare say in its time had often said to the house, Here is the green farthingale* (*Great Expectations* by Charles Dickens)

favours NOUN here favours is an old word which means ribbons ❏ *A group of humble mourners entered the gate: wearing white favours* (*Oliver Twist* by Charles Dickens)

feigned VERB pretend or pretending ❏ *not my feigned page* (*On His Mistress* by John Donne)

fence ■ NOUN a fence is someone who receives and sells stolen goods ❏ *What are you up to? Ill-treating the boys, you covetous, avaricious, in-sa-ti-a-ble old fence?* (*Oliver Twist* by

Charles Dickens) ■ NOUN defence or protection ❑ *but honesty hath no fence against superior cunning* (*Gulliver's Travels* by Jonathan Swift)

fess ADJ fess is an old word which means pleased or proud ❑ *You'll be fess enough, my poppet* (*Tess of the D'Urbervilles* by Thomas Hardy)

fettered ADJ fettered means bound in chains or chained ❑ *"You are fettered," said Scrooge, trembling. "Tell me why?"* (*A Christmas Carol* by Charles Dickens)

fidges VERB fidges means fidgets, which is to keep moving your hands slightly because you are nervous or excited ❑ *Look, Jim, how my fingers fidges* (*Treasure Island* by Robert Louis Stevenson)

finger-post NOUN a finger-post is a sign-post showing the direction to different places ❑ *"The gallows," continued Fagin, "the gallows, my dear, is an ugly finger-post, which points out a very short and sharp turning that has stopped many a bold fellow's career on the broad highway."* (*Oliver Twist* by Charles Dickens)

fire-irons NOUN fire-irons are tools kept by the side of the fire to either cook with or look after the fire ❑ *the fire-irons came first* (*Alice's Adventures in Wonderland* by Lewis Carroll)

fire-plug NOUN a fire-plug is another word for a fire hydrant ❑ *The pony looked with great attention into a fire-plug, which was near him, and appeared to be quite absorbed in contemplating it* (*The Old Curiosity Shop* by Charles Dickens)

flank NOUN flank is the side of an animal ❑ *And all her silken flanks with garlands dressed* (*Ode on a Grecian Urn* by John Keats)

flip NOUN a flip is a drink made from warmed ale, sugar, spice and beaten egg ❑ *The events of the day, in combination with the twins, if not with the flip, had made Mrs.*

Micawber hysterical, and she shed tears as she replied (*David Copperfield* by Charles Dickens)

flit VERB flit means to move quickly ❑ *and if he had meant to flit to Thrushcross Grange* (*Wuthering Heights* by Emily Brontë)

floorcloth NOUN a floorcloth was a hard-wearing piece of canvas used instead of carpet ❑ *This avenging phantom was ordered to be on duty at eight on Tuesday morning in the hall (it was two feet square, as charged for floorcloth)* (*Great Expectations* by Charles Dickens)

fly-driver NOUN a fly-driver is a carriage drawn by a single horse ❑ *The fly-drivers, among whom I inquired next, were equally jocose and equally disrespectful* (*David Copperfield* by Charles Dickens)

fob NOUN a small pocket in which a watch is kept ❑ *"Certain," replied the man, drawing a gold watch from his fob* (*Oliver Twist* by Charles Dickens)

folly NOUN folly means foolishness or stupidity ❑ *the folly of beginning a work* (*Robinson Crusoe* by Daniel Defoe)

fond ADJ fond means foolish ❑ *Fond worldling* (*Doctor Faustus 5.2* by Christopher Marlowe)

fondness NOUN silly or foolish affection ❑ *They have no fondness for their colts or foals* (*Gulliver's Travels* by Jonathan Swift)

for his fancy PHRASE for his fancy means for his liking or as he wanted ❑ *and as I did not obey quick enough for his fancy* (*Treasure Island* by Robert Louis Stevenson)

forlorn ADJ lost or very upset ❑ *you are from that day forlorn* (*Gulliver's Travels* by Jonathan Swift)

foster-sister NOUN a foster-sister was someone brought up by the same nurse or in the same household ❑ *I had been his foster-sister* (*Wuthering Heights* by Emily Brontë)

fox-fire NOUN fox-fire is a weak glow that is given off by decaying, rotten wood ❑ *what we must have was a lot of them rotten chunks that's called fox-fire* (The Adventures of Huckleberry Finn by Mark Twain)

frozen sea PHRASE the Arctic Ocean ❑ *into the frozen sea* (Gulliver's Travels by Jonathan Swift)

gainsay VERB to gainsay something is to say it isn't true or to deny it ❑ *"So she had," cried Scrooge. "You're right. I'll not gainsay it, Spirit. God forbid!"* (A Christmas Carol by Charles Dickens)

gaiters NOUN gaiters were leggings made of a cloth or piece of leather which covered the leg from the knee to the ankle ❑ *Mr Knightley was hard at work upon the lower buttons of his thick leather gaiters* (Emma by Jane Austen)

galluses NOUN galluses is an old spelling of gallows, and here means suspenders. Suspenders are straps worn over someone's shoulders and fastened to their trousers to prevent the trousers falling down ❑ *and home-knit galluses* (The Adventures of Huckleberry Finn by Mark Twain)

galoot NOUN a sailor but also a clumsy person ❑ *and maybe a galoot on it chopping* (The Adventures of Huckleberry Finn by Mark Twain)

gayest ADJ gayest means the most lively and bright or merry ❑ *Beth played her gayest march* (Little Women by Louisa May Alcott)

gem NOUN here gem means jewellery ❑ *the mountain shook off turf and flower, had only heath for raiment and crag for gem* (Jane Eyre by Charlotte Brontë)

giddy ADJ giddy means dizzy ❑ *and I wish you wouldn't keep appearing and vanishing so suddenly; you make one quite giddy.* (Alice's Adventures in Wonderland by Lewis Carroll)

gig NOUN a light two-wheeled carriage ❑ *when a gig drove up to the garden gate: out of which there jumped a fat gentleman* (Oliver Twist by Charles Dickens)

gladsome ADJ gladsome is an old word meaning glad or happy ❑ *Nobody ever stopped him in the street to say, with gladsome looks* (A Christmas Carol by Charles Dickens)

glen NOUN a glen is a small valley; the word is used commonly in Scotland ❑ *a beck which follows the bend of the glen* (Wuthering Heights by Emily Brontë)

gravelled VERB gravelled is an old term which means to baffle or defeat someone ❑ *Gravelled the pastors of the German Church* (Doctor Faustus 1.1 by Christopher Marlowe)

grinder NOUN a grinder was a private tutor ❑ *but that when he had had the happiness of marrying Mrs Pocket very early in his life, he had impaired his prospects and taken up the calling of a Grinder* (Great Expectations by Charles Dickens)

gruel NOUN gruel is a thin, watery cornmeal or oatmeal soup ❑ *and the little saucepan of gruel (Scrooge had a cold in his head) upon the hob.* (A Christmas Carol by Charles Dickens)

guinea, half a NOUN a half guinea was ten shillings and sixpence ❑ *but lay out half a guinea at Ford's* (Emma by Jane Austen)

gull VERB gull is an old term which means to fool or deceive someone ❑ *Hush, I'll gull him supernaturally* (Doctor Faustus 3.4 by Christopher Marlowe)

gunnel NOUN the gunnel, or gunwhale, is the upper edge of a boat's side ❑ *But he put his foot on the gunnel and rocked her* (The Adventures of Huckleberry Finn by Mark Twain)

gunwale NOUN the side of a ship ❑ *He dipped his hand in the water over the boat's gunwale* (Great Expectations by Charles Dickens)

Gytrash NOUN a Gytrash is an omen of misfortune to the superstitious, usually taking the form of a hound ❏ *I remembered certain of Bessie's tales, wherein figured a North-of-England spirit, called a 'Gytrash'* (*Jane Eyre* by Charlotte Brontë)

hackney-cabriolet NOUN a two-wheeled carriage with four seats for hire and pulled by a horse ❏ *A hackney-cabriolet was in waiting; with the same vehemence which she had exhibited in addressing Oliver, the girl pulled him in with her, and drew the curtains close.* (*Oliver Twist* by Charles Dickens)

hackney-coach NOUN a four-wheeled horse-drawn vehicle for hire ❏ *The twilight was beginning to close in, when Mr. Brownlow alighted from a hackney-coach at his own door, and knocked softly.* (*Oliver Twist* by Charles Dickens)

haggler NOUN a haggler is someone who travels from place to place selling small goods and items ❏ *when I be plain Jack Durbeyfield, the haggler* (*Tess of the D'Urbervilles* by Thomas Hardy)

halter NOUN a halter is a rope or strap used to lead an animal or to tie it up ❏ *I had of course long been used to a halter and a headstall* (*Black Beauty* by Anna Sewell)

hamlet NOUN a hamlet is a small village or a group of houses in the countryside ❏ *down from the hamlet* (*Treasure Island* by Robert Louis Stevenson)

hand-barrow NOUN a hand-barrow is a device for carrying heavy objects. It is like a wheelbarrow except that it has handles, rather than wheels, for moving the barrow ❏ *his sea chest following behind him in a hand-barrow* (*Treasure Island* by Robert Louis Stevenson)

handspike NOUN a handspike was a stick which was used as a lever ❏ *a bit of stick like a handspike* (*Treasure Island* by Robert Louis Stevenson)

haply ADV haply means by chance or perhaps ❏ *And haply the Queen-Moon is on her throne* (*Ode on a Nightingale* by John Keats)

harem NOUN the harem was the part of the house where the women lived ❏ *mostly they hang round the harem* (*The Adventures of Huckleberry Finn* by Mark Twain)

hautboys NOUN hautboys are oboes ❏ *sausages and puddings resembling flutes and hautboys* (*Gulliver's Travels* by Jonathan Swift)

hawker NOUN a hawker is someone who sells goods to people as he travels rather than from a fixed place like a shop ❏ *to buy some stockings from a hawker* (*Treasure Island* by Robert Louis Stevenson)

hawser NOUN a hawser is a rope used to tie up or tow a ship or boat ❏ *Again among the tiers of shipping, in and out, avoiding rusty chain-cables, frayed hempen hawsers* (*Great Expectations* by Charles Dickens)

headstall NOUN the headstall is the part of the bridle or halter that goes around a horse's head ❏ *I had of course long been used to a halter and a headstall* (*Black Beauty* by Anna Sewell)

hearken VERB hearken means to listen ❏ *though we sometimes stopped to lay hold of each other and hearken* (*Treasure Island* by Robert Louis Stevenson)

heartless ADJ here heartless means without heart or dejected ❏ *I am not heartless* (*The Prelude* by William Wordsworth)

hebdomadal ADJ hebdomadal means weekly ❏ *It was the hebdomadal treat to which we all looked forward from Sabbath to Sabbath* (*Jane Eyre* by Charlotte Brontë)

highwaymen NOUN highwaymen were people who stopped travellers and robbed them ❏ *We are high-waymen* (*The Adventures of Huckleberry Finn* by Mark Twain)

hinds NOUN hinds means farm hands, or people who work on a farm ❑ *He called his hinds about him* (*Gulliver's Travels* by Jonathan Swift)

histrionic ADJ if you refer to someone's behaviour as histrionic, you are being critical of it because it is dramatic and exaggerated ❑ *But the histrionic muse is the darling* (*The Adventures of Huckleberry Finn* by Mark Twain)

hogs NOUN hogs is another word for pigs ❑ *Tom called the hogs 'ingots'* (*The Adventures of Huckleberry Finn* by Mark Twain)

horrors NOUN the horrors are a fit, called delirium tremens, which is caused by drinking too much alcohol ❑ *I'll have the horrors* (*Treasure Island* by Robert Louis Stevenson)

huffy ADJ huffy means to be obviously annoyed or offended about something ❑ *They will feel that more than angry speeches or huffy actions* (*Little Women* by Louisa May Alcott)

hulks NOUN hulks were prison-ships ❑ *The miserable companion of thieves and ruffians, the fallen outcast of low haunts, the associate of the scourings of the jails and hulks* (*Oliver Twist* by Charles Dickens)

humbug NOUN humbug means nonsense or rubbish ❑ *"Bah," said Scrooge. "Humbug!"* (*A Christmas Carol* by Charles Dickens)

humours NOUN it was believed that there were four fluids in the body called humours which decided the temperament of a person depending on how much of each fluid was present ❑ *other peccant humours* (*Gulliver's Travels* by Jonathan Swift)

husbandry NOUN husbandry is farming animals ❑ *bad husbandry were plentifully anointing their wheels* (*Silas Marner* by George Eliot)

huswife NOUN a huswife was a small sewing kit ❑ *but I had put my huswife on it* (*Emma* by Jane Austen)

ideal ADJ ideal in this context means imaginary ❑ *I discovered the yell was not ideal* (*Wuthering Heights* by Emily Brontë)

If our two PHRASE if both our ❑ *If our two loves be one* (*The Good-Morrow* by John Donne)

ignis-fatuus NOUN ignis-fatuus is the light given out by burning marsh gases, which lead careless travellers into danger ❑ *it is madness in all women to let a secret love kindle within them, which, if unreturned and unknown, must devour the life that feeds it; and, if discovered and responded to, must lead ignis-fatuus-like, into miry wilds whence there is no extrication.* (*Jane Eyre* by Charlotte Brontë)

imaginations NOUN here imaginations means schemes or plans ❑ *soon drove out those imaginations* (*Gulliver's Travels* by Jonathan Swift)

impressible ADJ impressible means open or impressionable ❑ *for Marner had one of those impressible, self-doubting natures* (*Silas Marner* by George Eliot)

in good intelligence PHRASE friendly with each other ❑ *that these two persons were in good intelligence with each other* (*Gulliver's Travels* by Jonathan Swift)

inanity NOUN inanity is sillyness or dull stupidity ❑ *Do we not wile away moments of inanity* (*Silas Marner* by George Eliot)

incivility NOUN incivility means rudeness or impoliteness ❑ *if it's only for a piece of incivility like to-night's* (*Treasure Island* by Robert Louis Stevenson)

indigenae NOUN indigenae means natives or people from that area ❑ *an exotic that the surly indigenae will not recognise for kin* (*Wuthering Heights* by Emily Brontë)

indocible ADJ unteachable ❑ *so they were the most restive and indocible* (*Gulliver's Travels* by Jonathan Swift)

ingenuity NOUN inventiveness ❑ *entreated me to give him something as an encouragement to ingenuity* (*Gulliver's Travels* by Jonathan Swift)

ingots NOUN an ingot is a lump of a valuable metal like gold, usually shaped like a brick ❑ *Tom called the hogs 'ingots'* (*The Adventures of Huckleberry Finn* by Mark Twain)

inkstand NOUN an inkstand is a pot which was put on a desk to contain either ink or pencils and pens ❑ *throwing an inkstand at the Lizard as she spoke* (*Alice's Adventures in Wonderland* by Lewis Carroll)

inordinate ADJ without order. To-day inordinate means 'excessive'. ❑ *Though yet untutored and inordinate* (*The Prelude* by William Wordsworth)

intellectuals NOUN here intellectuals means the minds (of the workmen) ❑ *those instructions they give being too refined for the intellectuals of their workmen* (*Gulliver's Travels* by Jonathan Swift)

interview NOUN meeting ❑ *By our first strange and fatal interview* (*On His Mistress* by John Donne)

jacks NOUN jacks are rods for turning a spit over a fire ❑ *It was a small bit of pork suspended from the kettle hanger by a string passed through a large door key, in a way known to primitive housekeepers unpossessed of jacks* (*Silas Marner* by George Eliot)

jews-harp NOUN a jews-harp is a small, metal, musical instrument that is played by the mouth ❑ *A jews-harp's plenty good enough for a rat* (*The Adventures of Huckleberry Finn* by Mark Twain)

jorum NOUN a large bowl ❑ *while Miss Skiffins brewed such a jorum of tea, that the pig in the back premises became strongly excited* (*Great Expectations* by Charles Dickens)

jostled VERB jostled means bumped or pushed by someone or some people

❑ *being jostled himself into the kennel* (*Gulliver's Travels* by Jonathan Swift)

keepsake NOUN a keepsake is a gift which reminds someone of an event or of the person who gave it to them. ❑ *books and ornaments they had in their boudoirs at home: keepsakes that different relations had presented to them* (*Jane Eyre* by Charlotte Brontë)

kenned VERB kenned means knew ❑ *though little kenned the lamplighter that he had any company but Christmas!* (*A Christmas Carol* by Charles Dickens)

kennel NOUN kennel means gutter, which is the edge of a road next to the pavement, where rain water collects and flows away ❑ *being jostled himself into the kennel* (*Gulliver's Travels* by Jonathan Swift)

knock-knee ADJ knock-knee means slanted, at an angle. ❑ *LOT 1 was marked in whitewashed knock-knee letters on the brewhouse* (*Great Expectations* by Charles Dickens)

ladylike ADJ to be ladylike is to behave in a polite, dignified and graceful way ❑ *No, winking isn't ladylike* (*Little Women* by Louisa May Alcott)

lapse NOUN flow ❑ *Stealing with silent lapse to join the brook* (*The Prelude* by William Wordsworth)

larry NOUN larry is an old word which means commotion or noisy celebration ❑ *That was all a part of the larry!* (*Tess of the D'Urbervilles* by Thomas Hardy)

laths NOUN laths are strips of wood ❑ *The panels shrunk, the windows cracked; fragments of plaster fell out of the ceiling, and the naked laths were shown instead* (*A Christmas Carol* by Charles Dickens)

leer NOUN a leer is an unpleasant smile ❑ *with a kind of leer* (*Treasure Island* by Robert Louis Stevenson)

lenitives NOUN these are different kinds of drugs or medicines: lenitives and palliatives were pain relievers; aperitives were laxatives; abstersives caused vomiting; corrosives destroyed human tissue; restringents caused constipation; cephalalgics stopped headaches; icterics were used as medicine for jaundice; apophlegmatics were cough medicine, and acoustics were cures for the loss of hearing ❑ *lenitives, aperitives, abstersives, corrosives, restringents, palliatives, laxatives, cephalalgics, icterics, apophlegmatics, acoustics (Gulliver's Travels* by Jonathan Swift)

lest CONJ in case. If you do something lest something (usually) unpleasant happens you do it to try to prevent it happening ❑ *She went in without knocking, and hurried upstairs, in great fear lest she should meet the real Mary Ann (Alice's Adventures in Wonderland* by Lewis Carroll)

levee NOUN a levee is an old term for a meeting held in the morning, shortly after the person holding the meeting has got out of bed ❑ *I used to attend the King's levee once or twice a week (Gulliver's Travels* by Jonathan Swift)

life-preserver NOUN a club which had lead inside it to make it heavier and therefore more dangerous ❑ *and with no more suspicious articles displayed to view than two or three heavy bludgeons which stood in a corner, and a 'life-preserver' that hung over the chimney-piece. (Oliver Twist* by Charles Dickens)

lighterman NOUN a lighterman is another word for sailor ❑ *in and out, hammers going in ship-builders' yards, saws going at timber, clashing engines going at things unknown, pumps going in leaky ships, capstans going, ships going out to sea, and unintelligible sea creatures roaring curses over the bulwarks at respondent lightermen (Great Expectations* by Charles Dickens)

livery NOUN servants often wore a uniform known as a livery ❑ *suddenly a footman in livery came running out of the wood (Alice's Adventures in Wonderland* by Lewis Carroll)

livid ADJ livid means pale or ash coloured. Livid also means very angry ❑ *a dirty, livid white (Treasure Island* by Robert Louis Stevenson)

lottery-tickets NOUN a popular card game ❑ *and Mrs. Philips protested that they would have a nice comfortable noisy game of lottery tickets (Pride and Prejudice* by Jane Austen)

lower and upper world PHRASE the earth and the heavens are the lower and upper worlds ❑ *the changes in the lower and upper world (Gulliver's Travels* by Jonathan Swift)

lustres NOUN lustres are chandeliers. A chandelier is a large, decorative frame which holds light bulbs or candles and hangs from the ceiling ❑ *the lustres, lights, the carving and the guilding (The Prelude* by William Wordsworth)

lynched VERB killed without a criminal trial by a crowd of people ❑ *He'll never know how nigh he come to getting lynched (The Adventures of Huckleberry Finn* by Mark Twain)

malingering VERB if someone is malingering they are pretending to be ill to avoid working ❑ *And you stand there malingering (Treasure Island* by Robert Louis Stevenson)

managing PHRASE treating with consideration ❑ *to think the honour of my own kind not worth managing (Gulliver's Travels* by Jonathan Swift)

manhood PHRASE manhood means human nature ❑ *concerning the nature of manhood (Gulliver's Travels* by Jonathan Swift)

man-trap NOUN a man-trap is a set of steel jaws that snap shut when trodden on and trap a person's leg

❑ *"Don't go to him," I called out of the window, "he's an assassin! A man-trap!"* (*Oliver Twist* by Charles Dickens)

maps NOUN charts of the night sky ❑ *Let maps to others, worlds on worlds have shown* (*The Good-Morrow* by John Donne)

mark VERB look at or notice ❑ *Mark but this flea, and mark in this* (*The Flea* by John Donne)

maroons NOUN A maroon is someone who has been left in a place which it is difficult for them to escape from, like a small island ❑ *if schooners, islands, and maroons* (*Treasure Island* by Robert Louis Stevenson)

mast NOUN here mast means the fruit of forest trees ❑ *a quantity of acorns, dates, chestnuts, and other mast* (*Gulliver's Travels* by Jonathan Swift)

mate VERB defeat ❑ *Where Mars did mate the warlike Carthigens* (*Doctor Faustus Chorus* by Christopher Marlowe)

mealy ADJ Mealy when used to describe a face meant palid, pale or colourless ❑ *I only know two sorts of boys. Mealy boys, and beef-faced boys* (*Oliver Twist* by Charles Dickens)

middling ADJ fairly or moderately ❑ *she worked me middling hard for about an hour* (*The Adventures of Huckleberry Finn* by Mark Twain)

mill NOUN a mill, or treadmill, was a device for hard labour or punishment in prison ❑ *Was you never on the mill?* (*Oliver Twist* by Charles Dickens)

milliner's shop NOUN a milliner's sold fabrics, clothing, lace and accessories; as time went on they specialized more and more in hats ❑ *to pay their duty to their aunt and to a milliner's shop just over the way* (*Pride and Prejudice* by Jane Austen)

minching un' munching PHRASE how people in the north of England used to describe the way people

from the south speak ❑ *Minching un' munching!* (*Wuthering Heights* by Emily Brontë)

mine NOUN gold ❑ *Whether both th'Indias of spice and mine* (*The Sun Rising* by John Donne)

mire NOUN mud ❑ *Tis my fate to be always ground into the mire under the iron heel of oppression* (*The Adventures of Huckleberry Finn* by Mark Twain)

miscellany NOUN a miscellany is a collection of many different kinds of things ❑ *under that, the miscellany began* (*Treasure Island* by Robert Louis Stevenson)

mistarshers NOUN mistarshers means moustache, which is the hair that grows on a man's upper lip ❑ *when he put his hand up to his mistarshers* (*Tess of the D'Urbervilles* by Thomas Hardy)

morrow NOUN here good-morrow means tomorrow and a new and better life ❑ *And now good-morrow to our waking souls* (*The Good-Morrow* by John Donne)

mortification NOUN mortification is an old word for gangrene which is when part of the body decays or 'dies' because of disease ❑ *Yes, it was a mortification–that was it* (*The Adventures of Huckleberry Finn* by Mark Twain)

mought PARTICIPLE mought is an old spelling of might ❑ *what you mought call me? You mought call me captain* (*Treasure Island* by Robert Louis Stevenson)

move VERB move me not means do not make me angry ❑ *Move me not, Faustus* (*Doctor Faustus 2.1* by Christopher Marlowe)

muffin-cap NOUN a muffin cap is a flat cap made from wool ❑ *the old one, remained stationary in the muffin-cap and leathers* (*Oliver Twist* by Charles Dickens)

mulatter NOUN a mulatter was another word for mulatto, which is a person with parents who are from different races ❏ *a mulatter, most as white as a white man* (*The Adventures of Huckleberry Finn* by Mark Twain)

mummery NOUN mummery is an old word that meant meaningless (or pretentious) ceremony ❏ *When they were all gone, and when Trabb and his men–but not his boy: I looked for him–had crammed their mummery into bags, and were gone too, the house felt wholesomer.* (*Great Expectations* by Charles Dickens)

nap NOUN the nap is the woolly surface on a new item of clothing. Here the surface has been worn away so it looks bare ❏ *like an old hat with the nap rubbed off* (*The Adventures of Huckleberry Finn* by Mark Twain)

natural ■ NOUN a natural is a person born with learning difficulties ❏ *though he had been left to his particular care by their deceased father, who thought him almost a natural.* (*David Copperfield* by Charles Dickens) ■ ADJ natural meant illegitimate ❏ *Harriet Smith was the natural daughter of some-body* (*Emma* by Jane Austen)

navigator NOUN a navigator was origi-nally someone employed to dig canals. It is the origin of the word 'navvy' meaning a labourer ❏ *She ascertained from me in a few words what it was all about, comforted Dora, and gradually convinced her that I was not a labourer–from my manner of stating the case I believe Dora concluded that I was a navi-gator, and went balancing myself up and down a plank all day with a wheelbarrow–and so brought us together in peace.* (*David Copperfield* by Charles Dickens)

necromancy NOUN necromancy means a kind of magic where the magician speaks to spirits or ghosts to find out what will happen in the future ❏ *He surfeits upon cursed necro-mancy* (*Doctor Faustus chorus* by Christopher Marlowe)

negus NOUN a negus is a hot drink made from sweetened wine and water ❏ *He sat placidly perusing the newspaper, with his little head on one side, and a glass of warm sherry negus at his elbow.* (*David Copperfield* by Charles Dickens)

nice ADJ discriminating. Able to make good judgements or choices ❏ *consequently a claim to be nice* (*Emma* by Jane Austen)

nigh ADV nigh means near ❏ *He'll never know how nigh he come to getting lynched* (*The Adventures of Huckleberry Finn* by Mark Twain)

nimbleness NOUN nimbleness means being able to move very quickly or skillfully ❏ *and with incredible accuracy and nimbleness* (*Treasure Island* by Robert Louis Stevenson)

noggin NOUN a noggin is a small mug or a wooden cup ❏ *you'll bring me one noggin of rum* (*Treasure Island* by Robert Louis Stevenson)

none ADJ neither ❏ *none can die* (*The Good-Morrow* by John Donne)

notices NOUN observations ❏ *Arch are his notices* (*The Prelude* by William Wordsworth)

occiput NOUN occiput means the back of the head ❏ *saw off the occiput of each couple* (*Gulliver's Travels* by Jonathan Swift)

officiously ADJ kindly ❏ *the governess who attended Glumdalclitch very officiously lifted me up* (*Gulliver's Travels* by Jonathan Swift)

old salt PHRASE old salt is a slang term for an experienced sailor ❏ *a 'true sea-dog', and a 'real old salt'* (*Treasure Island* by Robert Louis Stevenson)

or ere PHRASE before ❏ *or ere the Hall was built* (*The Prelude* by William Wordsworth)

ostler NOUN one who looks after horses at an inn ❏ *The bill paid, and the waiter remembered, and the ostler not forgotten, and the chambermaid taken into consideration* (*Great Expectations* by Charles Dickens)

435

ostry NOUN an ostry is an old word for a pub or hotel ❑ *lest I send you into the ostry with a vengeance* (*Doctor Faustus 2.2* by Christopher Marlowe)

outrunning the constable PHRASE outrunning the constable meant spending more than you earn ❑ *but I shall by this means be able to check your bills and to pull you up if I find you outrunning the constable.* (*Great Expectations* by Charles Dickens)

over ADJ across ❑ *It is in length six yards, and in the thickest part at least three yards over* (*Gulliver's Travels* by Jonathan Swift)

over the broomstick PHRASE this is a phrase meaning 'getting married without a formal ceremony' ❑ *They both led tramping lives, and this woman in Gerrard-street here, had been married very young, over the broomstick (as we say), to a tramping man, and was a perfect fury in point of jealousy.* (*Great Expectations* by Charles Dickens)

own VERB own means to admit or to acknowledge ❑ *It's my old girl that advises. She has the head. But I never own to it before her. Discipline must be maintained* (*Bleak House* by Charles Dickens)

page NOUN here page means a boy employed to run errands ❑ *not my feigned page* (*On His Mistress* by John Donne)

paid pretty dear PHRASE paid pretty dear means paid a high price or suffered quite a lot ❑ *I paid pretty dear for my monthly fourpenny piece* (*Treasure Island* by Robert Louis Stevenson)

pannikins NOUN pannikins were small tin cups ❑ *of lifting light glasses and cups to his lips, as if they were clumsy pannikins* (*Great Expectations* by Charles Dickens)

pards NOUN pards are leopards ❑ *Not charioted by Bacchus and his pards* (*Ode on a Nightingale* by John Keats)

parlour boarder NOUN a pupil who lived with the family ❑ *and somebody had lately raised her from the condition of scholar to parlour boarder* (*Emma* by Jane Austen)

particular, a London PHRASE London in Victorian times and up to the 1950s was famous for having very dense fog–which was a combination of real fog and the smog of pollution from factories ❑ *This is a London particular . . . A fog, miss'* (*Bleak House* by Charles Dickens)

patten NOUN pattens were wooden soles which were fixed to shoes by straps to protect the shoes in wet weather ❑ *carrying a basket like the Great Seal of England in plaited straw, a pair of pattens, a spare shawl, and an umbrella, though it was a fine bright day* (*Great Expectations* by Charles Dickens)

paviour NOUN a paviour was a labourer who worked on the street pavement ❑ *the paviour his pickaxe* (*Oliver Twist* by Charles Dickens)

peccant ADJ peccant means unhealthy ❑ *other peccant humours* (*Gulliver's Travels* by Jonathan Swift)

penetralium NOUN penetralium is a word used to describe the inner rooms of the house ❑ *and I had no desire to aggravate his impatience previous to inspecting the penetralium* (*Wuthering Heights* by Emily Brontë)

pensive ADV pensive means deep in thought or thinking seriously about something ❑ *and she was leaning pensive on a tomb-stone on her right elbow* (*The Adventures of Huckleberry Finn* by Mark Twain)

penury NOUN penury is the state of being extremely poor ❑ *Distress, if not penury, loomed in the distance* (*Tess of the D'Urbervilles* by Thomas Hardy)

perspective NOUN telescope ❑ *a pocket perspective* (*Gulliver's Travels* by Jonathan Swift)

phaeton NOUN a phaeton was an open carriage for four people ❑ *often* *condescends to drive by my humble abode in her little phaeton and ponies (Pride and Prejudice* by Jane Austen)

phantasm NOUN a phantasm is an illusion, something that is not real. It is sometimes used to mean ghost ❏ *Experience had bred no fancies in him that could raise the phantasm of appetite (Silas Marner* by George Eliot)

physic NOUN here physic means medicine ❏ *there I studied physic two years and seven months (Gulliver's Travels* by Jonathan Swift)

pinioned VERB to pinion is to hold both arms so that a person cannot move them ❏ *But the relentless Ghost pinioned him in both his arms, and forced him to observe what happened next. (A Christmas Carol* by Charles Dickens)

piquet NOUN piquet was a popular card game in the C18th ❏ *Mr Hurst and Mr Bingley were at piquet (Pride and Prejudice* by Jane Austen)

plaister NOUN a plaister is a piece of cloth on which an apothecary (or pharmacist) would spread ointment. The cloth is then applied to wounds or bruises to treat them ❏ *Then, she gave the knife a final smart wipe on the edge of the plaister, and then sawed a very thick round off the loaf: which she finally, before separating from the loaf, hewed into two halves, of which Joe got one, and I the other. (Great Expectations* by Charles Dickens)

plantations NOUN here plantations means colonies, which are countries controlled by a more powerful country ❏ *besides our plantations in America (Gulliver's Travels* by Jonathan Swift)

plastic ADV here plastic is an old term meaning shaping or a power that was forming ❏ *A plastic power abode with me (The Prelude* by William Wordsworth)

players NOUN actors ❏ *of players which upon the world's stage be (On His Mistress* by John Donne)

plump ADV all at once, suddenly ❏ *But it took a bit of time to get it well round, the change come so uncommon plump, didn't it? (Great Expectations* by Charles Dickens)

plundered VERB to plunder is to rob or steal from ❏ *These crosses stand for the names of ships or towns that they sank or plundered (Treasure Island* by Robert Louis Stevenson)

pommel ■ VERB to pommel someone is to hit them repeatedly with your fists ❏ *hug him round the neck, pommel his back, and kick his legs in irrepressible affection! (A Christmas Carol* by Charles Dickens) ■ NOUN a pommel is the part of a saddle that rises up at the front ❏ *He had his gun across his pommel (The Adventures of Huckleberry Finn* by Mark Twain)

poor's rates NOUN poor's rates were property taxes which were used to support the poor ❏ *"Oh!" replied the undertaker; "why, you know, Mr. Bumble, I pay a good deal towards the poor's rates." (Oliver Twist* by Charles Dickens)

popular ADJ popular means ruled by the people, or Republican, rather than ruled by a monarch ❏ *With those of Greece compared and popular Rome (The Prelude* by William Wordsworth)

porringer NOUN a porringer is a small bowl ❏ *Of this festive composition each boy had one porringer, and no more (Oliver Twist* by Charles Dickens)

postboy NOUN a postboy was the driver of a horse-drawn carriage ❏ *He spoke to a postboy who was dozing under the gateway (Oliver Twist* by Charles Dickens)

post-chaise NOUN a fast carriage for two or four passengers ❏ *Looking round, he saw that it was a post-chaise, driven at great speed (Oliver Twist* by Charles Dickens)

postern NOUN a small gate usually at the back of a building ❏ *The little servant happening to be entering the* *fortress with two hot rolls, I passed through the postern and crossed the drawbridge, in her company* (*Great Expectations* by Charles Dickens)

pottle NOUN a pottle was a small basket ❑ *He had a paper-bag under each arm and a pottle of strawberries in one hand . . .* (*Great Expectations* by Charles Dickens)

pounce NOUN pounce is a fine powder used to prevent ink spreading on untreated paper ❑ *in that grim atmosphere of pounce and parchment, red-tape, dusty wafers, ink-jars, brief and draft paper, law reports, writs, declarations, and bills of costs* (*David Copperfield* by Charles Dickens)

pox NOUN pox means sexually transmitted diseases like syphilis ❑ *how the pox in all its consequences and denominations* (*Gulliver's Travels* by Jonathan Swift)

prelibation NOUN prelibation means a foretaste of or an example of something to come ❑ *A prelibation to the mower's scythe* (*The Prelude* by William Wordsworth)

prentice NOUN an apprentice ❑ *and Joe, sitting on an old gun, had told me that when I was 'prentice to him regularly bound, we would have such Larks there!* (*Great Expectations* by Charles Dickens)

presently ADV immediately ❑ *I presently knew what they meant* (*Gulliver's Travels* by Jonathan Swift)

pumpion NOUN pumpkin ❑ *for it was almost as large as a small pumpion* (*Gulliver's Travels* by Jonathan Swift)

punctual ADJ kept in one place ❑ *was not a punctual presence, but a spirit* (*The Prelude* by William Wordsworth)

quadrille ■ NOUN a quadrille is a dance invented in France which is usually performed by four couples ❑ *However, Mr Swiveller had Miss Sophy's hand for the first quadrille*

(country-dances being low, were utterly proscribed) (*The Old Curiosity Shop* by Charles Dickens) ■ NOUN quadrille was a card game for four people ❑ *to make up her pool of quadrille in the evening* (*Pride and Prejudice* by Jane Austen)

quality NOUN gentry or upper-class people ❑ *if you are with the quality* (*The Adventures of Huckleberry Finn* by Mark Twain)

quick parts PHRASE quick-witted ❑ *Mr Bennet was so odd a mixture of quick parts* (*Pride and Prejudice* by Jane Austen)

quid NOUN a quid is something chewed or kept in the mouth, like a piece of tobacco ❑ *rolling his quid* (*Treasure Island* by Robert Louis Stevenson)

quit VERB quit means to avenge or to make even ❑ *But Faustus's death shall quit my infamy* (*Doctor Faustus 4.3* by Christopher Marlowe)

rags NOUN divisions ❑ *Nor hours, days, months, which are the rags of time* (*The Sun Rising* by John Donne)

raiment NOUN raiment means clothing ❑ *the mountain shook off turf and flower, had only heath for raiment and crag for gem* (*Jane Eyre* by Charlotte Brontë)

rain cats and dogs PHRASE an expression meaning rain heavily. The origin of the expression is unclear ❑ *But it'll perhaps rain cats and dogs to-morrow* (*Silas Marner* by George Eliot)

raised Cain PHRASE raised Cain means caused a lot of trouble. Cain is a character in the Bible who killed his brother Abel ❑ *and every time he got drunk he raised Cain around town* (*The Adventures of Huckleberry Finn* by Mark Twain)

rambling ADJ rambling means confused and not very clear ❑ *my head began to be filled very early with rambling thoughts* (*Robinson Crusoe* by Daniel Defoe)

raree-show NOUN a raree-show is an old term for a peep-show or a fairground entertainment ❑ *A raree-show is here, with children gathered round* (*The Prelude* by William Wordsworth)

recusants NOUN people who resisted authority ❑ *hardy recusants* (*The Prelude* by William Wordsworth)

redounding VERB eddying. An eddy is a movement in water or air which goes round and round instead of flowing in one direction ❑ *mists and steam-like fogs redounding everywhere* (*The Prelude* by William Wordsworth)

redundant ADJ here redundant means overflowing but Wordsworth also uses it to mean excessively large or too big ❑ *A tempest, a redundant energy* (*The Prelude* by William Wordsworth)

reflex NOUN reflex is a shortened version of reflexion, which is an alternative spelling of reflection ❑ *To cut across the reflex of a star* (*The Prelude* by William Wordsworth)

Reformatory NOUN a prison for young offenders/criminals ❑ *Even when I was taken to have a new suit of clothes, the tailor had orders to make them like a kind of Reformatory, and on no account to let me have the free use of my limbs.* (*Great Expectations* by Charles Dickens)

remorse NOUN pity or compassion ❑ *by that remorse* (*On His Mistress* by John Donne)

render VERB in this context render means give. ❑ *and Sarah could render no reason that would be sanctioned by the feeling of the community.* (*Silas Marner* by George Eliot)

repeater NOUN a repeater was a watch that chimed the last hour when a button was pressed–as a result it was useful in the dark ❑ *And his watch is a gold repeater, and worth a hundred pound if it's worth a penny.* (*Great Expectations* by Charles Dickens)

repugnance NOUN repugnance means a strong dislike of something or someone ❑ *overcoming a strong repugnance* (*Treasure Island* by Robert Louis Stevenson)

reverence NOUN reverence means bow. When you bow to someone, you briefly bend your body towards them as a formal way of showing them respect ❑ *made my reverence* (*Gulliver's Travels* by Jonathan Swift)

reverie NOUN a reverie is a day dream ❑ *I can guess the subject of your reverie* (*Pride and Prejudice* by Jane Austen)

revival NOUN a religious meeting held in public ❑ *well I'd ben a-runnin' a little temperance revival thar' bout a week* (*The Adventures of Huckleberry Finn* by Mark Twain)

revolt VERB revolt means turn back or stop your present course of action and go back to what you were doing before ❑ *Revolt, or I'll in piecemeal tear thy flesh* (*Doctor Faustus 5.1* by Christopher Marlowe)

rheumatics/rheumatism NOUN rheumatics [rheumatism] is an illness that makes your joints or muscles stiff and painful ❑ *a new cure for the rheumatics* (*Treasure Island* by Robert Louis Stevenson)

riddance NOUN riddance is usually used in the form good riddance which you say when you are pleased that something has gone or been left behind ❑ *I'd better go into the house, and die and be a riddance* (*David Copperfield* by Charles Dickens)

rimy ADJ rimy is an adjective which means covered in ice or frost ❑ *It was a rimy morning, and very damp* (*Great Expectations* by Charles Dickens)

riper ADJ riper means more mature or older ❑ *At riper years to Wittenberg he went* (*Doctor Faustus chorus* by Christopher Marlowe)

rubber NOUN a set of games in whist or backgammon ❑ *her father was sure of his rubber* (*Emma* by Jane Austen)

ruffian NOUN a ruffian is a person who behaves violently ❑ *and when the ruffian had told him* (*Treasure Island* by Robert Louis Stevenson)

sadness NOUN sadness is an old term meaning seriousness ❑ *But I prithee tell me, in good saḍness* (*Doctor Faustus 2.2* by Christopher Marlowe)

sailed before the mast PHRASE this phrase meant someone who did not look like a sailor ❑ *he had none of the appearance of a man that sailed before the mast* (*Treasure Island* by Robert Louis Stevenson)

scabbard NOUN a scabbard is the covering for a sword or dagger ❑ *Girded round its middle was an antique scabbard; but no sword was in it, and the ancient sheath was eaten up with rust* (*A Christmas Carol* by Charles Dickens)

schooners NOUN A schooner is a fast, medium-sized sailing ship ❑ *if schooners, islands, and maroons* (*Treasure Island* by Robert Louis Stevenson)

science NOUN learning or knowledge ❑ *Even Science, too, at hand* (*The Prelude* by William Wordsworth)

scrouge VERB to scrouge means to squeeze or to crowd ❑ *to scrouge in and get a sight* (*The Adventures of Huckleberry Finn* by Mark Twain)

scrutore NOUN a scrutore, or escritoire, was a writing table ❑ *set me gently on my feet upon the scrutore* (*Gulliver's Travels* by Jonathan Swift)

scutcheon/escutcheon NOUN an escutcheon is a shield with a coat of arms, or the symbols of a family name, engraved on it ❑ *On the scutcheon we'll have a bend* (*The Adventures of Huckleberry Finn* by Mark Twain)

sea-dog PHRASE sea-dog is a slang term for an experienced sailor or pirate ❑ *a 'true sea-dog', and a 'real old salt,'* (*Treasure Island* by Robert Louis Stevenson)

see the lions PHRASE to see the lions was to go and see the sights of London. Originally the phrase referred to the menagerie in the Tower of London and later in Regent's Park ❑ *We will go and see the lions for an hour or two–it's something to have a fresh fellow like you to show them to, Copperfield* (*David Copperfield* by Charles Dickens)

self-conceit NOUN self-conceit is an old term which means having too high an opinion of oneself, or deceiving yourself ❑ *Till swollen with cunning, of a self-conceit* (*Doctor Faustus chorus* by Christopher Marlowe)

seneschal NOUN a steward ❑ *where a grey-headed seneschal sings a funny chorus with a funnier body of vassals* (*Oliver Twist* by Charles Dickens)

sensible ADJ if you were sensible of something you are aware or conscious of something ❑ *If my children are silly I must hope to be always sensible of it* (*Pride and Prejudice* by Jane Austen)

sessions NOUN court cases were heard at specific times of the year called sessions ❑ *He lay in prison very ill, during the whole interval between his committal for trial, and the coming round of the Sessions.* (*Great Expectations* by Charles Dickens)

shabby ADJ shabby places look old and in bad condition ❑ *a little bit of a shabby village named Pikesville* (*The Adventures of Huckleberry Finn* by Mark Twain)

shay-cart NOUN a shay-cart was a small cart drawn by one horse ❑ *"I were at the Bargemen t'other night, Pip;" whenever he subsided into affection, he called me Pip, and whenever he relapsed into politeness he called me Sir; "when there come up in his* *shay-cart Pumblechook."* (*Great Expectations* by Charles Dickens)

shilling NOUN a shilling is an old unit of currency. There were twenty shillings in every British pound ❑ *"Ten shillings too much," said the gentleman in the white waistcoat.* (*Oliver Twist* by Charles Dickens)

shines NOUN tricks or games ❑ *well, it would make a cow laugh to see the shines that old idiot cut* (*The Adventures of Huckleberry Finn* by Mark Twain)

shirking VERB shirking means not doing what you are meant to be doing, or evading your duties ❑ *some of you shirking lubbers* (*Treasure Island* by Robert Louis Stevenson)

shiver my timbers PHRASE shiver my timbers is an expression which was used by sailors and pirates to express surprise ❑ *why, shiver my timbers, if I hadn't forgotten my score!* (*Treasure Island* by Robert Louis Stevenson)

shoe-roses NOUN shoe-roses were roses made from ribbons which were stuck on to shoes as decoration ❑ *the very shoe-roses for Netherfield were got by proxy* (*Pride and Prejudice* by Jane Austen)

singular ADJ singular means very great and remarkable or strange ❑ *"Singular dream," he says* (*The Adventures of Huckleberry Finn* by Mark Twain)

sire NOUN sire is an old word which means lord or master or elder ❑ *She also defied her sire* (*Little Women* by Louisa May Alcott)

sixpence NOUN a sixpence was half of a shilling ❑ *if she had only a shilling in the world, she would be very lilkely to give away sixpence of it* (*Emma* by Jane Austen)

slavey NOUN the word slavey was used when there was only one servant in a house or boarding-house–so she had to perform all the duties of a larger staff ❑ *Two distinct knocks, sir, will produce the slavey at any*

time (*The Old Curiosity Shop* by Charles Dickens)

slender ADJ weak ❑ *In slender accents of sweet verse* (*The Prelude* by William Wordsworth)

slop-shops NOUN slop-shops were shops where cheap ready-made clothes were sold. They mainly sold clothes to sailors ❑ *Accordingly, I took the jacket off, that I might learn to do without it; and carrying it under my arm, began a tour of inspection of the various slop-shops.* (*David Copperfield* by Charles Dickens)

sluggard NOUN a lazy person ❑ *"Stand up and repeat ''Tis the voice of the sluggard,'"* said the Gryphon. (*Alice's Adventures in Wonderland* by Lewis Carroll)

smallpox NOUN smallpox is a serious infectious disease ❑ *by telling the men we had smallpox aboard* (*The Adventures of Huckleberry Finn* by Mark Twain)

smalls NOUN smalls are short trousers ❑ *It is difficult for a large-headed, small-eyed youth, of lumbering make and heavy countenance, to look dignified under any circumstances; but it is more especially so, when superadded to these personal attractions are a red nose and yellow smalls* (*Oliver Twist* by Charles Dickens)

sneeze-box NOUN a box for snuff was called a sneeze-box because sniffing snuff makes the user sneeze ❑ *To think of Jack Dawkins — lummy Jack — the Dodger — the Artful Dodger — going abroad for a common twopenny-halfpenny sneeze-box!* (*Oliver Twist* by Charles Dickens)

snorted VERB slept ❑ *Or snorted we in the Seven Sleepers' den?* (*The Good-Morrow* by John Donne)

snuff NOUN snuff is tobacco in powder form which is taken by sniffing ❑ *as he thrust his thumb and fore-finger into the proffered snuff-box of the undertaker: which was an*

ingenious little model of a patent coffin. (*Oliver Twist* by Charles Dickens)

soliloquized VERB to soliloquize is when an actor in a play speaks to himself or herself rather than to another actor ❏ "*A new servitude! There is something in that,*" *I soliloquized (mentally, be it understood; I did not talk aloud)* (*Jane Eyre* by Charlotte Brontë)

sough NOUN a sough is a drain or a ditch ❏ *as you may have noticed the sough that runs from the marshes* (*Wuthering Heights* by Emily Brontë)

spirits NOUN a spirit is the nonphysical part of a person which is believed to remain alive after their death ❏ *that I might raise up spirits when I please* (*Doctor Faustus* 1.5 by Christopher Marlowe)

spleen ■ NOUN here spleen means a type of sadness or depression which was thought to only affect the wealthy ❏ *yet here I could plainly discover the true seeds of spleen* (*Gulliver's Travels* by Jonathan Swift) ■ NOUN irritability and low spirits ❏ *Adieu to disappointment and spleen* (*Pride and Prejudice* by Jane Austen)

spondulicks NOUN spondulicks is a slang word which means money ❏ *not for all his spondulicks and as much more on top of it* (*The Adventures of Huckleberry Finn* by Mark Twain)

stalled of VERB to be stalled of something is to be bored with it ❏ *I'm stalled of doing naught* (*Wuthering Heights* by Emily Brontë)

stanchion NOUN a stanchion is a pole or bar that stands upright and is used as a buidling support ❏ *and slid down a stanchion* (*The Adventures of Huckleberry Finn* by Mark Twain)

stang NOUN stang is another word for pole which was an old measurement ❏ *These fields were intermingled with woods of half a stang* (*Gulliver's Travels* by Jonathan Swift)

starlings NOUN a starling is a wall built around the pillars that support a bridge to protect the pillars ❏ *There were states of the tide when, having been down the river, I could not get back through the eddy-chafed arches and starlings of old London Bridge* (*Great Expectations* by Charles Dickens)

startings NOUN twitching or nighttime movements of the body ❏ *with midnight's startings* (*On His Mistress* by John Donne)

stomacher NOUN a panel at the front of a dress ❏ *but send her aunt the pattern of a stomacher* (*Emma* by Jane Austen)

stoop VERB swoop ❏ *Once a kite hovering over the garden made a swoop at me* (*Gulliver's Travels* by Jonathan Swift)

succedaneum NOUN a succedaneum is a substitute ❏ *But as a succedaneum* (*The Prelude* by William Wordsworth)

suet NOUN a hard animal fat used in cooking ❏ *and your jaws are too weak For anything tougher than suet* (*Alice's Adventures in Wonderland* by Lewis Carroll)

sultry ADJ sultry weather is hot and damp. Here sultry means unpleasant or risky ❏ *for it was getting pretty sultry for us* (*The Adventures of Huckleberry Finn* by Mark Twain)

summerset NOUN summerset is an old spelling of somersault. If someone does a somersault, they turn over completely in the air ❏ *I have seen him do the summerset* (*Gulliver's Travels* by Jonathan Swift)

supper NOUN supper was a light meal taken late in the evening. The main meal was dinner which was eaten at four or five in the afternoon ❏ *and the supper table was all set out* (*Emma* by Jane Austen)

surfeits VERB to surfeit in something is to have far too much of it, or to overindulge in it to an unhealthy degree ❏ *He surfeits upon cursed* necromancy (*Doctor Faustus chorus* by Christopher Marlowe)

surtout NOUN a surtout is a long close-fitting overcoat ❏ *He wore a long black surtout reaching nearly to his ankles* (*The Old Curiosity Shop* by Charles Dickens)

swath NOUN swath is the width of corn cut by a scythe ❏ *while thy hook Spares the next swath* (*Ode to Autumn* by John Keats)

sylvan ADJ sylvan means belonging to the woods ❏ *Sylvan historian* (*Ode on a Grecian Urn* by John Keats)

taction NOUN taction means touch. This means that the people had to be touched on the mouth or the ears to get their attention ❏ *without being roused by some external taction upon the organs of speech and hearing* (*Gulliver's Travels* by Jonathan Swift)

Tag and Rag and Bobtail PHRASE the riff-raff, or lower classes. Used in an insulting way ❏ *"No," said he; "not till it got about that there was no protection on the premises, and it come to be considered dangerous, with convicts and Tag and Rag and Bobtail going up and down."* (*Great Expectations* by Charles Dickens)

tallow NOUN tallow is hard animal fat that is used to make candles and soap ❏ *and a lot of tallow candles* (*The Adventures of Huckleberry Finn* by Mark Twain)

tan VERB to tan means to beat or whip ❏ *and if I catch you about that school I'll tan you good* (*The Adventures of Huckleberry Finn* by Mark Twain)

tanyard NOUN the tanyard is part of a tannery, which is a place where leather is made from animal skins ❏ *hid in the old tanyard* (*The Adventures of Huckleberry Finn* by Mark Twain)

tarry ADJ tarry means the colour of tar or black ❏ *his tarry pig-tail*

(*Treasure Island* by Robert Louis Stevenson)

thereof PHRASE from there ❏ *By all desires which thereof did ensue* (*On His Mistress* by John Donne)

thick with, be PHRASE if you are 'thick with someone' you are very close, sharing secrets—it is often used to describe people who are planning something secret ❏ *Hasn't he been thick with Mr Heathcliff lately?* (*Wuthering Heights* by Emily Brontë)

thimble NOUN a thimble is a small cover used to protect the finger while sewing ❏ *The paper had been sealed in several places by a thimble* (*Treasure Island* by Robert Louis Stevenson)

thirtover ADJ thirtover is an old word which means obstinate or that someone is very determined to do want they want and can not be persuaded to do something in another way ❏ *I have been living on in a thirtover, lackadaisical way* (*Tess of the D'Urbervilles* by Thomas Hardy)

timbrel NOUN timbrel is a tambourine ❏ *What pipes and timbrels?* (*Ode on a Grecian Urn* by John Keats)

tin NOUN tin is slang for money/cash ❏ *Then the plain question is, an't it a pity that this state of things should continue, and how much better would it be for the old gentleman to hand over a reasonable amount of tin, and make it all right and comfortable* (*The Old Curiosity Shop* by Charles Dickens)

tincture NOUN a tincture is a medicine made with alcohol and a small amount of a drug ❏ *with ink composed of a cephalic tincture* (*Gulliver's Travels* by Jonathan Swift)

tithe NOUN a tithe is a tax paid to the church ❏ *and held farms which, speaking from a spiritual point of view, paid highly-desirable tithes* (*Silas Marner* by George Eliot)

towardly ADJ a towardly child is

dutiful or obedient ❏ *and a towardly child* (*Gulliver's Travels* by Jonathan Swift)

toys NOUN trifles are things which are considered to have little importance, value, or significance ❏ *purchase my life from them bysome bracelets, glass rings, and other toys* (*Gulliver's Travels* by Jonathan Swift)

tract NOUN a tract is a religious pamphlet or leaflet ❏ *and Joe Harper got a hymn-book and a tract* (*The Adventures of Huckleberry Finn* by Mark Twain)

train-oil NOUN train-oil is oil from whale blubber ❏ *The train-oil and gunpowder were shoved out of sight in a minute* (*Wuthering Heights* by Emily Brontë)

tribulation NOUN tribulation means the suffering or difficulty you experience in a particular situation ❏ *Amy was learning this distinction through much tribulation* (*Little Women* by Louisa May Alcott)

trivet NOUN a trivet is a three-legged stand for resting a pot or kettle ❏ *a pocket-knife in his right; and a pewter pot on the trivet* (*Oliver Twist* by Charles Dickens)

trot line NOUN a trot line is a fishing line to which a row of smaller fishing lines are attached ❏ *when he got along I was hard at it taking up a trot line* (*The Adventures of Huckleberry Finn* by Mark Twain)

troth NOUN oath or pledge ❏ *I wonder, by my troth* (*The Good-Morrow* by John Donne)

truckle NOUN a truckle bedstead is a bed that is on wheels and can be slid under another bed to save space ❏ *It rose under my hand, and the door yielded. Looking in, I saw a lighted candle on a table, a bench, and a mattress on a truckle bedstead.* (*Great Expectations* by Charles Dickens)

trump NOUN a trump is a good, reliable person wo can be trusted ❏ *This lad Hawkins is a trump, I perceive* (*Treasure Island* by Robert Louis Stevenson)

tucker NOUN a tucker is a frilly lace collar which is worn around the neck ❏ *Whereat Scrooge's niece's sister˜the plump one with the lace tucker: not the one with the roses˜blushed.* (*A Christmas Carol* by Charles Dickens)

tureen NOUN a large bowl with a lid from which soup or vegetables are served ❏ *Waiting in a hot tureen!* (*Alice's Adventures in Wonderland* by Lewis Carroll)

turnkey NOUN a prison officer; jailer ❏ *As we came out of the prison through the lodge, I found that the great importance of my guardian was appreciated by the turnkeys, no less than by those whom they held in charge.* (*Great Expectations* by Charles Dickens)

turnpike NOUN the upkeep of many roads of the time was paid for by tolls (fees) collected at posts along the road. There was a gate to prevent people travelling further along the road until the toll had been paid. ❏ *Traddles, whom I have taken up by appointment at the turnpike, presents a dazzling combination of cream colour and light blue; and both he and Mr. Dick have a general effect about them of being all gloves.* (*David Copperfield* by Charles Dickens)

twas PHRASE it was ❏ *twas but a dream of thee* (*The Good-Morrow* by John Donne)

tyrannized VERB tyrannized means bullied or forced to do things against their will ❏ *for people would soon cease coming there to be tyrannized over and put down* (*Treasure Island* by Robert Louis Stevenson)

'un NOUN 'un is a slang term for one– usually used to refer to a person ❏ *She's been thinking the old 'un* (*David Copperfield* by Charles Dickens)

undistinguished ADJ undiscriminating or incapable of making a distinction between good and bad things ❏

their undistinguished appetite to devour everything (*Gulliver's Travels* by Jonathan Swift)

use NOUN habit ❑ *Though use make you apt to kill me* (*The Flea* by John Donne)

vacant ADJ vacant usually means empty, but here Wordsworth uses it to mean carefree ❑ *To vacant musing, unreproved neglect* (*The Prelude* by William Wordsworth)

valetudinarian NOUN one too concerned with his or her own health. ❑ *for having been a valetudinarian all his life* (*Emma* by Jane Austen)

vamp VERB vamp means to walk or tramp to somewhere ❑ *Well, vamp on to Marlott, will 'ee* (*Tess of the D'Urbervilles* by Thomas Hardy)

vapours NOUN the vapours is an old term which means unpleasant and strange thoughts, which make the person feel nervous and unhappy ❑ *and my head was full of vapours* (*Robinson Crusoe* by Daniel Defoe)

vegetables NOUN here vegetables means plants ❑ *the other vegetables are in the same proportion* (*Gulliver's Travels* by Jonathan Swift)

venturesome ADJ if you are venturesome you are willing to take risks ❑ *he must be either hopelessly stupid or a venturesome fool* (*Wuthering Heights* by Emily Brontë)

verily ADJ verily means really or truly ❑ *though I believe verily* (*Robinson Crusoe* by Daniel Defoe)

vicinage NOUN vicinage is an area or the residents of an area ❑ *and to his thought the whole vicinage was haunted by her.* (*Silas Marner* by George Eliot)

victuals NOUN victuals means food ❑ *grumble a little over the victuals* (*The Adventures of Huckleberry Finn* by Mark Twain)

vintage NOUN vintage in this context means wine ❑ *Oh, for a draught of*

vintage! (*Ode on a Nightingale* by John Keats)

virtual ADJ here virtual means powerful or strong ❑ *had virtual faith* (*The Prelude* by William Wordsworth)

vittles NOUN vittles is a slang word which means food ❑ *There never was such a woman for givin' away vittles and drink* (*Little Women* by Louisa May Alcott)

voided straight PHRASE voided straight is an old expression which means emptied immediately ❑ *see the rooms be voided straight* (*Doctor Faustus 4.1* by Christopher Marlowe)

wainscot NOUN wainscot is wood panel lining in a room so wainscoted means a room lined with wooden panels ❑ *in the dark wainscoted parlor* (*Silas Marner* by George Eliot)

walking the plank PHRASE walking the plank was a punishment in which a prisoner would be made to walk along a plank on the side of the ship and fall into the sea, where they would be abandoned ❑ *about hanging, and walking the plank* (*Treasure Island* by Robert Louis Stevenson)

want VERB want means to be lacking or short of ❑ *The next thing wanted was to get the picture framed* (*Emma* by Jane Austen)

wanting ADJ wanting means lacking or missing ❑ *wanting two fingers of the left hand* (*Treasure Island* by Robert Louis Stevenson)

wanting, I was not PHRASE I was not wanting means I did not fail ❑ *I was not wanting to lay a foundation of religious knowledge in his mind* (*Robinson Crusoe* by Daniel Defoe)

ward NOUN a ward is, usually, a child who has been put under the protection of the court or a guardian for his or her protection ❑ *I call the Wards in Jarndyce. The*

are caged up with all the others.
(*Bleak House* by Charles Dickens)

waylay VERB to waylay someone is to lie in wait for them or to intercept them ❑ *I must go up the road and waylay him* (*The Adventures of Huckleberry Finn* by Mark Twain)

weazen NOUN weazen is a slang word for throat. It actually means shrivelled ❑ *You with a uncle too! Why, I knowed you at Gargery's when you was so small a wolf that I could have took your weazen betwixt this finger and thumb and chucked you away dead* (*Great Expectations* by Charles Dickens)

wery ■ ADV very ❑ *Be wery careful o' vidders all your life* (*Pickwick Papers* by Charles Dickens) ■ *See* wibrated

wherry NOUN wherry is a small swift rowing boat for one person ❑ *It was flood tide when Daniel Quilp sat himself down in the wherry to cross to the opposite shore.* (*The Old Curiosity Shop* by Charles Dickens)

whether PREP whether means which of the two in this example ❑ *we came in full view of a great island or continent (for we knew not whether)* (*Gulliver's Travels* by Jonathan Swift)

whetstone NOUN a whetstone is a stone used to sharpen knives and other tools ❑ *I dropped pap's whetstone there too* (*The Adventures of Huckleberry Finn* by Mark Twain)

wibrated VERB in Dickens's use of the English language 'w' often replaces 'v' when he is reporting speech. So here 'wibrated' means 'vibrated'. In Pickwick Papers a judge asks Sam Weller (who constantly confuses the two letters) 'Do you spell it with a 'v' or a 'w'?' to which Weller replies 'That depends upon the taste and fancy of the speller, my Lord' ❑ *There are strings . . . in the human heart that had better not be wibrated*' (*Barnaby Rudge* by Charles Dickens)

wicket NOUN a wicket is a little door in a larger entrance ❑ *Having rested here, for a minute or so, to collect a good burst of sobs and an imposing show of tears and terror, he knocked loudly at the wicket;* (*Oliver Twist* by Charles Dickens)

without CONJ without means unless ❑ *You don't know about me, without you have read a book by the name of The Adventures of Tom Sawyer* (*The Adventures of Huckleberry Finn* by Mark Twain)

wittles ■ NOUN vittles is a slang word which means food ❑ *I live on broken wittles–and I sleep on the coals* (*David Copperfield* by Charles Dickens) ■ *See* wibrated

woo VERB courts or forms a proper relationship with ❑ *before it woo* (*The Flea* by John Donne)

words, to have PHRASE if you have words with someone you have a disagreement or an argument ❑ *I do not want to have words with a young thing like you.* (*Black Beauty* by Anna Sewell)

workhouse NOUN workhouses were places where the homeless were given food and a place to live in return for doing very hard work ❑ *And the Union workhouses? demanded Scrooge. Are they still in operation?* (*A Christmas Carol* by Charles Dickens)

yawl NOUN a yawl is a small boat kept on a bigger boat for short trips. Yawl is also the name for a small fishing boat ❑ *She sent out her yawl, and we went aboard* (*The Adventures of Huckleberry Finn* by Mark Twain)

yeomanry NOUN the yeomanry was a collective term for the middle classes involved in agriculture ❑ *The yeomanry are precisely the order of people with whom I feel I can have nothing to do* (*Emma* by Jane Austen)

yonder ADV yonder means over there ❑ *all in the same second we seem to hear low voices in yonder!* (*The Adventures of Huckleberry Finn* by Mark Twain)